Never Close Your Eyes

Also by Emma Burstall

Gym and Slimline

Emma Burstall

Never Close Your Eyes

preface
publishing

Published by Preface 2009

10 9 8 7 6 5 4 3 2

Copyright © Emma Burstall, 2009

Emma Burstall has asserted her right to be identified as
the author of this work under the Copyright, Designs and Patents Act 1988

First published in Great Britain in 2009 by Preface Publishing
20 Vauxhall Bridge Road
London SW1V 2SA

An imprint of The Random House Group

www.rbooks.co.uk
www.prefacepublishing.co.uk

Addresses for companies within The Random House Group Limited
can be found at www.randomhouse.co.uk

The Random House Group Limited Reg. No. 954009

A CIP catalogue record for this book is available from the British Library

ISBN 978 1 84809 047 7

The Random House Group Limited supports The Forest Stewardship Council
(FSC), the leading international forest certification organisation. All our titles
that are printed on Greenpeace-approved FSC-certified paper carry
the FSC logo. Our paper procurement policy can be found at
www.rbooks.co.uk/environment

Mixed Sources
Product group from well-managed
forests and other controlled sources
www.fsc.org Cert no. TT-COC-2139
© 1996 Forest Stewardship Council
FSC

Typeset in Palatino by Palimpsest Book Production Ltd,
Grangemouth, Stirlingshire
Printed and bound in Great Britain by CPI Bookmarque, Croydon CR0 4TD

For my parents, Sue and Christopher Burstall.
Thank you for everything.

'There are literally thousands of writing groups across the country. It seems as though in every street in Britain someone is writing a book.' Alan Samson, Publisher

Characters

❧❧❧

Evie Freestone: a wedding-dress designer
Neil: her estranged husband, a consultant obstetrician and gynaecologist
Freya and Michael: their children
Helen: Neil's new live-in partner
Margot: Evie's former boss
Bill: Evie's neighbour, a former university professor
Jan: his dead wife
Galina: a Ukrainian student, taught by Bill
Steve: Evie's boyfriend, a celebrity writer
Jacob: Steve's baby son
Lucy: Freya's best friend
Abigail, Chantelle and Gemma: schoolgirl bullies
Liam: Abigail's boyfriend
Richie: Chantelle's ex-boyfriend
Cal Barton: Freya's online friend

Becca Goodall: Chief Investment Officer for a large international company
Tom: Becca's husband, a sports journalist
Alice and James: their children
Monica: their au pair
Gary Laybourn: Becca's old schoolfriend, who works for a human rights charity
Michelle: Gary's wife
Dawn Mackey: a schoolgirl from Newcastle
Jude: her sister
Maureen: their mother, a cleaner

Nic Quinton: a freelance journalist
Alan: her husband, an accountant
Dominic: their son
Marie: Nic's oldest friend

Tristram: chairman of the St Barnabas's Creative Writing Group
Carol, Pamela, Russell, Jonathan, Angela and Tim: members of
  the writing group
Griselda: Carol's sister

Zelda: a clairvoyant
Miss Addison: her former class teacher
Derek: Zelda's former boyfriend

Chapter One

Benwell, Newcastle upon Tyne, 1978

'Look at yersel'! Ye're such a fuckin' saddo.'

Jude was standing in the bedroom doorway, her face fixed in a mean sneer. Dawn could see the red freckles on her nose, the pale, ugly eyebrows, the clogged mascara. She wondered for a moment why Jude didn't paint her eyebrows black, too, to match the lashes. There again, there wasn't much point. She'd always be hideously ugly whatever she did.

Dawn turned away from her sister and back to the exercise book on the end of her bed. She didn't have a desk; she had to kneel on the floor.

'Was the collapse of the Weimar Republic inevitable?' she read. She picked up the black Biro again and put the end in her mouth. She always did that; it helped her think.

She heard Jude leave her position in the doorway and pad in bare feet across the tatty blue carpet to her side of the room. The thought of Jude's feet made Dawn feel sick. Jude hardly ever cut her toenails, which were long, yellowish and dirty, with bits of red chipped nail varnish that had been there for months. Dawn didn't know how Jude's lover boy could stand them. There again, it wouldn't be her feet he was after. Dawn didn't like to think about that, either.

Jude started opening her bedside drawers and banging things around, humming loudly. Dawn wanted to cry. It was so unfair. The essay was due in tomorrow and she'd been enjoying writing it. Mam would be home from work soon, then she and Jude would have to help get the tea, though Jesus knows what they were going to eat. Chips and that disgusting tinned ham again probably.

'Please, Jude,' she said, 'can Ah just finish this?'

Jude stopped banging. Dawn waited for something, more sneers, but nothing came. The silence was almost worse than the humming and banging. It was creepy.

She looked up to see Jude leap from her bed on to Dawn's and then on to the floor. Jude was still in her school uniform, though she'd taken her tights off and her rolled-up navy-blue skirt was so short that you could see right up her fat white legs to her dirty grey knickers.

Dawn sprang to her feet, whipped her essay away from the end of the bed and hugged it to her chest. 'Ye nearly trod on me work.' Her whole face felt hot.

Jude smirked, turned her back and started fiddling with the things on Dawn's bedside table: her travel clock in the shiny brown case; the little pink flowery porcelain pot in which she kept the two pairs of gold studs that she'd bought with her paper-round money.

Dawn winced. Her bedside table was precious. It was white and plasticky and it wobbled but it was hers, her own private property. Jude had no right to touch it. She kept her diary locked up in the top drawer and her watch, given to her two years ago on her tenth birthday by Nana, in the bottom. 'Double figures!' she'd written on the card in big, bold letters. 'With lots of love to my special girl.' She'd kept that, too, and the case with 'TIMEX' on it that the watch had come in.

Jude had Dawn's school photo in her hand now and was poking her finger in some of the faces, laughing. 'Look at the conk on that!'

'Give me that,' Dawn said, trying to grab the photo back. But Jude was taller – though Dawn was catching up fast – and held it above her head out of reach.

'Ahh, little Dawn in her hockey photo,' Jude teased. 'At her posh grammar school.'

Dawn jumped on the bed and made another lunge for the photo, but Jude had it behind her back now. Dawn wondered, for a second, why she cared about it so much. She was only in the B-team. But she was so happy when they picked her. It showed that she wasn't just good at essays, she was OK at sport, too. And she wanted to go on a hockey tour with the other girls. She'd hardly ever been off the estate, let alone out of Newcastle. She wouldn't tell them that, though.

'Give it me, ye big fat cow,' Dawn muttered again. 'It's mine.'

'Ye're just a stupid little girl with ye stupid little hockey,' Jude taunted. 'I'm gonna rip it up.'

Dawn's head was throbbing, ready to explode. The photo was probably doomed one way or another. She jumped off the bed, reached out and seized two great clumps of her sister's long, ginger hair and pulled as hard as she could.

'Bitch,' Jude shrieked, dropping to the floor and pulling Dawn down with her. Jude was kicking and squirming but Dawn held on tight. She was almost enjoying this.

'Get off!' Jude yelled again. 'I'll fuckin' kill ye.'

Dawn couldn't see the photo. Jude wasn't using her hands to defend herself so she must be clutching it. She was so hard.

'I'll only let go if ye give it me now,' Dawn screeched, yanking viciously on her sister's hair again. Good job she'd got Mam's thick fair mop, not Jude's pathetic, orange wisps.

Dawn felt a sudden sharp pain. Jude's foot in her stomach. She fell back, winded. Jude was on top of Dawn immediately, sending her crashing backwards. She started thumping and scratching, her knees digging into Dawn's sides. Jude was much heavier. Dawn knew that she couldn't beat her with brute strength alone.

She was on her back beside the bed. She registered the frayed pink base of the bed-frame, which sagged in the middle. There was a gap between it and the floor and she could see the outline of various objects hidden away underneath in the dark.

Anything precious that Dawn couldn't put in the bedside table went there: her Monopoly board; her shoes for best. If she put them in the small, rickety wardrobe that she shared with Jude they wouldn't last long.

Jude was straddling her, thumping up and down on her stomach as hard as she could. Her long nails scraped down Dawn's cheek, making her eyes water. She snapped them shut in case Jude decided to gouge them out; she wouldn't put it past her.

3

Dawn was hurting so much that she could hardly feel it any more. She wondered if she was going to die. She managed to pull her left arm out from underneath Jude's right leg without her noticing and slid her hand under the bed, reaching round until her fingers felt something rubbery: the end of her hockey stick?

'I hate ye,' Jude was saying. 'I'll always hate ye. Ye think ye're so fuckin' clever but ye're not. Ye're so ugly no lad'll ever want to shag ye. Ye'll never get a job neither. Ye'll end up cleaning toilets just like me mam.'

Dawn inched her fingers along the stick until they felt wood. Then she managed to drag the whole thing towards her so that it was close enough for her to lever it round in an arc until it was lying beside her.

Dawn's head was pounding and she was gasping for breath. She squeezed her eyes open and registered Jude's pink, sweaty neck, her heavy, jutting jaw as she bounced up and down. Dawn managed to raise her head a couple of inches off the floor and the second that Jude looked down she spat as hard as she could. Bingo! The spit landed on Jude's cheek and dribbled down, leaving a disgusting foamy trail.

Now she'd be for it.

Jude's eyes flashed. 'Ye'll be sorry for that.' She grabbed Dawn's head in both hands and banged it up and down, up and down on the carpet. Dawn wanted to be sick. She knew she had to get out fast or Jude probably would kill her.

Still clutching the hockey stick, she mustered just enough strength to wriggle on to her side, knocking Jude off balance. Jude toppled sideways, hitting her head on the bed, and lay sprawled on the floor for a second, her skirt up round her middle, her revolting fat stomach spilling all over.

But she rallied surprisingly quickly. She twisted, put her hands on the floor and started to pick herself up. Dawn could see the photo underneath her, all crumpled and torn. She didn't have much time. She sprang to her feet, picked up the hockey stick in both hands and brought it down on Jude's body with all her force.

One, two, three. Jude screamed, curling into a little ball,

pulling her arms up to protect her head. Dawn wanted to laugh. She felt so good, mighty, powerful. Made a change.

She took a step forward, closed her eyes tight and brought the stick down again: one, two, three. It made a dull thudding noise. Jude deserved it.

Dawn lost count of the number of times she struck. When her arms started aching she stopped and opened her eyes. Jude was no longer screaming and thrashing around. Good, it had obviously hurt. Dawn paused, took a step forward and then hit one more time without looking. 'One for luck.'

There was a funny sound, a sort of gurgle, like bath water going down the plughole, then a sigh. Dawn dropped the stick and looked down. Jude was lying on her side now, her eyes staring, her hair spread around her in a knotty orange mess, her mouth open. Something seemed to be oozing from the side of her head and nose on to the tatty blue carpet. Blood?

Me mam's gonna kill us.

Dawn squatted down. 'Jude?' There was no reply.

She gave her sister a shake. 'Jude? Stop funning, will ye? We're gonna have to clear this lot up quick before me mam gets back. We'll get wrong . . .'

Jude's shoulder looked a bit weird, sort of wonky. And her ear was bleeding. Dawn sat back. She needed to think about this.

She noticed the frayed edges of the carpet round the scuffed skirting board and the faded brown duvet cover, all rumpled and falling off the end of the bed. She saw the dirty cream walls with stickers and crayon marks on them and the ends of the thin, pale pink curtains fluttering in the summer breeze where the window was open.

All these familiar things. The room seemed so quiet.

Her hands reached up to her mouth. She jumped, startled. Someone was screaming, shattering the silence. It was a high-pitched scream. The hairs on her arms prickled, but she didn't know where it was coming from. Not from Jude. She was sleeping.

There were noises outside the window. Voices. A key turning in the lock: Mam getting back from work; people coming upstairs.

5

'Oh my God!' someone shouted. It was a man. The screaming went on, boring into her unconscious, making her brain hurt. The hockey stick was still on the floor beside her. She looked at her hands, stared at them. They were covered in blood.

Then Dawn realised she was the one screaming, saying the same thing over and over again: 'I didn't mean to, honest to God, I didn't mean to.'

What was she talking about?

Then there were hands on her. Someone was lifting her up. 'Call an ambulance . . . get the coppers.'

Who were these people? What were they doing? Everything was weird.

Someone was carrying her downstairs into a car. It wasn't Mam. She wanted Mam. Where was she?

Then she blacked out.

Chapter Two

**London Borough of Richmond upon Thames.
Present day**

'"The handsome face of Spiculus, turned brown by the sun, moved closer to hers. Cornelia had an overpowering urge to run her fingers through his thick, dark locks. His lips were dangling there, like ripe cherries . . ."'

There was a cough. Evie stopped reading and looked up from the page. She sighed. There was an unwritten rule that no one should speak until whoever was reading out loud had finished. But this was the third interruption in as many minutes.

'Did you want to say something else, Pamela?' Evie asked. It came out slightly more sharply than she'd intended. After all, the whole idea of the writing group was that it was supposed to be friendly and collaborative, not confrontational: the last thing Evie wanted was to get into an argument, and with Pamela of all people.

Pamela, who was sitting up ramrod straight in the front row, nodded. The half-moon glasses slid down her long thin nose a little further. Evie hoped they'd drop off.

'Do lips really dangle?' Pamela enquired. She made it sound like an innocent enough question but the expression on her face gave her away: she was smug, no doubt about it, delighted to have found fault. She really didn't have the right attitude.

'And why on earth don't you say hair rather than locks?' Pamela went on. 'Nobody says locks in real life.' She scanned the rest of the group for approval.

The ten or so others sitting in front of Evie glanced at their feet, embarrassed. Several cleared their throats.

At last Tristram raised a hand. 'Let, erm, er . . .'

7

'Evie,' someone stage whispered.

I've only been coming here for four years.

'Evie, of course,' Tristram continued, straightening his tie. 'Let Evie finish, please.'

Pamela sniffed.

Tristram was self-appointed chairman of the St Barnabas's Creative Writing Group, so called because of the church hall where they met each month. But members didn't hold him in particularly high regard.

For a start, he was forever going on about the army and his old boarding school, wasting valuable time. And being rather hard of hearing, he tended to get the wrong end of the stick, too. At least he'd had the good sense to intervene now, though. It was really bad manners of Pamela to have jumped in like that. She should have waited till the end.

Evie felt crushed. She couldn't help it. She was trying so hard to finish *The Roman's Wife*, her historical romance. It wasn't coming easily to her and she knew that she was making a lot of mistakes. But it was her dream to get published one day and, let's face it, we all have to dream.

The only person whose writing Pamela seemed to have any respect for at all was Becca, and Becca already had a high-powered job. Writing was just a hobby to her. It really wasn't fair.

Evie looked down at the page again and tried to find the spot where she'd left off. Suddenly a voice piped up from the back of the hall: 'Well, I think "lips dangling like ripe cherries" is rather a nice, sensual image.'

It was Nic, confident, outspoken Nic, who could always be relied on to leap to Evie's rescue at moments like this. Evie peered over Pamela's stiff helmet of grey hair into the rows beyond and smiled at her friend.

Nic beamed back and did a furtive thumbs up. But Pamela had the bit between her teeth and would not be constrained. She gave a bitter little smile.

'It's, ahem, a bit of a cliché though, isn't it?' she said.

Evie saw Nic look down at her lap and start to flick furiously through a book. 'Hold on a moment,' she said, her blond bob

8

quivering. 'Here we are. It says in my dictionary that a cliché is "a phrase or word that's lost its original effectiveness or power from overuse". Well, how often do people talk or write about lips dangling like ripe cherries?'

There was silence.

'Precisely,' Nic said triumphantly. 'So I think Evie's perfectly justified in choosing the simile, even if you may have heard it once or twice before.'

Pamela's lips pursed, her mouth set in a thin, jagged line. Evie found herself wondering for a moment if she'd ever kissed anyone, really kissed them – a proper snog. She guessed not. There was nothing ripe and cherry-like about Pamela's lips. In fact she didn't really have any.

Neil, now, was a different matter. He knew how to kiss. His kisses were sexier even than making love. But when was the last time he'd kissed her? She scrabbled around her mind, like someone desperate to recall the blurred face of a long-dead loved one.

But Neil wasn't dead. Oh no. He was giving all his kisses to someone else. Evie felt a stab of misery. She straightened up, pulled down her shoulders, forced herself back to the present. No point dwelling on that. She must look forward to the future. Everyone said so.

'Shall I continue?'

Tristram waved his hand grandly. 'Of course, of course.' He glanced at his watch. 'Good Lord, you'd better get a move on, too. It's half past nine. When I was at boarding school it was lights out at half past nine every night even in the sixth form. Of course we all read under the blankets until Matron came and smacked our bottoms and confiscated our torches.'

No one laughed.

Carol, a woman in the second row who was probably in her late fifties, clicked her tongue. 'He's such a bore, isn't he?' she said loudly, flicking her straggly, shoulder-length grey hair off her face. Tristram didn't seem to hear.

Pamela scraped back her chair theatrically and turned away from Carol. The two women must be of a similar age, Evie guessed, but they could hardly be more different. While Pamela

9

was outwardly genteel and damned only in snide, veiled terms, Carol had a wild, anarchic, tell-it-as-it-is streak.

She was quite batty, of course. She rode her bicycle in all weathers and wore ancient cardies covered in cat hair. There was always a faint whiff of something about her, too – cat pee? Evie didn't like to think about it.

Pamela, on the other hand, favoured neat slacks and twin-sets and never had a hair out of place. She smelled of Yardley Lily of the Valley eau de toilette spray. She could scarcely bring herself even to look at Carol, let alone speak to her, and made no secret of the fact that she thought her a fool. But Evie rather liked Carol. She was eccentric but there was also something deep about her.

Evie caught Nic's eye and found herself starting to giggle. She sucked in her cheeks. She was aware of a few other titters coming from different parts of the room, like the beginnings of a Mexican wave.

Carol, picking up on the atmosphere, threw back her head and roared with laughter herself. 'It's all right,' she snorted, showing off a set of yellowy, stained teeth, 'the old fool's deaf as a post.'

'God, I need a drink,' Nic whispered as she, Evie and Becca pushed open the heavy wooden doors of the church hall and stepped out into the night.

'Me too,' Evie agreed. 'I'm sorry but I loathe Pamela. She's a mean cow. It's not as if she's God's gift to writing either. She's got such a gloomy outlook on life. Her writing makes me want to slit my wrists.'

'I know,' Nic agreed. 'But don't let her get to you. You just keep at it. I love the way you describe how Neil – er, sorry, Spiculus the gladiator is suddenly seeing your heroine in a totally different light. It's as if he'd never looked at her – really looked – before.'

Evie pretended not to notice Nic's slip of the tongue. It's true, she did find herself thinking of her husband whenever she described Spiculus, Cornelia's dishy love interest. But she'd tried to make them different. For instance, Neil had dark-brown hair while Spiculus's was black. And the novel was set in Rome in 60 BC, for heaven's sake, not London suburbia.

She hugged her cardigan around her. It was only September, but the evenings were getting chilly.

'Hey, gurrrls!'

The women swung round. It was Russell, another member of the writer's group. Russell was small and slight, with pale skin, longish, thinning black hair and a wicked sense of humour. He had written several rather difficult literary novels, all unpublished.

'Going for a beverage?' he asked, starting to unpadlock his bike, which he'd chained to a bike rack just beyond the church hall.

Evie smiled. 'Fancy coming?'

Russell shook his head. 'Nah, I should get back.'

'How's the job?' Evie enquired. 'Any interesting tales to tell us?'

Russell worked in a genito-urinary clinic or, as he preferred to put it, he was a 'willy-and-fanny doctor'. He could be deliciously indiscreet.

'Wee-ell,' he said, cocking his head on one side and fastening his helmet. 'We had a newly pregnant woman and her husband in the other day. They were terribly worried because he'd lost his wedding ring in an awkward place and they were afraid it might strangle the baby.'

Evie squealed. 'So what did you do?'

Russell grinned. 'Oh, I just fished around a bit and got it out. It wasn't difficult. Then I gave them a quick anatomy lesson and showed the husband how to do it himself next time. Bob's your uncle!'

Nic guffawed. She had a surprisingly loud, dirty laugh for someone so small; she was only about five feet three and tiny with it, like a sparrow. 'God, how embarrassing. Don't you find it embarrassing when people do things like that?'

Russell shrugged. 'I'm used to it. I'll tell you about the bloke with the penile piercings next time – if you're good.'

'Oooh, yes,' Becca giggled. 'Where exactly—?'

Russell put his hand up. 'Gotta shoot.' He swung a canvas bag over his shoulder and climbed on his bike.

11

'See you next month,' Evie called out as he pedalled off down the street. 'Lovely man,' she went on, turning to the others. 'What a job, though. Wouldn't suit me. Shall we go to the Swan? It's not exactly glamorous but at least you can get a seat.'

'Good idea,' Becca replied, in that rather precise way that she had of talking, as if she were reciting lines. 'Don't let me stay too long, though. I've got a plane to catch in the morning. I'm hoping to clinch a multi-million-pound deal with a company in San Francisco.'

Evie whistled. Why wasn't she clinching multi-million-pound deals rather than fretting about how she was going to pay the gas bill?

Something had definitely gone wrong somewhere.

Chapter Three

The women strolled along the main road in the direction of the station before turning left down a narrow, cobbled side road which led to the River Thames. The pub, about halfway down, was set back slightly from the other buildings and had an old-fashioned-looking sign with a painted swan outside.

Inside there was just one dimly lit room and a few elderly men were propped up on bar stools in the corner. They looked up and stared when Becca, Nic and Evie strode in.

'God, you'd think they'd never seen a woman in here before,' Nic whispered.

Becca smirked. 'Praps they think we should all be at home washing the dishes and ironing shirts.'

Evie grinned up at her. At five feet ten, Becca was by far the tallest of the group. She had long, slim arms and legs but she wasn't model-perfect. She was a typical English pear, with a small bust and wider hips that she tended to disguise by wearing long jackets. She was very attractive, though, rangy, with a long, thin face that was interesting rather than beautiful, and a surprisingly small, upturned nose.

'Ironing, what's that?' Evie quipped.

'Evening, ladies, what can I get you?' The young barman gave them a pleasant smile.

Nic pushed forward. 'Red or white?' she asked, turning to the others.

'White,' they chorused.

'A bottle of Pinot Grigio,' Nic said with an air of authority. 'Actually, make that two.'

Evie started to protest. 'We'll never—'

'It'll be last orders soon,' Nic interrupted, pointing to the large square silver watch on her thin wrist. 'They'll stop serving.'

They sat round a wooden table near the fireplace. Nic filled three glasses nearly to the brim and smiled. 'I'm quite relieved there wasn't time for me to read what I'd written. I dread to think what Pamela would have made of my paltry offerings.'

Evie took a sip of wine. 'How's it coming on?'

Nic grimaced. 'I reckon it's the most unthrilling thriller ever. I read the first few chapters again the other night and decided it was a pile of poo.'

Becca put her glass down. 'Don't be so hard on yourself, I'm sure it's not.' She smiled. 'You should let Evie and me take a look sometime. We'll give you constructive feedback.'

Nic shook her head. 'Thanks, but to be honest I've really not made much progress. For some reason I keep fannying around, finding other things to do and not getting down to it. I've started going for runs in the park and taking loads of time out for swims and walks with the dog. Dizzy's exhausted and the pair of us have never been fitter but the book's just languishing.'

Evie laughed, revealing a big gap between her front teeth. 'I know what you mean. It is hard to get down to it even though once I've cleared the decks and made space in my mind to write, I absolutely love it. But hey, running sounds fab. I wish I could join you but my stupid boobs would get in the way.'

Evie glanced down at her ample chest. She was a 34DD. Neil had never complained but to her, they were the enemy. She'd always envied women like Nic and Becca who could wear T-shirts in the summer and strappy little dresses with no bra and look so free and chic.

Becca shook her head. 'Honestly, Evie, all you need is a good sports bra.'

'Too right,' Nic chipped in. 'I wear two – and a support top as well. Workmen used to shout "they're bouncing well" even though I'm not exactly voluptuous. Not any more.' She leaned forward, glancing left and right to make sure that no one else was listening. 'Guess what?'

Evie and Becca bent over, too; their three heads were practically touching.

'I've had Botox,' Nic whispered conspiratorially.

Evie stared. 'You haven't?'

'No!' said Becca rather loudly. Nic's glare made her wince. 'Sorry.'

Nic nodded. 'I'm surprised you haven't noticed. It's not like either of you to miss a trick. There's this woman who does it really cheaply. She's a trained nurse – I think. I couldn't resist.'

Evie frowned. Cheap Botox didn't sound great. 'Where did you have it done?'

'Ealing.'

'No, you moron, I mean where on your face?'

'Oh.' Nic pushed her blond fringe up. 'Here . . . and here . . . and here,' she said, pointing to her forehead, the gap between her pale eyebrows and her crow's feet, except that she didn't have any and her forehead looked baby smooth.

'Hmmm,' said Evie disapprovingly. 'You didn't need it. It's injecting poison into you. Gross.' She wrinkled her nose. 'What does it feel like?'

Nic thought for a moment. 'Well' – she put her elbows on the table and cupped her chin in her hands – 'I like the fact that the lines have gone but I can't move my forehead at all.' She tried to frown, by way of demonstration, but nothing budged.

Evie giggled. 'That must feel weird.' She and Becca practised wrinkling their foreheads a few times to check that their muscles were in good working order.

'And there's another thing,' said Nic. She looked embarrassed. 'One eyebrow seems to be higher than the other.'

'What?' said Becca and Evie in unison. They peered at Nic more closely.

'Look,' she said, indicating. Her left eyebrow did, indeed, seem to have a more pronounced arch than the other.

Evie snorted; she couldn't help herself. 'It doesn't show,' she lied.

Nic glowered. 'Oh yes it does. And I'll have to wait three months now for it to wear off.'

'Good job you've got a fringe,' Becca said seriously.

'You could always try covering one of your eyebrows up with foundation and painting a new one on to match the other,' Evie said helpfully.

'Or just shaving them both off and starting again,' Becca added.

Nic shot them a look. Her lips had gone very thin and slot-like.

'Er, how's your journalism going?' Evie asked, changing the subject quickly.

Nic's shoulders relaxed. The others took a deep breath. 'I'm stuck doing a piece on the best potties for *Mums* magazine at the moment.' She managed to raise her eyes ceilingwards despite the frozen forehead. 'I do get some turkeys.'

Becca frowned, lifted her eyebrows and frowned again, just to be certain. 'Best potties?' she said. 'Why don't you tout yourself round, try to write for some different publications? Now that Dominic is older you must be fed up with writing about toddlers.'

Nic took a slug of wine and topped everyone up. Evie admired the coloured bangles around her wrists that jangled when she moved.

'It's all right for you' – Nic shrugged – 'you're so dynamic. If you want something, you just go for it. But I'm no good at freelancing. I hate having to hustle for work. *Mums* gives me lots of features and I can practically do them standing on my head so it makes sense for me to stick with them. Anything for an easy life.'

Evie glanced at Becca, who looked irritated. She knew why. Becca was a 'can do' person who had no patience with defeatism. Becca opened her mouth to tick Nic off, but closed it again. Evie took a deep breath. She wasn't satisfied with Nic's explanation either but the conversation was moving on.

'Talking of potties,' Becca said, 'Tom insisted on throwing out James's old buggy the other day. It was getting in the way of his golf clubs. It made me feel quite sad. I realise how little I took James out in it.'

'But you had weekends with him when you weren't working,' Nic insisted. 'You shouldn't feel guilty.'

Becca sighed. 'I know, but I do.'

Evie suddenly felt her eyes filling with tears. They'd been doing that a lot recently. 'God, it's so difficult,' she sighed. 'Here am I not doing much work and feeling guilty that I don't bring in more money and that I'm a bad example to my kids, while you've got an amazing job and you're fretting away about neglecting yours. Why can't we get it right?'

Becca shrugged. 'Don't ask me. But I wouldn't call it an amazing job. It pays well but they buy you body and soul.' She thought of something. 'That reminds me. I've got this colleague at work, Moira, whose daughter's getting married. I told her you designed wedding dresses. Shall I give her your number?' Her eyes were shining.

Evie made a face. 'I don't know. Thanks for thinking of me but I've already got a dress on the go. I'm not sure I can take on anything else right now.'

Becca tipped her head on one side and looked at her friend closely. 'But I thought you wanted more work?'

Evie groaned. 'I do – and I don't. I'm so confused. To be honest I'd bite somebody's hand off to go back into a job instead of working for myself. I like being around people. I miss the stimulation so much. But I've been out of the fashion world so long, I've lost confidence. Besides, the kids have been through so much, I couldn't go waltzing off to work and leaving them.'

She ran a finger round the rim of her glass. 'I'd love to set up my own shop, but it's such a gamble and you need capital. And then I think, What on earth am I saying when I can't even cope with having more than one dress to make at the same time? I must be mad.'

'Stop agonising and just get on with it,' Becca said. 'Being negative will get you nowhere.'

She sounded sharp. Evie bit her lip.

Becca must have noticed. 'Things still hard with Neil?' she asked more gently.

Evie tried to smile. 'Ish.'

Nic topped up her glass again. 'It'll get easier but it's going to take time. Is he still dropping round a lot?'

Evie nodded. 'Almost every day. I don't know which is worse: the days when I see him or the days when I don't.'

Nic pulled a face. 'I'd like to strangle him, Evie, really I would.'

Becca rummaged in her handbag, took a hankie out and blew her nose. 'I've got a cold coming.'

Evie noticed her hair. It had been blow-dried completely smooth. 'You've been to the hairdresser's.' Becca was always having her hair done.

'You're observant,' she said. 'I nipped out at lunchtime.'

'Nice,' Evie fibbed. She hated Becca's hair. It was thick, straight and nearly black – to match her perfectly arched eyebrows – and parted rather severely at the side. It didn't do her justice. It was obviously dyed and looked so unnatural against her pale skin.

Evie had wanted to say something for ages, ever since the three had met at ante-natal classes nearly ten years ago when they were expecting their boys, but she'd never dared.

Maybe the wine was giving her courage. 'Have you ever thought of trying a slightly lighter shade?' she asked tentatively. 'I've always thought you'd suit light brown, or even—'

'I agree!' Nic chipped in rather too eagerly. 'What colour are you really? I imagine . . .'

Becca's look stopped them both in their tracks. She could do that. 'I like this colour.'

Evie swallowed. 'Of course, it's lovely.'

'Yes, lovely,' echoed Nic.

The bell rang, punching a hole in the awkward silence.

'Time, please,' the barman called.

Becca rose.

Nic squealed. 'Look, we've left nearly a whole bottle of wine. What a waste!'

'You paid for it, you take it,' Evie insisted, picking the bottle up and passing it to Nic. 'It's a screw top. You and Alan have it.'

Nic winked. 'If you insist.'

'Mind how you go, ladies,' one of the men shouted after them.

Nic turned and shot them one of her most dazzling grins.

She's so gorgeous, Evie thought, and she really doesn't know it.

She and her friends wandered out into the night.

Chapter Four

Evie fiddled with the front-door key, gently nudging it in and out of the lock trying to find the right position. Damn. It was playing up again. What if this time it had properly broken and she couldn't get in? At least the children were home but she didn't want to ring the bell and wake them.

Finally, after more twisting and turning, the key slid into its appointed grooves and the door creaked open. Evie found herself thinking for the umpteenth time that she really must get someone to fix the mechanism.

The overhead lamp in the hall cast a dingy glow. It was a lovely, wide hall with a high ceiling and elaborate cornicing, but the unflattering light seemed to emphasise all the bad bits. The wooden floor had long since lost its polished sheen and was now scuffed and worn, and there were dirty marks on the walls.

Evie's eyes fell on the thin crack, running almost from ceiling to floor, on the left-hand wall by the mirror. She couldn't help herself. There was a new sheet of plain paper over the crack in a nondescript, off-white. You could tell it was new because the paint was brighter and cleaner than the rest. It was obvious that it had been slapped on to try to hide what was behind. Only it hadn't worked. The crack had come through again.

It depressed Evie. She remembered how worried she'd been when the crack had first appeared, fearing subsidence or some other major problem. She'd begged Neil to investigate, or at least to let her pay someone to do so, but he'd refused, insisting he'd do it himself – when he had time.

Eventually, fed up with her nagging, he'd gone out one Saturday morning and bought a roll of wallpaper and some glue from a DIY shop. It had taken him about half an hour to plonk a sheet over the crack and another half-hour to paint it. The paper looked dreadful, all bobbly. A botched job. And he knew it. Evie was upset, she'd have to live with that, but Neil really didn't care.

'Do it yourself if you don't like it,' he'd snapped.

Well, the penny had finally dropped. It had taken her all those months to face up to the truth and now it was staring her right in the face: he didn't care about the house because he didn't love her any more. She'd tried so hard to ignore the signs: the bad temper, the never wanting to go out with her on their own, the longer and longer working hours, the turning away from her at night.

It was several months more, however, before he'd sat her down on the shabby sofa in the sitting room and told her that he'd fallen for someone else. The way he'd spoken, you'd honestly have thought that it was her fault.

'We've got nothing to talk about any more,' he'd said, refusing to meet her gaze. 'You're so wrapped up in the children, whereas Helen has an interesting career and really understands my work.'

Helen, of course, had every reason to understand his work, being a nurse at the hospital where he was a consultant obstetrician and gynaecologist. She was also twenty-five, childless and beautiful. Neil had always liked beautiful women.

Ironically, he was the one who'd persuaded Evie to give up her job thirteen years ago when she had Freya. He'd said that she could always go back to designing and making wedding dresses when the children were older.

Evie felt a painful lump in her throat. She tried to swallow it down. It was so cruel. She felt washed up, discarded like an old shoe.

She dropped her keys on the hall table and caught sight of the white envelope, still unopened, addressed to Mr Neil Freestone. She must remember to give it to him next time he dropped by. Tomorrow, probably.

She tugged off her coat and threw it over the banisters. Kicked off her shoes too, and left them there in an untidy pile along with the others. At least she had Nic and Becca – and the children, of course. He couldn't take them away from her. She swung round, glanced at herself in the mirror and smoothed down her fair hair, which had been blown out of place by the wind. She wasn't bad-looking, really. But her eyes were sad.

She felt the tears welling again and bit her lip. If she could only hate him. Then it would be easier. Instead, she hated herself for hoping like some stupid, lovestruck fool that he'd change his mind. She stuck her tongue out at her reflection and turned away. She was tired, that's all. She needed to sleep. She'd feel better after a good sleep.

There was no sound from upstairs, which was a relief. Michael was supposed to go to bed at 9 p.m. on weekdays and Freya no later than ten, but when Evie went to check on her she was often awake still, chatting to her friends on the computer. No wonder she found it so hard to get up in the mornings.

Evie didn't like leaving Freya to babysit – she'd only just turned thirteen – but there wasn't a lot of choice. Money was tight now. It was either that or not go out.

She tiptoed into the kitchen and turned on the light. That empty feeling in the pit of her stomach had returned: a strange, gnawing sensation. It wasn't hunger but she needed to fill it. She opened the fridge and peered inside. There were yoghurts, milk, cheese and a piece of old quiche on a plate covered in clingfilm.

She pulled out the quiche and took a bite. It was so cold that it hurt her teeth and the cheese tasted sharp. She pulled a face, wrapped the clingfilm back over the plate and shoved it in the fridge again.

She got a glass of water, turned out the light and padded upstairs, past the hole in the wall made by Michael's cricket ball. Seven years they'd lived in this house and how long had the hole been there – five? She'd had such big plans when they'd moved in, too. It was her dream home: Victorian, with six big bedrooms and a large, south-facing garden. But it had needed a lot of work even before the kids had given it a battering and Neil hadn't been prepared to pay.

Evie shivered. She'd felt so angry and frustrated. She simply hadn't been able to understand his attitude. What a fool! It was all so clear now she knew that he'd started seeing someone else and didn't know how much longer he'd be around. She felt herself sway slightly. She closed her eyes and steadied herself on the handrail.

The bathroom door was open on the first floor and the light was on. Someone had left a wet towel on the lino. She bent down to pick it up. There was scum around the bath, too, and hairs on the soap in the sink. She put the soap on the edge of the bath and brushed her teeth quickly. She'd do a big clean-up tomorrow.

Across the landing, Freya's room was in darkness. Evie poked her head round the door and waited until she could hear her daughter's soft breathing, in and out, in and out. She felt a rush of love – her big girl. Freya was such a support, always asking if she was OK. Evie pulled the door to gently.

Michael, in the next room, had left his radio playing quietly. For company, probably. Even at nine years old he still didn't like it when his mother went out. She tiptoed in and turned the music off, taking care not to wake him either.

Evie went up another small flight of steps to the third floor in the attic and her heart gave a little skip as she entered her own bedroom. It was the one place that she'd managed to decorate before Neil left and it was gorgeous: her haven. She'd chosen a thick, coffee-coloured carpet and a queen-size bed with a squishy brown suede headboard that was really comfortable to lean against when she was reading.

There were full-length, cream silk curtains across the bay window with a motif of trellis and classical vases overflowing with flowers. She'd taken ages choosing that curtain fabric. It had cost a fortune but it was just right – cool and elegant without being boring. And she'd gone for lots of silk scatter cushions in different greys, browns and creams.

The rest of the ramshackle house made Evie's head ache, but her bedroom felt peaceful and soothing. The only problem was that Neil was no longer there to share it with her.

She slipped off her clothes, dropped them on the dumpy little armchair in the corner and pulled on her white cotton nightie. Then she climbed into bed and grabbed the phone beside her. She knew the number off by heart.

A deep, throaty voice answered immediately: 'Zelda speakin'.' She didn't sound surprised even though it was midnight.

'Hi Zelda, it's Evie, Evie Freestone.'

There was a pause.

'I hope it's not too late?'

Evie heard the sound of a match being lit. Another pause. She knew Zelda smoked. She waited.

'Of course not, darlin',' the voice came back at last. Zelda had a distinct cockney twang. Evie could almost smell the tobacco smoke wafting through the handset. 'What can I do for you?'

Evie badly wanted to pour her heart out but she didn't know where to begin. 'I've just come home from an evening out with friends,' she started. 'We went to a meeting then for a drink . . .'

Tears started to well in her eyes again and trickle down the back of her throat, making her splutter. She couldn't finish. She hadn't expected this; she hadn't realised quite how upset she felt.

Zelda made a cooing noise. 'There, there,' she said huskily. 'You had a nice evenin' out and now you've got back to an empty house?'

'Yes,' Evie whispered. 'Well, the children are asleep. I feel so lonely. I miss Neil so much. I don't know what to do.' The last words came out as a sort of wail. She reached for a tissue and blew her nose. There was a box to hand at the side of the bed.

'Come now,' Zelda said softly. 'No need to cry. Would you like me to do a readin'?'

Evie felt her spirits lift. 'Yes please. I could do with some good news.'

'Shall I put it on yer usual card?'

Evie didn't like to think what this would cost. At £1.50 a minute it wasn't cheap. She'd already spent a fortune on Zelda but she was worth every penny.

'Now close yer eyes,' Zelda went on, 'and concentrate very carefully while I make a connection.'

Evie sank back on the pillows and did as she was told. It was such a relief to put herself in someone else's hands, not to have to think for herself.

'Ah yes,' Zelda said at last, 'I can see why you're upset. Someone wasn't very kind to you today?'

Evie gulped. 'No.' She waited, ears pricked, for more.

'A woman?' Zelda asked.

'Yes.'

'An older woman – with glasses? I think I can see glasses.'

'Yes,' Evie repeated. 'Pamela, that's her name. She was horrible to me at my writing group. Picked my work apart.'

Zelda tutted. 'Stay away from her, sweet'art,' she warned, 'she's a negative influence. She has a bad aura. You must surround yourself only with positive people who'll make you feel better, who'll help you heal.'

Evie breathed in deeply and clasped the phone tighter to her ear. Zelda was so perceptive. She was always right. Pamela was no good for her. She took a deep breath. 'What about the future?' she whispered. 'Can you see . . . will Neil ever come back?'

She had butterflies in her stomach. Was she making a mistake – pushing Zelda too far?

Zelda was silent for a few moments. It felt like an eternity. 'No, darlin',' she said finally. 'I've told you before.'

Evie's brain started to swim. That sounded so definite. Surely there was some hope?

'But you will meet someone else,' Zelda went on. 'Someone who'll be better for you, a healin' influence.'

Evie was surprised. 'Are you sure?'

'Quite sure. I can see him now. He's travelled a lot, some sort of explorer perhaps.'

Evie was intrigued. 'What does he look like?'

Zelda paused. 'I can see quite a lot of hair, broad shoulders. He's tall, yes, and good-lookin'.'

'When will I meet him?'

'Quite soon. In the next twelve months or so.'

Twelve months? That seemed a long time to wait. 'Does he have children?' It was unlikely that she'd meet someone without children at her age. Whoever it was would be bound to have a past.

Zelda made a sucking-in sound. She was having another drag. Evie was sitting straight up in bed now, all agog.

'I can't be certain, darlin',' Zelda continued. 'But I think, yes, I think he has. I'm seein' one or two children.'

Evie sighed. That would be complicated. But anything was possible. Blended families were so common these days.

'What's his name?'

Zelda coughed. 'It begins with a T – or a P. Or is it a W? One of those.' She paused. 'The picture's fadin',' she said suddenly. She sounded anxious. 'I can see somethin' else . . . oh!'

Evie was startled. 'What is it?'

Zelda started to speak again slowly. Her voice sounded different, low and strange. 'I can see blackness,' she said. 'Badness.'

Evie shuddered. 'What sort of badness?'

'Somethin' terrible,' Zelda went on, 'hate, somethin' wicked . . .'

She shrieked. Evie jumped and dropped the phone on the bed. Her heart was hammering. She wanted to stop listening but couldn't. She picked the phone up again warily.

'You must be careful,' Zelda hissed. 'Very, very careful.'

Evie waited, frightened. She knew not to disturb Zelda when she was in the middle of a trance. At last, however, she could stand it no longer: 'What is it?' she begged. 'Who do I need to be careful of?'

'I'm sorry, love,' Zelda whispered. She sounded weary. 'The connection's gone. I can't see no more. I shouldn't have told you. Don't worry about it; it's not important. Just think about nice things, happy things now.'

Evie knew she wouldn't be able to sleep after that. She closed her eyes but kept the light on and the radio playing. What did Zelda mean about something terrible? What if it were true? She wished that Neil were here beside her to comfort her. He'd tell her it was all a load of nonsense, there was nothing in it.

She tried to think positive thoughts about this strange but interesting other man that Zelda had mentioned. She painted a mental picture of his smile, his eyes, his hands. Their lips met, but it was Neil's face she saw looking into hers, Neil's hair that she felt beneath her fingers.

She pulled the pillow over her head and squeezed her eyes

tight shut to blot out the image. The pieces of his face scattered, like a broken jigsaw. But as soon as she stopped squeezing, they started to re-form piece by piece. Soon her husband was right there in front of her again, laughing at her.

'Just go away,' she whispered. 'Please leave me alone.'

But he wouldn't.

Chapter Five

'Don't touch that, Alice. Omigod, look what you've done now!'

Becca stared at the thick splodge of creamy-brown foundation on the bedroom carpet. It was the expensive Clarins foundation that gave her pale skin a lovely warm glow. But more importantly, how the hell was she going to get it out?

She grabbed a piece of cotton wool from her dressing table and rubbed it into the once greenish patch of carpet. Bits of white fluff now stuck to the gloop creating an almost artistic effect. What did it remind her of? Ah yes, that was it, a sheep. An impressionistic sheep in a grassy field. If it were Easter time, one of the children could cut the sheep out, stick on two black eyes and some legs and give it to somebody as a nice card.

But what the hell was she doing thinking about Easter? The fact was that she'd made the stain much worse and now she was definitely going to be late.

'You naughty girl,' Becca said, snatching the pot of foundation from her daughter's hand. 'I've told you not to play with Mummy's make-up, and what have you got on your face? Oh, Christ. You've been at my blusher too, haven't you?'

Becca tried to scrub the red powder off her daughter's cheek with another piece of cotton wool, only it didn't work.

She scurried to the bedroom door. 'Tom? TO-OM, where the hell are you?'

'He can't hear you, Mummy, he's downstairs on the loo,' Alice said gravely.

Becca swung round. Alice's eyes were very wide.

'He's been there ages,' the little girl went on. 'I think he's reading the paper.'

'I'll bet he's reading the paper,' Becca spat. 'He's always on the bloody loo when I need him. I asked him to give you break-fast. Don't tell me you haven't had breakfast?'

Alice looked guilty.

Becca checked herself in the mirror and ran a brush through her thick, shoulder-length, almost black hair one last time. She'd only recently had her eyebrows and eyelashes retinted, which meant that she didn't need black mascara. One less job. She grabbed Alice by the arm.

'Come on, young lady,' she said, steering the little girl towards the stairs. 'I'm going to flush out that no good sonofabitch dad of yours if it's the last thing I do.'

Tom was sauntering into the kitchen, a newspaper under one arm, when Becca caught up with him. He scratched his head and gave her a wide, relaxed smile, flashing two dimples in his plump cheeks.

'Hi, Becks, I thought you'd left,' he said casually. He was still in his dressing gown – the silk purple and gold kimono that she'd bought on one of her business trips to Japan. On his feet were the soft beige leather slippers she'd found in Morocco. Small, round and ruddy-faced, with a mass of once black, now rapidly greying curls, he looked quite the relaxed, trouble-free gentleman of leisure. It annoyed her immensely.

Becca looked daggers at him. 'I haven't left because Alice has just tipped foundation all over the bedroom carpet,' she snarled. 'And she says she hasn't had breakfast either.'

Tom looked surprised. 'I thought I asked you to get some cereal?' He looked at his daughter affectionately.

Becca jumped in before Alice had time to answer. 'She can't get her own cereal,' she spat, 'because she can't reach. In case you haven't noticed, she's only six.'

Tom ruffled Alice's mop of curly fair hair. She looked like a little angel with her big blue eyes; everyone said so. 'You can reach the cereal if you get a stool, can't you, Ally-Pally?'

Alice looked from Mum to Dad, uncertain of what she was supposed to say.

'No she can't,' Becca snapped. 'And don't call her Ally-Pally, you know I hate it.'

James came into the hall now brandishing an exercise book.

28

He had straight hair, like his mother, but it was the same colour as his sister's – pale yellow – and cut very short above the ears. Becca noticed that he was still in his blue and white checked pyjamas. Had the au pair forgotten to iron his school shirts? Bloody Monica. She was hopeless. Becca would have to have another word with her.

'Can you sign this for me?' James said, shoving the exercise book under her nose. 'I'm going to finish my review in a minute.'

Becca wished that she was three and could fling herself down and throw a temper tantrum. 'No, I can't sign it,' she screeched. 'I'm going to miss my plane and why haven't you finished your review and why can't you ask your dad for once who's been sitting on the toilet for the last half-hour having a nice read?'

Tom cleared his throat. 'Ahem, loo or lavatory, my darling, not toilet.' He grinned.

Becca took a deep breath and counted silently to herself. It usually worked. James's mouth had started to quiver at the corner. He was nine and tall and grown-up-looking for his age, but he still cried very easily. And he hated it when his parents argued – which was rather a lot.

Tom, registering, took the book from his son. 'Don't take any notice of her,' he said, turning the pages until he found the right place. 'She was out last night with the girls and she's in a foul mood. Here, give me a pen. Where shall I sign it?'

Becca was almost in tears as she jumped in the taxi and headed for the airport. She loathed leaving the children in a panic like that and she hadn't even kissed them goodbye. Why couldn't Tom be more supportive? He knew that she had an early start and now the kids would be thinking that she was the bad fairy as usual while he was the nice, cuddly one. And she wouldn't see them for four days.

In some respects it was easier when she was away. At least then she had only herself to think of. But that was an awful thing to feel. She spent three or four months of the year abroad and missed the children so much. If Tom pitched in and helped as he should the mornings would go more smoothly.

She checked her watch: 7.40 a.m. The traffic didn't seem too bad – so far. She was going to be all right but she might have to run when she got to Heathrow. Mind you, she was used to cutting it fine. She settled back in the leather seat. There was no point stressing about it now, it was out of her hands. She'd have plenty of time on the plane to gather her thoughts and study the papers she'd brought with her.

Thank God she was flying with British Airways. She felt safe with them. Well, safer. That flying course she'd been on hadn't exactly conquered her phobia. She was bloody terrified. They said it was all to do with her fear of letting go, of losing control. It was true she was a control freak, that's why she'd got where she was. Knowing it didn't make flying any easier, though.

She unzipped her black leather briefcase, checked all the information was there: the mission statement for PSR Pharmaceuticals Inc., the company's annual report, investments to date, a biography of the chairman and so forth. In truth, she hadn't wanted to take on any new clients right now, her portfolio was big enough already. But it would have been difficult to turn down.

Her BlackBerry pinged. Email from James. 'Don't worry, Mummy, review all done. Love you xxx'.

Dear James.

'Well done, darling, have a good day,' she emailed back. 'See you Tuesday. Give A a big kiss.' There, now she felt better.

She pulled out her mini iPod and put on her relaxation album: *Balance Your Life: Ten Easy Steps to Emotional Health*. The woman's soothing tones filtered through Becca's brain.

'Now, close your eyes. Breathe in gently through the nostrils, breathe out gently through your nostrils,' the woman said. 'Become aware of how the cool air enters the nostrils and how the air feels a little bit warmer when you exhale. Find your own rhythm. After doing this for a little while, breathe in gently and hold your breath for a few seconds . . . Now breathe out with a sigh like this – herrrr. And again. Herrrr. Repeat this exercise fifteen times.'

Becca breathed in and out fifteen times as instructed.

'Now,' the soothing voice continued, 'concentrate on the noises inside and outside this room. Just accept them for what they are, let them pass by like clouds . . .'

Becca could hear the purr of the car's engine and a motor-bike overtaking. She felt drowsy. She'd gone to bed later than intended last night.

'Relax all the muscles in your face, your eyebrows, your cheeks, your jaw, your mouth, your tongue, your whole face. Let it go loose and limp, loose and limp.'

Her face felt liquid, muscle-free.

'Your whole face is feeling simply relaxed,' the woman went on. 'And remember, on every out-breath you're feeling a little bit more relaxed than before. Now relax all the muscles in your back, down to your buttocks. Relax. Now let this feeling of relaxation move to your shoulders. Let both your shoulders drop down. Loose and limp, loose and limp.'

'We're here, miss.'

Becca's eyes sprang open. For a moment she had no idea where she was. Then she remembered. She must have nodded off. She sat up quickly and straightened her jacket. There was a wet patch on the lapel. Oh God, she'd been dribbling.

The taxi driver opened Becca's door and pulled her wheelie suitcase from the boot. He produced a receipt from his pocket which she signed hurriedly. Then she grabbed the suitcase and her briefcase and ran. She had no idea what she looked like. Her hair was probably sticking up all over the place but there was no time to muck about.

She plonked herself down in the aircraft with just a few moments to spare and breathed a sigh of relief. She fastened her seatbelt and waited for lift-off. There was a smell of cooking and she realised that she was hungry. On a good day she'd get to the airport a little early and have her favourite Eggs Benedict for breakfast in the plush Concord Room at Terminal 5. But this morning there'd been no chance.

She was pleased to be tucked away in a window seat out of sight. She pulled out her BlackBerry furtively, ignoring the announcement about turning off all electronic equipment, and switched on. There were the usual 149 emails but nothing urgent.

31

She glanced quickly down the list at the sender and subject and started deleting junk messages. This would save her a few minutes when she arrived at her hotel, the Mandarin Oriental in San Francisco.

She continued scanning down the email list and was pleased to find one from Nic. It had been sent at 1.30 a.m. She must have typed it after she got home last night. Blimey, she stayed up late.

The subject was 'Howdy Doody!' Becca opened up the text. 'Good luck, babe, sock it to 'em! See you very soon. Nic x'.

Becca smiled and wrote back: 'I have two books with me, something edifying about the spread of Liberalism in Europe and another called *The Smart Girl's Guide to Looking Good and Feeling Great*. I know which I'll read first! Becks x'.

The plane started to taxi slowly towards the runway and the air steward started the safety routine. Becca closed her eyes and gripped the armrests. How many times had she seen this? She couldn't bear to watch it again, it just made her more nervous.

She tried to imagine that she was at home, curled up on the sofa with the children watching a DVD. Taking off and landing were the worst. It helped if she tried not to hear the engine sounds but focused on something else entirely.

She cast her mind back to the writing group last night. It had been some meeting. Pamela had behaved even more badly than usual and Carol was shocking. But Russell was as sweet and incisive as ever. He was such a nice man. She really valued his comments.

She felt annoyed with herself for having made so little progress in the last few months. Evie was deadly serious about her novel, but she, Becca, had only been playing at it really. But it was all mapped out. She just needed to get down to it. A series of six kids' mysteries, a touch of the Enid Blytons, a sort of modern-day Famous Five. She was sure it would work.

The bit she enjoyed most was describing the house in Devon where the children were holidaying, with its endless rooms and sprawling orchards surrounded by fields. So different from her own, poky childhood home.

She shivered. Maybe she'd find some time to write some more on this trip. She could become a famous author and get off the hamster wheel. It wasn't impossible. J. K. Rowling had done it.

J. K. had been on her own when she'd started – a single mum. Becca thought of Tom. She hadn't mentioned her dream, her fantasy of giving up work, to him. He'd just laugh and say that she couldn't write for toffee. He, being a sports journalist, was the writer in the family. Her job was to make money and keep him in the lifestyle to which he was accustomed. She pictured him in that purple and gold kimono. She wished to God she'd never given it to him.

She opened her eyes and was just about to switch off her BlackBerry when another email caught her attention. It was from Facebook.

Gary Laybourn added you as a friend on Facebook. We need to confirm that you know Gary in order for you to be friends on Facebook.

To confirm this friend request, follow the link below:
http://www.facebook.com/n/?reqs.php

Thanks,
The Facebook Team

Becca read the message again to be sure. Her breath started to come in short gasps. Gary Laybourn? From primary school? It couldn't be. But she didn't know anyone else with that name. It must be – but how had he found her? More importantly, how the hell had he recognised her?

She smoothed her nearly-black hair and tucked it behind her ears – an involuntary movement. She should never have joined Facebook. She was a fool. She should have trusted her instincts. But everyone at work had been talking about it. It would have seemed odd if she hadn't signed up. Besides, she looked totally different now.

Not as different as she thought.

She licked her lips and glanced around, half expecting a lynch mob to appear. No one had moved from their chairs; everything looked perfectly normal. The blood was pounding in her temples. She felt as if she was going to be sick.

Gary Laybourn. What did he want? To sell her story to the *News of the World*? She'd liked him once. He'd been nice to her. They were sort of going out, in a silly, twelve-year-old way, until . . . well.

It was so long ago, in another life. She'd shoved all those memories in a box, buried it and thrown away the key.

She switched off the BlackBerry quickly, took a deep breath, pulled *The Smart Girl's Guide to Looking Good and Feeling Great* out of her handbag, but she couldn't concentrate. It was impossible. As soon as the plane reached ten thousand feet she grabbed her iPod. She needed the relaxation CD again. She'd known something like this would happen one day. It was bound to. She wasn't prepared, though. How could you be?

She closed her eyes and tried to clear her brain, calm herself down. She'd bin the email and never hear from him again. She was shivering, she felt so cold. She'd liked him so much. He'd written to her a couple of times but she hadn't written back. She tried to imagine what he was doing now. Was he married? Did he have children? She'd like to know – but could she trust him?

'Good morning, madam, have you decided what you'd like for breakfast?' The male air steward's smile seemed to have been pinned on his face and abandoned there.

Becca shook her head.

He frowned. 'Do you need any assistance?' She must have gone white.

'No thanks.' She tried to smile. 'I'm not hungry.'

She plugged in her earphones again. 'Loose and limp, loose and limp,' the woman on the CD said. But Becca couldn't concentrate, the soothing tones were just an irritation, like a wasp in her ear. The flight would seem interminable. She flicked the iPod off. She was going to have to deal with this on her own.

When they finally arrived, she switched her BlackBerry back on, logged on to Facebook and reread the message. Her finger hovered over the delete key but she couldn't press it.

Her palms felt sweaty. She wiped them on her skirt and hit 'reply': 'Rebecca Goodall has accepted your invitation to become friends.'

There was no going back now.

Chapter Six

Nic poked a finger in her mouth and fished out a small piece of plastic. Pah. It had broken off the end of the Biro she'd been chewing. She made a face and dropped it in the bin beside the desk.

She rubbed her eyes. So, which potty should she 'highly recommend'? Her panel of testers – three mums from different parts of the country – seemed to like the one that made flushing sounds. It was also splash-proof, musical and there was a pull-out, portable potty underneath. It really was all-singing, all-dancing.

And to think that Dominic hadn't ever even used a potty. Hadn't liked them. Preferred to go on the big loo straightaway. Better keep that to herself.

She started to tap on the computer. *Mums* had already commissioned her next piece after this one: kiddies' toothpaste. She was grateful for the work, really she was. She remembered being obsessed with all this sort of thing when Dominic was small. She could talk for hours to other mothers about cloth versus disposable nappies, teething gels, baby massage and suchlike. It had seemed fascinating back then.

She should have moved on but she hadn't the energy to come up with original ideas, to get on the phone to commissioning editors and introduce herself, sell herself. She pushed back her chair, stood up and stretched. Dominic would be home before long. Maybe she should forget the potties feature and do a bit of her novel.

She scratched her head. She needed coffee first. She wandered downstairs to the kitchen. It was a big, square room at the back of the house with a large rectangular oak table at one end and a squishy cream sofa against one wall. The table was almost completely surrounded by glass walls and looked out over a neat, symmetrical garden. At the other end of the kitchen were the sink, cooker, dishwasher and pale oak worktops. The whole room was painted white and there were various carefully selected modern paintings on display. Nic had picked them up at affordable art fairs. She loved collecting paintings.

She'd had the kitchen designed by a first-class architect about three years ago. She'd wanted a feeling of space, light and, above all, harmony. She couldn't bear clutter. She'd been delighted with the result at the time but somehow, now, the room seemed to have lost its lustre. It didn't give her so much pleasure any more.

Her eyes fell on the breakfast plates still on the table. She quickly bundled them into the sink. Then she filled the stainless-steel kettle and put two big spoonfuls of dark-brown coffee into a small cafetière. She breathed in and the smell filled her lungs. She really should cut down on caffeine. There again, there were more important things to worry about.

She glimpsed the open bottle of red wine in the corner beside the sink, next to the jars of rice and pasta, and looked away quickly. She pulled a bottle of Chardonnay from the wine rack below and put it in the American-style stainless-steel fridge. Then she took out a litre of milk and poured some in her favourite pink flowery mug along with the coffee.

Upstairs again she sat down, closed the potties document and opened up her book. Reading the title, as she had done so often before, still gave her a tickle of excitement:

THE GIRL FROM NIGER
by
NIC QUINTON

She checked the word count: 30,375 words. Getting on for a third of the way through. Once she reached the 50,000-word mark she'd feel that she was really making progress.

She scrolled down to Chapter Ten and started to reread. 'A wave of shock surged through Beattie's body. She stared again at the man over the top of her newspaper. It couldn't be. It was!

He was the man she'd seen hanging around outside her hotel that day. And again in the bar last night. But who was he?'

Nic felt a tingle of pleasure. The action was hotting up. She continued to read until she got to the bit where she'd left off the day before yesterday. She began to type:

'Beattie finished her drink quickly and paid the bill. She decided to call on Adamou on her way home to see what he thought.'

Nic loved writing about Beattie, a beautiful, mixed-race investigative journalist with long black hair that she smothered in oil so that it went ringletty. Beattie was everything that Nic would like to be: brave, adventurous, brimming with self-confidence.

She'd sent Beattie to Niger to investigate the gruesome discovery of a child's body – a girl – in the River Severn, with her liver and kidneys removed. Police reckoned that the girl might have been killed for her body parts. A number of other children had gone missing from the area where the girl came from and rumours abounded locally that the parts were being sold to rich westerners for transplantation.

In Niamey, Niger's capital, Beattie had become friendly with Adamou, a handsome young artist she'd met in a bar who seemed keen to help her with her investigations. They'd soon started a steamy affair.

Nic thought for a moment.

'He came to the door in his shorts and sandals – and nothing else. When he saw that it was Beattie, he grinned with delight.

'"Come in, beautiful," he said, pulling Beattie by the arm into the dark interior. "I've been thinking about you."'

The doorbell rang. Bugger. Nic quickly closed the document and raced downstairs two at a time. 'Coming,' she shouted.

She could hear Dominic pushing against the door. Why did he do that? He was so impatient. She pulled the door open and he fell forwards, practically knocking her over as he barged into the hallway.

'Careful,' Nic scolded. She smiled at Evie, standing behind Dominic. Evie was taller than Nic, but only by a couple of inches, and rounder. She wasn't fat, far from it, but she did have this large bust that she tried – and usually failed – to disguise.

Today she was wearing a long-sleeved, pale-pink T-shirt that suited her pretty, peaches-and-cream complexion. There was a good inch of cleavage peeping out of the V-neck. You couldn't avoid it. She grinned back, revealing the endearing gap between her two front teeth.

'Thanks for giving him a lift,' Nic said. 'Coffee?'

Evie shook her head. 'I promised I'd get new school shoes for Freya. Her old ones are wrecked.'

Nic glanced over Evie's shoulder and caught sight of Freya in the passenger seat of the battered silver Renault Espace. Michael was in the back. Freya turned and gave a half-smile.

'Michael can stay here,' Nic said brightly. 'I'll give him tea. I imagine shoe shopping isn't his idea of a good time?'

'Too right.' Evie frowned. 'But you're always—'

Nic raised a hand. 'Dom will be delighted and it's no trouble, honest. Maybe you can stay for a glass of wine later?'

Evie smiled. 'That's really kind . . .'

'Settled.' Nic grinned. Michael was already getting out of the car.

'Am I staying?' he asked hopefully. He must have clocked something in the women's body language. 'Please, Mum?'

'All right.' Evie ruffled his hair. 'You're saved from the shoe torture – this time.'

'Yesssss!' Michael punched the air.

Nic hummed as she spread out the oven chips on a baking tray and took the peas and fishfingers out of the freezer. It was hardly cordon bleu but at least the boys would eat it. She wondered what to do for Alan and opened the fridge. There were prawns and lots of vegetables. She could do a curry. She liked cooking curries. There again, he'd probably have had a big lunch at work and there was no point cooking curry just for her. She pulled a ready-made moussaka out of the freezer. It'd do. She'd just have a bit of salad.

She checked the kitchen clock: 5.50 p.m. Ten minutes to go. She tipped some peanuts into a bowl and opened a packet of port and stilton crisps. She sniffed and wrinkled her nose. She picked three of her favourite glasses from the cupboard – the green and silver party ones that she'd found in a catalogue – and then she laid the table.

The boys were very quiet upstairs, probably on the PlayStation. The clock hands slid to the 6 and 12. Nic breathed in and out slowly, padded to the fridge and removed the bottle of Chardonnay. Her fingers trembled slightly as she uncorked it and poured herself exactly half a glass.

The wine was pale gold, thick, almost oily-looking. She took a sip and sighed. Her body seemed to melt into the liquid. She took another sip and closed her eyes.

The oven pinged. Her eyelids fluttered open. 'Boys!' she called. 'Supper.'

They trooped into the kitchen and sat, silently gobbling down the food that she'd put in front of them. She watched with amusement while Dominic, his dark head bent over the plate in concentration, separated his food into three parts: peas, fishfingers and chips. Then he ate the peas and fishfingers, leaving the chips, his favourite, till last. He'd always done that, ever since he was old enough to hold a spoon and fork.

Evie's Michael was the opposite, though. He ate the chips first, dipping them again and again into the tomato ketchup, his mouth soon smeared red, making smacking noises with his lips. Then he ate the fishfingers and finally the vegetables – his least favourite. He was rather quiet and reserved when he didn't know people but Nic was glad that he felt at home here.

'Eat up your peas then you can have pudding,' she said firmly.

Gradually the volume in the kitchen started to increase. Soon, it was almost deafening. The two boys were laughing and shoving each other. Dominic almost fell off his chair.

'Watch it,' Nic warned. She recognised the signs. They'd had their fuel boost, now they were hopping with energy. She unlocked the glass door and slid it open.

'Go,' she laughed. 'Go outside and run a few laps round the garden.'

They burst out like whippets from the traps.

40

'Race you to the tree at the end,' Dominic screamed.

'My shoelace has come undone,' Michael wailed. But Dominic had already set off. Michael tore off the shoe in frustration, threw it across the grass and raced, with one shoe on, one shoe off, after his friend.

Nic turned back inside and slid the door closed again. Her wine glass was sitting on the worktop near the sink. It was nearly empty now. She drained the last drop. She was annoyed. Where was Evie? She started to clear the table. She could hear the boys shouting outside. She took a handful of peanuts, opened and closed the dishwasher several times finding more things to put in.

At last the doorbell rang and she raced down the hall. 'Did you get the shoes?' she asked, smiling.

Freya, standing behind Evie, held up a plastic bag. 'Ta da.'

Evie grimaced. 'We must have gone to about ten shoe shops and tried on practically every single pair.' She looked meaningfully at Nic. 'In the end we reached a compromise.'

Freya shrugged her shoulders and grinned. She would be such a pretty girl, Nic thought, if only she didn't dress so oddly.

Nic took the plastic bag. 'Come inside and show me,' she said to the girl. 'Evie, I should think you need a nice glass of wine after that.'

She poured Evie a glass and another one for herself. Evie didn't seem to notice that the bottle was already open. The women sat round the kitchen table and Freya produced a pair of big, black, very masculine-looking Dr Martens.

'They're great,' Nic lied. She glanced nervously at Evie. 'Very trendy.'

Evie smiled back weakly.

Freya nodded without making eye contact. This, Evie had already explained to Nic, was all part and parcel of being an emo – short for emotive or emotional – a cool young subset of the Goths, apparently. Generally, emos worked hard at looking – and being – miserable, introspective and misunderstood.

Freya had dyed black hair and wore heaps of mascara. Today she was in her school uniform but at weekends she favoured skinny jeans and tight, printed, band T-shirts. She tended to slouch so that her slender body resembled a question mark. Despite attempting to look as unappealing as possible, however, there was a sweetness about her that she couldn't disguise, and a vulnerability. She had big blue eyes, a peaky little chin and a full mouth. In a few years, Nic thought, she'd be a beauty.

Nic felt that Evie was remarkably sanguine about the emo business. Evie's view was that it was just a phase and Freya would come out the other end. She'd been through a lot with her dad leaving home and needed to express herself.

The boys opened the glass door and burst into the kitchen. 'We're going up to watch telly,' Dominic explained, racing past.

'Take your shoes off first,' Nic called after them.

Finally, Evie took another sip of wine and rose. 'I must go. Freya's got homework for tomorrow.'

'But we haven't finished the bottle yet,' Nic protested. 'You can always leave the car here and pick it up in the morning.'

Evie was about to reply when Nic's husband, Alan, appeared in the kitchen doorway. He was a small, slightly awkward-looking man with short, straight hair that was greying at the sides and combed neatly off his face with a side parting. He was wearing a navy-blue raincoat over his dark suit, which looked just a little too big for him. He hovered uncomfortably for a second or two.

'Darling!' Nic smiled, beckoning him over. 'We were setting the world to rights. Glass of wine?'

He walked over to Nic and pecked her on the cheek. 'No thanks. Good to see you, Evie.' He took off his raincoat, laid it on a chair and started loosening his tie.

'And you're . . . ?' He looked at Freya.

'My daughter, Freya,' Evie explained quickly.

Nic watched him carefully. His left eye flickered.

'Of course. How do you do, Freya.' He held out his hand, which she took. 'I didn't recognise you.'

She didn't meet his gaze.

'The last time we met you were just a little girl with bunches.'

At that she gave a half-smile.

He turned back to Nic. 'I've got a bit of work to do.' He patted her on the shoulder.

Nic glanced at Evie and took a big glug of wine, draining the glass. 'Work, work, work, it's all he does.' She poured herself more wine.

Alan was already on his way out of the door. 'Bye, Evie. Bye, Freya.'

'He slaves away in that study of his till all hours,' Nic went on. 'I honestly don't think he'd notice if I pranced around in nothing but a pair of fishnet stockings.'

'You should try to go away together for a weekend or something,' Evie suggested. 'It sounds like you need it.'

Nic didn't seem to hear.

'I almost wish he had some secret lover hidden up there,' she said, taking another sip of wine. 'At least then I could understand why he doesn't want to be with me.'

Chapter Seven

Neil's Alfa Romeo was outside the house when Evie and the children returned. She shivered. She hated that car: his tart cart. He'd bought it soon after he'd walked out, leaving her with the ancient Renault Espace. She'd like to run a fifty-pence piece all along that horrible, sleek, shiny black side.

He'd let himself in as usual and had his back to them when they entered the kitchen. There was a strong smell of toast. He'd obviously been making himself at home. She felt a prickle of irritation. That was her coffee and her bread he was using, but she couldn't say anything. She mustn't upset the kids.

He turned to face them and grinned. Evie registered the full, soft mouth surrounded by day-old stubble and the dimple in his chin. Her insides fluttered. Why did he still have this effect on her?

'Hey, Michael, where have you been?' He ruffled his son's hair, which was dark brown like his own. Freya hung back with her mother.

'C'mon. Give your old dad a kiss,' Neil said. Freya allowed him to peck her on the cheek.

'I've got to do my homework,' she said, moving quickly towards the door.

'Supper will be about half an hour,' Evie called after her.

Neil fetched himself a plate from the cupboard and sat down at the kitchen table with two slices of buttered toast.

'Want some?' he asked Michael, who shook his head.

'I had tea at Dominic's.'

Evie got out the salmon pieces she'd defrosted in the fridge and stuck them in the oven. Then she made a salad and fetched knives, forks, glasses and put them on the table. She made it take longer than necessary. She needed something to do.

She listened to the pair of them discussing Michael's day, and then the big football match coming up and which side they wanted to win. She wanted to cry. It sounded so artificial, like small talk. Before, when Neil was at home, he didn't need to ask questions like that, he just knew whom Michael would be supporting.

'Haven't you got any homework?' she asked Michael eventually. Neil had had long enough. Michael sloped upstairs. She waited for Neil to leave but he didn't.

'I've got something to tell you, Evie,' he said.

Her heart started beating faster.

'Sit down,' Neil said. 'Please.'

'I'd rather stand.' She needed to retain some sense of control.

'Helen's pregnant,' he told her. 'The baby's due in April. We're very pleased.'

She felt herself sway slightly and put her hands on the worktop to steady herself.

'I wanted to tell you first, of course,' he went on. 'Then Helen and I would like to tell the children together. We might take them to a restaurant, have a bit of a celebration.'

Evie bit her lip. She wanted to cry but she was determined not to give him the satisfaction. Instead, she fetched herself a glass of water.

'Congratulations,' she said, deadpan.

'Don't be like that,' he replied, coming up behind her. 'It'll be nice for the children to have a baby brother or sister.'

He started to put his hands on Evie's shoulders but she squirmed away, raising her flattened palms. 'Don't touch me . . .'

He backed off.

'I'm very happy for you, Neil,' she went on, as steadily as she could. 'But I'd like you to be careful with the children. They're still very upset about us and this'll be a big shock.'

Neil made to sit down again but Evie knew that she couldn't hold it together for much longer. 'Please go now,' she said quietly. 'I need to get supper.'

He sighed. 'OK. I should be able to pop round again tomorrow, bar emergencies.'

'Please don't,' she said under her breath. 'Please do.'

'What?'
'Nothing.'

Freya knew something was wrong the minute she walked in. 'Are you OK?'

Mum was standing at the sink running her finger under the cold tap. She looked pale. 'I cut my finger,' she said, putting it in her mouth.

Freya moved to be by her side.

'It's all right,' Mum said reassuringly. 'I'll be fine. It was stupid, I was cutting the bread and somehow missed. I'll be OK in a minute.'

Freya took her mother's hand and examined the cut. It was bleeding quite a lot but it was only a nick.

'Oh Mum.' She put her arms around her mother, who clamped the finger back in her mouth. 'Do you need a plaster?'

Mum shook her head. She wouldn't look Freya in the eye.

Freya peered at her. 'Has something else happened?'
'No.'

Freya scanned the room; she didn't know what she was looking for. 'Has Dad gone?'
'About ten minutes ago.'
'That's a relief.'

Mum laughed and Freya felt reassured. Sort of.

Evie jumped when the doorbell rang. She was supposed to be watching the ten o'clock news except that she wasn't able to concentrate. Nothing was sinking in. It couldn't be Neil again, surely? She'd seen enough of him for one day. Before opening the door she whipped off her round, tortoiseshell NHS glasses and smoothed her fair hair, which was tied back in a ponytail. She hated those glasses, they were so ugly.

'Bill!' She realised that she must look startled.
'Am I disturbing you?'
'No. I thought you were someone else.'

Bill was her next-door neighbour. She'd known him for years, ever since she and Neil had moved in. She saw that Bill was holding a brown paper bag, which he thrust into her hands.

She peered inside. The porch light was on and she could see three smooth, round onions still dusted with earth.

'I dug them up today,' he explained. 'I've got masses, a bumper crop. I'll bring you a pot of my onion relish when it's ready. It's going to be the best.'

She was touched. He often brought her little presents from his allotment – some potatoes here, a bag of apples there – especially since Neil's departure.

'I'm not that keen on relishes, to be honest, but thanks for these.' She smiled. 'They're huge.'

'Ah yes,' he said, 'I am rather pleased with them. Mushroom Mack's dead jealous.'

Bill, a widower in his early fifties, was a former university professor, fearsomely intelligent. He'd taken early retirement and seemed to spend most of his days either with his nose buried in a book or at the allotment. Mushroom Mack, a fellow allotmenteer, appeared to be the bane of Bill's life. Bill claimed that he was outrageously competitive while Bill himself couldn't give two hoots about whose leeks were bigger, but Evie wasn't fooled.

'Come in,' she said.

Bill was about to say no, she could tell.

'Please.' There was a giveaway crack in her voice. She dug her nails in the palms of her hands.

He frowned. 'Are you all right?'

She didn't reply but led him quickly into the kitchen and put on the kettle. 'Neil's girlfriend's pregnant,' she blurted while her back was turned. It just slipped out.

'Oh,' he said.

She put a mug of tea in front of him. It was an Emma Bridgewater mug, covered in different coloured spots. She chose the Cath Kidston one for herself, with the tiny pink and yellow flowers and the chip on the handle.

She sat at the kitchen table, nursing the warm cup in her hands, and glanced at him. He had that intense look on his face that made her slightly nervous. He had deep-set, piercing blue eyes with creases round them and short, silver-grey hair. He was always tanned, throughout the year, because he spent so much time out of doors.

Often he had a wide, amused smile that made the creases round his eyes deepen. But when he was serious, as now, he tended to go very still and quiet and concentrated. Evie felt like one of his students at a university tutorial. She fiddled with the silver chain around her neck.

'That must be difficult for you,' he said at last. She was staring at her tea but she was aware that he was still scrutinising her. She felt tears pricking and starting to trickle down her cheeks. She couldn't help herself. She reached for a piece of kitchen roll.

'I know it's silly,' she spluttered. She wished that she didn't sound so girlish. 'I mean, of course we're separated and everything but I feel, well, gutted. I suppose it just makes everything so final.'

To her surprise, Bill moved his chair closer to hers and put an arm, slightly awkwardly, around her shoulder. She felt her body relax a little.

'You've had a shock,' he said. His voice was low and sympathetic, which made her want to cry even more. 'Of course you're upset.'

'I'm so sorry.' She blew her nose. 'I bet you wish you'd never called.'

Eventually she calmed down. He took his arm away gently and moved his chair back to its original position. 'Please don't apologise. A trouble shared and all that.' He shot her an understanding smile. 'I've got broad shoulders.'

He leaned back in his chair, crossed his arms and rested a foot on his knee. 'Have you spoken to anyone else about this? Your parents, perhaps?'

She made a face. 'I couldn't talk to *them*.'

He scratched his head. 'Why not?'

'I must have told you about them?'

'I don't think so.'

'But you know I'm adopted?'

He nodded.

'They're small business people,' she went on, 'they own several furniture shops. All they care about is money and making sure I screw as much as I can out of Neil. They're furious with him. They think I should take the dosh and cut him out of my life completely. They don't seem to understand that he was my husband for all those years and I still have feelings for him. I can't just switch them off like a tap. Plus, I still want him to be a father to the kids. They'll hate him even more when they find out about the baby,' she added grimly.

Bill knitted his brows. He seemed to be pondering something. 'Would you like to come to the Orange Tree Theatre with me?' he said at last. 'There's a play on called *Chains of Dew*, by an American writer I hadn't heard of. It's had great reviews. It might take your mind off things.'

Evie smiled gratefully. 'It's kind of you but I don't think I'm up to doing anything right now. I'd be terrible company.'

Bill shook his head. 'Don't worry about that. You don't even need to say anything if you don't want. Go on, it might do you good.'

She laughed. 'Is that your idea of the perfect date: a totally silent woman?'

He looked wounded. 'Not at all. I just thought—'

She put a hand on his arm. 'I was joking. Of course I'll come. Thank you for asking. I can do virtually any evening. Just let me know when you can get tickets.'

'You're on.' He rose. 'You know you can call on me anytime, don't you?'

'You're so kind,' Evie replied.

'Sure you'll be all right?'

She nodded. 'Thanks again, Bill.'

'Don't mention it,' he said, taking his Barbour jacket off the back of the chair and heading towards the door. 'Pleased to be of service.'

Chapter Eight

Tears poured down Freya's cheeks as she reread Lucy's words.

Sorry, Lucy wrote. *thought id better warn u. there saying u gave liam a blow job in the boys toilets.*

Freya felt sick. Liam was Abigail's boyfriend. Abigail used to be her friend. She'd hate her now, too. How was she going to face school tomorrow?

This had been going on for weeks. Almost every day Gemma and Chantelle and the others were spreading more rumours on MSN. If only Richie, Chantelle's ex, had never asked Freya out. They'd only snogged once and Chantelle had chucked him already anyway. But still, she and Gemma had decided Freya was a man-stealer and that was that.

She glanced at her new shoes in the box and kicked the lid shut. She didn't feel excited about them any more. She felt guilty. Poor Mum. She'd spent a fortune on them. Gemma and Abigail had the exact same ones but it probably wouldn't make any difference. They complimented other girls who wore them, but they'd just say Freya was copying or something. In the past few weeks they'd called her a slag, liar and a thief, and they'd said she'd fuck anyone in sight. It was getting too much.

Even Freya's best friends were starting to distance themselves from her, probably because they were scared of what would happen to them otherwise. Lucy was all right, though she had to pretend that she was still friends with Gemma and Chantelle and Abigail at school. Freya understood why. But Lucy messaged Freya every night to tell her what was going on. Sometimes she rang and recited exactly what they were saying. It made Freya ill.

u should tell your mum, Lucy wrote.

But Freya would never do that. Mum had enough to deal with. Freya was worried about her. She seemed especially sad tonight, as if she was going to have a nervous breakdown or something. That was scary.

want me 2 come round? Lucy asked.

nah, im all right, Freya lied. *thanks anyway.*

She sniffed, wiping her eyes and nose on the sleeve of her school blouse. Life was shit. She picked up the compact mirror on her desk and stared into it. Her face was all red and blotchy and she had a huge zit on her chin. She never knew she could be so unhappy.

She put in her earphones and switched on her iPod. The first track was Funeral for a Friend's 'Red is the New Black'. It seemed appropriate. She wondered what Cal was doing. It was past nine so she wouldn't look too keen if she messaged him. She started to type: *crap day. wubu2?* (What have you been up to?) She hoped he was online.

'Can I come in?'

She looked up. Michael, her brother, had poked his head round the door. He didn't wait for an answer. She could see that he'd been crying, too. They were a right pair. And Mum had been weeping. They were a right family. His cheeks were red and his eyes looked puffy. She turned off the music and took out her earphones. She felt all mother hen-ish.

'Hey, bruv,' she said. 'You should be in bed. What's the matter?'

He slumped on to her bed, elbows resting on his knees, his head bowed. He didn't even notice the new black and white poster on the wall of the man with a dagger in his heart. Normally he'd have said 'Gross!' or something like that.

'I miss Dad,' he said. His straight brown hair hung down, covering his face.

Freya left her desk and sat beside her younger brother on the purple duvet, putting her arm round his thin shoulders. 'I know,' she said. 'I do too.'

'But I wish he wouldn't keep coming round because it upsets Mum,' Michael said fiercely. 'He pretends it's to see us but I

51

don't believe it. It's like he doesn't want her but he won't let her go either.'

Freya felt a lump in her throat. Michael was so young yet he understood everything. 'He still loves you, you know,' she said, trying to sound comforting like Mum. 'Just because he's left doesn't mean he doesn't love you any more.'

Michael growled. He must be sick of hearing it. He started jiggling his leg up and down. Something flashed in the corner of Freya's screen. Cal?

'Why don't you get us a biscuit?' she said brightly. 'There're chocolate ones in the cupboard.'

Michael frowned. 'Mum's downstairs with Bill. She won't let me.'

'Tell her they're for me,' Freya suggested. 'I need them to help me concentrate on my homework.'

Michael perked up. 'I'll get the packet.'

'Good idea.' Food always worked with him.

She waited until he'd left the room to check her laptop. 'Cal Barton' it said in the little box in the corner. Her heart fluttered. *hey, it's me*, she read. *why was yr day crap?*

She sighed with pleasure. Thank God she had Cal. Every day she worried that he'd go off her like the others and every evening he came back to her. She could tell him everything and he never took the piss. Most of the boys she hung out with hated talking about feelings and stuff like that, but not Cal.

She'd never met him but she felt as if she had. He was the same age as her, but he didn't live in London and knew nothing about her school or friends, which was a good thing. Funny that his parents were separated, too. And his dad kept coming round making his mum upset so he knew exactly what Freya was going on about. She began to tell him all about Gemma and Abigail.

fucking losers, he wrote. *ur so much better than them. u shouldnt let them get to u then they'll have won.*

She talked a bit about Mum and Dad, too. Then they got on to music and clothes.

wot u wearing? he asked. *bet u look buff?* (Sexy.)

She smiled. *sorry, just my school uniform,* she replied. *wot bout u?*

school uniform, he wrote back. *gonna get a new haircut at the weekend. shorter on the sides and sort of spikey on top.*

cool, she said. It sounded nice. She wished she could see it.

got to go, he said. *Pir.* (Parent in room.)

ok, she said, *hak.* (Hugs and kisses.)

hak. cul8r. (See you later), he replied.

Nic plodded upstairs, spilling tea as she went. 'Bugger.'

She knew that she was drunk again and wished she'd never opened that second bottle of wine. Or the first, for that matter. She knocked on Alan's door.

'Come in.' He sounded distracted, nose buried in some tedious spreadsheet or other, no doubt.

She turned the knob and pushed open the door with her foot. 'Whoops!' Brown tea sploshed on to the cream carpet. 'I brought you some tea,' she said. 'I'll clean it up.' She bent down and dabbed at the wet stain with the corner of her skirt.

Alan looked irritated. 'Just put it there,' he said, pointing to the top of the grey filing cabinet beside his desk. She rose carefully, using her hands to steady herself. He didn't seem to notice that she was having trouble getting from one side of the room to the other without tripping.

'There,' she said, pleased that the mug was still half full. She turned and smiled at him, willing him to speak to her. 'What are you doing?'

She peered over his shoulder. He seemed to be writing an email or something. She noticed he'd typed something weird. She caught sight of the letters c and u and the number 8.

'What does that mean?' she asked.

'Nothing. Accountancy-speak,' he said vaguely, pressing 'send'. He logged off. 'I'm finished for the night,' he sighed, sitting back in his seat and stretching. 'Think I'll watch TV for a bit downstairs to unwind. You go to bed.'

Her shoulders drooped. 'You're always working.'

He got up and turned his laptop off, winding up the leads

and putting the whole thing into its case, ready for the morning. Then he pecked her on the cheek, smiling. 'I'm sorry, we're having a particularly busy patch at the moment.'

'You're always having a busy patch,' she replied.

Chapter Nine

'Who's a beautiful girl then?'

Carol popped the saucer of roast chicken scraps on the yellow lino and ran her hand along Victoria's soft, gingery fur. The cat, purring loudly, sniffed the food, picked up a chunk of white meat and put it on the floor beside the saucer where she began chewing greedily. Albert, who was black and white, was jumping up around Carol's ankles, yowling.

'All right, all right,' she said, flicking her long grey hair out of her eyes, 'yours is just coming. I've only got one pair of hands.'

She put another saucer of food beside Victoria's, and Albert set to with gusto. Carol grinned and gave them both another stroke. 'There now,' she said. 'Good kitties.'

She turned to the chicken carcass on the white plastic work-bench, tore the rest of the meat and jelly off the bones and put the scraps in a big blue plastic dish. Then she went down her narrow hallway to the small sitting room at the back of the house, opened the glass door and placed the bowl on the grass by the compost heap.

She knew that at least two wild cats came to her for food but there might be more. And the foxes and the odd badger would polish off any leftovers. She must remember to leave some broken peanuts out later for the hedgehogs, too.

She sniffed the air. There was a sweet smell coming from the few remaining white roses climbing up the rickety wooden fence to her left. They were very late. It was mid-September now. Carol looked around and thought how lucky she was. The garden was only tiny but it was almost completely secluded, thanks to the tall bushes on either side. And when she looked up all she could see were trees and sky. It was amazingly quiet, too. In Richmond, just up the road, you were bothered by the constant drone of planes overhead. But here, usually the only audible noises were birdsong and the shouts of children in their gardens.

She went back inside and closed the glass door. There was nothing left on the chicken carcass worth keeping, so she wrapped it in a plastic bag and dropped it in the bin in the corner of the kitchen. Then she piled up the various dishes that she'd used, stuck them in the red bowl in the sink and ran cold water over them. She couldn't be bothered to wash them now. They could wait till later, or tomorrow even.

Carol glanced out of her kitchen window. A couple of children were still playing football in the road outside but most had gone in. It was pretty safe on the estate. Few cars passed by and most tended to belong to locals who knew to drive slowly.

It was a lovely place for children to grow up. Quiet streets and lots of trees. Some of the modern houses, including hers, were a bit small and poky, but at least they had decent-sized windows that let in lots of light.

Carol recognised one of the boys from two doors down but the other she'd never seen before. The football rolled on to the pavement in front of her window and the boy she knew ran to fetch it. He stooped to pick it up and as he rose, he caught her eye. She smiled and waved. He waved back shyly before running back to his friend.

He was a nice lad. They mostly were around here, apart from the odd one who could be a bit cheeky. Carol would often stop and chat to them while she was watering her pots by the front door. She liked children.

She sighed and switched the wireless on to Classic FM. She tended to do that in the evenings when it started to get dark. She liked listening to music while she wrote. She was getting on quite well with her novel. It was a bit complicated, though – science fiction. Sometimes she wasn't sure that she understood it herself. She wondered if she should ask someone from the creative writing group to take a look. Not Pamela, obviously. She really was the limit. She'd been so rude to Evie at the last meeting about that line of hers: 'lips dangling like ripe cherries'. It wasn't that bad and Pamela needn't have been sarky. Carol could have punched her.

She glimpsed the big pile of papers on the worktop in the right-hand corner beside the fridge. It was where she put all the newspaper and magazine clippings she wanted to keep, the recipes, scraps of paper with telephone numbers on, letters that needed answering. The pile just got bigger and bigger.

On top was a letter from the local council, with a form to fill in if she wanted an extra recycling box. She needed one with all those cat food tins she accumulated. She'd better do it now, she'd been putting it off for too long.

She slipped on her specs, which were hanging round her neck on a piece of string, and registered the photo stuck to the side of the old white fridge with Blu-Tack. She peered at it, as she had so many times before. It was a small, square, black and white photo in a white cardboard frame with a picture of a newborn baby wrapped in a white blanket. Carol could still remember the photographer. He'd visited all the mums on the maternity ward that day and asked if they'd like a picture. She'd ordered just one decent-sized print, plus a tiny, passport-sized photo. It was all she could afford. Mother wasn't going to give her any money.

The tiny infant was almost bald, with just a wisp of fair hair on the top of its head. Its little hands were curled up in front, like a squirrel or a rabbit. It had a wrinkled face and its eyes were scarcely open. The photo was faded and the frame was bent at the edges.

Carol smiled at the baby. 'I'm going to answer a few letters then I'll get down to my writing,' she said. 'But I think I'll have a nice cup of tea first.'

She picked up the kettle and filled it with water. Victoria and Albert had finished their meal now and were rubbing themselves against her legs, asking for more.

'You've had your supper,' Carol chided. 'I'm not giving you any more because you'll get fat.'

The phone rang, making Carol jump. She wasn't used to the phone. People didn't tend to ring that often. It was an old-fashioned one, white and a bit mucky, with a curly cord. Carol picked up the receiver and the main bit fell on the floor because the cord was twisted and too short.

'Bother.' She had to manoeuvre herself round her bicycle, propped against the kitchen table, to sit down on the other side.

'Hello,' she said, trying to unwind the cord so that she could relax back in the chair. 'How nice to hear you!'

She listened while her younger sister gabbled on about this and that. Griselda was getting a bit doo-lally, Carol reflected. Come to think of it, she'd always been a bit doo-lally. But Carol loved her all the same. As children, it had been them against their parents and the world and they'd clung to each other for comfort.

It was a shame Griselda had moved to the other side of London. It meant they saw so little of each other. But they both knew they'd always be there for each other. In an emergency, Griselda would come running and vice versa. Funny how neither of them had ever married. Something to do with their weird upbringing, no doubt.

'I saw Mother the other day,' Griselda was saying on the phone. 'Sittin' on the end of me bed.'

'Did you?' Carol said. Mother had died years ago, but Carol took the view that it was best to go along with Griselda. She was always claiming she could see things, feel the presence of dead people around her and so on. It was creepy but she didn't actually do any harm. And she certainly wasn't going to change now, at her age. Challenging her just made her upset.

'She said she was sorry for what she did to you. She sent her love,' said Griselda.

Carol swallowed. 'That's nice.'

'We sat and chatted for quite a while,' Griselda went on. 'She said Aunty Vi was there with her, but I couldn't see her. Mother said—'

'Please, Griselda,' Carol interrupted. This was getting too much.

Griselda tut-tutted. 'You should listen to her,' she chided. 'She's different now, she wants to help.'

She said 'elp' instead of 'help'. And she tended to leave the

58

ends off her words. She'd developed quite a cockney accent having lived so long in the East End. Carol didn't approve.

'There's an "h" at the beginning of "help", Griselda,' she corrected her. Griselda would always be her baby sister, even though they were knocking sixty, the pair of them.

'Oh, you and your bloody elocution lessons,' Griselda cackled. 'Just leave off, will you? And stop callin' me Griselda. You know I don't like it.'

'Sorry, Zelda,' Carol added.

Zelda put down the phone, lit a cigarette and reflected on the conversation. Carol was quite batty, what with all her cats and that. Getting battier by the minute.

She'd wanted to tell Carol about all them visions she'd been having, as well as the conversation with Mother. But Carol would never listen properly. She mistrusted the spirit world. In fact, she tried to pretend it wasn't there. She went to church every Sunday, said her prayers like a good girl and hoped for the best. Bit of a Miss Goody Two-Shoes actually. Or pretended to be, more like. Bit of a joke considering what she'd done.

Zelda looked at the sky outside. The evenings were drawing in fast. It'd be winter before she knew it. She'd better go for her walk soon or it'd be too dark. She pulled her green cardy over the blue kaftan, tied a pink and white silk scarf round her head and opened the heavy front door. The air was cool and she was glad of the cardy. She glanced back at the dark-red front door just to make sure she'd closed it properly.

It was in a state, that door, no two ways about it. All peeling. She couldn't remember the last time it was painted. How long had she lived here? Must be getting on for forty years. Well, it had maybes only been painted once in all that time, not that it bothered her.

She'd been lucky to get a flat right opposite Victoria Park, she thought, fastening the buttons on her cardy. It'd probably be worth a fortune now to some yuppy from the City with more money than sense. Good job the landlord didn't want to sell. He had houses all over London. He couldn't be bothered to do them up, he liked the rent.

She'd seen enough people come and go over the years. She didn't mind the young couple with a baby above her, but the grumpy old geezer right at the top was a bit of a pain. He made a heck of a fuss about the baby's crying but it didn't worry her. She could just zone out and think of other things.

She turned right along the pavement past the blue iron railings till she got to the park gate. Most of the roses in the rose garden were over now, but there were a few tired red blooms. She followed the little path through the garden till she reached the open grass, beyond which was the big, round pond. It looked grey and murky today. Zelda shivered.

There were lots of ducks and Canada geese swimming around. On the left-hand side was the little café, where she often treated herself to a cup of coffee and a Chelsea bun. It would be closed now though. Anyways, she'd be having her tea soon.

She took some stale bread out of the plastic carrier she'd brought with her, tore off a few pieces and threw them in the water. Some ducks and a couple of Canada geese whooshed over, squawking, and dived for the bread.

Zelda laughed. 'Don't get yer knickers in a twist, I've got plenty.'

She tore off more bread, making sure nobody was left out. 'Wait yer turn, you greedy so-and-sos.'

A couple of geese heaved themselves out of the water and started waddling towards her. She picked up a stick from the ground and gently prodded them until they plopped back in the pond. 'You won't get no dinner unless you stay in the water,' she warned them. 'I don't want you nipping me bum.'

Two kids who'd been sitting on a green bench a few feet away got up and strolled towards her. They were wearing tracksuit bottoms, trainers and baseball caps back to front. One was black, the other white. Zelda checked them out. She was used to doing that. They must be about sixteen or seventeen. They didn't look like trouble but you could never be sure. She kept her eye on them as they approached.

'You got a light?' the white one asked.

'Sorry,' Zelda said. 'Don't smoke.' She wasn't going to dig

in her pockets for her lighter. She wasn't that stupid. They might get ideas about what else could be in there.

'You still got your slippers on,' the black boy pointed out.

Zelda looked down and saw the royal-blue fluffy nylon slippers Carol had given her one birthday. She'd forgotten to change them.

She shrugged. 'Nothing wrong with that, they're comfy.'

The two boys shook their heads and walked off, sniggering.

Zelda finished throwing the bread and strolled around the pond. Apart from the youths, hardly anyone was about now. She came to Victoria Park virtually every day at different times. Sometimes, though, when it was sunny, instead of visiting the pond she'd stroll across the road and watch the children in the adventure playground. She'd take a sandwich with her and a flask of tea and sit on the grass or a park bench. She enjoyed doing that. She didn't have a garden to sit in. Victoria Park was her garden.

She thought about her clients. The phone usually started ringing around 8.00 p.m. and kept going until eleven or twelve. Later sometimes. She must have about twenty regulars now; she'd built up quite a business. She'd never planned to get into psychic lines but when her breathing got bad and she couldn't work in the old people's home any more, she had to find some other way of making a living.

Lucky she'd spotted that ad in the local paper. 'Genuine psychics wanted', it said. Well, that was her all right. They'd invited her for an interview. She'd been dead nervous but it wasn't too bad. The man asked her a few questions, told her to give him a reading and that was that. The job was hers. It was a bit of a swizz. She had to give him half her earnings, that was the deal. But she still made a fair whack. People kept coming back, they wanted her specially. Particularly that Evie. She must have spent a fortune on readings.

Zelda had walked all round the pond now and she could feel her chest getting tight. Time to go home and sit down. She retraced her steps through the little garden and along the pavement, passing a few people in suits on their way back from work. She kept her head down. She didn't want to be distracted by the spirits. She wasn't in the mood; she needed to conserve her energy for tonight.

Sometimes complete strangers would pass by with the dead sitting on their shoulders or walking by their side. The spirits would try to attract her attention by whispering rude comments or issuing warnings. They'd expect her to answer, the cheeky bastards. She couldn't help all of them. She was only human.

She was glad when she reached the house again. It was getting chilly. She took off her scarf and cardy and opened a tin of soup, warming it on the cooker in the corner of the lounge. She didn't have a kitchen as such. Just a sink, a cooker and a mini fridge. It was quite sufficient.

She ate the soup from a bowl sitting on the armchair beside the electric fire. She'd lit one ring. She needed it this evening. Then she dropped a piece of bread in the bowl and scraped it round the edges to get the dregs. It was tomato, her favourite.

The phone rang.

'Here we go,' she muttered, putting the bowl on the floor beside her chair and picking up the handset. She cleared her throat and put on her telephone voice. 'Zelda speakin'.'

It was one of her regulars, the woman whose husband had topped himself. Zelda had spoken to the husband several times but the problem was, he didn't seem very keen on the wife. In fact he was really rude about her. Zelda couldn't repeat some of the things he said, so she had to use her imagination and make up something nice.

'He's missin' you really bad, darlin',' she said. 'He wishes you weren't on your own with the kiddies, he just couldn't cope with the stress at work no more.'

The woman was sobbing on the end of the line. 'If only he'd told me, I could have done something, we could have got professional help . . .'

The man was being really annoying, whistling in Zelda's ear, calling his wife a nag and a harridan.

'Stop doing that, will you?' Zelda hissed, before she could check herself.

'What?' the woman asked, surprised.

'He says he loves you very much,' Zelda said quickly.

The man whistled even louder in her ear. It hurt. She moved her head away.

'Does he really?' the woman asked hopefully. She'd stopped sobbing. 'Tell him I love him back.'

'I will, darlin',' Zelda said. 'He's blowin' kisses and askin' you to give the kids a cuddle for him.'

She felt a sharp pain in her upper arm. 'Ouch.' She could swear he pinched her. He must be in the room though she couldn't see him. She hoped he wouldn't hang about, keeping her awake all night. She'd better let him alone and he might go away.

'Oh,' she said, 'I'm losin' the connection. It's fadin'.'

There was a sharp intake of breath at the other end.

'I'm sorry, darlin',' she told the woman. 'He's gone.'

The woman was disappointed but nevertheless hung up sounding much happier than before. Zelda was relieved. She felt sorry for her, even if she had driven her old man to his grave. She wouldn't have meant to. And maybe he was a rotten husband. He wouldn't tell her that now, would he?

The next call was from a man whose daughter had died twenty years earlier. Zelda couldn't find the girl at all so she had to dream it up. The truth was, she couldn't always make a connection. Sometimes the spirits just didn't want to be disturbed. But she was providing a service and her clients were paying good money. She couldn't let people down. They weren't to know whether it was all a load of old bollocks or not. So long as they went away satisfied, what was the harm?

At last Evie phoned. Zelda knew it was her before she heard the voice. She reached for the grey shawl on the back of the brown chair, wrapping it round her as best she could with one hand.

'I want to know more about what you told me – about that terrible, bad thing,' Evie said. She sounded anxious. 'I've been thinking about it all week.'

Zelda closed her eyes and breathed in and out slowly. She tried to focus on Evie. She'd never met her, of course, she didn't need to, but she had a clear enough picture of her and she could see her essence, her core. It was agitated.

63

Zelda's mind started to go blank and an image began to form. She saw strange figures arguing, saying terrible things to each other. Burning with hate.

'What can you see?' Evie's voice cut through the silence.

'Danger,' Zelda moaned. She was rocking back and forth in her chair. 'Terrible danger.' The hand in which she held the receiver felt clammy. She switched it into the other hand and wiped the damp one on her skirt.

Evie started to cry. 'What sort of danger? You've got to tell me. What can I do?'

Zelda was trying so hard to talk to the figures, but she couldn't get through. 'I don't know,' she sighed, slumping forwards in her chair and putting her head in the free hand. 'I can't tell you no more.' She felt exhausted. Her whole body was heavy and aching.

Evie was still crying at the other end. Zelda wanted to go and lie down, have a rest, but she couldn't leave the woman like this. 'I can see something else.' She tried to sound bright. 'It's that man again, the tall handsome one, the one you're going to meet.' She slid a cigarette from the box lying on the little table beside her, lit it and took a long drag.

'Tell me more.' Evie had perked up; the crying seemed to have stopped. 'Where does he live? What exactly does he do for a living?'

Zelda racked her brains. 'I can see a beautiful hotel, darlin', with palm trees outside. Blue sky, the ocean. I think you're going to travel. Do you like travelling?'

Evie sounded pleased. 'Oh yes. I love it.'

'And I can see a white dress, flowers, lots of people.'

'A wedding?' Evie said, startled. 'You mean we're going to get married? Goodness, I never thought I'd get married again.'

Finally she hung up. Zelda made sure she'd left her in a good mood. She was exhausted, now, drained – and troubled. She wished she could put Evie out of her mind for once.

She got up slowly, turned off the electric heater and switched out the little light on the table. Then she shuffled into her tiny bedroom next door, drew the faded blue curtains and put on her nightie. She hopped into bed quickly, pulling the blankets around her for warmth. Right now, she wished she'd never been born with the gift. It felt more like a burden. Why couldn't she be like ordinary people? Life would be so much simpler.

'G'night, Derek, love you,' she said, rolling on to her side. He was the young man she'd been engaged to once. He'd let her down badly, though. Left her heartbroken. But they'd become close again since he'd crossed over.

'Goodnight, Mother, goodnight, Father,' she whispered. She never went to sleep without wishing them sweet dreams, too.

She thought of Evie Freestone, pretty, blonde Evie Freestone. She had a lot to cope with. Well, she wasn't alone. Lots of people had heavy burdens to bear. Zelda had done the business: she'd warned her of the dangers. But she couldn't go on about them, could she? You weren't allowed to dwell on bad things with clients. And quite right too.

Her boss had been very firm about it. It was against the rules.

Chapter Ten

Zelda was five and had just started school when she realised that she was different from other little girls. She remembered making the discovery as clearly as if it were yesterday.

The teacher, Miss Addison, was at the front of the class telling them about how plants grew. Miss Addison had short, yellow, curly hair and glasses. She seemed very old, though she was probably only about twenty-five. Zelda liked her.

Miss Addison had asked some of the children to help her put three broad-bean seeds in plastic see-through cups with a little water.

'Now,' she said, 'we're going to put one of the cups in the stationery cupboard, one on my desk and one on the windowsill. Which bean do you think will grow the fastest?'

Several children put their hands up, but not Zelda. She was too busy staring at the little boy sitting cross-legged on Miss Addison's desk. He was wearing funny clothes: brown lace-up shoes, grey shorts, long grey socks, a white shirt and a navy-blue striped tie. He had a cap, too, but he wasn't wearing it. He'd taken it off and put it on the desk with his navy-blue jacket.

His fair hair was very short and he had freckles on his nose. He was being naughty, putting on a silly voice and imitating Miss Addison, pretending to be her. Zelda tried not to laugh because she knew she wasn't allowed to. She glanced at the other children, who were watching Miss Addison, their faces completely serious. She wondered how they managed to concentrate.

The little boy jumped up and stood on the desk, waving his arms around. He really was very bad. Zelda was surprised that Miss Addison didn't send him out.

'Let's see if you're right,' Miss Addison said. 'Mary, will you please put this cup in the cupboard? And, Jessie, you can put this one on the windowsill.'

The girls got up obediently.

Zelda tried not to look, but the little boy suddenly turned around to face the blackboard and did something really rude: he wiggled his bottom at the whole class and they didn't even seem to notice. She giggled; she couldn't help it. Then he spun round again, put his pinkies in his cheeks and pulled, giving himself a funny mouth. That made her laugh out loud. He looked like a clown.

'What is it, Griselda? Would you like to share what's so funny with the rest of the class?' Miss Addison seemed really annoyed.

'Sorry, miss,' Zelda said. 'It's just that boy sitting on your desk.' She stood up and pointed. She thought she was being helpful. 'He's making funny faces at me.'

Miss Addison frowned. 'There's no boy on my desk; don't be silly. Now, will you please sit down, open your book and pay attention like everyone else.'

The little boy jumped on to the floor now and stood behind Miss Addison, waving. Zelda couldn't understand why Miss Addison was pretending that he wasn't there.

'He's behind you, waving his arms about,' she blurted.

The other children started to laugh.

'He's got grey shorts on and a white shirt and a blue hat with a gold—'

Miss Addison stared. 'What did you say?'

'It's a hat, miss, with gold on it. And he's got really short hair. I think it's your brother, the one you told us about.'

Miss Addison went a bit weird after that. She walked over to Zelda's desk and pulled her up by the arm – quite hard. 'Come with me.'

Zelda didn't like the tone in her voice and started to cry. Why was Miss Addison cross? Zelda thought Miss Addison liked her brother. She'd told them lots of stuff about him, how they used to go tadpoling and things.

Miss Addison closed the classroom door behind them and immediately the children inside started laughing and shouting.

67

Zelda wished she was in there with them. Outside in the corridor Miss Addison bent down, put her face right up close to Zelda's and hissed: 'If this is your idea of a joke, young lady, it's not funny. You should never make jokes about the dead. It's very, very bad. You're a very naughty little girl.'

Miss Addison's face was scary. Zelda had never seen her like that. Normally she was smiley and kind. Zelda wanted to go home. She wanted Carol.

Miss Addison took her to see Miss Perry, the headteacher, and she was angry, too. She told Zelda that she'd hurt Miss Addison's feelings. Zelda wept and wept. She liked Miss Addison, she never wanted to upset her. But how was she to know that Miss Addison's brother was dead? Zelda didn't remember her saying so.

She didn't really understand what dead meant anyway; she thought it was like sleeping, only you didn't wake up. Well, the little boy seemed very much awake to her. Why was Miss Addison lying? Grown-ups weren't supposed to lie. It was very confusing.

After that, she learned to be more careful. She often saw strange people about. One minute they were there, the next they weren't, but she didn't tell. Sometimes they spoke to her, sometimes they didn't. Mostly she wasn't scared, but occasionally they did nasty things like jump out and frighten her. But she kept her mouth shut because people might get cross, like Miss Addison and Miss Perry.

The only one she did tell was Carol. She didn't get angry, but she didn't want to hear about it much either. When they were in bed, Zelda would sometimes whisper across the room: 'Aunty Vi says hello,' or, 'Scruffy wants to give you a lick.' Scruffy was their cocker spaniel who died when Zelda was four. Mother said they couldn't have another dog.

'There's no one there,' Carol would whisper. She was three years older than Zelda.

'There is, really there is,' Zelda would reply. Occasionally she'd get upset and start crying. Then Carol would climb in her bed and give her a cuddle and make her feel better.

'There there,' she'd say, stroking her little sister's dark hair.

'Never mind. I believe you. But don't tell anyone. Don't tell Mother or Father, OK?'

'OK,' Zelda repeated.

Zelda and Carol were dead scared of Mother and Father. He used to be a bank manager but Zelda could only vaguely remember him going into London in his suit in the mornings. They lived in Teddington then, in a little house near the river with an apple tree in the garden that she and Carol used to climb. Zelda could only have been three or four when they left, but she could still picture the apple tree.

Something happened with the bank, Zelda never did know what. She knew it was bad, though, and she wasn't allowed to talk about it with anyone, Mother said. The next thing, they were moving to Harrow, to a poky flat on an estate so Father could be near his job at RAF Northolt.

He'd been in the RAF before when he was a young man. He was a pilot officer, he told them. He went back to the same job – pilot officer – but this time looking after accounts. Zelda guessed he didn't really like it much; he was always bad-tempered when he got home. But he was lucky to have a job at all. Mother said that sometimes in a gloomy sort of way.

He didn't like children. She and Carol used to annoy him. If they didn't do well in a school test or something he'd get out his belt, put them over his knee, pull down their knickers and beat them.

Mother didn't like them much, either. She was always picking on them: 'Tidy your room,' she'd say, even though they'd just tidied it. 'Pick up your shoes, dry the dishes, stop making a noise.' She was always finding something wrong.

Zelda thought she probably hated living on the estate and hated the other women, too. She used to sniff and say they were common. Zelda and Carol weren't allowed to play with the other children on the green outside. They had to stay inside, doing their homework or helping with the chores. It was a good job they had each other or they'd have been really miserable.

Zelda sighed. Mother was sitting right beside her on the bed now, nudging her in the ribs. She wouldn't let her go to sleep.

'Carol's all right,' Zelda said. 'She knows you're sorry.'

'I thought it was for the best,' Mother said for the umpteenth time. 'She was only sixteen. How could she have looked after a baby?'

'We all could have helped, I suppose,' Zelda replied. She brought her knees up to her chest. Hunched up in a little ball.

'You mean your father and I could have? You were only thirteen, you wouldn't have been able to do much.'

'I would when I got in from school,' Zelda protested.

'Besides,' said Mother, 'think about the neighbours. Things were different in those days, remember. There was a lot of shame.'

Zelda thought of Carol in her little house. Zelda never saw the baby before it was taken away, she wasn't allowed to. She put a corner of sheet into her mouth and sucked on it.

'Don't do that,' Mother said crossly. Zelda took it out again.

'And you need to give this room a good clean,' Mother went on. 'It's disgusting. I didn't bring you up to live in a disgusting room like this.'

Zelda's brain ached. She guessed Mother would be at it for hours. She was in one of those moods. There was no point trying to argue back, it would only make her worse. She turned over and tried to think about her walk earlier, the ducks and Canada geese. She tried to think about which way round the pond she'd go tomorrow. Maybe she'd pop over to the café in the morning and have one of their nice, frothy coffees.

She pictured Derek's face. His brown moustache, his crisp white shirt with the spotless cuffs. Funny how he always looked so young, just as he was when she knew him. He wasn't here tonight. Probably off somewhere having fun with his mates. He was a bit of a lad, that Derek, always had been.

She scrunched her hands into a tight fist and dropped off at last, with the sound of her mother's voice droning in her ears.

Chapter Eleven

'Shall we meet for a drink after work sometime? It'd be good to catch up after all these years.'

Becca swallowed. It was so tempting. Gary looked lovely in his Facebook picture. Kind, friendly, even if he was thinning on top. Cute snaps of his kids, too.

She realised that she was greedy for information, for any scraps he could give her. He'd opened the lid and unleashed a swarm of emotions. She didn't know if she'd be able to put the lid back on.

He worked for a human rights charity. That fitted. She remembered that he was always a bit different, sensitive, even at the age of twelve or thirteen. Not like other boys. Suppose he told his wife, though, or his friends? Once out, information had a habit of leaking all over the place no matter how careful you tried to be.

She read on. 'You look great in your profile picture.' It was an email. She'd told him not to write on Facebook any more. Too risky.

'Very different, though,' he continued. 'I recognised you by your nose, believe it or not. You always had a cute little upturned nose. I've often wondered what happened to you. I'm glad things have worked out for you.'

Becca decided not to reply. She ate the last bite of the salade Niçoise wrap that her PA had brought her and took a swig of English Breakfast tea. She glanced out of the window. It was still pouring with rain and there was no point having her usual stroll around the block before getting back to business.

Some of her colleagues in the big, open-plan office were at their desks like her, but most were out. In the canteen, probably. There tended to be an exodus around 1.15 to 1.30 p.m.

There was a pile of newspapers on her desk that she hadn't had a chance to look at yet. She picked up the *FT* first – her bible – and turned to the Lex column. Then she switched to the *Independent*'s financial pages, followed by *The Times*. She was adept, by now, at scanning through and speed-reading just the bits she needed to know. It only took about ten minutes.

Now she opened the *Telegraph* and turned to the sports pages. She was relieved to see a small piece in there by Tom about the Spanish defender leaving Chelsea to rejoin Barcelona. Tom hadn't had anything in there for days, which always worried her.

He was so lazy. He couldn't pull the wool over her eyes. She was terrified that one day he'd get the boot and the awful thing was, he probably wouldn't even care. He'd love to slob around all day in his bloody dressing gown doing nothing.

Irritated, she turned to the middle pages for some light relief. There was a colour photo of a well-known actress leaving a top London nightspot. The paper detected 'tell-tale dimpled skin' on the back of her thighs. She was rarely without a cigarette in hand, the paper tutted, and that might explain it.

Becca groaned. Give her a break. They hardly ever subjected men to this treatment. She looked more closely at the photo. It was true, though, the actress did have cellulite. And she was so young, too. She resolved to buy some of that expensive anti-cellulite cream that Nic recommended the next time she was in John Lewis. It was worth a try.

Becca checked the clock on her computer screen. Nearly time for her conference call with a UK property analyst. She'd have to engage her brain. Her team was divided by asset classes: Dave headed up the equities team, Rob bonds and cash, while she took a special interest in alternatives, including derivatives and property.

As Chief Investment Officer, she was involved with the management of almost $57 billion of assets globally on behalf of pension funds and other institutional investors. UK commercial property appeared to have peaked and the IPD index in July showed negative capital returns for the first time in a long time.

The smart investors had been trying to reduce volatility and raise cash since the beginning of this year but properties were getting harder to sell and yields had already shifted up by 1 per cent. With the turmoil in the credit markets it would be interesting to see how the highly leveraged investors (who had taken the market away from institutional investors) would react.

The half-hour call went reasonably well. She wrote up the notes immediately afterwards and posted them on the intranet. Since hers was a global company, they posted all fund-manager meeting notes on to a global site so that members of the four regional investment teams (Australasia, Europe, North America and Emerging Markets) could review them straightaway.

She caught up with her management team on her way to get a cup of tea from the canteen. Back at her desk, she did a quick Ocado shop. She felt a bit guilty but the children had to eat and when else was she supposed to do it? Besides, it didn't take long. She was an expert. Then she rang Rob, who was based in New York, to catch up with him, too. He'd been touching base with some specialist credit hedge fund managers to see how they'd fared in the market turmoil.

It was 7.30 p.m. before she finally left the office. Because of the US time difference she'd had to wait to speak to several clients. She'd saved a few of the market updates that had come in by email during the day on her BlackBerry to read on the train. Before heading home she'd checked Bloomberg to see where European markets closed and how the US was going that day.

She was relieved, when she stepped out into the cool evening air, to find that it had stopped raining. She wouldn't need to get her umbrella out. She scurried along the darkening streets, click-clacking in her high heels towards Bank tube station, before dropping down into the sweaty bowels of London to catch the drain back to Waterloo.

She hadn't thought about James and Alice all day, she'd been too busy. But now she felt a stab of longing; she hoped Alice would still be awake when she returned, even though it would be naughty of Monica, the au pair, not to have got her to sleep earlier.

The tube was full, despite the time of night, and Becca couldn't get a seat. She held on to the rail overhead, bumping occasionally into the short woman beside her in a beige mac.

'Sorry,' Becca apologised.

The woman smiled. 'No problem. Is it always this packed? I'm not used to these crowds. I'm only in London for a couple of days for meetings.'

Becca started. The woman was from the North-East, you could tell by her soft Geordie accent. You rarely heard accents like that in London. A wave of longing crashed through Becca, making her gasp. She'd never been back, not once. Never would; it would be too dangerous. She swayed slightly, managing to steady herself.

'I'm afraid it is – always this busy,' she said to the woman carefully. 'I'm used to it.'

'I could never get used to it,' the woman replied. 'I like a bit of peace and quiet, me. The countryside around Newcastle, Durham Cathedral, Whitley Bay. They're my spiritual home.'

Becca practically ran out of the train station down the high street towards home. Her feet were killing her and she was aware that people were staring. She must look a strange sight in her high heels, long dark hair streaming behind her, black Donna Karan mac flapping at her shins. They must be wondering why she was in such a hurry. Her laptop felt very heavy. She just wanted to get home, to throw her arms around her children and breathe in their sweet, comforting smell.

She didn't care that Tom wouldn't be home for hours, nor that it might take ages to get James and Alice to sleep. She didn't care that she was tired and hungry and that she'd have to eat supper alone. She'd have given anything to sit down with that woman and ask if Fenwick's was still in the same place in Newcastle city centre. Was the Metro working and could you still buy stotty cake and slabs of pease pudding in that baker's off the main square?

She knew now that she was going to meet up with Gary and ask him all those questions and more. She was going to start

74

to piece the jigsaw puzzle back together, wherever it might lead her, whatever the outcome.

She had no alternative. There was no going back. After all these years, a brief exchange with a strange woman on the train had swept all her hard-won choices clean away.

Chapter Twelve

❧❧❧

Evie admired the two little round box trees in square terracotta pots on either side of Nic's black front door. She wished that she had a pair of secateurs, though. They could do with a trim. They were getting out of shape.

She rang the bell. Nic seemed to take an age to answer. Evie pressed her nose against the stained glass and peered through. At last she saw Nic's silhouette coming down the hall.

Evie did a double take when she saw her friend. 'What's the matter?' she asked. She couldn't help it.

Nic looked terrible: she was wearing a baggy beige cashmere jumper and dark-blue jeans that showed off her tiny, neat figure but her face was white and pasty and there were beads of sweat on her upper lip and forehead. Her eyes were bloodshot, too.

'You ought to be in bed,' Evie went on, concerned.

Nic laughed. 'I'm fine. Just had a bit of a late night, that's all.'

She led Evie into her large, bright kitchen at the back of the house. It's where she always took friends. She and Alan rarely seemed to use the other downstairs rooms. Evie looked around. The place was a tip, with dirty mugs, glasses and plates on virtually every surface. There was a stale smell of food and alcohol, too.

'Blimey. You must have had quite a night. Midweek, too. Who came over?'

Nic had to move some of the dishes in the sink out of the way so that she could fill the kettle. 'Fiona and Natalie,' she said nonchalantly. 'The kids came for tea and everyone ended up staying rather longer than intended.' She gave Evie her naughty-little-girl look.

Evie shook her head. She wasn't impressed. Nic was always

doing this, kidnapping mothers, including her, and plying them with wine on a school night.

'I don't know how you do it,' Evie went on. 'I wouldn't be able to get up in the morning. It's not good for you, you know.'

Nic sat at the rectangular oak table looking out over the garden while she waited for the kettle to boil. She rubbed her eyes. 'I need a facelift,' she said suddenly. 'Where's a good place to go, do you know?'

'You do not need a facelift,' Evie said crossly. 'You need an early night. You're beautiful as you are.'

'No I'm not,' Nic moaned. 'I don't want to go down the Botox path again after my last experience but I need something done. Look.' She pinched the bags under her eyes. 'They don't spring back any more. The pinch mark just stays there.'

'If you have a facelift Becca and I will have to have one, too,' Evie said. 'And I can't afford it, so it's not fair. I'm not going to go round looking like your grandmother whatever you may think.'

Nic laughed. She had a surprisingly big mouth and her smile seemed to fill her face. 'OK, OK, it was only an idea. Actually, I don't just need a facelift, I need a whole new life.'

Evie looked at her. 'That bad? Do you want to talk about it?'

Nic bit her lip. 'Not really. But thanks anyway.'

Evie felt this was her cue to change tack. 'I was wondering if Michael could borrow one of Alan's waistcoats,' she asked. 'You know he's in *Oliver*? He needs to look like a Victorian urchin. I seem to remember Alan has quite a collection. Do you think he'd mind?'

'Of course not,' Nic said. 'He hasn't worn them for ages. I wish Dom had auditioned, but he hates acting.'

'He may change.'

Nic was picking at a piece of fluff on her jumper. Her hands were trembling. Evie frowned.

The kettle switched itself off. Evie sprang up. 'Let me get the coffee. Where do you keep it?'

Once the drinks were made, Nic took the mug from Evie and cupped her hands around it. 'I do feel pretty ghastly,' she admitted. 'Maybe I'm going down with something.'

Evie took a swig of coffee. 'You should go back to bed. I'll collect Dominic.'

'I'll be all right. I've got things to do today. This coffee's a godsend.'

'Was Alan with you last night?' Evie asked, noticing the crushed crisps on the floor.

Nic laughed. 'What do you think? He went straight up to his study the minute he got in. Hardly even took time to say hello. You know what he's like. But hey!' she added. 'We managed to have quite a party without him!'

Evie realised now probably wasn't the right time but she couldn't help it. It was the thought of people partying that did it. She looked down at the table. 'Helen's pregnant,' she blurted.

'What?' Nic looked really shocked. 'Oh God. When did you find out?'

'Monday, after coming back from yours. Neil was there waiting. I haven't told the children yet. He says he wants to take them out for dinner with Helen and tell them then. Have a celebration.' She made a face.

'Bastard,' said Nic. 'Oh, Evie, I'm so sorry.' She put her hand on her friend's and gave it a squeeze. 'How do you feel?'

'Pretty crap,' Evie admitted. 'I'm worried about the kids, too, Freya especially. I think they'll take it badly. They haven't accepted Helen at all.'

Evie got up and tried to put some plates in the dishwasher. Speaking about it was making her feel worse.

'Leave that,' Nic said firmly. 'Let's talk about something else. Sit down and tell me about your book.'

Evie closed the dishwasher, sat back down and sighed. 'There's this handsome gladiator, right, called Spiculus, who's been granted his freedom by the emperor and he's now like a freelance bodyguard for wealthy families. My heroine, Cornelia, thinks she's falling in love with him, only she's married to Marcellus.'

Nic rested her elbows on the table and cupped her face in her hands. 'Mmm?'

'Cornelia thinks Marcellus doesn't love her,' Evie went on. 'Why?'

'I'm getting to that. Because they've only been married a year and he's been spending most of his time at their country villa outside Rome and ignoring her and she's really hurt. So when drop-dead-gorgeous Spiculus comes to work for the family, it's easy to see why she's bowled over. He pays her lots of attention and she's really smitten. The only thing is . . .' Evie looked stricken.

'What's the matter?' Nic cried. 'It sounds great so far.'

Evie shook her head. 'The problem is I was going to make Spiculus turn out to be a rat and Marcellus, the husband, was going to be lovely all along, he just thought Cornelia didn't love him, which was why he was in the country villa.' She put her face in her hands. 'And now,' she said, weeping, 'I'm going to have to change my whole plot. Because Neil's girlfriend's having a baby and he's never going to come back.'

Nic got up and put her arms around Evie. 'Oh, honey,' she said. 'You still love him, don't you?'

Evie nodded miserably.

'You know what?' Nic said, standing up. 'I think you *are* going to have to change the plot. I think you should make Spiculus the true hero who rescues Cornelia from her vile husband who's a bully and a gambler and a love rat.'

Evie looked up with a tearstained face. 'You think?' she said. 'It'll take a lot of rewriting.'

Nic nodded firmly. 'Definitely. Never mind the rewriting, it'll be worth it in the end.'

Evie looked thoughtful. 'Maybe you're right.' She wiped her nose on a piece of crumpled hankie that she'd fished from her jeans pocket and brightened. 'Hey, Zelda says I'm going to meet a new man, some sort of explorer.'

Nic looked puzzled. 'Zelda?'

Evie was embarrassed. She'd forgotten that she hadn't told Nic or Becca about Zelda. Somehow she didn't think they'd approve.

'She's a psychic,' Evie confessed. 'I talk to her sometimes on the phone. She's very good.' She glanced at Nic. 'Honestly.'

Nic tried to frown but couldn't so she twisted her mouth instead. 'You don't believe in all that rubbish, do you?'

'Not really,' Evie said quickly. 'But there's no harm in it.'

Nic looked at her seriously. 'You say that, but I think psychics can be dangerous. They play with people's minds, particularly vulnerable people. You should be careful.'

'Don't worry,' Evie promised. 'It's only a bit of fun.'

'I must admit I'm a little scared.'

The orthodontist patted Nic on the shoulder. 'Relax. It'll be worth it in the end. Just focus on that million-dollar smile.'

He was a big man, clean-shaven and rather handsome, with longish brown hair that came down over his ears and curled slightly at the white collar of his tunic. He must be in his forties and had a slight Australian accent. He looked like an outdoors type: strong and hearty, but his voice was low and reassuring.

He'd been through the procedure with her very carefully but she still had butterflies in her stomach. She closed her eyes, wishing that the dental surgery didn't smell so clinical. It just added to her nerves. The orthodontist's gloves reeked of anti-septic, too.

He'd put some Beethoven on in the background, which was soothing. She thought again that she really should have eaten something before she came because she'd been warned that she'd only be able to manage soft foods for several days.

The dental nurse put some plastic glasses on Nic. 'Now open your mouth.' She did as she was told.

'I'm going to put some little triangles in your cheeks,' the nurse said. They felt soft, like cotton-wool padding. She passed the orthodontist a spray which he squirted in Nic's mouth. 'This'll make it dry inside so the glue will stick,' he explained.

The nurse was a pretty little thing in her twenties with squiggly auburn hair tied back in a ponytail and lots of freckles. She talked quite a bit to Nic, explaining what the orthodontist was doing.

'This plastic bracket is to keep your mouth open while we put the braces on,' she said pleasantly. Nic's jaw was beginning to ache already. 'Now we're going to put a special liquid on your teeth to get them ready for the braces. It's going to sit on them for thirty to sixty seconds. Then we're going to rinse the teeth out, spray a lot of water.' She looked at her watch while she waited for a minute to be up. 'You might get some funny looks for a few days.' She laughed. 'Have you told your friends what you're having done?'

Nic shook her head and made a grunting noise. In truth, she hadn't told anyone that she was going to get braces, mainly because she didn't want to be dissuaded. Even Alan had no idea. He'd say that she didn't need them.

The nurse produced something that looked like a hairdryer and gave it to the orthodontist, who puffed hot air in her mouth. It didn't hurt, it just felt peculiar.

'OK,' the nurse went on, 'then we have this little lollipop with a special liquid on it. It really gets on the teeth well.'

The blow-dryer went in Nic's mouth again. This was all taking what felt like a very long time. Her head was aching and her stomach straining. She was dismayed that the painkillers she'd taken earlier for her hangover were wearing off so quickly.

It wasn't the money Alan would be angry about; he'd always been generous with cash and rarely questioned her about her spending. It was silly to be anxious. Unnecessary. She tried to shove him to the back of her mind and focus on something else.

The nurse must have read her mind. 'Think about a lovely beach with yellow sand and palm trees,' she suggested. 'This is the tray that has the braces on. We're going to go ahead and put it in your mouth and press down a little bit. You OK? Can you give me a thumbs up?'

Nic just about managed one. She wasn't happy, though. Her teeth and gums were protesting; they didn't like the brutal treatment. Good idea, she thought, to focus on a beach. She tried to remember their holiday last summer in Barbados. Dominic had loved it; there had been a boy roughly his own age staying at the hotel, an only child, too. They'd teamed up and spent hours snorkelling and playing table tennis. It had been perfect. Alan had had his nose buried in a book for virtually the entire two weeks. She'd read about five books herself and there had been a plentiful supply of free cocktails.

'Now we're going to shine a light that will help us harden the glue on the braces,' said the nurse.

Nic's mind clouded over. That call from her mother had cast rather a pall over the final few days. Mummy had slipped and broken her wrist. She was lonely, Nic knew, since Daddy had died, but tried so hard not to show it. Nic's siblings weren't much help. Her sister lived in Dubai with her husband and family and her brother, the single one, was in Cornwall.

He was worse than useless in any family crisis; he only thought of himself. Sure enough, when Nic had rung to see if he could take a few days off work and stay with Mummy in Hampshire until she returned, he'd claimed he couldn't get away.

'Don't even think about cutting short your holiday,' Mummy had said. 'I'm fine, truly. My neighbour's being such a help. She went shopping for me yesterday and stocked up the fridge. So kind of her. You have a lovely time and I'll see you when you get back. Give Dominic a big kiss.'

Nic *had* considered flying home, but she knew it would only make Mummy cross. Nic knew she'd cope all right; she was tough. She'd had to be, bringing up three kids on her own when Daddy was with the Army overseas, often in some of the world's hottest spots. It had made Nic feel guilty, though, to think of her struggling on her own. She shouldn't have to.

Nic pictured Daddy's face: so strong and kind. He hadn't stood any nonsense from them when they were little, but she had always been secure in his affection, always known that he wanted what was best for them.

She tried to swallow. It wasn't easy when her mouth was wide open and there was someone poking and prodding around inside.

'You're doing really well,' the orthodontist said. 'We're ready to put the upper braces on now. We're going to push up on the teeth, you'll feel a slight pressure . . .'

Slight pressure? She felt as if her upper jaw might crack.

'Now we're going to shine the light that's going to help us harden the glue on the braces again, OK?'

Nic nodded. Daddy would be so worried if he knew what a mess she was in. Thank God he'd never find out. Nor would Mummy. Of that Nic was determined. Mummy was too old to be burdened with her problems.

'Now we're going to take off the top part off the soft tray,' said the nurse.

Nic felt more tugging. They must be nearly finished now. Daddy had warned her about the dangers of drinking; he said he'd seen at first hand in the officer's mess what harm it could do. He and Mummy rarely drank themselves: just a glass or two of wine on special occasions, some champagne for a celebration. He wouldn't understand, he'd have told her just to stop. 'Have a bit of self-discipline.'

'And the bottom part,' said the nurse. 'Good.'

Nic took a deep breath. If only it were that easy.

The nurse took the bracket out and the pillows from her cheeks. Nic's mouth felt sore and bruised, but there was no pain.

'Sit up now and have a good rinse,' said the nurse, passing her a plastic cup. The pink liquid tasted weird. Nic had difficulty swooshing it round her mouth. Her teeth were numb and jangling at the same time.

The dentist took his mask off and smiled. He had a perfect set of teeth himself: white and very straight. He was an excellent advertisement.

'All done!' he said. 'It's going to feel a little tender for the first week or so. We'll give you some pain relief.'

He walked over to the sink in the corner of the room and took off his gloves. Nic was still sitting upright on the reclining chair.

'Would you like to have a look?' The nurse smiled, reaching for a little round mirror on the worktop behind. Nic nodded. The moment of truth.

She took the mirror in both hands, opened her mouth and grinned widely. She'd gone for turquoise-coloured braces; she'd decided that black would look as if she had decay, red as if her teeth were bleeding and yellow as if her teeth were covered in egg or something. She'd been warned against white because they would get dirty. Turquoise seemed quite fun, as if she were making a statement rather than trying to pretend that the train tracks weren't there.

They were startling, though. She stared at them for some

time. She looked like an overgrown teenager. She just needed a few spots and pigtails to complete the bizarre look. She closed her mouth quickly.

'It'll take a little while for your mouth to adjust to the feeling of them being there,' said the nurse, taking the mirror from Nic. 'You may experience a tingling sensation that makes it feel as if your teeth are itching. That's quite normal. Also, as the teeth shift the wire may poke out of the back of the brackets on your molars so we'll give you some wax for that. Occasionally the brackets can irritate your cheeks and lips. Put a small amount of wax on the face of the bracket and you'll have instant relief.'

Nic started to get up. She felt wobbly. The nurse took her arm.

'Try eating foods like macaroni, mashed potato, ice cream and soups for the first week or so,' she went on. 'Make an appointment at reception for a month's time when we'll tighten the braces, but if you have any problems in the meantime please don't hesitate to give us a call.'

'Thank you,' Nic managed to mumble.

For a second she wondered why on earth she'd done it, why she'd chosen to put herself through so much discomfort. It wasn't as if the twisted tooth was that noticeable. She brushed the thought from her mind. She was looking after herself, that was it. Her teeth had always bugged her; she'd feel better once they were straight. Maybe it would encourage her to get herself straight, too.

She decided to stop at the supermarket on the way home and buy some tins of soup.

'Bit nicer out there today,' the cashier said pleasantly. She was a plump woman in her fifties with a short, curly brown perm and glasses. Nic saw her quite often when she popped in for something or other.

She piled the tins of soup into a single plastic bag; she'd forgotten to bring her environmentally friendly canvas one.

'Yes,' she said. 'Not quite so cold.' She handed the cashier her card and smiled.

The woman jumped. She couldn't help herself. 'Oh.'

Nic had momentarily forgotten about the braces. 'I've just

had them put on,' she explained, closing her mouth quickly. 'There's no getting away from them, is there?'

The cashier looked flustered. 'I'm sorry, I wasn't expecting . . .'

'It's all right,' Nic reassured. 'I know they're a bit obvious.'

Great, she thought as she headed towards the car park. So much for funky turquoise. Now she was going to have to wear a bleeding paper bag over her head for the next twelve months . . .

Chapter Thirteen

'Follow me.'

Evie led the young woman up the two flights of stairs to her bedroom. She'd laid the wedding dress out on her bed all ready to be tried on.

'It's beautiful,' said the young woman, taking off her navy-blue coat. 'I'm sorry I couldn't get here any earlier. I was really busy at work today.' She had short, dark hair, a pretty, round face – rounder than Evie remembered – and her cheeks were rosy. She looked awfully young to be getting married.

Not for the first time Evie was struck with the irony of the situation: here she was creating a dream dress for the bride-to-be's perfect day while her own marriage had been an absolute disaster. On reflection, she really ought to have picked a different career. Like a divorce lawyer.

'No problem.' She smiled, hanging the coat on a hook on the back of her bedroom door. 'Here, would you like to slip your clothes off behind this screen and I'll help you put it on.'

The young woman went behind the blue and gold silk screen in the corner of the room and Evie could hear her unzipping something. She'd picked the screen up for virtually nothing in an antiques market and re-covered it herself. It was very useful on occasions like this.

The young woman stepped out in her white bra and knickers, looking slightly embarrassed. Evie couldn't help noticing her bust – it seemed to have grown since the first fitting a month ago. And the tops of her arms were plumper.

Evie straighted her shoulders. 'Right,' she said in her most matter-of-fact voice. 'I'll hold the dress up while you step into it. Don't worry if it doesn't fit, it's only tacked. I can easily alter it.'

The dress, in gold, crushed taffeta, was strapless, with a fitted, boned bodice which fastened at the back with lacing. It was supposed to ruche down gently to hip level and flare slightly to a two tier A-line skirt with a train. Evie prided herself on managing seemingly to interpret exactly what the bride-to-be wanted, whilst subtly steering her away from anything unflattering. On occasions, it required a high degree of diplomacy.

'Is it a bit tight?' The young woman sounded worried.

Evie didn't even try to do the laces up at the back. She took a deep breath. 'No problem, there's plenty of fabric. I, er, I can't help noticing though, that you've gone up a cup size or two. Have you, by any chance . . .' She steeled herself, '. . . thought of taking a pregnancy test?'

The young woman spun round, wide-eyed. 'Oh,' she said, covering her mouth with her hands, 'do you think I could be . . . ?'

Evie nodded. 'I'd say so.'

'That night of the dinner party . . . I must ring Matt . . .'

Evie did a quick calculation on her fingers. It was the first week in October. If the woman was, say, eight weeks pregnant now, she'd be nearly due by the time of the wedding in April. Tricky. They'd have to go for a different style of dress. She might even want to postpone.

'Shall I make us a cup of tea while you get dressed?' Evie smiled. 'You look like you need one.'

The young woman appeared dazed. 'We weren't planning to start a family for a year or two . . .'

Evie patted her on the shoulder. 'Sometimes babies have their own ideas about timing. It's not bad news, is it?'

'Oh no. We definitely want kids. It's just . . .' The young woman smiled ruefully. 'Well, I didn't want to be a fat bride.'

Evie gave her a friendly hug. 'Don't worry, we can have a rethink. You'll look gorgeous.'

The young woman didn't leave till 6.30 p.m. and Evie wasn't in the mood for going out now. But she'd promised her neighbour, Bill, and he'd bought the tickets, so that was that. She didn't have time for a shower so she pulled on a clean pair of dark-blue jeans, which she tucked into her flat black knee-length biker books, and a sloppy black V-necked jumper that almost disguised her ample chest; she couldn't cope with the impertinent comments that it tended to attract today.

She added some earrings and a chunky black and white necklace to jazz the ensemble up. Her fair hair was looking a bit flat, so she tied it back in a French ponytail and slapped on some brown eye-shadow, blusher and lip gloss. She took a last look in the bathroom mirror. 'That'll have to do.'

The children were watching TV. She felt guilty about leaving them. 'Darling, can you make sure Michael's in bed by nine thirty?' she asked Freya. 'I'll be home by eleven at the latest.'

Neither of them looked up.

Evie knocked on Bill's door at seven o'clock. 'I'm a terrible mother,' she said, practically tripping over a pile of books in the middle of his hall as she went in.

'Sorry,' Bill said, shoving the pile to one side with his foot. 'There doesn't seem to be room for them anywhere else.' He took his jacket off one of the hooks on the wall and started to put it on. 'A terrible mother?' he said. 'Nonsense. I've just been rereading Charles Dickens's *Bleak House*. Mrs Jellyby, now she was a terrible mother, obsessed with her African project while her house is strewn with rubbish and her son's head is stuck between the banister railings.'

Evie laughed. Bill was always quoting some great work or other and his house was full of literature. Too full, in her opinion. There were shelves in every room and they were all bulging. With no more space left, he'd taken to stacking piles of books in every available corner, too.

'Come on, we have to go or we'll be late,' she said, taking his arm.

'All right, all right,' he replied, buttoning up his shabby brown leather jacket with his free hand. 'Dash, I've forgotten my wallet.'

Evie took a deep breath. He was so absent-minded. Typical professor, though he didn't look like one. She always imagined professors to be small and round with white hair and glasses. But Bill was tall and lean. She supposed he got his muscles from all that digging at the allotment. He bounded up the stairs two at a time to retrieve his wallet.

They decided it would be easier to get a bus to the Orange Tree as parking was difficult in Richmond. They arrived just in time to take their places in the little theatre in the round. If you sat on the wooden benches in the front row, where they were, the actors practically perched on your lap. As the lights went down, she dug the tortoiseshell glasses out of her handbag and slipped them on, hoping that Bill wouldn't notice.

It was an amusing, madcap play by American writer Susan Glaspell, surprisingly modern given that it was written in 1922, and with a strong feminist message. Evie found herself laughing more than she had in ages, though she was aware that there was a powerful, suffused anger, too. She even managed to forget about Neil and the baby.

With his smart, liberal New York friends, Seymore Standish, one of the main characters, was a banker and frustrated artist whose poetic ambitions were hampered, he claimed, by the fact that he had a mother, wife and children to support in the conservative Midwest.

The real picture, however, was rather different. His wife, Diantha, whom he patronisingly called Dotty Dimple, wasn't in fact the small-minded character that he painted, and when Nora Powers arrived from New York, spouting radical ideas about birth control, Diantha jumped on the feminist bandwagon. Seymore, who was secretly attracted to Nora, was appalled by what he regarded as his wife's wild behaviour and exposed himself as a snobbish hypocrite.

The play ended with an unexpected twist: Diantha, realising that her new-found liberal ways were destroying her husband, decided to turn her back on Nora and return to her narrow, stifling existence.

There was a stunned silence at the end of the show, as people processed what had happened. Then the audience broke into applause. Evie wondered what Neil would have thought of it. They used to go to quite a lot of plays together, though he always said that he preferred the cinema.

She declined Bill's offer of a drink afterwards. She wanted

to get back to the children and she wasn't in the mood anyway. They walked side by side to the bus stop round the corner.

'Thoroughly enjoyable,' Bill commented, 'though I found the ending disappointing.'

'Did you?' Evie asked. 'Why in particular?'

'I just thought it was unconvincing, somehow, that Dotty would have chosen to go back to her repressed life with her vain, misogynistic husband after being exposed to all those enlightened ideas. She didn't need to.'

'Oh, but I think she did,' Evie said.

'Why?'

'Because for all his faults, she knew he needed her, that he was nothing without her. He'd just shrivel and die.'

Bill went quiet for a moment. 'What a terrible indictment of the female condition,' he said finally, 'that a woman would choose to stay with her husband simply because he needed her.'

Evie felt her face go red. 'Well, yes, but there was another very good reason too, don't you see?'

'No.'

Was Bill being deliberately difficult?

'What was that?' he asked. 'I can't see any good reason at all.'

'Dotty loved him, *silly*,' Evie said. 'It was obvious. For all his faults, she was still desperately in love with him.'

They sat in silence on the top deck of the bus as it trundled towards home. Evie wondered if she'd offended Bill by calling him silly. She felt bad, but she couldn't quite believe that he could be so blinkered. To her it was what the whole play was essentially about: the mad, inexplicable power of marital love.

They parted at her garden gate. Evie could see the light was still on in Freya's room. She frowned. Freya really shouldn't stay up this late. She'd be so tired in the morning.

'Thanks, Bill,' she said. 'It was a lovely evening.' She gave him a peck on the cheek.

'Don't mention it,' he replied, turning on his heel and walking swiftly away.

* * *

She paused in front of Freya's door. She must remember to knock before entering. Teenagers needed their privacy.

She thought of her own parents, who had been so controlling. They'd never knocked, ever. She'd felt under constant scrutiny. She'd hardly been able to move without one of them saying: 'Shouldn't you put your slippers on?' or: 'Have you finished your homework?'

Perhaps it was because they couldn't have children themselves. They'd tried for years, but nothing happened. So in the end they decided to adopt and what they got was her: their one and only precious child.

They loved her, she knew that, but the three of them were, in many ways, a terrible match. They were entrepreneurs, practical, businesslike – and totally lacking in imagination. It had made her think that as regards the whole nature versus nurture debate, nature tended to win out. But the adoption agencies could hardly be expected to take that into account along with everything else.

Her parents had made some money early on with a printing business, then lost it all. Later, when they were back on their feet, they turned to furniture shops and enjoyed some success but it was hard work and unpredictable. They were desperate for their only child to embark on a more solid career.

It was all right when she was little, but as she grew up they hardly knew what to do with this wild, temperamental girl who dyed her hair purple and begged for a sewing machine so that she could make her own wacky, bohemian clothes.

They tried to persuade her to do business studies at university. Instead, she insisted on going to art college, then the London College of Fashion, where she put her passion to good use and learned about clothes design. Everyone said she had lots of talent; she even won a couple of awards. But her parents remained unimpressed.

'How are you going to earn a decent living doing that?' they sniffed. 'It's only the lucky few who make any money.'

She was thrilled when she landed her first job with a lingerie designer in Kensington, but still they were disapproving. She spent her days cutting out, fitting, pinning, running around after the boss and being paid a pittance.

'You'd earn more if you came to work with us,' they tutted.

But she loved what she did; at shows she rubbed shoulders with all the major names: Betty Jackson, Jean Paul Gaultier, Jasper Conran. And she managed to make a bit of cash on the side, making brightly coloured ball gowns for friends with teeny strapless bodices and huge net skirts.

After the lingerie job she'd gone to work for Margot, a top wedding-dress designer in Holland Park. Thanks to her good eye for detail and sympathetic manner with customers, Evie soon rose through the (admittedly small) ranks and found herself working side by side with the boss herself.

One of her tasks was to help with fittings in the vast changing room at the top of the shop. She loved the gold silk curtains, gilt mirrors and heaps of heavily perfumed fresh flowers. After the fitting she'd cut out the dresses then bag them up for the machinists. Then she'd do most of the alterations, sometimes having almost to redesign the dress when brides-to-be lost unusually large amounts of weight.

The dresses cost more than a thousand pounds, which was a lot in those days, but business was booming. When Evie married Neil, Margot designed the ivory, hand-beaded silk dress herself and gave it to the couple as a wedding present.

After she fell pregnant with Freya, Evie hoped that she'd be able to go back to work part-time but Margot refused. At first Evie was upset, but Neil persuaded her that it was for the best.

'I don't want my children to be looked after by some stranger,' he said, 'I want them to be looked after by their mum.'

She'd set up her own business and started making bespoke wedding dresses from home. It had gone rather well at first, she'd had quite a few orders, but what with one thing and another she'd let it drift. Neil had never given her much encouragement or seemed remotely interested in her work. Ironic, then, that he'd cited her lack of career as one of the reasons why she bored him and he was leaving her.

She knocked on Freya's door and entered. The room was pretty dark as Freya had only her desk light on. There were posters all round the walls, mostly of sickly-looking pop stars with big black hair and heaps of eyeliner. The blackout blind was down, so that you couldn't see the moon or any light from the streetlamps outside. She kept the blind down most of the time and the window closed. Evie thought the long, thin room felt like a coffin. She couldn't bear it, but Freya seemed to prefer it that way.

She was lying on her bed staring at her laptop. Her face, lit up by the screen, had a strange, bluish tinge.

'Hello, darling,' Evie whispered.

Freya continued typing. 'Hi.' She didn't look up. 'How was the play?'

She was wearing her night gear: a grey vest top and baggy red drawstring bottoms. Her dyed black hair was tied up on top. Evie thought she looked very small and young and vulnerable. She felt a rush of love. She sat down on the end of her daughter's purple duvet.

'Excellent,' she said. 'Did Michael go to bed OK?'

'Yeah, no probs.' Freya carried on typing.

'Who are you talking to?' Evie asked, curious. Freya seemed very absorbed.

'Just a friend,' she replied. 'Cal.'

'Who's he?'

Freya remembered something. 'Dad called,' she said, looking up. 'He asked me and Michael to go to lunch with him and Helen. I said I didn't want to.'

Evie's throat tightened. 'You should go.' She tried to sound bright. 'It'd be nice to get to know Helen better.'

'I have absolutely no desire to get to know Helen better,' Freya said hotly. 'I hate her, and I hate Dad too, for that matter.'

'Shhh,' Evie replied, 'you mustn't say that. It's nobody's fault what happened. It's just one of those things.'

Freya sat bolt upright, her blue eyes flashing. 'Of course it's somebody's fault. That cow should never have even looked at him. He was a married man, for God's sake. She had no right.'

Evie swallowed. This was going to be even harder than she'd feared. 'It takes two to have an affair,' she pointed out. She cleared her throat. 'I think he wants to tell you something.'

Freya stared at her mother. 'What sort of thing?' she said suspiciously. 'God, they're not getting married, are they?

Well, I'm definitely not going to the wedding. No way. How disgusting! She's practically young enough to be his daughter.'

Evie shook her head. 'No, they're not getting married as far as I know.' She felt totally at sea. She had no idea how you were supposed to deal with a situation like this. There were no rules.

'What then?' Freya demanded.

'I can't tell you,' Evie said, staring down at her nails and pushing back the cuticles. 'He'd be furious with me. He wants to tell you himself.'

Freya's mouth set in a thin, hard line. 'Don't tell me then,' she hissed. 'I don't want to know anyway.'

Evie started to cry; she couldn't help it. 'Please don't be angry with me. It's hard enough as it is.'

Freya put her laptop on the floor and shuffled over to be beside her mother. She gave her a hug. 'I'm sorry, Mum. I didn't mean to upset you.' She lay down and put her head on her mother's knees.

Evie sat there for several minutes, stroking her daughter's hair and staring into the blackness. She knew Freya was going to be shocked by the news. She wished she could absorb some of the misery.

At last, Freya sat up. 'Are you OK now?'

Evie felt guilty. 'I'm fine. You should go to bed. Will you ring your father tomorrow?'

'If I have to,' Freya said. 'But I'm not going to be pleased for him, whatever it is he's going to tell me.' She picked her laptop off the floor. 'I just have to speak to someone for a second.'

'It's late, you really must sleep,' Evie protested.

'One minute more. I didn't say goodbye.'

Evie didn't stop her. She was glad Freya had plenty of friends, boys and girls. Friends could be crucial at a time like this. Evie remembered how much she'd relied on hers when she was locked in a battle with her parents about going to art school. She'd won in the end, but, boy, it had been a mammoth fight!

Yes, friends were good news, and Freya was going to need all the support she could get.

* * *

94

Nic ran herself a deep bath, poured in a generous dollop of her favourite orange-blossom bath oil and lit the candle in the special holder on the metal bath rack which Dominic had given her for her last birthday. There was also a useful slot for a glass of wine and she'd fixed herself a particularly large Sauvignon Blanc.

She took off her clothes and sank down in the warm water right up to her chin. She'd been shivery all afternoon since she'd had the braces put on. Her whole head and face felt super-sensitive. She couldn't imagine that she'd ever get used to having a pile of metal in her poor sore mouth.

She lay right back, letting the water cover her hair, and closed her eyes. She'd planned to have a bath, take another painkiller and go to bed really early, as soon as Dominic's light was out. Alan had called to say he'd be extra late and not to wait up. Somehow now, though, it was nearly midnight.

After a few minutes she rose and took a sip of wine. She could hear noises in the bedroom next door: Alan getting changed? Bugger, he was earlier than expected. She stayed stock-still. Presently she heard him closing his wardrobe door and leaving the room. She slipped under the water again, relieved for once that he hadn't come to say hello.

When the water began to feel cold, she got out and wrapped herself in a big, mink-coloured towel. Then she padded next door and put on her brushed cotton, blue and pink spotty pyjamas. They were her comfort pyjamas: there wasn't a whiff of sensuality about them.

She folded down the green bedspread and started to read; she was halfway through a Jackie Collins romp. It helped to take her mind off things. She thought that she heard Alan come upstairs and was about to switch out the light when she realised that he'd gone the other way into his study. She squeezed her eyes shut. So he wasn't going to say goodnight? There again, she'd done her best not to alert him to her presence in the bath-room, either.

She took another swallow of wine from beside her bed, draining the glass. The second bottle downstairs was empty now. That, and the heavy-duty painkiller from the orthodontist, should knock her out. She started to read another page but her eyes were blurry. She put her book face down on the duvet. At last, oblivion beckoned.

'You're up late. I thought you said you were having an early night?'

She started, looking up. Alan was at the end of the bed. He'd changed out of his suit into his striped pyjamas and burgundy dressing gown. She smiled. In a flash, she realised what she'd done and closed her mouth again but it was too late. Her heart fluttered.

'Good day?' he asked, tightening his dressing-gown belt.

'Fine. You?'

'Not bad,' he said, scratching his head. 'Busy, you know. How's Dom?'

She licked her lips, which felt as if they stuck right out with the metal behind them. 'Great. He had piano after school.'

Alan shifted slightly. 'That's nice.'

She put a finger in her mouth, bared her lips slightly and picked at some imaginary particle of food. 'Ow.' The bedside light was quite bright; he'd surely notice now.

'I've got to go in early tomorrow,' he said, turning to leave.

She couldn't believe it. 'Alan?'

'Yes.'

'I've had braces put on.'

There was a pause. 'What did you do that for?'

Nic sniffed. 'I've always hated my crooked tooth . . .' She wanted him to come and sit beside her and listen while she explained everything: how long it would take for the treatment to work, what it cost, why having straight teeth was important to her. How much her mouth hurt tonight.

Instead he moved to her side of the bed, bent down and pecked her on the forehead. His lips were dry. 'I have to finish some work.'

She waited until he'd left the room before turning out the light.

'Goodnight,' she called softly.

He didn't hear.

Chapter Fourteen

'I have something exciting to tell you!' Tristram looked really pleased with himself.

Evie, Nic and Becca exchanged glances. 'He's been asked to give a talk at his bloody boarding school?' Nic whispered. 'That'll give the pupils a thrill – not.' She smiled, revealing a mass of turquoise and metal in her mouth. Evie was shocked.

'What . . . ?'

Nic looked embarrassed. 'I'll tell you later.'

'I have the forms here for a national writing competition,' Tristram went on. It was the October meeting of the Creative Writing Group and he was standing at the front of the class, clutching a pile of papers. The room fell silent.

'The winner will receive five hundred pounds and the guarantee of being taken on by top agent, Palmer Brooke.'

There was a murmur of excitement.

'I think we should all enter,' Tristram said. 'It'll be a good incentive to finish our manuscripts. What do you say?'

Nic put her hand up. 'It sounds great but I'm not nearly finished yet. When's the closing date for applications?'

Tristram nodded. 'Good question.' He peered at the small print on the top sheet of paper. 'It says here the first of June. It might seem tight but that actually gives us nearly eight months. Ian Fleming used to produce the first drafts of his Bond books in just six weeks.'

Several people groaned.

'Yeah, but I bet he didn't have children to pick up from school and a house to run,' Evie muttered.

Tristram ignored her. 'The winner will be announced sometime around December next year,' he added with a flourish.

Pamela was clearly desperate to speak. She was sitting right at the front, as usual, and her helmet of immaculate grey hair was bobbing up and down in excitement.

'I think it's a marvellous idea,' she announced, turning to face the others. 'I can easily get my manuscript in by then. In fact I'm just about to begin the first edit.' She gave a smug little smile.

Carol, sitting beside Evie, yawned theatrically. 'Old clever clogs,' she whispered. She grinned, exposing her stained teeth.

She's a one-off, Evie thought. She liked her. Carol said what everyone else was thinking. Evie nudged her. 'Shhh.'

'I'll leave the forms on the chair here,' said Tristram. 'You can collect them at the end of the meeting.' He cleared his throat. 'Now, this month I thought we should talk about "Show Don't Tell".'

'What's that?' Carol asked.

Tristram looked at her sternly. 'I'm coming to it. This is a very common writing problem,' he went on. 'I'm going to read a passage to you here from a well-known book on creative writing.' He pulled a slim paperback from the pocket of his tweed jacket and straightened his tie.

'"Show Don't Tell is one of the fundamental rules of writing,"' he read. '"Picture yourself, for a moment, in the cinema watching a film. There's a battle scene and two knights are going at it like hammer and tongs. It's so effective that you feel as if you're actually there, experiencing every thrust of the sword, every punch, every blow. That's showing. You're with the characters, smelling their sweat, feeling their fear.

'"Now imagine that a narrator is standing in front of the screen describing what is happening: 'Sir Hector lashed out with his fists and Sir Guillaume swayed for a moment, before drawing his sword and plunging it in his opponent's side.' That's telling. Here the narrator is describing the events to the reader rather than letting them experience things for themselves."'

He finished the passage and looked up. 'Now, who's going to volunteer to read from their manuscript?'

Pamela's hand shot up. Carol shuffled noisily in her seat but as no one else offered, Pamela it was.

She stood at the front of the class and cleared her throat. '"A car drew up outside Serena's gate,"' she read. '"Her husband got out from behind the wheel. Her sister's frustration evaporated immediately. She breathed out a long gasp. But Serena held her feelings in. She was full of pent up anger and frustration."'

'Can you stop there?' Tristram said. Pamela's eyelids fluttered in irritation. 'There are several examples of Show Don't Tell,' he went on. 'Can anyone identify them?'

There was an embarrassed silence. No one, except Pamela, much liked pointing out other peoples' mistakes.

Finally, Carol stood up. '"Her sister's frustration evaporated immediately,"' she said, plonking herself down again.

Pamela's eyes narrowed.

'Quite right.' Tristram nodded. 'What would have been a better way of putting it, anyone?'

Pamela's mouth was thin and pursed. Hah! Served her right, Evie thought, for being so mean about her writing last month.

Russell chipped in. 'Would a better way of putting it be: "Her sister's shoulders relaxed and she breathed a sigh of relief"?'

'Absolutely,' Tristram said. 'Let the readers interpret for themselves. Much more effective. Any other examples?'

Several members of the group spotted further errors. Evie thought Pamela looked close to tears. She felt almost sorry for her.

'Well, I think it's all nonsense,' Pamela said when the dissection had finished. 'Quite frankly there needs to be a narrator guiding the reader. Think of Jane Austen – she was ever-present.'

Carol leaned over and whispered loudly in Evie's ear: 'She thinks she's Jane Austen now.'

Evie had to stifle a giggle.

She, Nic and Becca stayed behind for a few minutes at the end of the class. Evie couldn't contain her curiosity about Nic's train tracks.

'So what's this all about?' she asked. The braces were so bright, the sort of thing you usually see on teenagers. They were rather startling.

Nic shrugged. 'Didn't I tell you? I've always hated my crooked tooth.' She opened her mouth and pointed to where her right canine was, behind a mass of metal. 'I just decided now is as good a time as any to have it straightened.'

Becca raised her perfectly plucked, almost black eyebrows. Evie thought how she *would* love to know what her natural hair colour was. There was no way she was going to ask again, though.

'How long will the braces be on for?' she asked Nic, who was tucking a strand of blond hair behind an ear, revealing a delicate diamond stud.

'Up to a year,' she replied.

'A year?' Evie gasped. 'Gawd. Mind you, they are sort of fetching, I suppose. I remember I longed for braces when I was at school but I didn't need them. I used to put metal paperclips across my teeth and pretend.'

Evie heard a cough. She turned to the back of the room. It was Carol, fiddling in her basket looking for something. Evie had been so engrossed in talking to Nic and Becca that she hadn't realised Carol was still there.

'Have you lost something?' Evie asked.

Carol looked flustered. 'I can't find my bicycle key.'

Evie couldn't help smiling. Carol had spilled what looked like the entire contents of her basket on the floor. There were paper hankies, a purse, a hairbrush, a pair of tan tights (for some reason), and a surprising number of pens and pencils.

'Ah, here it is!' Carol cried, brandishing a key. 'I knew it was in here somewhere.' She stuffed everything back in her basket and stood up.

'We're going for a drink. Fancy coming?' Nic asked.

Carol moved closer to the women. 'Thank you for asking, dear,' she said. 'It's very kind of you. But I'd better get home to let my cats out.'

Evie hadn't noticed before, but Carol was wearing jeans and trainers and a flowery shirt with a surprisingly jaunty red tank top. The youthful effect was somewhat spoiled, however, by her straggly grey hair.

To Evie's surprise, Carol came right up close and peered in

her face. 'Are you all right, dear?' she asked. She looked really concerned.

'Fine, thanks,' Evie replied, taking a step back. 'Why d'you ask?'

Carol reached out and touched her cheek. Evie flinched. She certainly hadn't been expecting that.

'You look so tired,' Carol said, her forehead wrinkled. 'I know you've been having a hard time. You must take care of yourself.'

Evie felt a lump in her throat. She hadn't realised it was so obvious, even to a relative stranger like Carol. 'No, I'm fine, honestly,' she said. 'But thanks anyway.'

Carol sighed, put on her blue anorak, which had fallen on the floor beside Evie, and picked up her basket. 'Well, I'll be going. Have a nice drink.' She gave Nic a funny look. 'Have you done something to your teeth?'

Nic sighed. 'Yes, I've got braces.'

'How extraordinary! I thought they were just for teenagers. Well, I've seen everything now.'

Evie winced. She didn't dare look at Nic. Carol did have a habit of putting her foot in it. She reached the door and turned.

'And look after Evie, you two,' she said, wagging a finger at Nic and Becca, who glanced at each other, surprised. 'She needs you, you know.'

Becca felt slightly drunk as she opened the heavy iron gate and tottered up her garden path. She'd been tempted to take a taxi but her house was only a short walk from the pub. She might be on a million pounds a year but she'd worked incredibly hard for her money and she didn't want to throw it away.

She fumbled for her key and put it in the lock. She hiccuped, thinking she'd allowed Nic to top her up at least once too often. Becca cursed herself. She hated being drunk, that feeling of being out of control. She'd regret it when the alarm went off at 6 a.m., too.

Nic herself had seemed fine, not at all squiffy, just more voluble than usual – if that was possible. Becca marvelled at her capacity. It was quite impressive, particularly for one so small.

To her surprise Tom was home already, sitting on the sofa in the downstairs television room watching football in the inevitable dressing gown. His bare feet were resting on the low mahogany coffee table, and there was a bowl of half-eaten crisps on the chair beside him. He didn't look up. Becca felt hugely irritated.

'I'm home,' she said, slipping off her high heels and navy mac. She'd had to go straight to the writing group from work. 'In case you hadn't noticed.'

'Hello, darling,' he replied, his eyes still glued to the TV screen. Suddenly he lurched forward, his fists clenched. 'Ooh, ooh,' he said. 'Yesss!' He leaped up, punching the air, his dressing gown flapping open to reveal rather more than Becca wanted to see right at this moment.

'Sorry,' he replied sheepishly, closing the dressing gown and sitting down. 'Great goal.'

Becca plonked herself on to the brown leather bucket chair opposite him. She'd bought it from Liberty several years ago and she loved it.

'Good day?' he asked, grabbing a handful of crisps and shoving them in his mouth. Some crumbs fell on the sofa. Becca bit her lip, hoping they wouldn't leave greasy marks.

'Busy,' she replied. 'You?'

'Good laugh,' he said. 'Had a leaving do at the Lamb at lunchtime that went on most of the afternoon.'

Becca prickled with annoyance. 'Didn't your boss mind?'

Tom snorted. 'Nah, fortunately we've got this new reporter who's extremely keen. He's always more than delighted to cover for us.'

Becca sniffed. 'It doesn't sound very professional. You should be careful.'

At last Tom looked at her. 'You're in a bad mood. What's the matter?'

She wanted him to turn off the TV, ask her to sit beside him, put his arm around her and listen while she talked. But once she started, she mightn't stop. Then where would she be? She couldn't tell him. Not any of it. She straightened her shoulders and stood up.

'Nothing's the matter,' she said. 'I'm just tired, that's all.'

'Well, go to bed then.' He turned back to the football. 'I'll be up in a minute, when this has finished.'

'I'll be asleep by then,' she replied.

Chapter Fifteen

Her heart was thumping and there were butterflies in her stomach as she turned the corner into Roupell Street. It was dark, but the lights of the old-fashioned lamp-posts gave off a warm glow and halfway down the road she could see the usual cluster of men and women in suits outside the King's Arms.

There were always people drinking outside, unless it was pouring with rain. Tonight wasn't wet or cold, but it wasn't warm either. It was blowy; a typical autumn evening. Becca wouldn't have wanted to stay out. She was glad that she was wearing a cardigan under her office mac.

Normally she'd take her time to walk down the narrow little road, past the charming Victorian cottages which opened straight on to the pavement. Roupell Street was like a little oasis after the hustle and bustle of Waterloo Station. She loved it.

She usually enjoyed, too, strolling into the picturesque pub with its cosy wood-panelled rooms and bizarre memorabilia, including a collection of ancient sewing machines. But today she was too nervous to notice any of it. She just hoped that she wouldn't need to rush to the loo. Her stomach was churning. In stressful situations, it was always the first thing to react.

She pushed past the office workers on the pavement and walked slowly into the bar. It was reasonably full for a Monday night but there were a few empty tables. She wondered, momentarily, if she looked all right. She'd reapplied her brown lipstick several times on the train but there had been quite a wind. She tucked her long hair behind her ears in two quick movements – too late to comb it now – and scanned the room.

A middle-aged man with grey, balding hair was sitting on his own in a corner. He was wearing a dark, shabby suit and was slumped over his pint in a way that suggested defeat and world-weariness. Not Gary, surely? In his Facebook picture he looked much younger. But it might have been an old photo.

The man looked up. He had a fleshy nose that seemed to retreat into the folds of his cheeks. Becca sighed with relief. It certainly wasn't Gary, so where was he? They'd agreed to meet at 8 p.m. and it was now ten past. Maybe he'd been held up. Maybe he wouldn't show at all.

She wandered into the conservatory at the back of the pub and checked the faces. No Gary, she was pretty certain. But she waited for a few moments to make it obvious that she was looking for someone. One or two people gazed at her with mild interest before turning back to their companions and drinks. The room was cramped and noisy and Becca had a sudden urge to get out fast, into the fresh air, and scuttle home.

Instead, she went back to the main bar and ordered a gin and tonic. She needed it. She took a gulp and sat down at an empty table on the right of the room. From here, she had a pretty good view of the door and would be able to scrutinise anyone coming in.

She was still wearing her coat, so she slid it off. She was quite warm now and decided to remove her pale-blue cashmere cardigan, too. She was wearing a white cotton shirt underneath, tucked into a navy-wool pencil skirt by Armani. She'd spent longer than usual this morning choosing the outfit. She'd opted at first for a silk, flowery Chloé shirt but decided at the last minute that it was too flashy. Luckily the white shirt was still fairly crisp.

The wooden door swung open and Becca knew him immediately. He was smaller than she'd imagined but he looked strong and athletic. His receding hair was cut extremely short, and there was the suggestion of mid-brown-coloured sideburns, worn in the fashionable, longer way. Becca quite liked them. They made him look streetwise and slightly edgy.

He was wearing a black leather jacket and an open-necked shirt, with a black and red rucksack over his shoulder. He looked totally different from the City types that she worked with – more casual. He caught her eye and gave her a big, friendly grin. Becca's heart skipped. This was going to be all right after all.

'Hey there!' he said, approaching her table. She got up and he leaned across to kiss her. She hesitated, wondering whether to expect two kisses or just one. He seemed to hesitate, too. In the confusion, their lips almost met. They laughed with embarrassment.

'Sorry,' Becca said. 'I never know what the etiquette is these days.'

He laughed back. 'Me neither.'

He swung his bag off his shoulder and put it on the floor. Then he took off his jacket and hung it on a chair. 'Another one?' he asked, motioning to her gin and tonic, which was still half full.

She shook her head. 'I should get you one.'

He raised a hand. 'I'm nearest the bar.' Which was true. Becca sat down again.

It was several minutes before he was served, which allowed her to take a closer look at him from behind. On reflection he wasn't small at all, just average – five foot tenish? The same as her. He was wearing a relaxed blue and white striped shirt over dark-blue jeans and thick-soled, brown leather lace-up shoes that looked more suited to weekend rambles than the office. Although his jeans were quite loose-fitting, she could see that he had a nice little bum.

He turned and smiled, a warm, open smile, and carried a pint of what looked like lager with him to the table. 'At last,' he said, sitting opposite Becca. His gaze rested on her face for a moment. 'You look great. Now you're here in the flesh, I can see you've hardly changed.'

She noticed that his Geordie accent had mellowed since he was a boy, but it was still there. Not like hers. She'd worked so hard at getting rid of it. Now everyone assumed that she was from London. She realised that she was shaking. She folded her arms, crossed her legs and attempted a smile. She hoped it didn't look unnatural.

'Hardly changed?' she said. 'In thirty years? I wish.'

He laughed. 'No, honestly. Obviously your hair's a different colour – and I don't remember those black eyebrows. But I can still see the little girl I kissed in the park.'

He laughed again but she frowned. 'Yes, well, an awful lot's happened since then.'

'Do you want to talk about it?'

Becca swallowed. She was sick of being careful. How lovely it would be to pour out her whole story: those first days when it was all a dream. When she thought she'd wake up and everything would be back to how it was.

Then the gradual realisation that this was for real, that it wasn't going to go away. The fear and loneliness that threatened to crush her. A young girl alone in a strange place, surrounded by strange people. New rules, new ways of behaviour.

The terrible, gnawing homesickness, the way she missed her mam, missed Jude, even missed her crummy little bedroom. All those familiar objects gone for ever. She was never going home again. The guilt and self-hatred that came in waves and left her gasping for breath. At those times she'd wanted to join Jude so badly. If they'd given her a gun she'd have put it in her mouth and pulled the trigger.

Some of the other kids didn't care, didn't understand what they'd done, but Becca did. She knew about death; she'd watched her beloved nana die of cancer. She knew that Jude wasn't ever coming back. They wouldn't let her go to the funeral or visit the grave. That was part of her punishment. Besides, they said, it would be too risky. There'd be a media frenzy.

Becca didn't know anything about that but she found out later, when she was older. The tabloids gave it pages and pages: 'Grammar-school girl batters sister to death with hockey stick.' 'A sustained and vicious attack,' the judge called it. 'She's dangerous. She needs to have a very close eye kept on her.'

Mam gave them an interview, saying she'd always been odd and different. That hurt. The neighbours said she was weird, too, not like other kids. 'There was something cold about her,' they insisted. 'She had an icy stare.'

She wanted to describe the different secure units, the dormitories and schoolrooms, the therapists who snipped her open and tried to delve into her soul, picking over it, poking and prodding, trying to identify why, to understand the anger that had driven her to do it, the trigger that had sent her over the edge. They'd delved till there was nothing left to discover. Then they'd taught her how to stay calm. She'd been a model patient; she was brilliant. She never got angry now – not *really* angry. She had it all under control.

Later, much later, she'd explain, there was the dull ache of acceptance, the feeling that at least she was paying her dues. And at last, amidst her books, buried in her studies, she began to find a little peace.

Finally, there was the parole board. All those people sitting round, asking her questions, testing her, trying to catch her out. But she passed with flying colours – as she did all her exams. Then there was the intricate false identity, a new name, new city, university, a pre-history that foxed everyone, even her husband. She'd tell Gary that she never saw her mam again. Not once. Had never even been back to Newcastle. But she couldn't say any of this. Not one bit. Not yet, anyway.

'I've tried to put it behind me,' she said instead. She spoke slowly, choosing her words carefully in advance. 'What I did was ugly and terrible, but I realised long ago that I couldn't change what happened. The best I could do was try to move on and make a decent life for myself. I was guilty and I paid my dues and I believe that I've been forgiven where it matters. That's all I can say.'

He nodded. He'd been listening intently. 'I didn't mean you to rake all that up,' he said. 'I just wanted to find out how you've been. You've more than moved on. Looks like you've made a fantastic go of things. Congratulations. Champion.'

Champion. Becca hadn't heard that in a long while. She sipped her gin and tonic. She felt more relaxed now. He seemed sympathetic and easy to talk to.

'I've got a well-paid job,' she agreed. 'I worked like crazy when I was locked up. I'd always been pretty swotty, if you remember, and it was comforting to bury myself in my studies. I was determined to get to university, too, to make what I could of this second chance that I'd been given.' She tipped her head to one side. 'I'm not quite so successful at managing the rest of my life, though.'

He scratched his head. 'What do you mean?'

She frowned. 'Oh, crazy hours, never seeing enough of the kids, a lazy husband who doesn't pull his weight, you know the sort of thing.' She gave a wry smile.

He nodded. 'It's hard, I guess, for a lot of women, trying to do it all. Michelle would probably say the same thing. We're lucky because I work flexi-hours and I can pick them up from school. But I'm sure she'd tell you there are lots of other things I do wrong.'

Becca was surprised. He seemed to her to be pretty perfect: kind, handsome, a good listener. So unlike the alpha males that she met in the office. Unlike Tom, too, who couldn't even be bothered to look up from the telly when she entered the room. She didn't want to probe, though. She'd only been with him ten minutes. Strange how she felt as if she'd known him for ever. Well, in a way she had. Almost for ever, anyway.

'Marriage, eh?' she said. 'What does Michelle do?'

'She's a teacher,' Gary replied, taking a swig of lager. 'At a primary school in Hammersmith. She doesn't like it much but we need her salary. I love my job but it's not exactly well paid.'

Becca put her elbows on the table and leaned forward, cupping her face in her hands. 'It's funny,' she said thoughtfully, 'but I used to think money was so important. I was so envious of those middle-class girls at the grammar school. They seemed to me to have everything: nice homes, lots of clothes, ponies even, some of them. But now I've got plenty of money it seems kind of pointless.'

Gary pulled a face. 'I'd like it to be pointless. I hate consumerism, all that lusting after material things. But once you have kids, unfortunately, it does seem to take over rather. Michelle wants a bigger house for them, more of a garden. And London's so expensive. I've suggested moving out of town and I could commute but she's not interested.'

Becca felt a wave of sadness. He wasn't particularly happy, she could see that now. Somehow she'd hoped that he would be, hoped that for some people at least things could work out. Life was too full of sadness. So many people struggling away to earn a decent living and make a good life for their kids and then what? Old age and death.

She reached out and touched his arm. 'Well, it's lovely to see you,' she said. 'After all these years.' She rose. 'I'll get us another drink but I need to go to the loo first. Would you mind keeping an eye on my bag?'

She couldn't quite believe it when, glancing at her mobile, she saw that it was nearly 11 p.m. The time had flown. They'd talked non-stop about his job, hers, the children, their friends, what they liked doing and her book, too. He'd been very interested in that. 'Keep at it,' he'd said. 'It sounds like a great idea.' He'd offered to read it for her and give constructive feedback.

'If you're sure?'

He grinned. 'I'd love to. Why don't you email it to me?'

He was so different from Tom, she reflected. He'd never bother to read it even if she asked. He'd be too busy watching the football. She resolved to send it to Gary the next day. His input could be useful.

'I must go,' she said finally, smoothing down her skirt and pushing her empty glass to one side. She paused. She'd circled round it all evening. Did she dare bring it up now?

'Tell me,' she said, 'do you go home much – to Newcastle, I mean? Do you know anything about my mother?'

He glanced at her and nodded. She didn't like the look on his face. It was sort of uncomfortable; shifty even.

'I go back from time to time,' he said. 'My mother and father are still there, in the same house, and one of my sisters. Your mother moved away . . . after it happened. She still keeps in touch with my mother by phone. They write to each other occasionally, too. As far as I know she's fine.'

Becca's stomach turned. So Gary's parents knew where Mam lived. Her mouth felt dry. 'Does she, you know, ever mention me?' That must sound pathetic. She straightened her shoulders and tried to look casual.

Gary frowned. 'I don't think so. I'm sorry.'

Becca shrugged. 'It's all right. She told me she never wanted to see or speak to me again and I guess she's kept her word. Can't say I blame her.'

She pulled on her cardigan and rose. 'I've enjoyed meeting you.' She meant it. She kissed him – just once – on the left cheek.

'Me too,' he replied, helping her on with her coat. He looked at her closely, his eyes full of meaning.

She took a step back, startled by the intensity of his gaze.

'Can we meet again soon?' he asked. 'I'd really like to.'

She paused. Swallowed. 'I . . . I think so,' she replied.

She left him at the pub door, heading in the opposite direction from her towards Southwark tube. She needed to make her way back to Waterloo. She felt peculiar, dazed, not like herself at all.

Normally she'd be itching to get home, hoping that Tom would be in and that she'd get the chance to share at least some of the day's news with him. But not today. She found herself walking slowly, breathing deeply, looking down at her shoes, scarcely aware of what was going on around her. She needed time to think.

She'd hadn't told Tom anything about Gary. It was too risky. She'd just said casually before she left for work this morning that she was seeing a friend. He hadn't pressed her, which wasn't a surprise. Usually she'd have been annoyed, but today it was a big relief.

Funny how Tom had only ever quizzed her that once about the fact that she hadn't kept in touch with any of her childhood friends and hadn't invited a single one to their wedding. 'I hated school,' she'd told him. 'They were the worst days of my life. Couldn't wait to get away.' He'd seemed satisfied.

But if she'd mentioned now that she was meeting someone from her past it might have pricked his interest, so she'd kept stumm. Now, though, she realised that there was another reason why she wouldn't want to tell Tom about Gary: she wanted to keep him, and not just her secret, to herself. The thought disturbed her.

She was confused: excited and nervous in equal measure. She had a weird sense that this was just the start of something, though she had no idea what. She'd felt an immediate affinity with Gary, a magnetic pull, a sense that she could say anything to this man whom she really hardly knew and he wouldn't be shocked, wouldn't judge her.

She had this feeling that he really understood and liked her. She wanted to spend more time with him, even though it was almost certainly a mistake. In fact, she couldn't wait to see him again.

What would Gary say to Michelle when he got home? Becca hadn't asked him not to tell his wife about her and her story. In fact, she'd rather assumed he would. She trusted him not to betray her; she hoped that his wife wouldn't either. After all, they were a couple, and couples are supposed to back each other. But she had a funny feeling that Gary wouldn't say much about her to Michelle. Maybe she was fantasising that the meeting meant more to him than it really did, but she didn't think so.

She crossed over Waterloo Road and walked towards the escalator that would take her to the main concourse. There were still a fair number of people about, but nothing like the crowds at rush hour.

Something made her turn her head to the right and she spotted a familiar face coming out of the tube. It was Nic's husband in a dark overcoat. He seemed to be hurrying towards the station exit; there was a young girl at his side.

'Alan!' Becca called. It was strangely comforting to see someone she knew.

He turned and stared at her, clearly not knowing who she was. Then a shock of recognition crossed his face. The girl also turned and gazed at Becca. She had peroxide-blond hair, too much make-up and small, pinched features.

Becca glanced down; she couldn't help it. She had to stop herself gasping out loud. The girl was in a black leather bomber jacket, mini-skirt, black fishnet tights and high black patent heels that looked absurdly large on her thin little legs. She appeared foreign, Eastern European possibly. She was probably only eighteen. Younger even.

'I'm on my way home,' Becca explained, pointing helplessly

at the escalator. She couldn't think of anything else to say. Alan nodded, unsmiling. Then he grabbed the girl by the arm and hustled her away. Becca was so surprised that she stood rooted to the spot, watching them disappear round the corner.

Ohmigod, she thought. He was with a hooker. She checked herself. She was being ridiculous. The girl wasn't a prostitute, she was just his niece or something. They'd been out to the theatre or for dinner and he was taking her home, back to her parents. But that skirt, those heels, that thin, white little face with so much make-up . . .

Becca shuddered, all thoughts of Gary momentarily forgotten. What on earth was she going to say to Nic? Indeed, should she say anything at all?

Chapter Sixteen

'I so don't want to go.' Freya's face was set in firm, fixed fury.

Evie frowned, putting a hand on each of her daughter's shoulders. 'Please, darling, you agreed,' she said, looking deep into Freya's big blue eyes. 'And don't do this in front of Michael. He's quite looking forward to it. If he knows how you feel he'll probably say he's not going, too.'

Freya shook her mother off and backed away. 'I don't know why you're so keen for us to go anyway when Dad's so vile.'

Evie swallowed. She didn't really know either. The last thing she wanted was for Neil and that bloody Helen to have a happy family lunch with her children. For them to be made to toast this impending baby who'd quickly assume its place at the forefront of its father's affections, likely as not shoving them into the back seat.

But Evie had been determined right from the moment Neil left that the children would still have a relationship with him, come what may. Hard as it was, she wanted them to bond with the baby, too, to feel part of Neil's new life. It was important for them, for their future.

'Try to enjoy it,' Evie pleaded. 'After all, it's not every day you get taken to a nice restaurant.'

'Nice restaurant?' Freya laughed humourlessly. 'It'll probably be McDonald's like last time.'

Michael appeared at the bottom of the stairs. He was wearing his best pale-blue polo shirt, Evie noted, and the trendy brown velvet jacket that she'd picked up at H&M for kids. He looked a darling, so smart. Evie smiled. 'You look lovely.'

Freya, on the other hand, had gone out of her way to make herself as unappealing as possible. She hadn't washed her hair, which was greasy and scrunched up on the top of her head in a sort of bun. There was a tie-dye effect, too, because she hadn't coloured it recently and her natural fair hair was showing through at the roots.

She was wearing tight black jeans, a black V-neck jumper that was much too big for her and had a hole in the left elbow, and grubby white sneakers. All this was set off with white face make-up and lashings of black eyeliner.

The doorbell rang. Evie felt her heart flutter, as it always did when Neil arrived.

'Open it,' she said, pushing Freya forwards.

'No, you.'

'I'll do it,' Michael grumbled, shoving past his mother and sister, who hovered anxiously, their backs to the wall.

Neil was standing on the front step looking gorgeous, as usual, Evie thought: clean and well groomed and scrummy. She felt a stab of longing. If only he'd hold her in his arms, tell her he'd made a terrible mistake, kiss her, squeeze her to his heart. Stop it, she told herself.

'C'mon you two.' He sounded bright and jolly. Evie thought it seemed slightly forced, though. Underneath that chirpy veneer he was probably nervous as hell about how they'd react.

'The restaurant's booked for one o'clock,' he went on, giving Michael a playful punch on the arm.

'I've got to be back for three,' Freya growled.

Neil wasn't to be deflated. 'No problem.' He grinned at his daughter. 'You look trendy.'

Freya scowled.

'And Evie,' he went on, 'lovely top. I haven't seen that one before.'

Evie hated the expression on his face. It was something between a smirk and a leer. She also hated herself for being flattered.

'This old thing?' she said icily. '£3.99 from Primark.'

'Well, it's very pretty,' Neil replied. He motioned to the children. 'The car's just round the corner.'

Evie couldn't bear to be in the house on her own, twiddling her thumbs and brooding. She considered phoning Nic or

Becca but decided against it. It was Saturday and the husbands might pick up. Evie couldn't face having to make polite conversation. Anyway, they'd probably be busy doing family things.

It would be a good opportunity to get on with some sewing, but she knew she wouldn't be able to concentrate. She thought of Bill; he'd been so kind when she'd told him about the baby. She grabbed her black duffel coat, pulled a pale-blue knitted beanie down over her ears and hurried next door.

'I wondered if I could borrow some milk?' she asked. 'We've run out. I'll go to the shops later.'

Bill was wearing grubby brown corduroy trousers and an old red and green checked shirt with the sleeves rolled up to his elbows. His face and arms looked remarkably tanned for the time of year. 'Been doing some gardening,' he explained, rubbing his dirty hands on his knees. 'Blasted brambles taking over the place.'

A funny noise slipped out of the back of her throat. He gave her one of his intense looks. 'What's up?'

There was no point pretending. 'Neil's taken the children out to tell them about the baby,' Evie whispered. 'I've tried to be positive in front of them but it's so hard.'

Bill narrowed his blue eyes. 'Let's go for a walk and you can tell me about it. It's a beautiful day.' He pointed to her feet and chuckled. 'But you'll have to change your footwear. I'm not taking you out in those.'

She looked down. She was still wearing the stupid, pink fluffy cat slippers that Freya had given her last Christmas. She felt her face redden. 'I'll nip back and change.'

'What about the milk?' he called after her.

'I'll pick it up later.'

They strolled along the river towards Teddington Lock, watching the rowers speeding past, urged on by their noisy coxes. There were a lot of people out today, families mostly, with dogs and small children wobbling on bikes or trundling along on scooters. The water shimmered and sparkled in the late October sunshine and Evie felt her spirits lift as she stretched her limbs and breathed in gulps of cool, fresh air. She linked her arm in Bill's. She had to walk quite fast to keep up with him; his legs were so much longer than hers.

She found herself talking a lot about Neil, yet again, and the baby, how she thought the children would take the news, why she was so upset. Every now and then Bill would offer a comment, but mostly he just listened.

After a mile or so they stopped and rested on a wooden bench, set a little way back from the river on the grassy verge. Her gaze wandered to the houses on the opposite bank. There was one, in particular, that she'd always loved: a weird, gothic-looking building with a round turret. You almost expected to see Rapunzel leaning out of the window, her long golden tresses blowing in the breeze.

'I'd love to have a workroom there,' she said. 'The light must be fantastic. I'm sure I'd be really creative if I had a room like that.'

Bill nodded. 'It's amazing. Must be worth a fortune.' He pointed to a much smaller house on the left with a pretty little garden that sloped down to the water's edge. 'How about that one instead? It's not stunning like the other one, but it still has the view. I could see you in there with your tailor's dummy and your wedding dresses.'

'I had a customer recently – actually I think it was the day that we went to that play at the Orange Tree. She came for a fitting and I had to inform her that she was pregnant,' Evie said.

Bill laughed. 'How did you know?'

'I could just tell. She'd gone up a cup size and the tops of her arms were all chubby.'

'So how did you break the news?'

Evie screwed her face up. 'It's difficult to be subtle about something like that. I think I said: "Have you thought of taking a pregnancy test?"'

Bill shuffled on the bench. 'Awkward. How did she take it?'

Evie put her head on one side. 'She was a bit shocked. We sat down and had a cup of tea and a chat. She rang the next day to say she'd done the pregnancy test and I was right. By then she'd had a bit of time to get used to it and even sounded quite excited, thank goodness.'

'I bet you've got heaps of stories like that,' Bill said.

'Yes. I have to be a bit of a counsellor sometimes.' Evie grimaced. 'I tend not to tell them about my own failed marriage – wouldn't want to trample on their dreams.'

Bill ignored the last comment. 'What about the pregnant lady's dress? Is it expandable?'

Evie sighed. 'I'll have to start again. I can't quite see a bride who's eight or nine months gone in a strapless boned corset. But she's so sweet I don't mind.'

He paused. 'You should do some advertising, you know, charge a bit more, get someone in to help. Maybe set up your own shop.'

Evie shrugged. 'I'd love to but you need capital, which I don't have.' She stared at the ground.

'You could take out a loan.'

She shook her head. 'I doubt the banks would want to lend me anything.'

'You won't know until you try,' Bill said seriously. 'Listen Evie, I know you're going through a bad time but you've got options, you know. You've heaps of talent, plenty of experience and now the children are older, presumably you've a little more time. You need to pull yourself together and stop feeling sorry for yourself. The only thing stopping you from moving on and making a new life and career for yourself is you.'

She shrugged. 'I suppose so but—'

'You see.' He sounded exasperated. 'You're putting obstacles in the way already.'

She stiffened. 'It's not easy, you know, being on your own . . .'

He was silent.

'I'm so sorry,' she cried suddenly. 'How selfish of me, when you've been on your own for so long.' She cleared her throat. 'Do you still miss Jan terribly?'

Jan was his wife who died of cancer some years ago. He rarely mentioned her.

He picked at a piece of fluff on his corduroy trousers. 'Less as time goes by,' he replied. 'She was a lovely woman. You'd have got on well with her.'

'I'm sure I would,' said Evie. 'What was she like?'

'A little like you.' Bill smiled, staring into the distance. 'Small and pretty and lively.'

Evie was touched. 'Ahh.'

'She ran her own PR business,' he went on. 'She did rather well but it was bloody hard work. Kept going pretty much throughout her illness. I tried to persuade her to slow down but she wouldn't.' He scratched his head. 'She was convinced right till the very end that she was going to get better.'

Evie's shoulders drooped. She fiddled with the toggles on her duffel coat. Bill must think her so inadequate. Jan managed to stay positive and keep working even when she was *dying*.

He squinted. 'It looks as if there's a good crop of apples on that tree.' He pointed again to the little house across the river that he'd earmarked for her. 'You could do your sewing in the garden in summer and watch the boats go by. There's plenty of shade.'

Evie was still thinking about Jan, working away at her business when she was so ill. She pulled her blue woollen hat further down over her eyebrows.

'I'd be tempted to make cider,' Bill went on.

'Sorry?' She didn't understand.

'With the apples.'

'Oh,' said Evie, rising. 'But I don't like cider so there'd be no point.'

'Of course not.'

Neil's car was pulling up outside the house when they arrived back.

'Thanks for the walk,' Evie said.

'Any time,' Bill replied. 'Think I'll go over to the allotment now. Care to join me? Michael would love it down there. He could help with some digging.'

She imagined Michael in his wellies, trampling around in the mud. It's true, he probably would love it.

She shook her head. 'I've got things to do. I'm going to a party at my friend Nic's tonight – you know, the freelance journalist. Lives in Twickenham?'

Bill raised his eyebrows. 'You're going out?'

119

'You seem surprised.'

'I just thought, after the news today, that the children might . . .'

'They'll be fine,' Evie said quickly. 'I promised Nic I'd go. I can't let her down.' She gave him a quick kiss on the cheek. She had to go up on tiptoes because he was much taller than her. He smelled faintly of aftershave and woodsmoke.

'Have a nice evening,' he said. There was something in his tone of voice that made her uncomfortable. He could be so superior at times.

'You too,' she replied, turning swiftly away.

Neil was opening the rear door to let the children out. Helen was in the front, looking straight ahead. On the rare occasions that Evie had met her she had always been frosty. She seemed almost jealous, which was extraordinary, given that Helen had everything over her, including looks, youth – and Neil. She really had no reason to feel insecure.

Evie glanced anxiously at the children. Her heart sank. Michael, who got out of the car first, looked confused. Neil ruffled his hair and his son smiled, but it was a forced-looking smile. Freya, meanwhile, was giving nothing away, which seemed ominous.

Neil tried to give her a kiss but she backed off.

'Bye,' she said, emotionlessly. 'Thanks for lunch.'

'It's a pleasure,' Neil replied brightly. 'Helen and I so wanted you to share in our happiness.'

She brushed past her mother without looking at her and walked up the garden path.

'Yeah, right,' Evie heard her mutter.

Freya threw herself on her bed and buried her face in the pillow. Her insides felt hollow. There was a black, empty space where her stomach, lungs and heart should be. Dad was having another child. Now he and Mum would never, ever get back together. Poor Mum. Poor Michael. Poor me.

She tried to picture Dad holding a baby. The thought made her want to puke. He'd expect her to be thrilled and to be a nice big sister and play with it and stuff. Some hope.

She'd nearly walked out of the restaurant. The only reason she hadn't was because of Michael. He'd have been really upset, as would Mum when she found out. Typical that Dad had picked a posh Japanese place in Richmond. Michael didn't even like Japanese food. He'd ploughed his way through pork kato curry but she could tell he was nearly gagging. She'd pushed her sushi round the plate. She hadn't even pretended to want it.

It was almost funny the way Dad waited until pudding to make his announcement. She'd seen them putting the champagne in the ice bucket so she knew it was coming. She'd pretended not to notice, though. Like she cared.

She'd guessed it was a baby because Mum said they weren't getting married. What else could it be? But he might have got a new job or something. Dad might have been moving to Serbia. If only.

Helen was nauseating, all simpering with Dad and trying to be the sweet little stepmother. 'You must come and see the baby whenever you like,' she'd said.

Well, that would be never, then, Freya thought. But she didn't say it.

'What are you going to call it?' Michael asked. Freya wanted to stab him in the ribs. It was gross, the way he was sucking up to them.

Dad laughed. 'It's not "it" Michael,' he'd said, 'it's he or she. We don't know the sex yet. As for names, have you got any ideas?'

Freya zoned out at that point, tried to listen to the conversations going on at the other tables. She heard someone say 'Piccadilly Circus' and 'wasabi'.

'What do you think, Freya?' Dad said. 'Any suggestions for names?'

She paused. 'Wasabi.'

Michael giggled. Dad scowled. 'Don't be silly.'

Helen looked upset. Good.

'I think it's a nice name,' Freya said. 'And it would suit either sex.'

After that, the conversation fizzled out. She remembered Dad asking them both about school. Helen tried to talk to her about music. 'What do you think of Amy Winehouse?' she'd asked. 'I quite liked that song about rehab.'

'She's all right.' Freya wasn't falling for that one.

Helen wouldn't give up. 'I'm going to a Will Young concert,' she'd said. 'I hope the noise doesn't upset Junior in here.' She'd patted her stomach. Sick.

Freya was pleased with her response: 'Will Young?' She pulled a face. 'I doubt it. Anyway, it's just a bunch of cells, isn't it?'

Helen sniffed. She looked as if she was about to cry. Result!

Freya strained her ears. Mum was talking to Michael in the bedroom next door. She had on her soothing mummy voice. They both laughed. Michael was still young. He didn't understand what was happening. Just as well. Freya was knackered. She pulled the duvet round her, closed her eyes and felt herself drifting off to sleep.

When she woke, the house was silent. She blinked. There was a little gap between the edge of her blind and the window and she noticed that it was dark outside now. She wondered how long she'd slept. There was a wet patch on the duvet where she'd been weeping. She got up, padded over to her laptop and logged on. Please let Cal be there. She needed him so badly right now.

At least school was a bit better. She'd done the right thing, taking his advice not to look too upset when she was around Gemma and Chantelle and the rest, not to let them get to her. And she'd ditched Richie, not that there'd ever been much between them. That had probably helped.

Basically she'd kept her head down, tried to be nice to people, avoided arguments and the nasty MSNing had stopped. For now anyway. Gemma and co. weren't exactly being nice to her, but at least they were leaving her alone. That was a huge relief. But now this.

hey Cal – u there? i need to talk, she wrote.

It didn't take him long to reply. *wot bout? im listening.*

She told him about the baby, Helen's stupid expression, Dad's happiness, Michael's confusion. Mum, trying so hard to be positive.

i don't want a half brother or sister, she said. *they're gonna expect me to love it, do stuff with it. but i hate them both.*

listen, he said, *life's shit sometimes. but u know wot? ur the best. you've got a beautiful heart. ive never known a girl like u before.*

She felt warm all over, tingly. No boy had ever spoken to her like that. It was almost like he was in love with her!

Was it possible for two people to fall in love without ever having met? She tried to picture what he looked like. She imagined he was tall and quite thin, with cool clothes and messy fair hair. She'd love to know if she was right, but she didn't dare ask.

He must be a mind-reader.

will u send me a foto of u? he said. *But don't tell anyone. i want to keep u to myself.*

He was sooo romantic. She'd get Michael to take a picture on Mum's digital camera. She wanted to call Lucy to tell her. Normally they told each other everything – whom they fancied, what kind of kissers they thought they'd be. But this time she wouldn't.

It was *her* secret. If word got out, it might spoil everything. Gemma and everyone would tease her. And Mum wouldn't like that she was talking to a stranger. Lucy would start talking about sex or something, giggle about what they were going to do to each other. She wouldn't understand that this was different.

There was a knock. Mum's head appeared round the door. Freya quickly minimised.

'May I come in?'

She looked beautiful, Freya thought. She was wearing a sparkly silver halter-neck top over loose black trousers, and high black heels that made her look much taller. She'd blow-dried her fair hair and had pretty make-up on: pinky brown lips and lots of mascara.

The silver top had a V-neck but it was quite low. Freya frowned. It was pretty gross for your mum to go out with cleavage showing. But it would be difficult to hide her boobs unless she wore a burka or something. Freya was quite glad that she didn't have boobs like that. It'd be something else to tease her about.

'You were asleep, I didn't want to disturb you,' Mum said. 'How do you feel?'

Freya pulled a face. 'I'd guessed it was a baby,' she said. 'It's sick. Where are you going anyway?'

Mum came and sat on the end of her bed. 'Nic's party, remember? Michael's downstairs watching TV. There's lasagne in the oven. It's ready whenever you want it.'

'Oh yes.' Freya had forgotten about the party. She didn't mind, though. She was happy talking to Cal.

'Darling,' Mum said. 'I know it's a big shock for us all, especially you and Michael, but it's not the baby's fault, you know. You'll grow to love it. It'll be exciting having a new brother or sister.'

'It won't,' Freya snapped. 'I'm going to make sure I have as little to do with it as possible.'

Mum sighed. She looked so sad. Freya left her desk and sat beside her, gave her a hug.

'Don't look so worried,' she said. 'I'm just in a bad mood. Dad was stupid at lunch, he was like a schoolboy. And Helen was all lovey-dovey with him. I hated it. But I expect I'll like the baby when it's born. I'm just being grumpy.'

Mum's shoulders relaxed and the worry lines on her forehead dissolved.

'Go off and enjoy your party,' Freya said. 'Michael and I will be fine. I'll get supper and make sure he doesn't go to bed too late.'

'Sure you don't mind?' Mum rose. 'I can cancel if you'd prefer?'

Freya shook her head. 'By the way, where's the camera?'

Mum thought for a moment. 'By my bed, I think. Why?'

'No reason,' Freya replied.

Chapter Seventeen

Nic giggled, listening out for Alan as he came upstairs. He seemed to take an eternity. It was a bit chilly with no clothes on. She had goosebumps. She hugged her arms around her and gave them a rub.

At last he entered the room and she leaped out from behind the door. 'Boo.'

He jumped, startled. 'What the . . . ?'

She smiled mischievously, twirling the long, blue silk scarf in her hands in a Salome-like fashion.

He frowned. 'What are you doing?'

'Seducing you,' she said, moving right up close so that her breasts rubbed against his shirt, her thigh against his trousered leg.

He took a step back. 'Don't be absurd. They'll be here in a minute.'

She bit her lip, feeling suddenly foolish and very vulnerable.

His expression softened. 'Maybe later.'

Yeah, right. She walked quickly over to the gold-upholstered armchair in the corner of the bedroom and started putting on the black and pink underwear she'd picked out earlier. She peeped round, hoping he might be looking, but he had his back to her, choosing a fresh shirt from the cupboard.

She took a swig from the half-empty glass of white wine on top of her mahogany chest of drawers and sighed. Their love-making was so infrequent these days, she wondered what on earth she'd have to do to get him in the mood. When was the last time they'd had sex? She honestly couldn't remember. He always had some excuse or other.

She stood in front of the full-length mirror in the corner of the room and slipped on the black, lacy, figure-hugging dress she'd picked up in a chi-chi vintage shop. According to the shop owner it was made in the sixties. It was short, a couple of inches above the knee, with a scoop neck and three-quarter-length lace sleeves. Nic had good legs; she knew she could carry it off.

'Can you zip me up?' she asked without turning round. She watched his reflection coming up behind her. Her blond bob was only chin-length, so she didn't need to lift her hair up for him. She hoped he might kiss her neck, her shoulder or something. But he didn't. He looked distracted, a million miles away.

'There you go.'

She swivelled round. 'How do I look?'

'Lovely,' he replied, bending down to tie his shoelace.

She finished her glass of wine and then straightened the bedspread, which was dark green, to match the green carpet and curtains. It was a queen-size bed with an elegant, ivory-coloured antique French headboard which Nic had picked up at an auction. One wall was covered in striking Cole & Son green and pale-blue paisley wallpaper, while the rest were painted off white. She'd wanted something calm and sophisticated, a bit like a hotel room.

She checked the en-suite bathroom, too. It was unlikely that anyone would go in there but you never knew. The dress felt a bit looser round the waist than the last time she'd worn it. She'd better eat something tonight or she'd start to look scraggy.

She'd hired a catering company to do the food: some meat and fish, lots of different side dishes. But her stomach turned at the thought of all those creamy salads, buttery new potatoes, sweet puddings. She just didn't seem to have an appetite these days.

Nic left the bedroom. Alan had gone downstairs. Across the landing she noticed that, unusually, he hadn't closed his study door. She decided to check for dirty cups and glasses. He usually left at least one mug of half-drunk coffee or tea lying around.

She always felt a slight frisson when she entered his study, as if she were a naughty schoolgirl going somewhere she shouldn't. He certainly never made her feel welcome there. She tiptoed in and pushed the door to, practically bumping into the ugly grey filing cabinet that was hidden behind it.

The room was terribly tidy, as always. There was a black leather sofa against the right-hand wall facing Alan's large, rectangular desk on the left. The desk was Victorian, made of walnut, with oval brass plate handles and a brown leather top. Alan had chosen it himself from an antique shop in Surrey. There was nothing on it, save a squat little orange and blue glazed cup which Dominic had made some years ago in pottery classes at school. Alan used it as a pen-holder.

All around the desk were built-in shelves with rows and rows of financial books, plus a few biographies and thrillers. Alan wasn't a big reader: he was always too busy working. But he tended to catch up when they were on holiday.

Nic noticed that his laptop was tucked away in its black holder, resting against the wall. She scanned the room for empty cups and was surprised that there were none. The clock on the wall said 8.15 p.m. The guests were invited for around eight thirty.

Something made her reach out, tentatively, to try the drawers on the desk. Normally, she knew, Alan kept them locked. He said there was important, confidential information about clients in there.

The first two drawers were, indeed, impossible to get into. But to her surprise, the third slid open. She glanced over her shoulder just to check. No Alan. Dominic was on a sleepover so he wouldn't disturb her.

She peered in the drawer. It was the biggest, deepest one. There seemed to be a pile of old magazines in there. On top was *The Economist*. She picked it up and checked the date: June 2007. There must be an article he wanted to keep.

The next one down was *The Spectator*. She picked that up too and put it on top of *The Economist* by her feet. Still curious, she pulled out the whole pile. It was difficult because it was heavy. She plonked the lot on the floor, knelt down and started to go through them quickly. There were more *Economist*s, several issues of *Time*, a *New Statesman* or two.

She reached the middle of the pile and stopped. Her head swam. *Teen Babes*, she read. She stared. There, on the cover, was a picture of a naked young girl with bunches, cupping her tiny breasts in a provocative pose. 'Tons of teen pussy', screamed the coverline. 'No 1 source for teen sex!'

She didn't want to but she couldn't stop herself. She opened the magazine and flicked through. It was crammed with pictures of naked girls deliberately chosen, no doubt, because they looked so young, no more than about twelve or thirteen. They had very slender bodies, hardly any breasts or pubic hair, no hips. In the background were props such as dolls, teddies and pink, girly furnishings. But there was nothing sweet or innocent about what they were doing.

Nic's heart fluttered. There must be some mistake. He wouldn't look at this stuff. The magazine must have got stuck to one of the other ones somehow and he didn't realise it was there. She picked it up. Underneath was another. Different title, same vein. And another. She riffled frantically through the whole pile until she got almost to the bottom and they were spread around her in a messy heap.

All teen sex magazines, every single one of them.

She covered her face with her hands. Who was this man she was married to? She wondered if she even knew him.

She squeezed her eyes shut, but she couldn't get away from what was in front of her. She could see girls – lots of young girls – dancing, opening their legs, inviting, pouting. A mash of flesh and lurid colours, faceless men pushing their way into garish orifices.

She imagined Alan poring over the photographs, touching, coming, even. She shuddered. It would be bad enough if they were grown women, but these were just children. It was abusive, disgusting and shameful. They weren't so very much older than Dominic.

She wanted to go but couldn't. She had to check the bottom of the pile. She turned back to the drawer. The very last thing in it wasn't a magazine but an A4-sized scrapbook, the kind she had as a child. She used to press wild flowers, stick them in and label them.

She opened the first page. It was covered in crudely cut-out pictures of smiling girls in school uniforms, the kind you see in catalogues. She turned over. More pictures. Children in underwear, little pants and vests, mostly white but some with flowers and doll motifs.

Her heart stopped. She looked more closely. Some of the pictures weren't right. Different heads were stuck on to the bodies. Heads of children – young girls – taken from photographs. She squinted. Some of the heads looked familiar. Lily, the neighbour's daughter? She was mistaken. Her imagination was running riot. Freya?

She put her hands over her mouth to stifle her cry. The word 'monster' slipped through her brain like a spectre. Her whole body shook.

There was an innocent explanation.

She sat there for a few moments, thinking rapidly. She needed to have her wits about her. Whatever she did next, whatever path she chose, was going to be crucial. Her brain was ticking so loudly that she could almost hear it. They were just pictures. Static images. Fantasy. They had nothing to do with real life.

They were young girls. Grown men shouldn't even think about doing these things to them.

She thought she heard a noise outside, a creak. She gasped, turning round. Nothing happened. She waited, holding her breath, until she was sure there was no one there.

If Alan found her . . . it didn't bear thinking about. If Alan left her . . . Her heart started beating faster. She depended on him for her very survival.

No one must ever know. Ever. She didn't know. She'd never been in the study or opened the drawer. It was his little secret. She breathed in and out several times. She needed another drink. That would blank it out, calm her down. But she must tidy up first.

Swiftly, she gathered the magazines together and put them carefully back in the drawer, making sure the scrapbook was on the bottom and *The Economist* on the very top, just as he'd left it. She closed the drawer and glanced around her one more time to make sure that she hadn't missed anything. Then she crept out of the room, leaving the door open as she'd found it.

She heard the doorbell ring and jumped.

'Nic!' Alan called from the bottom of the stairs.

'I'll be down in a minute,' she replied.

Her thoughts were all over the place, darting to and fro, an undisciplined mess. One by one she tried to marshal them together and regain control. It had never happened. Everything was OK.

She realised that she hadn't put her make-up on and scurried into the bedroom. She sat down at her Venetian-style, mirrored dressing table and stared. Her eyes were bloodshot and her skin looked sallow, almost yellowy. Deep lines ran from her nose to the corners of her mouth. She hardly recognised herself.

She shook her hair and straightened her shoulders. That was better. Pull yourself together. Thank God for foundation, eye-shadow, mascara and blusher. She set to work with a feverish intensity, smoothing on here, dabbing and brushing there, like an artist at his easel.

Ten minutes later exactly, she appeared at the drawing-room door. Everything looked just so: dimmed lighting, pale-cream walls, wooden floor, a giant vase of fresh flowers on the Indian white metal console against the far wall. There were a handful of guests already but many more were expected.

She glided over to Alan's side and took his left hand. She could feel his wedding ring between her fingers, solid and comforting.

'Sorry I'm late.' She smiled, glancing from one person to another, challenging them with her eyes to focus on her dress, her immaculate make-up and hair, anything but the turquoise braces. She was quite the poised, elegant lady of the house. 'Has everybody got a drink?'

Chapter Eighteen

Evie felt suddenly claustrophobic.

The room had filled up rapidly and was hot, noisy and crowded. Her high, pointy black boots were uncomfortable and she wanted to sit down on one of the sofas that were pushed out of the way against the walls. But she knew that would look odd and anti-social.

She excused herself from the little group that she was in and squeezed past more guests into the kitchen next door. She was desperate to get away. They'd been talking about washing machines. She'd wanted to say that she couldn't care less about washing machines, that it was incredibly boring to be discussing them and couldn't they find something better to talk about? But she hadn't dared. Had Neil been there she might have been more outspoken and tried to steer the subject round. But she felt self-conscious enough without drawing more attention to herself.

She remembered how, when she and Neil used to go to parties together, she'd glue herself to his side. If he left her for more than a few minutes she'd be looking round, wondering where he was, missing him. It was her nature; she wasn't made to be on her own.

She'd have been amazed, back then, that she'd one day be able to come to events like this as a single person and cope as well as she was. Except that right now, she felt that she wasn't coping at all. She was miserable. She should have stayed at home with the children, as Bill had suggested.

Where were Becca and Tom? Evie was sure that Becca had said they were coming. Maybe something had cropped up and they wouldn't show at all. Evie couldn't wait all night for them. She was tempted to slip away and go home. But Nic would be upset when she found out.

There were fewer people in the kitchen and she could breathe more easily. She took in her surroundings. There was a delicious-looking array of untouched food laid out on Nic's long wooden kitchen table. Two extra tables covered in white linen tablecloths that she must have hired or borrowed from somewhere stood at either end of it, and they were laden, too.

Evie spotted a whole salmon, French bread, plates of cold meats and several different, brightly coloured salads. Her stomach rumbled. It was ages since she'd eaten. But she didn't want to look greedy and be the first to dive in.

She decided to kill time and go to the loo. She didn't need to but she could comb her hair or something. Besides, she enjoyed Nic's loos. They were all white tiles and interesting glass basins with gleaming taps that probably cost more than Evie would spend on an entire bathroom. She swivelled round, ready to leave – and collided with someone she'd never met before.

'I'm sorry,' she muttered, flustered.

He took a step back, holding his hands up in mock surrender. 'Whoa! You're in a hurry,' he said, amused.

At least she hadn't skewered his foot with one of her pointy boots.

Evie glanced up. A very tall man was looking down at her smiling. Her nose was just about level with his nipples. It was a disconcerting thought. Even from her disadvantaged position she could tell that he was handsome, in a conventional sort of way. He had a strong jaw, a suggestion of designer stubble, longish, swept-back, straight black hair that was streaked with grey and a wide grin.

He appeared to be on his own; his wife must be next door.

'I'm sorry,' she repeated. 'I was going to the bathroom.'

He made a face. 'What a pity. I was willing you to eat something because my stomach's digesting itself. I don't want to be the first to dig in.'

He had a deep, educated voice. She giggled, relaxing. 'I'm hungry, too. Tell you what, we can make a pact. I'll go to the bathroom quickly and when I come back, we'll grab a plate each and help ourselves at exactly the same moment. Then we won't feel so self-conscious.'

'It's a deal,' he said, shaking her hand. 'But only if you agree to sit down and eat with me afterwards.' He frowned. 'That is if you're . . .'

'On my own? Oh yes, I'm separated,' Evie blurted. Immediately, she wished that she could take the words back. She blushed, hoping that he didn't think she was being forward. She hadn't needed to give him so much information. She could simply have said that she'd enjoy a chat. But she found it so painful to admit she was separated that she'd trained herself to get it over with in company as quickly as possible. It was easier, somehow, than having to wait, on tenterhooks, for the inevitable questions, usually followed by looks of sympathy.

Her face and neck felt boiling hot. She was staring down at her boots. She wished she could run to the bathroom and pour cold water over her head.

'So am I,' he said. 'Separated, I mean.'

Surprised, she forgot her embarrassment and looked at him again. It hurt her neck to crane it so; he was very tall. 'I'm sorry. It's difficult, isn't it?' she said, frowning.

He shrugged, stooping now to make it easier for her. 'We'd been getting on so badly, in the end it was a relief. The right thing for both of us.'

There was something about him that touched her: he looked too thin and pale for someone so handsome. There were creases round his eyes and worry lines on his brow that she hadn't clocked at first glance. He's been through the mill too, she thought. She wanted to find out more about him.

'I won't be long,' she promised. He gave her the thumbs up.

Evie tried the handle on the downstairs loo but it was locked. She hoped the person in there wouldn't be long. She leaned against the wall and waited. Nic whooshed out of the sitting room smelling of alcohol and expensive perfume and banged into her.

'I'm afraid it's—' Evie started to say, but Nic was already beating on the door.

'Hurry up in there,' she shouted, crossing her legs theatrically.

'I'm bursting.' She grinned, revealing her turquoise train tracks.

She sounded drunk. Evie wished she wouldn't drink so much. She could hear the chain being flushed and decided to try her luck on the first floor instead. Nic's need was clearly greater than hers.

'You a'right, darling?' Nic slurred after her.

Evie hoped she'd switch to soft drinks soon, though she didn't think it likely. 'Yes thanks,' she said, starting to climb the stairs. 'I'll use the one up there.' She pointed. 'Lovely party.'

She was nearly at the top when she spotted Alan coming out of a room opposite what she knew to be Nic's bedroom. Perhaps that was his study. Nic said he spent a lot of time in there. She was always surprised by how small and slight he was. He was wearing a crisp, pale-pink shirt which was open at the neck, and navy-blue trousers that seemed to hang on him.

His body language was quiet and timid; he gave the impression of someone who felt that he needed to apologise for being there. Yet when he spoke, he sounded intelligent, confident, in control. Appearances can be deceptive, Evie thought.

'Hi!' she said brightly.

He closed the door behind him and glanced to the left and right; probably didn't want Nic to know that he'd been checking work emails or something. She'd be furious. 'I had to take an important call,' he explained unnecessarily and smiled thinly. 'To tell you the truth, I'm not mad about parties,' he went on, lowering his voice. 'Nic's the social animal. What about you?'

'I do find it quite difficult talking to strangers,' Evie admitted. Then she remembered the tall man – she realised that she didn't even know his name – waiting for her downstairs. 'But I'm having a lovely time tonight,' she added quickly. 'Great crowd.'

'Good,' Alan said. He cleared his throat. 'How's Freya?'

Evie was surprised, and then she remembered that they'd met when she and Freya had come to collect Michael after shoe shopping.

'Fine,' she said. 'Well, a bit sulky and teenagerish sometimes but she'll grow out of it.'

He smiled. 'I'm sure she will. I hope you've had some food?'

'Just about to.'

'Excellent. You make yourself at home. I'll see you later.'

Evie quickly checked her make-up in the bathroom mirror and combed her hair. She had an awful lot of cleavage showing. She pulled the V of her top up but it didn't make much difference. Too bad, she thought, it's the way I'm made.

She peeped into the sitting room to see if Becca had arrived yet. She hadn't. The man was waiting for her in more or less the same spot in the kitchen where she'd left him. He grinned when he saw her.

'I don't know your name,' he said, stooping again so that he could talk in her ear. 'Mine's Steve.'

The kitchen was much busier now and several people were helping themselves to food. They needn't worry about being the first any more. But Evie was glad there had been an excuse for them to strike up a conversation. She took a white porcelain plate and chose some salmon and several spoonfuls of salad. Normally she'd have grabbed a chunk of bread, too, but she didn't want him to think her greedy.

'That's rather a dainty selection you've got there,' he said, joining her. He looked uncomfortable. His own plate was piled high. 'I feel bad now.'

She laughed, taking a chunk of French bread after all. 'There, happier?'

There was nowhere to sit in the kitchen. Evie didn't fancy standing so she suggested the TV room. She'd always envied Nic's TV room. It was where Dominic and his friends could hang out and make a mess without disturbing the rest of the house. There was a piano in there, too, for him to practise on.

They squeezed past the other guests and started to cross the hall. The doorbell rang and Evie could make out two figures through the stained-glass panels. She rested her knife and fork on the plate so that she had a free hand and went to open the door. Becca was standing there with a face like thunder. Tom seemed to be hovering slightly behind.

'He went to a rugby match with his mates and only just got back,' she hissed, jerking her head back in Tom's direction to signify whom she meant, as if there were any doubt.

Evie made a sympathetic face. 'Come in, come in,' she said, smiling at Tom, too, who flashed his dimples. 'This is Steve. Steve, this is my great friend Becca and her husband, Tom.'

Steve smiled, a little coolly Evie thought.

'We were about to have something to eat,' she went on. She was keen to get away. She didn't want to leave Steve standing there with a plate of food any longer than necessary. Becca started to take off her coat. She looked handsome and statuesque in a dazzling cream woollen dress, fitted to the waist, with a tie at the back and long, slightly puffy sleeves.

Nic appeared from the kitchen and tottered past Steve, nearly knocking him over. He moved to one side quickly. 'Darling!' she said, throwing her arms around Becca. 'How lovely to see you. I thought you were never going to make it.'

There were five of them in the hall now. It was a bit of a squeeze. Nic grabbed Tom by the arm. He hadn't even taken off his coat yet.

'Come and say hello to Alan,' she insisted, pulling him with her. 'He's standing in a corner on his own refusing to talk to anyone. He hates parties, you know.' She giggled. 'He's been abroad on business all week and all he wants to do is catch up on boring old emails. He keeps trying to sneak off to his study but I'm on his case.' She tapped her nose knowingly.

'Abroad all week?' Becca repeated. She frowned. She seemed to be processing something. 'But I saw him—'

Nic gave her a strange look. 'It's ridiculous standing here in the hall,' she interrupted. 'For goodness' sake, come and have a drink.' She half pushed, half pulled Tom and Becca forward.

'I'll come and find you in a minute,' Evie called as the three of them disappeared into the kitchen.

The TV-room door was pulled to, presumably to discourage people from going in, but Evie decided to ignore it. 'What do you think?' she asked, looking gratefully at the empty sofa and chairs. Her boots really were uncomfortable.

'Perfect,' Steve replied, following her. 'Nice and quiet. But don't let anyone see,' he whispered, pushing the door almost shut behind them, 'or they'll all want to join us.'

The thick, floor-length cream curtains were closed, giving the room a warm, cosy feel. There was a silver angle-poise lamp on the piano but it wasn't on. The only light came from the standard lamp with a chocolate-brown shade in one corner, opposite the black flat-screen TV in the other. Soft classical music was coming from a hidden speaker, so Nic must have expected that some people would sneak in here.

Evie perched on an elegant little red chair with her back to the window. Steve sat on the corner of the sofa beside her. He began to eat hungrily. Evie noticed with amusement that he'd taken lots of cold beef, the potato and pasta salads but no green leaves. Typical boy, she thought.

His hair was somewhere below chin-length and every now and again he'd put down his knife and fork and run his hands through it, but it didn't seem to go in his face.

She picked at her salmon. Her appetite seemed to have disappeared. 'So how do you know Nic and Alan?' she asked. She hadn't heard Nic mention a very tall, delicious, separated man before. There again, Nic had lots of friends that Evie didn't know. She was, as Alan had pointed out, a social animal.

Steve finished his mouthful. He seemed to be thoroughly enjoying his food. Maybe he wasn't much good at cooking for himself.

'Through work,' he explained. 'I'm a journalist like Nic. She and I started out on the same local paper years ago. I hadn't seen her for ages, to be honest, then a mutual acquaintance gave me her email address and I dropped her a line. It was nice of her to invite me tonight. What about you?'

He listened, eating quietly, while Evie explained that their boys were the same age. They'd originally met at ante-natal classes, then they'd been on a creative writing course. She told him about the creative writing group, too.

'Where do you work now?' she asked when she'd finished her story.

He looked at her. She couldn't help noticing that he had very nice eyes: dark brown, with black lashes and thick – but not too thick – black eyebrows.

'I'm freelance,' he said. 'I do mostly celebrity interviews these days, which means I travel a fair bit. I have to go wherever they are. They never come to you, of course.'

Evie froze, replaying his words in her head. 'Travel a fair bit . . . travel a fair bit.' What had Zelda said about that new man she was going to meet? That he travelled a lot?

Steve was dark, or had been, before the grey crept in, and he had long hair. Zelda had mentioned quite a lot of hair and broad shoulders, too. 'He's tall, yes, and good-looking,' she'd said. Well, he was certainly both of those.

Evie thought Zelda had insisted that his name began with a T, P or a W, but she could have got it wrong. He'd singled Evie out and here they were having a quiet chat all alone in Nic's TV room. Ohmigod! He must be the man Zelda had told her about. He was The One!

'Are you all right?' Steve said. 'You look like you've seen a ghost.'

She snapped back to the present. 'Yes, yes, I'm fine,' she said quickly. Then: 'Do you mind if I ask, do you have children?'

Her stomach fluttered. This mattered a lot. This was crucial.

He sighed. 'Yes, one, a little boy. Jacob. I hardly ever see him though. His mother makes things as difficult as possible.'

'I knew it,' Evie said, practically jumping off her seat. Zelda had told her that he'd have one or two kids.

He raised his eyebrows. 'I beg your pardon?'

She checked herself. 'I'm sorry,' she said quickly. 'It must be terrible not being able to see your child.'

He put his now empty plate down. 'It is hard,' he agreed. 'I adore Jacob. He's eighteen months old.' He fished inside his jacket and pulled out a photo of a cute, chubby-cheeked boy.

Evie took it from him and stared. 'He's gorgeous.'

Steve nodded, putting the photo carefully away again. 'I miss him so much.'

She felt a rush of sympathy. He was so sensitive, gorgeous – and amusing, too. How could any woman reject him?

She put her plate down at her feet. She'd hardly touched her food but he didn't seem to notice. He leaned forward, resting his elbows on his knees. She had his full attention. She worried, momentarily, about her cleavage. Was she falling out?

She glanced down and pulled on the V of her halter-neck top. When she looked up again, her eyes met his for a second. There was a flash of amused comprehension and he smiled.

'Now,' he said, 'tell me all about you, your ex and what happened. I want to know all about you. Absolutely everything.'

Chapter Nineteen

'Do you want to come in?'

Evie couldn't believe that she was being so brazen. There again, if he was The One it was all right, wasn't it? They clambered out of the taxi, Evie first, followed by Steve.

He hunted in his pockets. 'Sorry, I've got no . . .'

'Don't worry, I've plenty of cash,' she said, opening her bag and fishing out her purse.

'Keep the change,' she told the driver. It was a bigger tip than she'd usually give, but she didn't want to hang about a minute more than necessary.

It had been so steamy in the back seat of the cab. He'd kissed her – gorgeously – on the lips. A proper snog, at first wet and slow, then harder and deeper. The kind that makes your lips burn hot with blood. The kind you remember always.

There was only one place they could go from here, Evie thought: bed. But standing here in the cold, fiddling around in the bottom of her bag for the door key, was a bit of a passion-killer. She was beginning to lose her nerve. She prayed the dodgy door lock wouldn't play up and she'd have to call Freya. That would ruin everything.

At last she managed to open up and they stumbled inside. Evie was pretty tipsy and she guessed Steve must be, too. They'd sat for ages in Nic's TV room discussing their respective marriage break-ups, and she'd felt a strange, powerful connection with this man.

He'd told her that he and his wife had split up six months ago after he discovered that she'd been having an affair with an old boyfriend. He'd tried to persuade her to go for marriage counselling but she wouldn't and in the end he'd felt obliged to leave.

He said he'd thought that she must have everything she wanted now, including the house, the car and their little boy. But it seemed not. For some reason she was bitter and vengeful, making it as difficult as possible for him to see the child. Evie felt desperately sorry for him; the ex sounded like a complete cow.

After a while he got up to fetch some white wine from the kitchen. When he returned with a bottle and two glasses, he'd brought a pile of tissues as well. It's true, she needed them. She'd been alternately crying and laughing, listening to his tale of woe and recounting hers. She was so grateful for the tissues, it made her cry again.

'What have I done?' he asked, half horrified, half joking.

'Nothing,' she said. 'You've just been so lovely and open and kind. I realise how little Neil gave of himself or listened to me, really. Our marriage was so one-sided.'

Steve poured two large glasses of wine and handed one to Evie.

'Well, I'd like to propose a toast: to moving on from rubbish exes.' They clinked glasses. 'And the future.'

'The future,' she said, suddenly too shy to look him in the eye.

They chatted some more, never running out of things to say, and polished off the bottle. Evie said they should go and talk to Becca and Nic but Steve seemed reluctant. She managed to persuade him, though.

'Just for a moment,' she promised.

He certainly seemed keen. She loved the fact that he wasn't playing games, acting cool. They stood in the doorway of the sitting room and stared. The music was up loud – it was an old ABBA hit – and a small huddle of women in the middle of the room were dancing. Everyone else had backed away, to make space. Most of the women were moving well, in time to the music, but Nic was stomping and staggering.

'Money, money, money,' she shouted, using weird, jerking movements.

Evie cringed. Couldn't someone stop her? Suddenly, Nic pulled up her dress to reveal stocking tops and a black thong.

141

She began to wave her bum in the air, moving round in a circle to make sure everyone could see. There was an embarrassed giggle. Even Nic's dancing partners stopped and stared.

Evie looked around desperately for Alan and caught sight of him in a corner. He seemed to be hiding, propped against the wall. She willed him to step forward, take Nic in his arms, stop her making a fool of herself. But he didn't. Becca and Tom were nowhere to be seen.

She thought she should do something herself, but what if Nic pushed her off, making more of a scene? Evie felt a pull on her arm. She swung around and it was Steve. She was surprised. She'd forgotten about him.

He bent down and whispered in her ear: 'Let's get out of here quick, before anyone notices.'

'But—' Evie protested.

He was insistent. 'Come on, let's go.'

And so they'd slipped away without saying goodbye to anyone. Evie felt guilty and deliciously naughty at the same time. And here they were, standing in her dingy hall shivering slightly, realising that they hardly knew each other after all.

'Would you like a drink?' she asked, putting down her bag and taking off her coat. She couldn't think what else to say.

'Are you having one?' He looked around for somewhere to hang his jacket.

'I suppose so.'

'Then I will too.'

Fortunately the kitchen wasn't too messy, though she feared that it smelled of burned toast and the overhead light was horribly garish. She turned it off and switched on the little downlighters above the worktops instead. For once, she was relieved that most of them were broken. They gave off a more forgiving glow.

She noticed that the stainless-steel bin in the corner of the kitchen was full to overflowing. Bloody Freya, why couldn't she ever empty it? There again, the bin was probably the last thing on Steve's mind.

She poured them both a whisky. She didn't even like whisky, but wasn't that what you did on occasions like this? She'd seen it in films, anyway. She was going to suggest that they wander into the sitting room. He took the glass out of her hand, put it on the table and lunged forward, squashing his lips against hers.

She was startled. His tongue slithered into her mouth and she closed her eyes quickly, determined to get back in the mood. His hands reached for hers. She wasn't sure what he wanted. He was feeling for her fingers, covering them, holding them, interlacing them with his. She squeezed his hand and he squeezed back. Reassured, she pulled away.

'Quick, let's go upstairs,' she whispered. She thought of something: thank God she'd had a bikini wax. Bloody hell, though, she was wearing her big white comfy knickers. It crossed her mind that she could sneak off and change into her full-on black lacy set, but she ruled it out as too disruptive. She'd just have to busk it.

She wished a magic carpet would whisk them up. The thought of climbing all those steps made her apprehensive again. She was still in her pointy boots but she didn't want to take them off. She'd instantly shrink three inches and probably trip over her trouser legs.

She led him by the hand up the first flight of steps, stopping only for a second on the landing to check that Freya's and Michael's lights were off. She put a finger over her mouth. 'Shhh.' He nodded.

By the time they got to the third floor she was out of breath. She couldn't bear to switch the lamp on in her bedroom, so she opened the curtains behind the bed to let in a chink of light from the street outside.

When she turned around he was right there in front of her, a dark, towering figure. She felt suddenly hopeless and incompetent. 'I haven't done this for a while.' Her voice sounded small, silly. 'Actually, I've only done it with one person – Neil – for, um, seventeen years.'

He didn't reply. He was fiddling with the bow at the back of her neck which held up the sparkly top. He managed to pull it undone and the top flopped down, threatening to reveal her strapless bra. Instinctively, she covered herself with her arms, but he gently prised them apart and pulled the top down to her waist. Then he quickly undid her bra, slipped it off and dropped it on the floor by her feet.

She felt exposed, far more so than she remembered feeling with Neil, though she supposed she'd been just as shy when they'd first met. But her saggy bits: would he find them a turn-off? Find her a turn-off? But he was kissing her breasts, licking her nipples, fumbling with the zip on her trousers.

She stayed his hand. She wasn't going to stand there like some passive little girl; she was a mature woman now. All those years with Neil must have taught her something, for God's sake.

Still half clothed, she started to undo the buttons on his shirt, his belt, the zip on his trousers, until he had just his boxer shorts on. She was relieved that they weren't Y-fronts. Neil never wore them. She thought she might have a problem with a man in Y-fronts.

Steve stepped out of his boxers and trousers and kicked them aside. Now he was fully naked, his penis standing right up in front of her. She pressed her thigh against the length of him, her body against his so that they were skin to skin, with no space between. She ran her hands over his back, his bum. He felt warm and alive and he smelled nice: clean and hot.

She knelt down and wrapped her arms around his thighs. His legs felt smooth and sinewy. Neil's were thicker, hairier. Stop thinking about Neil. Stop making comparisons.

She kissed the tip of him and he moaned appreciatively. She started: HIV, Aids. Why hadn't she thought of it? She was always drumming it into Freya: be responsible when the time comes, practise safe sex. But what to do? She didn't have any condoms, there hadn't been any need.

Steve was waiting, expectantly.

'One moment,' she whispered in a low, barely-there voice that she hoped wouldn't spoil the moment. 'Do you have, erm, a condom?'

To her relief he bent down, rustled around in his trousers and produced a small packet. He ripped it open with his teeth and expertly rolled it on. She wondered, vaguely, if all unattached men carried them around these days or if Steve was ever optimistic. Whatever, he knew what he was doing.

Finally, she lowered her head again and slipped him in her mouth. The bitter, pungent rubber made her gag. Bloody hell, shame it wasn't banana flavour or something. But it was clear from the sounds he made that he liked it so she carried on. After a few moments he pushed her away. Then they were on the bed and he was pulling off her boots, her trousers and her big, white knickers. He paused for a moment and she feared that he was going to say something but he didn't. Instead, he dived down and started using his fingers, his tongue, flickering forward and back in a way that was quite unlike anything she'd experienced before. Neil didn't do it like that.

She tried to lose herself, to focus only on the sensation, but unwanted thoughts wormed their way in, distracting her. She saw Neil making love to Helen. Was he doing that nibbling thing that he used to do with her thighs? She saw Michael, asleep. Could he hear anything? It was a mash of images, confusing, troubling.

Tears of frustration sprang in her eyes. Steve must be tired by now. She reached down and touched his head, his hair. He placed his hand on hers and guided it between her legs, urging her to finish.

She came with a peculiar, painful little shudder, a reflexive spasm. She was relieved all the same. He nudged her on to her tummy, raising her pelvis with his hands before he entered, slipping in easily. He started to pant in and out and she knew that it was about to be over. She raised her head for a second, glimpsed the empty street outside through the chink in the curtains. Everything looked so normal.

He gave a loud groan that made her want to cry with relief herself: it had been so long. Tears trickled down her cheeks but she wiped them away. She was just being silly. The weight of his slumped body on hers, the stickiness of his warm skin, the pumping of his slowing heart against her ribcage, these were the things that she'd missed as much as her own moment of release.

At last he rolled on to his back and put his arm around her.

She nestled into his body, aware of the bigness of him, the bulk. She looked up at the ceiling. She thought his eyes were closed.

'You'll have to sneak out before the children wake up,' she whispered. At least it was Sunday tomorrow. Even Michael tended to sleep in on a Sunday.

'Mmm?' He sounded barely awake.

'The children – they mustn't find you here. It wouldn't be fair.'

He turned on to his side, away from her.

'I'll wake you in the morning, before my kids are up,' she repeated.

He grunted. He'd heard.

She snuggled into his back, her nose against his shoulder blade, her arm around him, thinking of Zelda, thinking of the future.

She knew that she wouldn't get much sleep, not with so much to reflect on, not with having to remember to wake him early. But it didn't matter. He was The One. Zelda had foreseen it. Evie couldn't wait to speak to Zelda tomorrow.

Thank God it was over. She'd done it; she'd made love with someone who wasn't Neil. In one night everything had changed. The whole world had tilted, and the landscape ahead looked completely different.

Chapter Twenty

❧

Nic opened one eye, then the other, and closed them again. Her mouth was parched, grainy and bitter. The braces were digging into her gums, too. She had no idea where she'd left the wax that she was supposed to rub on the metal. She wanted to swallow but couldn't.

She remembered the glass of water beside the bed and started to lift her head but it was too heavy.

She flopped back on the pillow.

Last night. She had vague fragments of memory, like frayed scraps of fabric on a dressmaker's floor. She saw people. Lots of people. Ah yes, the party. Alan's face staring and inscrutable. What was he thinking? She must have made a fool of herself – again. But what had she done? She couldn't remember.

The magazines. She remembered those. Young girls, their mouths open, legs apart, being breached front and back by faceless men old enough to be their fathers. She opened her eyes and the half-light poured in. Even her eyeballs felt dry. Lucky the curtains were thick, shielding her from a more brutal assault.

She was here. Alan was beside her. She was still safe.

She propped herself on her elbow. There was a sharp pain on the left side of her forehead that made her teeth jangle. She must have water. There was no moisture in her body. She was an old towel that had gone stiff and hard in the sun. She took a few sips. She needed more, the whole cupful, but a few sips were all she could manage.

She could feel the liquid trickle down her throat into her stomach, which keeled like a ship. What was there to get up for, to look forward to today – any day? Just today would do. She scrabbled around, trying to recall a lunch date, a party, any distraction. It was Sunday. A day of rest. Only long, grey hours stretching ahead.

There was a lump in her throat but it would pass. She just needed to make it through the first part of the morning, then the colours would seep through, drip by drip, as they always did, and spread across the canvas.

Alan was still asleep, lying on his back, one arm tucked behind his head. Nic stared. Who was he? Who was she? She shivered. The big, black memory lapses were happening more often now. There was a giant hole right ahead and she was teetering on the brink.

She rose, grabbed her dressing gown from the chair and padded downstairs to the kitchen. She could hardly see. The pain at the front of her head was growing more intense. Dizzy the dog was barking frantically at her heels, but she'd have to wait. Nic made straight for the kitchen cupboard and groped for the painkillers, poured herself a glass of orange juice from the fridge and gulped the tablet down. It left a sickly-sweet aftertaste at the back of her throat, somewhere near where she thought her tonsils must be.

She looked around, waiting for the tablet to take effect, for the first time registering the empty bottles on every surface, the dirty glasses and plates, last night's detritus. The place was a tip; it would take all morning to clear up.

She put some dog food in Dizzy's earthenware bowl. The stench made her reel. Dizzy almost tipped the bowl out of Nic's hands as she bent down. 'Wait,' she scolded.

She plonked down on the cream sofa against the wall and glanced through the glass doors at the neat, symmetrical patio area outside. It was just as she'd wanted: even, harmonious, balanced.

There must be bottles of half-drunk wine around. She swallowed and licked her lips. It would make her feel better. She had only to look.

Mustn't go there. Must keep the boundaries: never drink before 6 p.m.; always wear make-up. Her boundaries made her feel safe. She was all right, in control.

She closed her eyes again. The Sunday papers dropped

through the letterbox and landed with a thud on the hall floor. There was her journalism, of course. And her book. She still had these, her anchors. It was true that most of the old friends from her magazine days who used to commission her had stopped calling. But the market was bad, advertising was down and everyone was doing more articles in-house. It wasn't her fault.

She rubbed her eyes, making them sting. OK, maybe once or twice she'd called a features editor too often and flapped about the problems she was having, the case histories she couldn't find. And she'd missed a few deadlines. But Annabel from *Mums* magazine still commissioned her so she must be all right. Good old Annabel.

Nic rose mechanically and started to collect the plates and glasses. The clank of china on china made her wince. Lucky there was no food left out. The girls from the catering company must have dealt with the leftovers. Weren't they supposed to clear the dishes up afterwards, too? She vaguely remembered paying for it, but she couldn't be sure.

Leftovers. Her stomach reeled. Her face and underarms felt sweaty. She took off her dressing gown so that she was just in her white cotton nightie. That felt better. Cooler.

It's not as if Alan didn't like to drink, she thought, turning away as she rinsed the old food off the knives and forks before putting them in the dishwasher. He almost always had a glass of wine or a gin and tonic in the evening. He never questioned her spending on alcohol or chastised her for boozing, either.

Well, he'd tick her off at parties sometimes if she was embarrassing him. 'You've had enough, Nic. Stop now please,' he'd whisper in her ear. But at home he didn't seem to notice – or mind. Do what you want but don't get found out.

She thought back to how they'd met. It was at a friend's barbecue. She knew that she was on dazzling form that day: witty, glamorous, extrovert. She'd enjoyed playing with this serious, diffident little man, watching him fall under her spell, reeling him in. He was mesmerised. She tended to have that effect on people when she was in the right mood. And, God knew, she'd needed an ego boost.

She'd been pretty tipsy. Her friend tried to chuck black coffee down her throat. 'You'll be arrested for being drunk and disorderly,' she giggled.

But no one thought her drinking was a problem back then. She was just a good laugh; always up for a party, always the first girl on the dance floor.

She finished filling the dishwasher. Dizzy was scratching on the glass door. Blast. She kept doing that. You could see dirty little paw marks that infuriated Alan. Nic slid the door open and the dog raced outside. She was in no position to take her for a walk right now.

She plodded next door to start on the sitting room. That barbecue. Colm. Bloody hell. Him again. Even now his name made her knees buckle. Her sense of self, the essence of her, seemed to slip through the gaps in the floorboards at the mere thought of him.

He was her first husband, the handsome Irish reporter. The big boozer. She'd tried to match him, glass for glass. But he could drink them all under the table. She was desperately in love. They'd married after just six months and then he'd got a job in Australia. It took her a few weeks to sort her visa and pack up. When he collected her from the airport he told her that he'd met someone else. She could still feel the pain, ice-cold, like whiplash.

There was nothing more to say to each other. She spent one sleepless night in a cheap hotel near the airport and turned round and came right back. She wept for most of the flight. She was in her own little world, her back turned to the other passengers, her cheek pressed against the window. By the time she got off the plane the tears had dried up, leaving just an empty hole waiting to be filled.

She managed to laugh when she recounted the story to friends and family. She was so brave, they said. She was coping so well. Except that inside she wasn't coping at all; she was drowning, gasping for air.

The barbecue was a couple of months later. She'd put on her best summer frock and her most glittering smile and Alan hardly left her side the whole afternoon. Steady, sensible Alan who worked for a big firm of City accountants and was surely heading for a partnership. He'd bought a flat in London's Docklands. He just needed a wife and a kid or two to complete the picture.

He reminded Nic of her father: dependable, kind, slightly dull. She grasped at him with both hands, like a shipwrecked sailor clinging to a raft.

They started going out and, to her surprise, Nic found herself falling in love. It wasn't the blind, hot, all-consuming passion that she'd experienced with Colm, but something calmer, less demanding. Alan was quiet, cool and reserved, but he seemed to thaw a little in her reflected warmth and she was vivacious enough for them both. Everyone said they were the perfect combination.

She was a slip of a thing, a mere seven and a half stone. She couldn't weigh much more than that now; she'd never had much in the way of womanly curves. 'A girlish figure,' people used to say. She shuddered, remembering something.

Don't think about those magazines. You never saw them.

Did she drink much then, after splitting up with Colm, after she met Alan? She frowned. Alcohol had always been part of her life; part of his, too. But she didn't think her intake had been excessive.

They moved to a substantial double-fronted Victorian house in Twickenham and Dominic came along a few years later. She was glad to give up freelancing for a while to be a full-time mum, but it wasn't at all what she'd imagined. Alan was kind to her when he was around, but that wasn't often. Of course she'd known he was a workaholic when she married him, but it hadn't seemed to matter when she was free to do her own thing in the evenings and meet up with friends.

Chained to the house with a baby who seemed to want to feed all day and never sleep, she plunged into post-natal depression. They gave her anti-depressants, which helped, then Daddy died unexpectedly. Without drink she didn't think she'd have made it. Wine was her friend, her medicine. As long as she had wine she didn't mind that Alan wasn't there, that he was always working, that he never seemed to want to touch her these days. She self-medicated every night.

As Dominic grew she met a new circle of friends, mothers who all enjoyed a glass or three come 6 p.m. when they collected their kids from playdates. Nothing wrong with that. The house was always brimming with people, a real Mecca. She liked it that way. Keeping busy, busy, busy, throwing parties, organising children's activities, never leaving herself time to peep into that big, black hole.

She carried a pile of plates into the kitchen and stacked them up beside the dishwasher. The pain in her head had gone now, leaving just a dull ache and a tangle of precise and unspecific worries. Snippets from last night were coming back now. Marie hadn't been there. Marie, her oldest friend. She was the only person Nic had ever confided in. Nic couldn't tell Evie and Becca, her family, anyone. The shame.

Marie liked a drink, too. Nic felt weak. Her head started to swim and she thought she might keel over. She went back to the sitting room and sat down on the olive-green sofa which had been pushed against a wall. She rested her elbow on the arm, her head in her hand. That felt better.

She and Marie had had a great time in Paris on their girls' weekend a year ago. Marie had picked a swanky hotel close to the Louvre. It had taken Nic ages to pluck up courage. They were on pudding by then, and their second bottle of wine.

'You know,' she said, leaning across the white tablecloth, 'I think I might have a drink problem.'

Marie threw back her head and laughed. 'You're not serious?'

Nic felt her face and neck go red. 'I am.'

She could picture Marie now, suddenly sombre, her head on one side, her brow furrowed. 'Do you ever wake up and reach for the whisky bottle?' she asked.

Nic shook her head. 'I never drink before six p.m.'

'Do you have the shakes?'

'No.'

'Well,' said Marie, digging into her sorbet. 'My father had binges that would go on for days. He'd close the bedroom door, draw the curtains and lie there, morning, noon and night, consuming bottle after bottle of whisky. He couldn't function without a whisky first thing. You're not an alcoholic, you silly cow. You're nowhere near it.'

Nic smiled, relieved, and they toasted not being alcoholics with a large brandy each.

Her arm was beginning to hurt from the weight of her head. She lay down on the sofa, drawing her nightie round her. The grey silk scatter cushion felt pleasantly cool against her cheek.

There was her GP, Dr Kelly, of course. Nic had been round there a lot recently, about her periods, her achy shoulder, that mole she was convinced hadn't been there before. About lots of problems, except the one thing she really needed to discuss.

Once, she'd been twice in the same week. She walked in the room and Dr Kelly looked up, surprised. 'Hello again. What can I do for you this time?'

Nic showed her the tiny, speckled mole on her left thigh.

Dr Kelly glanced at it through a magnifying glass. 'Do you drink?' she asked, putting the glass down. Just like that.

Nic's heart missed a beat. 'Yes.'

'How much?'

'Oh, two or three glasses of wine a day.' She couldn't tell the truth.

Dr Kelly looked back at her notes. 'Well, you should stick to no more than two drinks and have a couple of alcohol-free days each week.' She jotted something on a notepad. 'I'll make an appointment with the dermatologist about that mole but I'm ninety-nine per cent sure that it's benign.'

Stop worrying, Nic told herself. If Dr Kelly thought that she had a problem then she'd have said so.

Nic must have dozed off. She woke disorientated. It took a few moments to work out where she was. She sat up; she was supposed to collect Dominic from his friend's at twelve-ish. She checked the clock on the console. It was pretty hideous: gilt, an early-nineteenth-century French carriage clock with a brass dial and Roman numerals. It didn't fit with the contemporary feel of the room but it had been given to her father as a retirement present when he left the Army. It was of great sentimental value.

Nic was relieved to see that it was only 10 a.m. There was still no sound from Alan. She was lonely. She drew the curtains and plumped the cushions on the sofas before heading back into the kitchen to put the kettle on.

'What are you doing?' Alan asked when she plonked a mug of tea beside him.

She'd deliberately made a noise. She wanted him to wake up.

He raised himself on one elbow and looked at her suspiciously.

'I've been clearing up downstairs. There's still quite a bit to do,' she said brightly.

He didn't speak. Worry seeped through her. She wasn't sure why.

'Nic?'

'Yes.' She waited, hovering.

'You were totally pissed last night. You made a complete fool of yourself.'

She couldn't move. She was made of stone. He'd never spoken to her like that before.

'I didn't feel great yesterday,' she prattled. 'I told you I had a dodgy tummy, remember? I hadn't eaten all day. The drink must have gone straight to my head.'

'You were waving your bum in the air,' Alan replied.

'Was I? How awful.' She laughed. 'I hope I had knickers on.'

'Nic?'

'Yes?'

'I can't cope with this any more.'

Had she heard properly? She was lost, flailing. 'What?'

'If you don't cut back on the drink I can't answer for the consequences.'

Her eyes were full of tears. She couldn't see. The ground swooped and swirled. She slumped on the bed.

'I will cut back, I promise,' she said. 'Don't leave me.' Not that. Anything but that.

'Come here,' he said, his voice softer now.

She peeped through the tears. His arms were outstretched, waiting for her. Thank God. It didn't matter what he looked at in his study, it didn't matter how much time he spent in there. She didn't care that they rarely made love or that he was often

154

cool and distant with her – and not just physically; mentally he was a million miles away, too, but it didn't matter. He was her lifebelt. Without him she'd drown.

She buried herself in his bare chest, in the familiar cavity between his ribs. He kissed the top of her head lightly and patted her arm.

'You can do it,' he said, starting to get up. 'You're a clever girl.'

She knew she could. She must. She just wouldn't have the first drink tonight, or tomorrow. It couldn't be that difficult.

'You're going to see some changes, I promise,' she mumbled, the drying tears making her cheeks itch. 'Just you wait and see.'

Chapter Twenty-One

❦

'We dragged mattresses into the loft and made a den and Max's mum let us sleep up there. It was wicked.'

Dominic was twitching with excitement. It made Nic smile. She'd been taken aback when she picked him up; he was white-faced and dishevelled, with dark circles under his eyes. He'd clearly hardly slept and he'd be exhausted and grumpy later. But he'd had a great time, which was all that mattered.

'It's roast beef and Yorkshire pudding for supper,' she told him, steering into the supermarket car park. She shouldn't be driving. She was probably over the limit still. 'I just have to pick up a few things.'

Like, well, everything. She hadn't planned to make a roast. She didn't usually. But today she was going to be the perfect wife and mother. Exemplary. If only her brain weren't filled with sludge. The signals couldn't make it through the pathways properly. Every movement, every thought, required extra effort. All she really wanted was to lay her head on the pillow and sleep.

'That wasn't just a few things, it was a huge shop,' Dominic complained.

'Well, I bought lots of treats.' She piled the bags in the boot.

Her hands trembled as she peeled the potatoes and chopped the broccoli. She must be careful; she could do herself an injury. When it was all prepared, she unloaded the dishwasher: the last of the party mess. She mopped the floor and then started on the kitchen cupboards. She hadn't cleaned them for – who knew how long?

Alan strolled in and started to make himself a cup of tea. There were tins and jars and packets everywhere. He didn't seem to notice. It could be her daily routine.

'Leave it to me,' she said brightly, putting a tea bag in his cup. 'You go and read the papers. I'm having a spring clean.'

Dominic had homework. 'I'll do it later,' he grumbled. He was getting grouchier by the minute.

She pulled out two kitchen chairs. 'Come on, I'll help.'

He looked at her suspiciously. 'You're in a good mood.'

'I'm always in a good mood,' she lied.

She took another headache tablet. Her third of the day. It was still only 4 p.m. She'd work on her book, *The Girl from Niger*, tonight after Dominic went to bed. That would keep her busy, away from the wine.

'Dominic, take Dizzy round the block for me, will you?' she called upstairs. He'd finished his essay about his favourite object in the house at last. He'd chosen the antique French clock on the console in the sitting room. It was her idea because he couldn't think of anything. It had been like pulling teeth but she hadn't snapped at him. Well, only once.

No answer. She called louder.

'I'm busy,' he replied.

The poor dog was desperate, whining; she hadn't been for a walk all day.

'C'mon, Diz,' Nic said, pulling on her grey tweed coat and tying the belt.

She wandered, like a lost soul, round the green while Dizzy raced ahead, stopping every now and then to sniff at something. It was getting dark now, a chilly October evening. The place was almost deserted, which was just as well. Nic didn't want to see anyone she knew; she was in no mood for chatting. She felt a bit vulnerable, though, a lone woman and her little dog. She doubted Dizzy would be much protection. She turned around and started to scurry home, dragging Dizzy beind her.

'Come on,' she urged. 'I'm cold.' As if Dizzy cared.

The beef was slightly overdone and chewy, and Dominic was too tired to eat, really. But he enjoyed the roast potatoes. Alan was quiet for most of the meal. He helped himself to a glass of red wine from the open bottle beside the fridge. Usually Nic would have one beside her already and would sip from the

157

same glass for the rest of the evening. She hoped for a smile, some acknowledgement, but if he noticed that she was drinking only water he didn't say.

He got up and gave his wife a peck on the cheek. 'D'you mind if I leave the clearing up to you and Dominic? I've got work to finish off.'

'Of course not,' she said. Perfect little housewife. Her shoulders drooped.

She and Dominic carried the plates to the dishwasher. Her eye fell on the bottle of red wine by the fridge. There must be a couple of glasses left in there at least but she wouldn't have any. Oh no. Not when she'd lasted this long.

'Go and run your bath,' she told Dominic. 'I want you in bed by eight.'

He started to protest but thought better of it; he was knackered.

'I'll be up in a minute,' she promised.

She tiptoed past Alan's study on the way down. She'd make a cup of tea then settle down to some writing. Who was she kidding? She was drained, good for nothing. She'd make a cup of tea and go to bed.

She tapped on Alan's door. She hadn't meant to. It just sort of happened. There was a pause. Was he rustling something, putting his magazines away? She shivered. She was imagining it.

'Come in.'

He was at his laptop as usual. He smiled, his eyes still on the screen. Reassured, she took a step forward.

He clicked something and swivelled round to face her.

'I thought I'd go to bed and read,' she said.

'Good idea.'

'Alan?'

'Yes.'

'I'm sorry about last night, I really am. Will you come and join me soon?' She wanted a cuddle, to be held, squeezed tight. She could put up with anything if he'd do that. 'You must be tired, too,' she added.

'When I've finished this.' He turned back to the screen.

Couldn't he hear the need in her voice? Was he totally indifferent? He'd loved her once, definitely. Maybe he still loved her. Well, he had a funny way of showing it.

She walked out, closing the door behind her, went into the kitchen and poured herself a large glass from the bottle of red wine. And another. She'd eaten little of the roast and it went straight to her head, giving her a delicious buzz.

She popped upstairs to check that Dominic's light was out. Good. The study door was still closed. Now she could get down to drinking in earnest. She went into the TV room, flicked through the channels and chose an old film of *Pride and Prejudice*. She'd wanted to see it at the cinema but she couldn't concentrate now. She switched to UKTV Gold. *Fawlty Towers* repeats. They seemed to be speaking a foreign language. But the canned laughter was good, like being at a party.

Sod sobriety. If she drank herself into her grave he wouldn't notice.

Those pictures, those young girls. Drink would obliterate them.

She chinked her glass against the screen. 'Cheers.'

i need 2 tell u sumthing.

Freya flinched. This didn't sound good. He wasn't going to say he had another girlfriend, was he?

It was 11 p.m. She had school tomorrow. They'd been talking for hours. Why was he doing this now?

Her fingers hovered on the keyboard. *wot?*

im not who you think i am, she read.

She stared. Took a moment or two to compose herself. *wot do u mean?* She was confused. Nothing made sense.

im older than u think.

Her head reeled. The room was spinning. She closed her eyes for a moment. He was joking, having a laugh. She opened her eyes again.

ha ha.

no, i mean it.

It didn't sound like a joke. She was shaking. *how old?* she typed. She didn't want to know. Eighteen? Twenty-five?

48, let me explain

But there was no time. She gasped, pushed back her chair and ran to the bed, blinded by tears. She threw herself down on the duvet, scrunched the pillow in her fists and sank her teeth into her hand. Cal, her beautiful Cal. Forty-eight? How was she supposed to believe that?

She stopped crying. Maybe this was some kind of test. He wanted to see if she really loved him. Well she'd prove it to him. Her breathing was shallow and jerky. She walked slowly back to the computer and sat down again.

She was frightened, but she needed to sort this out. *bak*, she typed.

u ok?

no.

let me explain

go on.

i have a daughter your age.

Fuck. The walls of her bedroom were swaying, about to cave in on her. She didn't want to look but she couldn't help it. She was drawn to the screen like an insect to the light.

she uses chatrooms a lot. i was worried. i wanted to find out what went on.

She swallowed. She was nothing to him. She was so young, stupid. She didn't know anything. Her fingers were jelly. *r u a pedo?*

course not, gross.

Well that was something. *so ur married?*

divorced. i wanted to help you. i can still help you.

She paused. A moment ago they were boyfriend and girlfriend. A moment ago she loved him. She'd told him everything, all her secrets. He was her only reason for living.

He was an old man, someone's dad.

She wanted to scream, but that would wake her mum and Michael. Trembling, she managed to type: *FUCK OFF I NEVER WANT 2 C U AGAIN.*

Life really was shit.

She couldn't think straight. She groped her way to the bathroom, took the bottle of paracetamol out of the cabinet. There

160

must have been about ten in there. She poured a glass of water and, choking, tipped the pills, three or four at a time, down her throat. If she couldn't have Cal, there was no point.

She stumbled back to her room, lay down on her bed and waited. The ceiling was blurring up. Her eyelids were so heavy; her body was made of earth. How long would it take to die? She thought of the new baby, her stepbrother or sister. She'd never see it. It would never get to know her. Bloody baby. She didn't care. Dad would be sorry. She saw Chantelle smirking. Ha! There'd be an enquiry. It would all come out. Maybe she'd go to prison. Excellent.

Her mother's face formed in front of her, a myriad dots of light coming together like so many millions of pixels. Her eyes were wide, her mouth frozen in an uncomprehending O.

Freya gasped. 'I'm sorry, Mum. I really am. I love you.'

She tried to get up but couldn't. She called out, but her voice was a kitten's mew. Fear seeped through her. Maybe she didn't want to die after all. She'd miss Mum. Michael, too. It was awfully final.

What have I done?

Nic thought she heard a noise upstairs. Alan leaving his study? She turned the volume down and staggered to the bottom of the stairs. 'Is that you?'

'Nic?' he called down. 'I thought you were asleep?'

'In a minute,' she managed to say. 'I'm watching the end of a film.'

'OK. 'Night.'

She finished the bottle beside the sofa and zapped off the TV. Then she tiptoed into the front garden where the bins were and shoved the bottle right to the very bottom, underneath the other rubbish. Well done, Nic. Pat on the back. Alan will never know.

She stopped for a moment at the mirror in the hall and stared. The blurred reflection of an ugly, drunk woman stared back. She opened her mouth, parted her lips in a humourless grin: her teeth, behind the braces, were stained blood red. Is this what she'd become?

She hated herself, intensely, completely. She was a monster. She didn't deserve to live.

She'd think about it in the morning, do something in the morning. All she wanted now was sleep, escape, freedom. Non-being. Nothingness.

Chapter Twenty-Two

The bus was groaning as usual. Freya jostled her way past a group of other kids waiting at the stop. She remembered something and looked behind her quickly as she climbed on. 'Bye!' she called to the funny grey-haired lady, who waved back. She was often waiting there and they chatted sometimes. She wore a weird, fluffy coat and was a bit bonkers but quite sweet. She always seemed very interested in what Freya was up to. She hadn't been in the mood for talking today, though.

'Hey, we were here before you,' a boy said. Freya thought he was in the year above. She ignored him and swiped her Oyster card. The driver looked ready to kill her, to kill them all.

'No more,' he shouted, starting to close the doors after her. 'You'll have to wait for the next one.'

There was no chance of a seat. Freya clutched on to one of the metal poles and stood, swaying, beside a tall, droopy-looking boy. He was two classes above her. He had a gross black moustache. Bum fluff. She caught his eye by mistake and looked at her feet. The moustache made her feel sick.

She felt like crying. She was so weak she could hardly stand up. Not surprising after Sunday. She'd been amazed to wake up on Monday morning. She'd thought she was in heaven or hell or something.

She'd wiggled her fingers and then her toes. Scanned the room. Everything was just the same. She couldn't be dead. Her alarm clock was going off. She wanted to laugh. She was alive! Then she remembered Cal.

She'd got up slowly. She felt so tired. It was hard to keep her eyes open. Getting dressed was difficult, too. She couldn't seem to do up the buttons on her school shirt. She knew she had to act normally; she mustn't let Mum know. She'd be so worried and upset. She had enough problems.

She'd peered at Freya sort of oddly over breakfast. 'Are you all right?' Her voice was sharp and anxious. It made Freya flinch. 'You look exhausted.'

'I'm fine,' Freya said, staring at her Weetabix. It wasn't unusual. She was never exactly chatty at breakfast. She thought she could drop off to sleep at any moment.

She'd managed to drag herself into school and back again. She hadn't been able to concentrate, though. She'd felt so depressed and hopeless. Homework was piling up in her bag but she knew she wouldn't do it. At break she'd sat under a tree on her own. Lucy had come up once, to ask if she was all right. But everyone else ignored her. They usually did that anyway, when they weren't picking on her, that is. They just thought she was weird.

Now it was Wednesday and she was on the stinking bus again. There was this letter from the class tutor in her bag that she was supposed to have given Mum to sign. It said Freya was 'giving cause for concern'. They wanted Mum to call the school to make an appointment.

Freya had forged Mum's signature. She was good at that. She'd put a line on the bottom: 'I'm busy at work but I'll ring soon.' Miss Fischer wasn't exactly the caring, motherly type. She'd probably forget anyway.

Freya had checked her computer in the evenings. Cal, or whoever he was, did message her, but she ignored him.

PLEASE, PLEASE SPEAK 2 ME, he said.

She didn't reply.

I MISS YOU SO MUCH. WE NEED2 TALK.

It wasn't right for a man of forty-eight to speak to a girl like that.

She felt a bit sorry for him, though. He was kind. He couldn't have been acting the whole time. And he'd really helped her, given her awesome advice. But she was sorrier for herself. Talking to him was all she'd had to look forward to. Now there was nothing. Bastard.

The bus jolted to a halt outside the school and loads of kids started to spew out on to the pavement. There was lots of shoving and swearing. An old woman on one of the seats for the elderly and disabled at the front glanced at her neighbour and tut-tutted.

Stupid woman. Freya had no sympathy for her. She only had to suffer for a few minutes; Freya would be stuck with them all day.

She walked through the black iron security gates towards the gaping entrance. The main part of the school was old and smelled of cooking and furniture polish. It was usually quiet here because the headteacher's room was just off the atrium. She had a nasty habit of bounding out of her office when you were least expecting it. She had eyes in the back of her head, that woman.

Once you left the main building and stepped into the annexe at the back, however, it was a different story; it was everyone for themselves. The corridors were heaving with kids, all in their hideous grey trousers or skirts, white shirts, striped ties and maroon jumpers. Freya elbowed her way towards her class-room, shoving and jolting. It was the only way.

'Slow down!' hollered one of the teachers. 'Stop shouting!'

The noise died down for a moment, then started up just as loud as before.

Gemma and Chantelle were lurking outside the classroom, their backs to the wall, avoiding the rush-past. They were whispering, their heads together. Freya's heart sank, as it did each time she saw them.

Chantelle, the furthest away, spotted her and nudged her friend, who turned round. Chantelle was tall and slim, of mixed race, with black Afro hair that reached down to her shoulders. She was buff, Freya had to admit, with big brown eyes, long lashes and full lips. But she was thick and gobby. She hated anyone clever, laughed at them.

Unfortunately, Freya was quite clever, even though she never did any work. She'd also stood up once, in Year 7, for another girl in the playground when Chantelle was being mean to her. Big mistake. Chantelle had never forgotten it.

Then there was Richie. If only Freya had never gone out with

165

Richie. Well, it wasn't even going out, but Chantelle didn't see it that way. She still thought she owned him even though she'd dumped him. He'd been quite upset for some reason. The thing was, you were either with Chantelle or against her, and for a variety of reasons she'd decided that Freya was definitely against her.

Freya hated Chantelle, but she sort of admired her too, in a sick way, because she was pretty and dangerous. But Gemma was a different matter. Gemma was Chantelle's little lapdog, her puppet. Freya loathed her. Gemma was small and chubby, with dyed blond hair, big tits and crooked teeth. She thought Chantelle was the best. She'd do anything for her.

Freya avoided looking either of them in the eye. She was hoping to slip past into the classroom before they had a chance to say anything. Unfortunately, there was a jam in front.

'You weren't at the party on Saturday,' Chantelle said, all innocence.

Freya shrugged. Say as little as possible, give nothing away, don't get their backs up.

'You should've come.'

Freya had to stop or they'd say she was blanking them. 'Why?' As soon as she'd said it, she wished she could take it back.

''Cause Liam was there and you could've given him another blow job.'

Freya felt her face go hot. She mustn't show she cared.

They sniggered.

'Anyone want a blow job?' Chantelle called, signalling to the other kids in the corridor. Several people looked round. 'Freya here'll give you one in the toilets at break.'

Freya's face was burning. She was relieved to see Matthew. He was a misfit, like her. She snuck through the door and found a place beside him in the middle of the class where they'd be least noticeable. She sat with him at lunch, too, on one of the long tables for sad pupils who'd brought their own sandwiches. She remembered how she used to queue up for the cafeteria like the others, but it had got so bad with the pushing and snide remarks that she decided it was safer to bring her own food.

'I got a new PlayStation game at the weekend,' Matthew said, taking the plastic off some sort of wrap thing. He was small and weedy, with glasses and a nerdy hairstyle. And he was obsessed with PlayStation games. It wasn't difficult to see why no one wanted to be his friend.

'Did you?' Freya said. She shouldn't complain. At least she had someone to sit next to.

'Yeah, and I'm going with my dad to Silverstone at the weekend.' Oh God. She'd forgotten. That was another of his obsessions: car racing.

Freya opened her carton of orange juice and took a sip.

'Hi!' a voice said. She looked up. Richie was standing beside her. There was a group of girls behind him, including Gemma and Chantelle. They had smirky little smiles on their faces.

Freya's heart fluttered. 'Hi.'

Richie seemed hesitant. He was fiddling with the bottom of his jumper. He looked skinny today, young and a bit spotty. She wondered what she'd ever seen in him.

'Wanna come out with me again?' he said. His left eye twitched.

She was confused. They'd only had one date; they'd gone to the cinema. He'd snogged her afterwards but it wasn't that nice for either of them. One of those yuck, slobbery ones. She'd told him she didn't want to go out with him again and he hadn't seemed to mind. She thought that was all in the past. Why was he saying this now?

She caught sight of Lucy at the back of the group. She looked worried. Freya twigged. Her pulse started to race. This was a set-up; how was she going to get out of it? Gemma gave Richie a push. He staggered forward, laughing awkwardly. Freya tried to think what to say, how to escape.

'You're really hot,' Richie said, pushing his hips back and forth, licking his lips. 'Phwooarr!'

The other girls cackled.

'My mate said he wanted another go,' Richie went on. 'Maybe you can do his dad while you're about it.'

'Told you she was a slag,' one of the girls piped up. 'Told you she'd screw anything in trousers.'

Freya could hardly see for tears. She glanced at Matthew. He was just sitting there, pretending nothing was happening, tucking into a Mars Bar. He was worse than useless, a complete wuss.

'Why are you saying this?' she said. She stared at Richie through blurred lashes, willing him to take it back. 'You know it's not true.'

He put his hands in his pockets. He wouldn't look at her.

'Tell them we only went on one date,' she pleaded. 'We never shagged, you know we didn't.'

He shrugged.

Freya glanced around. It seemed as if the whole canteen were watching her. Even the staff seemed to have stopped serving and clearing tables and were gawping, judging her.

There was a beam of light, pulsing down on the top of her head, illuminating her thoughts, showing the whole world what a silly, frightened little girl she really was.

She pushed back the bench seat she was sitting on and got up, stuck out her elbows, held her arms in front of her face and fled, sobbing, from the canteen.

u there?

Freya plonked down at her desk. She was still in her uniform; she hadn't even taken her tie off. She could hear Mum clattering in the kitchen, making an early supper. She was going out later.

Freya didn't normally message Cal so early but this was an emergency. She had to talk to him. She crossed her fingers under the table. Answer me, answer me, or I don't know what will happen.

No one there. He was probably doing his homework or watching telly or something. She checked herself. Don't be stupid. Forty-eight-year-old men don't do homework.

It crossed her mind that she knew nothing about him. The image she'd had of him, the image that he'd created, was shot to pieces. What did he do, where did he live, what did he look like? She didn't even know what he was called.

The minutes ticked by. She felt jumpy, unable to concentrate.

Maybe she'd put him off. Maybe he wouldn't speak to her again. She brushed the thought away; it was too much to bear.

Her head was thumping. She hadn't eaten since breakfast. But how could she think about food now? She rose and fetched her iPod from the bedside table, pulled off her black tights, kicked off her shoes, put her earphones in and lay down on her bed. She chose 'Nine in the Afternoon', by Panic! At the Disco. Come on Cal, or whatever your name is. Speak to me.

Something like a feather brushed against her bare feet. She started and opened her eyes. Michael was standing at the end of the bed tickling her with his fingertips. He was mouthing something.

'What?' she said. It dawned on her that she had her earphones in. She took them out.

'Supper's ready!' he repeated. 'Mum's been screaming for ages.'

'I couldn't hear.' She got up slowly, checking her computer on the way out. Still nothing. Her insides felt hollow. Her bottom lip quivered.

She'd just have to try again later.

'How was school?' Mum asked.

Freya took a mouthful of fish pie. She wasn't keen on fish. Mum was always trying to shovel it down them. She thought she could disguise it by covering it in sauce but it didn't fool anybody.

She shrugged. 'OK.'

Mum helped herself to a green bean; she wasn't eating with them. 'Much homework?'

'Some.'

'What subjects?'

'Can't remember.'

Mum sighed. 'I wish you'd be a bit more giving. I'm not trying to interrogate you, I'm just interested, that's all.'

'Sorry. I don't like talking about school. I've been there all day. I'd rather think about something else.' Freya glanced at her mother. Mum looked different, somehow. Her hair was clean and shiny and she didn't seem to have so many lines. Sparkly, that was the word. Come to think of it, she'd been in a very good mood for the past couple of days.

'What have you been doing today?' Freya asked, curious.

Mum took a sip of water and smiled. 'Oh, working on my wedding dress – and I managed to write another chapter of my novel.'

'Well done.'

'What's it about?' Michael asked.

Irritating boy. 'Mum's told you so many times,' said Freya.

Mum ignored her. 'It's set in Roman times and it's about a rich woman who's married to a brute of a husband called Marcellus. She falls in love with a handsome gladiator-turned-bodyguard, Spiculus, but she can't marry him because he's too low class and she thinks he only wants her for her fortune. But it's all going to work out all right in the end.' She grinned, revealing the funny gap between her front teeth.

'Will you get lots of money for it?' said Michael, pushing bits of fish round the plate.

'God, you're so mercenary,' Freya said.

He scowled. 'Shut up.'

'I doubt it,' Mum replied.

'What's the point of doing it then?'

Mum pretended she hadn't heard. 'Eat that fish, please.'

He made a face. 'I hate fish.'

'I beg your pardon?' She glared at him.

'Nothing.'

Freya put her knife and fork together. 'I forgot to ask. How was your party on Saturday?'

'Lovely.'

Freya was surprised. Mum didn't normally like parties these days. 'Wicked,' she said. 'Why was it lovely?'

Mum pushed back her seat and stared at her lap, fiddling with her fingernails. 'Ooh, you know. Lots of nice people.'

Freya looked at Mum carefully. 'Anyone in particular?'

'No.' Mum tucked her fair hair behind her ears. She was blatantly hiding something.

'Mum?'

She got up. 'Who'd like pineapple for pudding?'

Freya and Michael shook their heads.

'Who are you going out with tonight?' Freya persisted.

'Just a friend,' said Mum, stacking up the plates.

Freya didn't press any further. To be honest, she wasn't sure she wanted to know. It was bad enough that Dad had a girlfriend. The idea of Mum having a boyfriend really was bad. It made her tummy feel funny, sort of knotted.

She carried her glass to the sink. 'Mind if I go up and finish my history?'

It was mean of her not to help; Mum was never going to stop her doing her homework.

'Of course not,' Mum said brightly. 'I'll bring you some hot chocolate later.'

Wow. She really was in a good mood today.

That was disturbing.

hi.

Freya's heart missed a beat. *hi.*

want 2 talk?

Freya swallowed. *yes.*

ask me anything u want.

why did u lie 2 me? she typed.

im sorry. like i said, at first i wanted to find out about chatrooms cos of my daughter. i was worried about her. then we got chatting and the more i got 2 know you the more i liked you and wanted 2 help.

That sounded OK. He'd certainly helped.

why didn't you tell me sooner who u really r?

cos i was scared of losing u.

She paused. *wot u did was wrong.*

i know.

r u really called cal?

no.

Whats ur real name?

Al.

Al? She rolled it round her tongue a few times, to test it out. She liked it. *how many kids u got?*

1.

u still love me?

yes.

u got a bald patch?

She was giggling now. She wondered if he guessed.

no. dark hair. im ok looking. That's wot people tell me anyway.

wot people? She didn't like that. It made her jealous. *u seeing other girls?*

no. its only u i want.

She sniffed back a tear. She needed to hear that.

im really down.

tell me about it.

She described everything that had happened: the blow-job taunts, the Richie incident in the canteen. *im really depressed. i dont know wot 2 do.*

do u know their mobile nos?

yes.

give them 2 me and ill sort it.

how?

i mean it. dont worry, you wont get into trouble. ill make sure they never bully u again.

She checked her mobile for the numbers and typed them out. Was she doing the right thing? She didn't know. She hoped so. It couldn't make things any worse, anyway.

Mum knocked on the door and came in with a mug of hot chocolate. 'How's the history?' she asked.

Freya grinned. 'All done!'

'You look happy,' Mum said, putting the mug down. 'You must have done a fab piece of work.' She winked.

'You look happy too,' Freya replied.

Mum had changed. She was wearing her best skinny dark-blue jeans and her favourite pink V-neck cashmere sweater. It was a bit tight and busty, but she looked pretty and surprisingly young.

'I have to leave in half an hour,' Mum said. 'I'll make sure Michael's finished his homework. He should be in bed by nine. You sure you're OK?'

'Course. Have a nice time.'

Suddenly, Freya didn't mind so much if there was a boyfriend. It'd do Mum good. She deserved to have some fun.

'Don't be late,' Mum said. 'You've been looking tired recently. You don't get enough sleep.'

'Stop fussing,' said Freya. She was desperate to get back to Cal, or Al.

'I'm only thinking of you,' Mum added, kissing the top of Freya's head. 'You're very precious, you know.'

Chapter Twenty-Three

❧

Her mobile rang just as Evie was leaving the house. She put her bag down and scrabbled around in it. The front door was half open. Everyone could see in. She shoved it closed with her foot. Damn. It was a ridiculous bag – far too big. She could never find anything in it.

At last she spotted the phone winking at her beneath her cheque book, keys and make-up bag. She pulled it out and it stopped ringing. Damn again. She checked missed calls. It was Becca. Probably going to wish her good luck tonight. Evie couldn't resist a quick chat. She pushed the call button.

'Hey!' she said, crooking the phone in her ear and standing up.

'Can I talk to you for a moment?' Becca sounded worried.

Evie was confused. She'd expected a joke about Steve. Something crude, probably. Becca always made out that she was rather superior but she could be downright disgusting at times, just like her and Nic. She shouldn't have answered. She was late already.

'Of course,' she said, returning to the kitchen. She hoped Michael wouldn't hear or he'd be in with some question or other, some task for her to do before she left.

She pulled out a kitchen chair. 'Listen, I haven't got long. I'm meeting Steve.'

'I forgot,' Becca said. 'We can leave it till tomorrow.'

She sounded disappointed. This wasn't an option.

'No, go on,' Evie said, sitting down. 'I've got a few minutes.'

'I was coming home from work last week – a week ago last Monday,' said Becca.

Evie listened carefully.

'It was quite late and I spotted Alan – Nic's Alan – walking out of Waterloo Station.' She paused. 'He had a girl with him. Evie, she was a prostitute,' Becca blurted.

'What?' said Evie. This was nonsense. 'How do you know?'

'You should have seen her,' Becca went on. 'She had to be. She was wearing a tarty mini-skirt, high heels, peroxide hair and she was plastered in make-up. She looked very young.'

'Maybe it was his friend's daughter or something,' Evie said. 'There could be a perfectly innocent explanation.'

'I've thought about that, of course,' Becca agreed. 'But then at the party, Nic told me Alan was abroad on business on that Monday, when I saw him. So what was he doing coming out of Waterloo Station anyway?'

Evie took a deep breath, processing the information.

'I can't stop thinking about it,' said Becca. 'I was going to keep it to myself. But then I thought, maybe Nic should know. Maybe as her friend I owe it to her to tell her. What do you think? Ought I to or not?'

Evie got up and walked around the kitchen. She was conscious of the time but this was important. 'I don't think you should tell her,' she said finally.

'Why not?'

'It might ruin your friendship.'

'But—'

'Maybe Nic knows already,' Evie interrupted. 'I mean, no one can tell what really goes on inside a marriage, can they? Maybe Nic doesn't mind, turns a blind eye or whatever.'

'You don't believe that, do you?'

Evie put the phone in the other hand, swapped ears. 'And if she doesn't know,' she went on, 'maybe it's better that way. Ignorance is bliss and all that.'

'But—'

'What a bastard,' Evie said.

'I know.'

'I always thought he was a bit of a dark horse,' she continued. 'I never imagined this, though.'

'Honestly, the girl was so young,' Becca said. 'You should have seen her.'

'How revolting,' Evie said. She shivered. 'Listen, I can't talk to you any more now. I'm late. I'll call you tomorrow, OK?'

'Yes.'

'You know what?' Evie added. 'I love Nic, I'd do anything for her. But as far as I'm concerned, what her husband does in his spare time is none of our business.'

Becca pushed open the wooden door of the salon and walked inside.

'Hello, Mrs Goodall.' The receptionist, a pretty girl of about nineteen, smiled blandly. Becca came most weeks for some treatment or other; she must be one of their best clients.

'Ralph's with someone at the moment,' the girl explained. 'He won't be long. Can I get you a drink?'

'Lemon and ginger tea please.'

Becca handed her coat to the girl and strolled into the waiting area. It was dark and womblike, lit only by white candles in glasses, one in each corner. There was a heady smell of aromatherapy oils – rosemary mixed with various other essences that Becca couldn't identify. Soft music was playing in the background. She breathed in deeply, feeling her forehead and throat relax, her shoulders droop. God, she needed this. She couldn't loosen up on her own; she was programmed not to unwind.

The walls were painted a soft beige colour and there was a black leather sofa on the right. She plonked herself down. There was a pile of glossy magazines on the floor beside her but she didn't even bother to pick one up. She closed her eyes, enjoying having clear, black space in her head for the first time all day.

The receptionist came in with the tea. Irritated, Becca's eyes flickered open.

'Shall I put it here?' said the girl, placing a sleek white mug on the low wooden coffee table in front of Becca.

She nodded and closed her eyes again, allowing the hot, spicy aroma of lemon and ginger to seep into her nostrils and permeate her pores. She could easily fall asleep.

'Mrs Goodall?'

She glanced up. Ralph was at the door in his usual white coat, dark trousers and soft shoes. She followed him into the treatment room, half wishing that she could go just for the massage and skip the acupuncture bit. She'd been having it for months. She wasn't convinced that it had much effect, but maybe she did feel a little less anxious.

They sat on either side of the slatted wooden table in the corner while Ralph asked her about her week and how she felt.

'My neck's incredibly stiff,' she said, rolling her head from side to side, which made her wince. 'I'm pretty stressed at work.'

He went outside while she removed everything but her bra and pants. She climbed on to the couch in the middle of the room and pulled the white towel over her. It was soft and fluffy and smelled of fabric conditioner. When he re-entered she could hear him opening several tiny packets, each with one sterilised needle in. She didn't watch.

'I'm going to start with the neck,' he said, taking her right arm and pushing a needle into the side of her hand, below the little finger.

She flinched. It always hurt more than she remembered. She lay completely still while he did the same on the other side. The pain shot up to her shoulder blade and then deadened.

'Now I'm going to give you something that will boost your energy and make you feel less tired and stressed.'

This time he put needles on the fronts of her legs, just below each knee.

She cried out. She couldn't help it. 'That really hurts.'

'Good,' he said, which was annoying. 'It means they're in the right place.'

By the time he'd finished, Becca had six needles in her body. She kept her eyes shut tight. If she looked she might panic and pull the needles out.

'I'll come back in twenty minutes,' he said.

She breathed in and out deeply and tried to think pleasant thoughts but the conversation with Evie kept replaying itself in her brain. She tried to flick an imaginary off button but it didn't work. She was troubled. The problem was, she wasn't sure if Evie was right. What if Tom visited prostitutes? Becca would definitely want to know. And she'd definitely chuck him out. No question.

Supposing she told Nic and she did the same – chucked Alan out? Becca would have destroyed their marriage. She couldn't take on that responsibility, not on her own. There was always the possibility, of course, that rather than thanking her, Nic might hate Becca for it. There again, she might hate her for not telling her. Becca hoped Alan used condoms. God, imagine if Nic caught something. Becca would never forgive herself.

The awful thing was, if Nic somehow found out Becca would have to act all innocent, pretend that she knew nothing, that it was a complete shock. She was in a lose-lose situation. She wasn't used to dealing with those. If only she hadn't spotted Alan with that girl at all.

The needles weren't hurting any more but it was a relief when Ralph returned to take them out. Now for the enjoyable bit: the full body massage. Becca slipped off her bra and flipped over on to her tummy. She wriggled with pleasure as Tara started to knead into her neck, her back, her shoulders, her magic hands slippery with oil.

Tara was only little, small and slight, but she was so strong. She sought out the knots and pressed into them, working and moulding with her fingertips until Becca imagined the muscles were smoothed out, the ligaments soft and stretchy. It hurt, but it was pleasurable, too.

The scent of chamomile, lavender and sandalwood made her feel almost drunk. She allowed her body to sink into the couch; it was heavy enough to fall through the floor. She wondered vaguely what James and Alice were doing. Probably in bed by now. They wouldn't wait up; she'd told them she'd be late. Tom? He'd be in the pub somewhere with the other hacks. It was a mystery how they ever got any work done; it seemed to her that they were permanently half cut. Gary? Her muscles tensed. Tara sensed the change and applied more pressure.

What about Gary? Becca tried to picture him at home with his wife. Maybe they were having supper? But he was only real to her in the way that she'd seen him: sitting opposite her in the pub, listening carefully, looking at her intently. She couldn't imagine him existing in any other sphere.

They'd had no contact since the morning after they'd met,

nine days ago now. There was an email, quite short, waiting for her when she arrived in the office. He said he'd very much enjoyed seeing her again and was glad that she looked so well. He reminded her that he'd like to read her book, what she'd written of it, anyway. He called it her 'oeuvre', which made her laugh. She'd thought about it for a moment, then emailed back saying that she'd enjoyed seeing him, too. She decided not to send the book, though. It had seemed like a good idea when he'd first offered, but she'd had second thoughts. She didn't want him to get too close.

Since then she'd heard nothing. It was a relief, really. True, she'd checked her emails constantly, half hoping, half dreading to read his name. On balance, though, she decided no contact was good. What had she been thinking of, allowing herself to get all worked up like that? Now she was calm again, more normal. Better just to forget the whole thing.

'There you go,' Tara said, gently lifting her hands from Becca's back.

She sighed, disappointed that it was over.

'I'll leave you to get dressed,' Tara went on. 'Take as long as you like.'

Becca lay there for a few minutes, unable to move. She felt deeply relaxed. She hated the thought of having to go back on the train. It would ruin everything. Maybe she'd grab a taxi.

Her BlackBerry pinged in her bag. She got up slowly, but she had a head-rush all the same. She waited, immobile, until the dizziness passed before putting her clothes on. She could hear the receptionist and Tara talking quietly outside. They were waiting for Becca to pay. She opened her bag, took out her BlackBerry and listened to the message.

'Hi, Becca, it's Gary.'

Her heart pitter-pattered.

'I wondered if you'd like to go for dinner sometime?'

Dinner? Her mouth felt dry.

'Call me back when you have a moment.'

But how had he got her number? She didn't remember giving it to him.

'Hope to hear from you soon.'

She stood still for a moment before putting the BlackBerry back in her bag. She realised that she wanted to see him again very much. She also wanted him to tell her everything: about the kids at the primary school they'd gone to, what had happened to them; about the neighbours; the man in the sweet shop who called her 'pet' and 'hinny'; that daft milkman who couldn't whistle in tune; his mam, his sisters. Her mam. Every last scrap of knowledge that he possessed.

She wasn't sure which she wanted more: to look in his brown eyes or to hear him talk about home. She just knew that the two were inextricably linked.

She waited until she'd paid and left the shop before returning his call.

Chapter Twenty-Four

There were crowds of people outside Sloane Square tube station and Evie had difficulty finding an empty spot. She stood under-cover, in as prominent a position as possible, and looked out for Steve.

She wasn't sure which direction he'd be coming from; he hadn't told her. She shivered and clutched her coat around her. The weather was miserable: cold and damp. She was regretting wearing her pointy boots again. Would she never learn? At least she'd remembered the black lacy Agent Provocateur underwear this time. She hoped that Steve had chosen somewhere nearby to eat as she wouldn't be able to walk far.

She watched the crowds scurrying by and tried to imagine who everyone was, where they lived, what sort of jobs they had. A lot of men and women were in suits and clutching brief-cases, obviously on their way home from work. But there were also a fair number of couples, all dressed up on a night out.

The women wore lipstick, had carefully blow-dried hair and left a trail of expensive perfume behind them. Their men had clean, newly shaven faces, smart-casual coats and the sort of soft leather loafers worn by City types or foreigners with plenty of money.

She felt a tingle of pleasure. She was on a night out, too. Could they tell? She checked her watch: 8.45 p.m. He was only fifteen minutes late. Problems with the buses, no doubt. She hoped that Michael would be getting ready for bed now. Should she phone? She decided not.

She thought of Becca and the strange phone call that they'd had earlier about Alan. She was sure that she'd given the right advice. Best not to interfere. She glanced across the road at Peter Jones. It was closed, of course, as were all the shops. But with the bars lit up and lights on all around the square, everything looked deliciously enticing.

She tried to picture Steve's face, his eyes, his lips. For some reason the details were vague. But she could remember his touch, the heat of him, his naked body against hers. She felt a rush of warmth around her neck, her face, between her legs. She shuffled uneasily from one foot to another. Please hurry up. The anticipation was killing her. She was going to explode.

She glanced left, towards the Royal Court Theatre, and saw a man who looked like him: tall and thin, with longish dark hair, a dark green jacket a bit like the one that he'd worn on Saturday night. But when he came closer she realised that he was nothing like Steve at all; this man had mean eyes and a slot for a mouth. She glanced away quickly.

He might have changed his mind and decided that he didn't fancy her. She recalled that kiss in the cab, the scorching intensity of it. Of course he fancied her.

She'd had to hustle him out so quickly on Sunday morning that they'd hardly spoken. 'You have to go now,' she'd whispered in his ear, shaking him gently in bed beside her. 'The children mustn't see you.' Reluctantly he'd got up, pulled on his clothes and she'd bundled him, bleary-eyed, downstairs. She'd checked Freya's and Michael's bedroom doors anxiously as they passed.

When they got to the hall, she'd gone on tiptoe, pulled his face towards hers and kissed him tenderly on the lips.

'Call me,' she said, thrusting his jacket in his arms. 'Thanks for last night.'

'I will,' he mumbled back.

She laughed, remembering his sleep-soaked eyes. If she'd let him, he'd probably have stayed in bed all morning.

He'd made her wait all day. She had his number too, of course, but she wanted him to make the first move. She'd tried to sound nonchalant in front of the children when she answered the phone. They were all watching TV in the sitting room.

'I'll go next door,' she told him, in a too-polite voice.

The kids were absorbed in the film. They didn't suspect a thing. She practically ran into the kitchen and closed the door.

'Hey,' he said. She'd forgotten already how deep and sexy his voice was. 'How are you?'

'Fine,' she said shyly.

'I miss you,' he said.

Her whole body was filled with air.

'Can I see you tonight?' he went on.

She was a balloon, practically floating! But the balloon popped. 'I can't – see you tonight,' she stuttered, remembering. 'The children . . .'

'Oh.' He sounded disappointed.

'I can't leave them for two nights in a row, it's not fair.'

'No problem,' he said. 'I can't do tomorrow or Tuesday. What about Wednesday?'

They'd settled on Sloane Square because he said he could get the bus there from Clapham, where he lived. It wasn't as easy for her, but she said she was keen to get right away from home.

She checked her watch again: 9 p.m. Her chest tightened. She'd better ring him and see where he was. She found her mobile and called his number. His phone was switched off. She must have got the wrong number. She tried again. Same thing.

He'd probably got some last-minute celebrity interview or other and it was going on longer than expected. He'd appear any moment, smiling, full of apologies. 'I'm so sorry . . .' She breathed deeply and pushed the backs of her knees out. It was a trick her father had taught her to do before exams; it was surprisingly calming. She was such a worrier. It was ridiculous. She wished she could sit down, though. Her feet were hurting.

'Bit nippy.'

She turned around. An elderly man in a tweed cap and grey anorak was standing beside her, rubbing his hands.

'I'm meetin' me daughter here,' he said, in a London accent. 'I'm supposed to be takin' her out for a meal. Know anywhere nice?'

She shook her head. She didn't feel like talking. A moment later a plump, middle-aged woman in a pink and grey plaid coat appeared and kissed the old man on the cheek.

'Bye,' he said. 'Enjoy yer evenin'.'

The woman took his arm and shot Evie a curious look over her shoulder. She stamped her feet a few times to keep warm. Her stomach rumbled; she was so hungry. She fancied fish tonight. And lots of vegetables. She was in a vegetables mood. It was after nine now. He was nearly three-quarters of an hour late. He hadn't phoned. People passing by seemed to be looking at her strangely. Were they thinking she'd been stood up?

Stood up. It had never happened to her, not even when she was a teenager dating silly, unreliable boys. She'd been dumped a couple of times, but they'd always bothered to tell her.

He'd been so keen, desperate to see her. He'd made love to her so tenderly. Her fingers and toes were numb with cold. She tried his number one more time. Still switched off. She swayed slightly and reached for the wall behind to steady herself. She couldn't believe it, but what other explanation was there? If he'd had a problem he'd have phoned or texted.

She pulled her shoulders down and straightened up. There was a lump in her throat, like a boiled sweet that's got stuck. She tried to swallow. It hurt so much. She dug her nails into the palms of her hands. She wouldn't cry, not yet.

She turned on her heels and walked back into the tube, down the steps and on to the dimly lit platform. There were crowds of people waiting. A woman standing beside her laughed. Evie turned her back. She was still doubtful. It made no sense. It was so cruel.

The train stopped and disgorged chattering passengers on to the platform. Evie elbowed her way into the carriage and sat down on the nearest seat. Zelda. She must speak to her. Zelda would know what to do. Evie stared past the heads through the windows at the blackness outside. The pain in her chest was intensifying. She could hardly breathe. She wanted Neil so badly. Her husband. The father of her children.

It was as if he'd cut out her heart himself and flung it, bloody and trembling, on to the railway line ahead.

She spotted Bill halfway down the road, under the street-light. He was hunched over his gate; he seemed to be fiddling with something. She prayed he'd go inside. She couldn't speak to him. The minute she opened her mouth the tears would gush out.

He heard her footsteps and looked up. 'Evie!' He smiled and the creases around his eyes deepened. 'I was trying to fix this latch,' he explained, pointing at the gate. 'There's something wrong with it.'

Stupid latch. As if it mattered.

She waved a hand at him as if to say, 'Not now.'

He took a step closer and examined her face under the lamplight. 'What's the matter?'

She shook her head. She was trying so hard to hold the tears back. Why was he giving her that intense look of his? Couldn't he see that she needed to be left alone?

He opened his arms and she stumbled into them. He didn't even move. He was a rock. He was in his old, falling-apart Barbour jacket, the one he usually wore to the allotment. It smelled of earth and woodsmoke.

She clamped her mouth shut and pressed it against the material to stop herself howling. He was very still, his arms wrapped around her, his body absorbing her shudders. Her hands sought out the gap between his jacket and his jumper and her own arms snaked around his middle. He felt strong, lean and sturdy, like a tree. She could have stayed there like that for ever.

After a few moments she realised what she was doing and pulled away. 'I'm sorry,' she said, wiping her tears with the sleeve of her coat. 'You must think I'm such an idiot.'

She was conscious of the empty space between them.

'I was supposed to be meeting this man in Sloane Square,' she rattled on. She felt that she owed Bill an explanation. 'I'd only known him since Saturday but I really liked him and I thought he really liked me. He stood me up.'

She didn't look at Bill; she was embarrassed. But she was aware that he was listening carefully. She carried on wiping her eyes with her sleeve.

'I can't believe he didn't even phone,' she choked. 'It's brutal. I feel so humiliated. I feel like no one will ever want me.' She started to cry again.

Bill seemed to want to say something. Maybe she'd made him

uncomfortable, told him too much. 'Cup of tea – or something stronger?' he said at last. His voice was measured and low.

She was torn; she'd like to very much, but she needed to speak to Zelda.

She shook her head. 'I have to call someone,' she said. 'This psychic person. She's brilliant, you should try her.' She managed a little laugh. It was bizarre to think of Bill talking to a clairvoyant. She couldn't imagine it.

He frowned. 'I don't like them. I think they're dangerous. Most of them are frauds. They take your money, spout a load of nonsense and put ideas in your head. I should stay away if I were you. It's the last thing you need.'

She put a hand on his shoulder. 'You're such a cynic.'

'I'm not.' He sounded cross. 'Quite the opposite. I just don't want you getting hurt.'

'I'll be all right.' She paused. 'Anyway, where have you been?' She was keen to change the subject. He must have been coming back from somewhere. He wouldn't be fixing the gate at this time otherwise.

'Working.'

'Working?' she said, surprised. 'What sort of work?'

'Private tutorial.' He put his hands in his pockets. 'I do a bit of coaching now and again. Sometimes I go there, sometimes they come here. I quite enjoy it.'

'I didn't know.' She crossed her arms. 'How many students do you have?'

He ignored her question. 'If I were you I'd give that man a wide berth. If he calls and tries to make up to you, I'd tell him where to go.'

'I will,' she said.

'Will you be all right?'

She nodded.

'Sure you don't want to talk?'

'I'm sure.'

He pushed open his wonky gate and walked slowly up the garden path. She heard him sigh. She wondered why, but she had other things on her mind.

Chapter Twenty-Five

'Shall I put it on yer usual card, darlin'?'

'Yes,' said Evie.

Zelda stubbed her cigarette out in the ashtray beside her and settled back in the armchair. Her back twinged. It wasn't so good these days. She shuffled around until she was comfortable. She was getting old. 'Now then,' she said. 'What can I do for you?'

Evie was crying a lot, making choking noises. It was difficult to make out what she was saying.

Zelda had to strain. She caught the words 'party', 'tall and handsome', 'stood up' and 'tube station'. She got the gist of it. Some bloke had stood her up. Zelda didn't have much sympathy. Blokes always let you down one way or another. Derek had gone behind her back and let her down big time, that's for sure. Then when the shit hit the fan he was nowhere to be found. He'd slunk off, the little creep, got some job in Kent. How convenient!

'Dear, dear,' she soothed. 'You've had a rotten day. Shall I give you a readin'?'

'Yes, please,' Evie replied.

Zelda took a deep breath and tried to focus. 'Now close yer eyes,' she said, 'while I make a connection.'

She paused. 'Good, that's good. I've got one of me favourite spirits.' She shuffled in her seat. 'Some of 'em are a bit naughty, see, they like to make mischief. But this one here, he's all right. He's a good boy.'

She felt a little puff of air behind her, like someone's breath. The hair on the back of her neck prickled.

'Now,' she said, 'this man, who stood you up. Was he tall, like I said?'

'Yes.'

'Is he called Peter – or Richard?'

'No.'

'George? Or Walter maybe?'

'No, Steve.'

'Steve?' Zelda was surprised. 'I'm not being funny darlin',' she said, 'but I don't think he's the one you're waitin' for.'

'Oh.' She could hear the disappointment in Evie's voice. She started to cry again.

This wasn't going well. Zelda would have to do something. She couldn't afford to lose Evie. She bent forward and lit another cigarette. 'Wait a tick,' she said, taking a puff, listening to the babble in her head, trying to separate one voice from another. 'I think I got it wrong.' She could sense a new energy surging along the pathway between them. 'Steve, this man of yours, he's been havin' a lot of problems recently. A lot of things to sort out?'

'Yes, he's divorced,' Evie said. Her voice was very small. 'And his wife won't let him see his baby son Jacob.'

Zelda sighed. 'That's it. He's got family trouble, that's what it is. Don't worry, darlin'. It'll all come right.'

'Thank God,' Evie sighed. She'd stopped crying. 'I knew he was The One. That's why I couldn't understand it, you see. It was just such a weird thing to do.' She paused. 'I don't know how I'd cope without you.'

Zelda glanced outside. It was very dark. She'd forgotten to close the curtains. She shivered. She could do with turning on another ring on the fire but it was too much trouble to get up again.

'What about this other thing? This bad thing?' Evie said. She sounded nervous.

Silly girl. What was she doing bringing that up now? Some people were gluttons for punishment.

'Can you tell me anything more about it?' she persisted.

Zelda put her half-finished cigarette in the ashtray. The smoke wafted up, making her eyes sting. She closed them again. 'Are you sure you want me to do this, darlin'?' she said. 'Maybe we should wait for another time?'

'No,' Evie replied. 'I need to know if I can . . .'

A siren wailed in the distance. Zelda thought she could sense a shadow pass by her window. Cold spread from her feet up her body, right the way to the top of her head. The room was full up now. It was crammed. She could hardly breathe.

'It's someone close to you,' she gasped. Where was her inhaler? Little flutters, like fairy wings, ran up and down her arms.

'Is it one of the children?' she heard Evie ask. 'I must know.'

'I don't know, I don't think so,' Zelda said. The flutters had turned into pinpricks. They hurt. She was batting them off with her free hand, but they buzzed right back, like bluebottles. Why wouldn't Evie just go away, leave her alone?

'I have to go,' Zelda said, pushing herself up from her chair. Her cigarette had burned right down. There was just a smouldering stub left. They asked so much of her, the lot of them. Too much. Didn't they realise she was getting on? It was unreasonable.

'Be careful,' she muttered, 'that's all I can say.' She'd fetch her inhaler from the bedroom. Then she'd make a nice cup of tea.

'But what am I supposed to be careful of?' Evie wailed.

Zelda shook her head. You had to be firm with them sometimes. 'I'm sorry darlin',' she said, 'you've had your time for tonight. You can't expect no more from me now.'

Evie snapped her eyes open. There it was, that rattling noise that she'd heard in her dreams. It seemed to be coming from outside. There was an empty house opposite. Intruders? She felt for her phone on the bedside table.

Another rattle. It sounded quite close. She sat up, pulling the duvet round her. She didn't want to but she knew that she'd have to look. She opened the curtain behind her just a chink and peered out.

There was a clatter which made her jump. She glanced down and a spray of what looked like pebbles landed on the brickwork some way below her window and scattered on the ground. She switched on the light and made a wider gap in the curtain.

A tall, shadowy figure stepped away from the house and walked down the path towards the gate.

She narrowed her eyes and pressed her nose against the window pane. The figure turned and waved. There was just enough light from the streetlamps outside for her to be able to make out his face. She pulled open the sash window and leaned out.

'What the hell do you think you're doing?'

Christ. She hoped the children wouldn't wake.

Steve moved closer, so that he was standing underneath, looking up. 'I'm sorry about earlier. Will you open the door?'

She paused. He'd hurt her so much. She could still feel it, like a knife in her side. Zelda's words rang in her ears: 'It'll all come right.' She breathed in deeply and smiled. Actually, it was quite romantic, looking down at him like this. She felt like Juliet on her balcony. She stifled a giggle. He'd better have a bloody good explanation, though.

'I waited in the cold for nearly an hour,' she hissed.

'I can explain.'

He looked cute, gazing up at her like that in the gloom. Sort of imploring.

'Nice view,' he said. 'But you could get done for indecent exposure. Just let me in, will you?'

What the hell was he talking about? The penny dropped. She was stark naked, flashing her boobs at the whole street. Something made her glance left, towards Bill's house. She knew he slept in the front room like her. Appalled, she bobbed back away from the window.

Bloody hell. No wonder Steve had that half-grin on his face the whole time. She'd thought it was nerves. She stuck her head out between the curtains, making sure the rest of her was hidden behind the fabric.

'Wait there,' she said.

Was she doing the right thing? Of course she was. He was her destiny. The spirits had told Zelda. She grabbed her dressing gown and ran, two steps at a time, downstairs to meet him.

Chapter Twenty-Six

He shuddered. 'Christ, that was good.'

Evie could feel the cold, hard wood digging into her coccyx. She wriggled slightly to make herself more comfortable. She half wanted him to move, but at the same time she couldn't bear the moment to end.

She wasn't quite sure how it had happened. One minute, it seemed, he was muttering something about a row with his ex and losing his mobile, the next he was pulling her dressing gown off and shagging her senseless on the kitchen table.

She remembered she'd been on the point of telling him about her painful, pointy boots and rumbling tummy outside the station. She wanted him to feel the full weight of what he'd done. She'd been intending to raise the subject of public phone boxes in the absence of mobiles, too.

Unfortunately, she'd opened her mouth and before she'd had time to utter a word, he'd launched into one of those snogs, his taxi-snog as she now thought of it. After that, her resolve had flown out of the window. And now she was feeling the full weight of him on her instead.

She ran her hands down his smooth, damp back and squeezed his bum. 'I love you,' she whispered. It just popped out. She didn't regret it, though.

He pushed himself up on to his elbows, looked down at her and grinned. It wasn't quite what she'd expected, but it was a pleased grin. She liked the little creases at the side of his mouth when he smiled.

He rose slowly and she wiggled on to one side and sat up, her feet dangling over the edge of the table. There was a noise upstairs, like a door slamming. She pricked her ears, hoping it wasn't one of the children.

'Quick, get your clothes on,' she said. He picked his boxers off the floor and climbed into them while she hopped off the table and pulled on her dressing gown. She stood at the kitchen door and listened again. Silence. It could have been the wind. She always left her bathroom window slightly open. She turned round and was surprised to see him peering in the fridge.

'What is there to eat?' he asked, his face illuminated by the inside light. 'I'm starving.' He pulled out a carton of eggs and some butter and put them on the worktop. 'Think I'll have two.'

Her body felt warm and tingly. He was so at home! She wiped the table, got out the saucepan, wooden spoon, a plate, knife and fork and turned on the hob. She stood, waiting for him to come over and start cooking. She wasn't hungry herself.

He pulled out a chair and sat down. So he wanted her to make it for him, then. She felt a flash of irritation. Typical man. No wonder he was so thin. He'd probably been waited on by his ex and didn't know how to cook for himself. She'd have to sort that one out pronto.

She felt tired suddenly. She realised that it must be very late. It'd be hard getting the children up for school in the morning.

'Who are you interviewing tomorrow?' she asked, melting the butter in the pan and stirring with the wooden spoon. She could just about see what she was doing, thanks to the glow from the downlighters.

'Not sure yet,' he said, resting his elbows on the table. 'I'll do a ringaround in the morning.'

Evie cracked two eggs into the saucepan and stirred. 'Ringaround?' she asked. 'How does that work, then?'

He scratched his head. 'Oh, I chat with the agents, ask them if they've got any stories. If they're any good I'll tout them round.'

Evie added a little milk to the pan and stirred again. 'How exciting! What sort of stories have you done recently?'

He cleared his throat. 'I got a page lead on Maddy Cooper's secret IVF treatment in *Hot Telly* magazine.'

'Maddy Cooper?'

'She plays Tina in *Emergency*.'

'Oh.' Evie didn't watch *Emergency*. 'Tell me some of the other celebs you've interviewed. It must be such a glamorous job.'

He paused. He was obviously going through all the famous people he'd rubbed shoulders with. And she, as his girlfriend, would no doubt meet some of them one day!

'Tommy Cruise, Helen Mirren, Jimmy McAvoy—'

'James McAvoy?' she said. 'Wow. I love him. What's he like in real life?'

'Really nice guy,' Steve said. 'Down to earth. I've met him quite a few times.'

'What's his accent like?' said Evie, adding a little salt and pepper to the saucepan. 'Is it really pronounced?'

'His accent? Nah. He just sounds like you or me.'

Evie stopped stirring. 'Really? I thought he was Scottish.' She took the pan off the hob.

'Scottish?' he said. 'Oh yeah. But you can't tell any more. They tend to lose the accent once they get famous.'

Evie buttered two pieces of toast, cut them in half, put the eggs on and passed the plate to him. She was pretty sure she'd read somewhere that James McAvoy sounded very Scottish. Maybe she'd got him muddled up with someone else.

She sat beside Steve while he wolfed down the eggs and polished off a big glass of milk. 'Would you like some more toast?' she asked. He did seem very hungry.

He pushed back his chair and stretched. 'Let's go to bed now.'

She frowned. 'I don't know. Is that a good idea? You'll have to get up really early again, before the children wake.'

He leaned forward and put his hands over hers. They felt warm and reassuring. 'They won't go in your bedroom, will they, surely? I mean, if I stay up there while you get them off to school?'

'Oh.' She hadn't thought of that.

'Then we can spend the day together,' he went on, giving her hands a squeeze. 'Just you and me.'

'But what about your work?'

He lifted her hand up, opened the fingers and kissed the palm gently. 'Work can wait.'

She thought of the unfinished wedding dress in her bedroom and her book begging to be written.

'Don't you want to?' he asked at last, a hurt expression on his face.

How unromantic of her.

'Of course I do,' she replied.

Freya slammed the bathroom door shut. That'd show them.

It was one thing for Mum to have a new boyfriend, but it was completely out of order for her to bring him back here. It was obvious what they were up to. It was sick. She strode back into her bedroom and plonked down at the computer. She felt tears welling in her eyes.

i think mum's brought someone bak, she wrote. *a bloke. i want to vomit.*

yuk, he said, *do u know who?*

no.

has she brought anyone bak b4?

no.

maybe he's ok?

It was a thought. *maybe,* she replied.

do u think she's lonely?

probably.

well if your dad left, isnt it nice for her 2 have someone else?

She pondered that for a moment. *i just don't want to think of my mum having sex with anyone.*

sex is ok u know – with the right person.

She turned that round in her head. *i know, well, i don't know but i guess.*

u scared of sex? he asked.

no.

what then?

dont want to talk bout it.

ok.

They chatted some more, about Chantelle and Gemma, mainly. And music. He was the easiest person to talk to. In the end she was so tired that she could hardly keep her eyes open.

got 2 go now, she said at last. *night xx.*

luv u, c u 2morrow, Al wrote back.

She hugged her arms around her, rereading it a few times. Then she unplugged the cable that connected her mum's camera to the laptop and folded it up. She'd taken loads of pictures of herself smiling, making silly faces, pouting like a model. He said he liked that one best; she looked beautiful. No one except Mum had ever said she was beautiful before.

She switched off the bedside light, climbed under the duvet and closed her eyes. Tonight had been awesome, the best night ever. She and Al loved each other for definite. And on top of that, according to Lucy, Gemma, Chantelle and Abigail were in a right state.

They'd had identical texts: *'IM WATCHING YOU. STOP BULLYING FREYA OR YOU'LL B SORRY. I MEAN IT.'*

No one recognised the number and when they tried to call back it was switched off. Lucy said they'd discussed the possibility that it was Freya using someone else's phone, but they didn't think she'd do that. She was too chicken.

'They're crapping themselves,' Lucy giggled. 'They think someone might tell about that thing with Richie in the cafeteria.'

'Good,' said Freya. She felt light; she could sing! Why hadn't she thought of it herself? But it's true, she'd never have dared. Al was wicked. She was almost looking forward to going into school tomorrow. That was a first.

Al. It was weird he was so old. I mean, what did he look like? He said he was OK. Maybe he was lying. She'd nearly asked him to send a photo but she was petrified. What if he was sick? He must be sick, for God's sake. He was forty-eight. Her dad was forty-six and he was gross. Well, Helen didn't seem to think so. She liked him enough to have a baby with him.

Freya shuddered. She didn't want to think about any of that. She shouldn't have to. Dad should still be with Mum, then Mum wouldn't be having sex with some weird bloke downstairs. She and Dad would be going to garden centres or something. That's what Lucy's parents did; that's what *normal* parents did.

It was hard to believe that she'd been so depressed. She couldn't believe she'd tried to kill herself. She didn't want to die now, no way. Al had been great. He said she must never, ever do it again. She must tell him how she was feeling and he'd help.

Who cared if he was sick-looking? He was the only one who was really there for her. Anyway, he couldn't be that bad. He didn't have a beer belly and man boobs, did he? God. She'd better ask him for a photo, just in case.

She heard whispering on the landing. Mum's voice – and a man's. Shit. They weren't going to go upstairs, were they? She put her hands over her ears. It was weird. Just as something went right, something else started to go wrong. She wished she could wake up and be twenty and everything would be sorted.

She couldn't imagine being twenty and going to university and stuff. Maybe she'd fail all her exams and never go to university. Maybe she'd have to live at home and sleep in this room until she was an old lady, dribbling and peeing everywhere. It was scary, all that stuff about the future. What if no one wanted her and she never got a job?

Al wanted her. He thought she was beautiful.

She turned over on to her other side and her limbs started to dissolve into the mattress. At least there was one solid thing in her life: Al. She wished he was here now. But he might go off her if he met her. She might go off him. He might not fancy her.

Maybe they should keep things as they were and never actually meet. They could just carry on talking like this for ever. She felt so close to him right now. They were like soulmates. But it would be nice just to see his face, his smile, feel his touch. Hold his hand.

She'd think about that some more in the morning.

Freya stumbled out of the front door and the cold seeped inside her collar and up her arms. Mum was right; she did need her jumper. Too late now. The air was a damp grey and the plants and shrubs on either side of the garden path were deep green and drooping with recent rain.

'Stop pushing,' she screamed. Michael was right behind, nudging her in the back.

Her bag, groaning with books, was on one shoulder, the car keys in her other hand. She pressed the button to unlock the doors, which made a satisfying clunk.

'Hurry up,' Mum shrieked from inside the house. What was she doing? 'I can't find my bloody keys!' No change there, then.

Freya didn't usually get a lift to school but today was an emergency. They'd all overslept, even Michael. She'd probably get a late. She didn't care, but she was annoyed she'd miss registration. For once in her life she was looking forward to seeing Gemma and Chantelle's faces.

She glanced to her left and saw Bill hunched over his front gate. There was a box of tools at his feet. That was odd, mending a gate at this time, or mending a gate at all for that matter. Some people were funny.

'Hi, Bill!' she said. She felt like being friendly; she was in a good mood, despite the rush.

He looked up and smiled. She liked his smile. It was a real, genuine smile, not like the kind that some adults give when they just pretend they're pleased to see you. 'Hello, Freya!'

Michael pushed past and the bag dropped off her shoulder, spewing its contents over the garden path. She hadn't done it up properly.

'Look what you've—'

But he'd already opened the car door, clambered into her seat in front and was deliberately looking in the other direction. Creep. Bill left his tools and helped her stuff the books back in her bag.

'Thanks so much,' she said. He was really kind. 'Bit of a rush. Late for school,' she explained.

'Ah,' he said.

She caught his eye. She was surprised. Normally he was happy but today he looked serious, as if his mind was on something else. Mum came bustling down the path.

'Get in the car,' she ordered. She nodded at Bill. 'Hi.'

She could be a bit more friendly, when he'd just helped Freya with her bag.

197

'Sorry about last night,' Mum said, 'bothering you with all that stuff, I mean.'

What was she going on about?

Bill stood up and brushed his hands on his trousers, which were a bit grubby. 'Don't mention it.'

'Everything's all right now,' Mum went on. 'It's all sorted.' She turned to Freya: 'Get in the car, quick!'

Freya hesitated. There was a weird atmosphere between them. She glanced from one to the other, she couldn't help it. Bill was looking hard at Mum. Something was up, blatantly.

'I'm glad,' said Bill, 'that it's all sorted.'

Mum's mouth looked like a cat's bum. She didn't reply.

Chapter Twenty-Seven

'How are we all getting on with our writing, then?'

Tristram beamed at the class in front. Evie looked at the ground. Nic, sitting on her left, seemed about to speak but clearly thought better of it. Becca, on her right, fished a hankie out of her bag and blew her small, upturned nose.

Carol rose to her feet. 'I'm really enjoying my writing,' she said in a loud voice. She hadn't taken off her coat – a rather grubby-looking tan-coloured sheepskin Afghan with red and orange embroidery on the shoulders and a shaggy collar. It looked like something she'd bought in the 1970s.

She probably had bought it in the 1970s, Evie thought.

'Good,' said Tristram, still beaming. 'Can you tell us a bit about it?'

Carol tucked some strands of grey hair behind her ears. 'To tell you the truth,' she said, 'I'm a bit embarrassed to say anything.'

'Why's that?' Tristram asked.

'Well, you see, I've scrapped my old book and started a new one – about my cats.'

Pamela, in the middle of the front row as usual, made a rude scoffing sound.

'Your cats?' Tristram asked, ignoring the interruption.

'Yes,' said Carol. 'They talk to me, you see, and I write down what they say. They're very intelligent.'

Pamela couldn't contain herself. 'Heaven help us!' she said, shaking her severe coiffure. 'The woman really is mad.'

Tristram gave her a stern look. 'Can we let everyone have their say, please. This is a democratic meeting.'

'It's all right,' Carol said huffily, plonking back down next to Becca. 'I don't want to give too much away. Someone with no ideas of her own might try to steal my plot.'

'As if,' Pamela muttered, resolutely refusing to look round.

There was an embarrassed silence while Tristram shuffled through some papers he was holding. 'Ah yes,' he said, clearly spotting what he wanted. 'What about anyone else before we move on to today's agenda? How are you others getting on?'

Nic raised an arm. 'The words are flowing.' She did an exaggerated gushing movement with her hands. 'But I'm getting in a hell of a muddle about the sequence of prevents – er, events.' She giggled, revealing her turquoise braces. 'I'm not sure what should happen where.'

Evie frowned. Nic sounded odd. Was she tipsy?

'Have you tried the stickies trick?' Russell asked, swivelling to face Nic. He was sitting to the left of Pamela.

Russell, the willy-and-fanny doctor, was as wispy and pale as ever and he'd grown a cute little goatee.

'The stickies trick?' Nic asked. Her lips stuck out awkwardly because of the train tracks.

'Get yourself a big piece of card or something,' Russell explained, 'then write out everything that happens, chapter by chapter, on Post-It notes and stick them on the card. The great thing is, you can see everything at a glance. And you can move them round as much as you like if you think the sequence of events isn't right.'

Nic smiled again. 'Great idea,' she said, swaying slightly in her seat. 'Thanks.'

'Excellent,' Tristram agreed. 'Any other tips, observations, problems? No? Then I thought I should mention that apparently there have been thousands of requests for application forms for the writing competition.'

Several people turned to each other and started murmuring.

'I don't think this should put any of us off.' Tristram had to raise his voice to be heard and the chunter stopped. 'But we must redouble our efforts and make sure our writing is of the highest possible standard.'

'I don't know why we're bothering.'

The voice came from the back of the class. Everyone craned to look. It was Angela, a mousy little woman with big, black, square glasses in her thirties who usually said very little.

She was writing a novel about a girl who'd been raped and was self-harming. Her previous book was about a mother who killed her baby and hid the body in a suitcase in the loft.

Angela always seemed rather depressed; Evie couldn't help thinking she might be happier if she were to pick lighter subjects. She never said so, though.

Tristram removed his dark-green corduroy jacket and hung it on a chair beside him. 'Now why do you say that, Angela?' he asked tetchily. 'That's a very negative view.'

'Well, what's the point?' she grumbled. 'I mean, realistically, none of us is going to win.'

Tristram ran a hand down his red silk tie and rested it on his paunch. 'You just never know,' he said. 'Someone has to win, and we don't know what they're looking for. Besides, competition is good. Now when I was in the Army—'

Carol coughed. 'Can we get on with tonight's agenda?' she said, glancing at her watch. 'We did start rather late.'

Evie looked at her fingernails and shuffled uncomfortably. Carol was so rude. She was a bit of a godsend, though. She was the only one who dared to say what they were all thinking.

'Oh, right,' said Tristram in a wounded voice, 'yes, of course.' Evie felt almost sorry for him. 'Um, this month I thought it would be a good idea to look at pacing. That is, if everyone agrees?'

There was a general murmur of assent.

'I have an interesting article here, taken from a book about how to write a bestseller,' he continued. 'The writer calls pacing "your story's heartbeat".'

He cleared his throat and started to read: '"Good stories seem to fly along during the exciting bits, then slow down so that a reader can catch his breath before picking him up and rushing forward again, all with a definite sense of purpose."'

He looked up. 'Now, who's going to volunteer to read first so that we can analyse their pacing?'

Tim, sitting just in front of Evie, put his hand up. Bloody hell, he's brave, Evie marvelled. Tim was in his forties, she guessed, and was something to do with market research. He was small and round, with thinning grey hair and glasses that seemed too big for his face. He hadn't explained much about his novel, a thriller, but there seemed to be a lot about cars in it. He was very knowledgeable about different makes.

He himself drove a Toyota Yaris; Evie knew because he'd spotted her one day on her way to the station and kindly given her a lift. During the short ride, he'd outlined the pros and cons of the Yaris in impressive detail.

He stood up, holding his printed manuscript in front of him. '"The Mitsubishi Shogun pulled up alongside Ralph's Lexus RX high-performance hybrid at the traffic lights,"' he read.

Ralph, cradled in leather-lined luxury, smiled. Being green has never been so easy, he thought. He glanced at the driver. In just two hours, one would become a killer, the other his victim. For one second, the men's eyes met. Ralph glanced away quickly.

The lights changed and the Mitsubishi roared ahead, but the Lexus accelerated with V-8 gusto and soon caught up. The age of the high-performance hybrid is well and truly here, Ralph thought, gripping the steering wheel. He was still good-looking, even though he was in his fifties, but there were worry lines round his eyes.

He screeched round a bend and headed after the Mitsubishi, which he knew from experience not only was – but felt like – a huge car. It leaned over uncomfortably in corners, and the steering wasn't accurate enough. The ride was disappointing, too.

'Stop please,' Tristram said. 'Now, I can see several pacing problems here. Has anyone spotted them?'

Evie raised her hand. 'I think it's a mistake to say: "In just two hours, one would become the killer, the other his victim."'

Tristram nodded. 'Why?'

'Because it slows the passage down,' Evie said, 'and also it's giving the plot away too soon.'

'Exactly,' said Tristram. 'Anything else?'

'Well,' Evie said carefully, 'I'm not sure if you need quite so much detail about the make and performance of the cars.'

She was trying very hard to be tactful. 'I think it reduces the excitement somewhat.'

Carol huffed. 'Some of us aren't that interested in cars anyway,' she said. 'I don't have one at all. I bet I'm the greenest one here!' she added with a flourish.

Evie cringed, hoping Tim wouldn't mind. She daren't look at him.

'Yes, well some of us aren't interested in cats either,' Pamela spat. 'Nasty, yowling creatures—'

Carol started to get up. 'Don't you dare criticise my cats!'

'Ladies, please,' Tristram said, exasperated. He raised his hands. Carol looked as if she were about to say something and then plonked herself down. Evie sighed with relief.

Tristram picked up a pile of paper from the table by his side. 'Now I'd like you all to get some paper and a pen and scribble down a similar passage about a car chase, but with better pacing. I'll give you fifteen minutes, then we'll exchange notes.'

Carol leaned over and whispered in Evie's ear. 'I think I'll write about a chase on my high-performance Raleigh.' She grinned, revealing her stained teeth.

Evie grinned back. 'Shhh,' she said.

There was a decent crowd at the pub for once. Carol, Russell and Jonathan came, as well as Evie, Nic and Becca.

Jonathan was in his mid thirties and taught English to foreign students at a local adult-education college. He had long blond hair, a droopy moustache which he tended to twiddle with forefinger and thumb, and a weathered face. He'd spent years teaching abroad and was writing a stream-of-consciousness novel about a young man's sexual adventures in Spain and Italy. He rolled his own cigarettes, rode a motorbike and said 'cool' a lot.

Pamela usually had an urgent call of nature whenever he started reading passages from his work. They did tend to get a little steamy.

Evie was sitting on a small, farmhouse-style carver chair. She wiggled, noticing to her dismay that it felt rather tight. 'I think I'm developing writer's bum,' she said, half to herself.

Jonathan's ears pricked up. 'I beg your pardon?'

'Writer's bottom,' she repeated, feeling her cheeks go red when she realised that everyone was listening. 'Don't tell me you all nibble on carrot sticks when you're typing? I'm afraid I tend to cram in junk food between chapter headings.'

Jonathan grinned. He was the wrong person to be talking to. Tall and skinny, he couldn't weigh much more than ten stone. And being obsessed with sex, the conversation would only encourage him. 'Oh dear,' he said. 'Writer's derrière, eh? Let's have a butcher's. I need to see the evidence.'

Evie sniffed. 'Certainly not.'

Becca came to her rescue. 'I've got writer's belly,' she said, patting her tummy. She was wearing a tight black polo-neck jumper tucked into grey work trousers and looked enviably slim. 'I find I can't write without chocolate,' she went on, in that precise way that she had of speaking. 'I reach for it whenever I hit a sticky patch. I always used to be a thin person, but not any more.'

'Rubbish,' said Evie, scrutinising Becca's virtually non-existent tummy bulge. Come to think of it, Nic was one of those irritating types who 'forgot to eat', too. Evie decided that she picked the wrong friends.

'Oh, I wouldn't worry about writer's bottom, dear,' said Carol, grinning. 'Some of us have writer's waist, thighs and underarms, too. Anyone for a Pringle?' She waved a tube at them.

Nic changed the subject. 'Any interesting stories, Russell?' she asked, swigging from her glass of red wine. Evie noticed that three-quarters of Nic's drink was gone already; most of the others had only had a sip or two.

Nic was sandwiched between Russell and Jonathan on the bench seat opposite, facing the bar. They'd chosen the Fox and Rabbit this time, not their usual pub. This one was slightly cosier in winter.

Evie clocked that Jonathan was sitting very close to Nic, who was looking glamorous in a mustard-coloured cashmere sweater, a very short black skirt that showed off her good legs, and opaque black tights and boots. She was so trim that she could get away with it; she didn't look tarty. Come to think of it, she could actually do with putting on a few pounds.

Evie guessed that their thighs must be rubbing against each other but Nic didn't seem aware of it. Jonathan tended to lean against you, practically falling into your lap, if you sat next to him in the church hall, too.

'Nah, usual run-of-the-mill stuff,' Russell said, running his fingers round the rim of his beer glass. 'Well, I did feel a bit sorry for one young man who came in today, but patient confidentiality means I can't really talk about it.' He looked at Nic mischievously. She swayed to her left and dug him in the ribs.

'You can't say that and then not tell,' she whined. 'Go on, spill the beans.'

'The poor lad was only eighteen,' Russell continued. 'It must have taken a lot of courage to make an appointment.'

'So what was his problem?' Nic persisted.

Russell sipped his beer. They were all agog. 'Well, he had this girlfriend, right, but the problem was, he could get going all right but he couldn't, you know, finish the job.'

Nic spluttered. 'What, he couldn't – you know?'

Russell nodded mournfully.

'I'd have thought his girlfriend would be delighted,' Nic said. 'I mean, most young men seem to have the opposite problem, don't they?' She looked around. No one replied but Jonathan opened his eyes wide as if to say that had never been an issue for *him*.

'No,' said Russell. 'She's worn out from all the trying. They're at it all night sometimes. He's worried she's going to chuck him.'

Jonathan twiddled his blond moustache. 'At it all night?' he mused, half talking to himself. 'Marvellous.'

There was a general sniggering. Nic flashed her turquoise train tracks.

'I don't think that's funny at all,' Carol interrupted in a loud voice. Everyone stared. She looked really cross. She leaned across the table towards Russell and practically put her face in his. 'What are you going to do to help him?'

'It's tricky,' Russell said, suddenly serious. 'There was no obvious medical cause so I had to refer him to a sex therapist. Could take years of counselling, I'm afraid.'

There was silence for a moment while they ruminated on the young man's misfortune.

Evie straightened up. 'Changing the subject,' she said, cheerily, 'I've got some news.'

They all looked at her.

'Becca and Nic know already, but I feel like I want to tell the whole world. There's a new man in my life!'

Russell beamed. 'Well done!' he said. 'What's he like? Where did you meet him? Go on, tell all.'

'He's an old friend of Nic's called Steve and I met him at her party.' Evie grinned. 'And he's completely gorgeous. A celebrity journalist. Divorced. It's early days but' – she lowered her eyes – 'I think he's The One.'

'Oh no, dear.'

They all stared at Carol, who had risen to her feet and was looking wildly at Evie. She had a red, sweaty face, which could be due to the alcohol or the fact that she was still wearing her Afghan coat. But there was no denying the agitation in her voice.

'What do you mean?' Evie asked. She was confused.

'I mean, dear,' Carol said, wagging her finger, 'that it's far too soon to be saying that. After all, how long have you known this man? A week, a month?'

'Er, about ten days,' Evie admitted.

Carol slammed her fist on the table. 'Ten days isn't nearly long enough to get to know someone properly!' She looked around for support. 'And what about the children? They've had such a lot to cope with recently, what with your husband leaving and all that. I hope you haven't foisted this new person on them?'

Evie's face felt hot. 'I really don't think . . .' She started to rise herself. But Carol had picked up her bag and was already heading for the door.

Becca put a hand on Evie's arm. 'Leave it,' she said gently. 'She's just a bit batty. She doesn't know what she's talking about.'

Evie sat back down again. 'You're right,' she sighed. 'But it's a bloody cheek. I'm really angry with her. I mean, what business is it of hers who I see and who I choose to introduce my children to?'

'Quite right, man,' Jonathan agreed, twiddling his blond moustache again. He said 'man' a lot, too. 'That was way out of order.'

'It's no business of hers at all,' Nic said, reaching for her tan Mulberry under the table and pulling it clumsily on to her lap. 'Don't give it a second thought. Now, who's for another drink? I reckon we all need one after that.'

Chapter Twenty-Eight

'Hello, my darlings.'

Victoria and Albert snaked around Carol's legs, rubbing their sides against the furry bottom of her Afghan coat. She stooped down to stroke them, leaving the front door open behind her.

'Have you missed me?' she said. Victoria started purring loudly.

Albert, the black and white one, darted off towards the kitchen, glancing behind to see if Carol was following. When he realised that she wasn't, he pranced back and rubbed himself against her again.

'I know, I know, you're hungry,' she said, taking off her coat and hanging it on a peg on the wall, 'but you'll just have to be patient. I need to bring in my bike.'

She went outside to fetch the bike and wheeled it down the hall into the little sitting room at the back of the house. The harsh, overhead light made her blink; it had been so dark outside. She propped the bike against the table.

'I expect you want your supper?' she said, catching her breath. She'd pedalled home as fast as she could from the meeting, shot through lights and everything. She'd been so cross. She felt a bit better now, calmer. She couldn't have stayed in that pub a minute longer, though, listening to that stupid prattling. What was Evie thinking of, behaving like a silly schoolgirl? Especially when there were the children to think of, poor little things.

Carol shuddered. What was *she* thinking of? She didn't know what had come over her. She was normally so discreet. Had been all these years. She hoped she hadn't blown it. She wouldn't have, though. Evie would never guess, none of them would; they just thought she was barmy.

Carol fed the cats, made a mug of tea and set it on the table.

Then she stooped over and pulled a fat white book from the bottom shelf of the bookcase. She scanned the room. 'Bother, where are my specs?'

She spotted them on top of the pile of newspaper cuttings near the fridge and put them on. Then she sat down on one of the kitchen chairs and opened the book.

Carol peered at the little girl with fair hair and chubby arms and legs in the photo. The picture was a bit blurred, but you could see that she was in a swing being pushed by someone with her back to the camera. The little girl, who was about two, was waving her arms in the air, happy as anything.

Carol chuckled. 'Ah,' she said, 'dear little thing.'

That was the first one that she had of Evie, not counting the hospital picture on the fridge, of course. Just as well she'd managed to get a peek at the social worker's notes when her back was turned, otherwise she might never have tracked her down on the other side of London. It hadn't been easy, with just a surname and his occupation to go on. Good detective work, that's what it was. She should have been a journalist instead of stuck in an insurance office all those years.

Still, she'd done all right in the job. Built up a nice little nest egg. She rubbed her hands. My! Evie would be pleased with her unexpected windfall when the time came.

Carol continued flicking through the album. There was Evie learning to ride a bike, feeding the ducks, playing with her friends in the park. All outside, of course, and usually from a long way off. Carol had no zoom in those days, nothing like that. Just a basic Kodak, the best she could afford.

She'd got the train to south-west London every single Sunday to take a peep. 'Where are you going?' her mother would ask. 'Just out, with friends,' she'd reply.

'What friends?' Mother was so nosy.

'Some girls from the office. No one you know. We're going to the park. For an ice cream.'

Mother didn't like that, but she couldn't say much. Carol was earning her own wage now, she was grown-up, even if she was still living at home, saving madly for her own place. Mother didn't know that, either.

Some Sundays Evie was nowhere to be seen and then Carol had to go home disappointed. She could still feel that ache, that longing, even now. She sighed. The journey home had seemed interminable when she hadn't caught so much as a glimpse of her darling. She'd feel down all week, until Saturday came and she knew there was just one more day to go.

But in summer especially, Evie was often out and about with that woman who called herself her mother. Carol stopped and peered at the one of Evie in her school uniform. She'd taken the day off work especially to get that one. Well, it was a milestone after all. She wouldn't have missed it for the world.

Evie was walking along on the other side of the road, holding her mother's hand. The grey tunic dress was much too long for her; it reached well below her knees. Carol tutted. They should never have sent her to that Catholic primary school. She didn't have a Catholic bone in her body. She'd have been better off in the Church of England school round the corner. Still, it had turned out all right.

She flipped over another page of the album. Now you could see how much bigger Evie was getting. She had long, skinny legs outside the supermarket. And there, she looked almost like a teenager in that mini-skirt in the bowling alley, but she was only eleven. Carol shook her head. She'd never have let her wear a mini-skirt like that. Far too revealing. Carol wasn't keen on the bowling alley either. Dark and noisy. She'd only popped in because she'd happened to spot Evie queuing outside with her friends. They were on their own. She had to make sure they were OK.

It was a stroke of luck, really, that she'd managed to get the job in Richmond. It was a good company in a very desirable area. They said lots of people had gone for it. Not that Carol cared about the area. She just wanted to be close to Evie, to keep an eye on things. The flat was such a good price, too – and it had soared in value. She couldn't believe it when the estate agent told her how much it was worth. She'd got the full asking price. She'd never have been able to buy her little house otherwise. Things hadn't turned out all bad, by any means.

Carol looked at the bowling-alley photo again. Everything

was so murky, even with the flash. That place wasn't Carol's cup of tea, with all that loud music. You wouldn't catch her in there again. But there didn't seem to be any harm in it.

She didn't have so many snaps of Evie as she got older. It was harder to take photos without being seen. There were a couple of hazy shots of her outside school, surrounded by friends, often as not draped around some young man or other. Carol shook her head. She did go through a rebellious phase, with that terrible purple hair and everything. It was quite a worry.

Victoria leaped up on Carol's lap and turned a few times. Then she stood, kneading Carol's jumper fiercely, before settling down.

'Not surprising, with those stupid, narrow-minded old parents, is it?' Carol said, tickling the cat under the chin. 'She's a creative girl, artistic, she's got so much talent. She needed to be nurtured and encouraged, not crushed.' She wiped away a tear with her sleeve. 'I've done what I could, you know. It wasn't for me to poke my nose in. She'll be glad of the money when I die.'

She turned to the wedding photo. It was the only one that she'd managed to get. Evie was in the car beside Neil, waiting to drive to the reception. Carol had sidled up to a group of guests who were taking photos at the same time. No one had noticed. Evie looked so happy and radiant. Carol touched her daughter's face, tracing the pretty veil drawn back off her shiny fair hair.

She flipped on to the next page quickly. 'I can't believe he did that to her,' she said, stroking the cat again rather brutally. It miaowed in protest but she didn't notice. 'Not to my lovely girl. If I could get my hands on him . . .'

She paused for a moment, then laughed out loud. Victoria jumped. 'Just look at Freya-chops!'

A big, A4-sized colour photo of a beaming baby Freya stared back. She was wearing nothing but a white frilly hat and a nappy and was clutching an ice cream, most of which was smeared around her mouth and cheeks. Carol had sneaked right up close this time when Evie's back was turned as she rootled around in her bag; looking for something to clean the baby's face with, no doubt.

It was risky all right, but how could Carol resist? Freya looked scrumptious. It had been almost all she could do to stop herself picking her up and having a cuddle. Carol closed her eyes. She'd never cuddled Freya or Michael. Not ever. She'd only cuddled her own baby the once. What did Evie feel like, smell like? Why couldn't she remember?

She remembered the little snuffling mouth, though, seeking out her breast. But she wasn't allowed to feed her. They said it would be a mistake; they might bond. Well, that was stupid. As if Carol hadn't bonded with her already.

She ran her forefinger round Freya's chubby cheeks and her podgy wrists that seemed to have elastic bands wound tightly round them. 'Little Freya,' she cooed. 'Little pumpkin.'

Reluctantly, she turned a few more pages but there were none as clear as that of Michael when he was a baby. She swallowed. That emptiness again. Evie didn't take him to the local park so much, they seemed to go everywhere in the car. It wasn't the same, looking at fuzzy snaps of him in his babyseat through the car window. You couldn't see all his lovely dimples. But it was a good one of him and Freya on the climbing frame in that pub garden. What were they? About four and eight?

Carol's stomach lurched. She'd nearly had it. That man at the table next to her had given her such a dirty look. He was about to say something, she could tell. Thank God the barman appeared at just the right moment to collect the dirty glasses and she'd managed to slip away, camera intact.

She was pleased with the shot of Freya coming out of secondary school. Shame she dyed her hair that awful black colour and wore so much make-up. So like her mother at that age. She was such a pretty girl, too. Evie shouldn't allow it. But she looked in high spirits, for once, smiling with her friend as if they hadn't a care in the world.

Carol frowned. Freya. She was worried about her because of little things she'd told her at the bus stop in the mornings. Carol usually went down there. It was a good way of keeping in touch.

Freya wasn't happy at school, that was clear. Although she did mention that those girls who'd been bothering her weren't as bad lately. She looked awfully tired, too, with big circles round her eyes. Why hadn't Evie noticed? Freya said she talked a lot to people on the computer. Carol didn't know much about computers.

Freya had one special friend – Cal, that was his name. Well, that was nice, but Evie shouldn't let her stay up so late. Carol didn't like to criticise Evie ever, but she did seem to have lost the plot lately. Truth was, she was being a bit selfish, Carol thought. It was too bad, Neil leaving her, but she'd got wrapped up in her own problems. Maybe Freya was worried about this new boyfriend of Evie's? Carol wouldn't be surprised. She didn't believe for a minute that Freya didn't know. Children pick up on things. She was a clever girl.

Carol took a swig of tea. 'What are we going to do about this boyfriend?' Albert, who had curled up on her feet, twitched slightly in his sleep. 'He seems shifty to me. And that nasty long hair. I don't like long hair on a man.'

Carol moved her feet and Albert rolled off. She felt cold without her furry slippers. She nudged Victoria off her lap, too, and the cat sloped away.

'The trouble is,' Carol sighed, closing the album and rising slowly from her chair, 'there's nothing I really can do.'

She shuffled over to the sink, rinsed her mug and put it on the draining board. The cats were right behind, at her ankles.

'You've no idea,' Carol said, bending down to give them another stroke, 'how awful it is to be so powerless.'

Victoria miaowed. Carol stooped down to pick her up and cradled her in her arms, tickling her furry tummy. She stood there, looking out of the window at the black street for some time, rocking the cat back and forth in her arms like a baby. Thinking.

Chapter Twenty-Nine

It was good of Gary to come all the way over to Kew for dinner, but right now Becca wished that she were anywhere but here. She'd suggested this particular pub because it served excellent food and it was just around the corner from the station. She'd been there countless times at weekends with Tom and the children.

It was an imposing nineteenth-century inn, which had recently been refurbished to look like a Victorian front room. Normally, Becca loved the muted pink and beige wallpaper, the heavy curtains, the oversized mirrors and dark-wood sideboards, tables and chairs. There was a beer garden at the back, too, where the children could let off steam on sunny days.

James and Alice. She missed them so much. She missed Tom, too. She wanted to be at home, sitting beside him on the sofa. She wouldn't even care if he was glued to the TV.

'You should bring your kids here and spend the afternoon in Kew Gardens,' she said, dabbing her mouth with her napkin. 'There are some great things for children to do, as well as looking at the plants. James loves Climbers and Creepers.'

She was making ridiculous small talk, she knew. She felt flat, monochrome. She'd been wildly excited before meeting Gary. Now, even the pale-pink rose in a little white vase on the table looked sad.

She was also uncomfortably full. They'd each had three courses, which was unusual for her, and the waistband of her skirt was cutting into her stomach. She glanced at Gary across the table. He seemed so much less attractive than before: blander and more ordinary. The first time they met she'd loved his sideburns. Now she decided they were silly, as if he were trying to be younger than he really was.

She was angry, that was the main problem. This time she'd abandoned caution and pumped him for information. It was clear from what he said now that he hardly ever went back to Newcastle. There was little that he could tell her about old classmates from primary school. He couldn't even remember half their names. And worst of all, he'd misled her about her mother, Maureen.

The phone conversations she'd had with his mother, June, had all been years ago, around the time of the trial. And when Becca had quizzed him he'd admitted that June had, in fact, received only one letter from Maureen, and that was soon after Dawn went away.

Dawn. Who came back as Becca. She could picture Mr Carr even now. He was the one who'd come to collect her from the remand centre with his wife, Sheila, to take her to the secure unit that they ran together and that was to be her home for the next five years.

Sheila was a little, round, cuddly thing while he was tall and thin. He wore a tweed jacket and brogues and had a military air, but his face was kind and gentle.

Dawn had been frightened of him at first, but she grew to love him. He convinced her that she could *be* somebody and make a new life for herself. When she was finally let out, it was his grown-up daughter's name – Rebecca, or Becca for short – that she decided to adopt. She liked that name. There was no one called Becca on the estate and she liked that, too.

When she thought of her childhood now, it was Mr Carr and his wife whom she pictured; it was their middle-class accents, manners, views on life that she tried to emulate. Often, she imagined that she *was* Mr Carr's daughter, that everything that had happened before had been a bad dream.

But Dawn was worming her way into Becca's subconscious, rattling the box, trying to get out, to be heard.

Becca stared at Gary. She felt let down. How could she ever have thought him attractive? She rubbed the corners of her eyes, hoping that she wouldn't smudge her make-up. Actually, she didn't care if she smeared it all over her face. She was so tired. She just wanted to leave.

Gary leaned across the table and touched her hand. She flinched and he took it away.

'I'd like to come here with you again,' he said in a low voice. 'Not with the children.'

'Oh.' She couldn't disguise her unease.

He smiled. 'You're so defensive, like a wild horse. I can see the fear in your eyes, as if you're ready to bolt at any moment.'

She tucked her dark hair behind her ears and started to pick at the candle wax round the base of the candlestick. 'It's lovely in summer especially,' she said, trying to redirect the conversation. 'Kew Gardens, I mean.'

He rested his hand on hers again. This time she forced herself to let it stay there – for a moment.

He looked straight at her. 'I wish you'd relax. You can trust me.'

She shivered. She wished she'd never agreed to dinner. She was a fool. She'd known it was a mistake. She'd let herself down. Put herself in a dangerous position.

'It's not surprising that I'm defensive.' She coughed, using it as an excuse to pull her hand away again. 'It's a pretty big secret I've been keeping all these years. I'm on my guard all the time. I've had to be.'

'Well, you don't have to be on your guard with me.'

She could sense his eyes boring into her. Her heart fluttered. She felt suddenly panicky. Her instincts told her that she needed to get away now.

'I must go,' she said, checking the gold watch on her wrist. 'I've got an early start and Tom'll be wondering where I am. What about Michelle? What time did you say you'd be home?'

'I didn't say.'

She glanced at him now. She couldn't help it.

He cleared his throat. He looked embarrassed. 'To be honest, Michelle and I haven't been getting on that well. I didn't want to tell you too much before. But I can't lie.'

'I'm sorry.' Becca felt trapped. She didn't want to be drawn into this. She didn't want to know about his marriage. But it would be rude to leave now. She cursed herself for mentioning Michelle.

He sighed. 'It's terribly sad, especially for the children.

216

I've tried my best but I can't see us still being together in a year's time.' He looked at his hands on the table. 'I'd be lying, of course, if I pretended that you weren't a significant factor.'

Had she heard him correctly? 'But, Gary . . .' she blurted. She checked herself. 'We've only met twice.' It was difficult to keep the anxiety out of her voice. This was madness. 'We hardly know each other.'

He shook his head. 'I feel as if I know you through and through,' he replied softly. 'The important bit of you, the part that really matters. Your essence. What else do I need to know? Your hobbies, where you go on holiday?' He sounded contemptuous. 'We've got all the time in the world to talk about the trivial stuff.' He looked up. 'Now I've found you, Becca, I don't intend to let you go.'

Becca's heart started thumping. There was something weird about him and his intensity. How could she not have spotted it before? She needed to think. Fast.

'Gary?' She touched his arm. She'd have to be careful. Tactful. She was on the alert now, with all her wits about her. 'I'm so glad we've re-established contact. I've really enjoyed talking to you and catching up. You're part of my past, my history, and as you know I've felt desperately cut off from that all these years. But you need to know something.'

His eyes widened. He looked uncomfortable, which gave her courage.

'Tom and I, well, we've our bad times,' she went on, 'and our marriage isn't perfect. But I do love him. He's been an amazing support to me. And he's a brilliant father to the kids. I'd never, ever do anything to hurt him.'

She blushed, thinking of the impure thoughts that she'd had about Gary earlier in the evening, on her way to meet him. Thank God he wasn't a mind-reader. If only she hadn't implied on their first date that her marriage was tricky. She'd been reckless and stupid. She'd opened the door to him. She crossed her fingers under the table, hoping that her words would get through, that he'd understand her drift. It was a silly habit that she'd kept from childhood. Soon, all being well, she'd be back home where she was meant to be: moaning about Tom, feeling stressed about work, complaining of her lot, but safe. That lovely word: safe.

'What are you saying?' he asked. 'That you don't want to see me again?'

She bit her lip. 'No, I'm not saying that. I want us to be friends but . . .'

'Dawn?'

Her stomach reeled. She hadn't been called that for so many years. She reached up and felt beads of sweat on her forehead. She glanced left and right. Luckily there was no one nearby. She glared at him: 'Don't ever make that mistake again . . .'

Something made her stop. He was leaning back in his seat, relaxed. His arms were behind his head, one foot resting on the other leg. A little smile was playing on his lips.

It wasn't a mistake.

Her eyes locked on to his. An invisible thread between them meant that she couldn't look away.

'Does Tom know what you did?' he asked. His voice was firm and commanding.

She felt a chill running down her spine. She shook her head, and immediately wished that she hadn't.

'It would be a shame if he found out.'

Becca swallowed. 'Are you threatening me?' Her voice was a croak.

Gary laughed, making her jump. The thread between them snapped.

'Of course not,' he said, scratching his head. 'Whatever are you thinking? Now, when shall we meet again?'

'Whenever you want,' she said dully.

Tears streamed down her cheeks as she sat in the back of the cab, staring out of the window into the blackness. Her mind was racing. What did he want of her? What was he up to? If only she could delve into his brain and discover what his plan was.

She felt sick with that feeling of being out of control. But this was worse, far worse than flying. She'd take a hundred flights rather than be in the situation that she was in now. He had so

218

much power – he could do almost anything he liked. It was terrifying.

It seemed likely that he intended to blackmail her and then sell her story to the highest bidder. Was that his game? He'd get a lot of money for it. The tabloids would love it. They'd have a field day. There'd be a huge scandal and they'd fire her at work. No doubt about it. They'd say clients could no longer trust her – and she wouldn't blame them.

They'd probably have to sell the Richmond house, and the farmhouse in Normandy that they hardly ever used. That would be no great loss. There was enough in the bank to pay the children's school fees. Their circumstances would be very different but they wouldn't exactly be on the breadline. She knew what poverty felt like. She wasn't afraid of having less money. But the kids . . . She scrabbled in her pocket for a tissue and wiped her eyes.

'You all right, madam?' The taxi driver must wonder what on earth was the matter.

'Yes,' she muttered, blowing her nose. It was all she could manage.

Alice and James would suffer dreadfully. They'd be so frightened and confused. She'd have to tell them everything. And Tom. She felt sweaty and cold at the same time. She realised that she was shaking. He'd leave her, for sure. He'd say he'd never known her, that he was married to a stranger. He'd be revolted by what she'd done. She sensed the carefully constructed edifice that she'd built around her slowly crumbling.

Hadn't she known this would happen one day? She was a fool for thinking she could get away with it. And she was the architect of her own destruction. How fitting!

The taxi drew up outside her house and she dug in her bag for her purse. The machine at the front said £11.38. She passed a fifty-pound note through the hatch. 'Keep the change.' She didn't care. It didn't feel like hers anyway. She dragged herself off the back seat and climbed out. She felt shaky, uncertain of her feet.

'Do you need a hand?' The cab driver sounded kind, concerned. It made things worse.

She shook her head. 'No.'

The car pulled away and she stood with her hand on the heavy iron gate, reluctant to go inside. The light was still on in their bedroom at the front of the house. Tom must be awake. She could walk away now, keep walking, get a train somewhere. Go abroad. Disappear. She had her credit cards.

She had the car keys in her bag. She could drive to Beachy Head. She didn't fancy jumping. Or Brighton. Swim as far as she could and wait till the cold and the current got her. That sounded preferable.

'Does Tom know what you did?' Gary had said. 'Shame if he found out.'

It was odd that he hadn't mentioned money. He was insistent about seeing her again. That's when he'd ask for cash, at their next meeting. He was softening her up, making her sweat a bit. She didn't understand, though, what all the stuff about his marriage was about. And the way he'd said that he knew her really well – the essence of her. That was weird.

She heaved. She could taste bile mixed with the garlicky chicken she'd had earlier. She swallowed and the bile burned her throat as it went down.

She was startled by a noise above her.

'Becks?' Tom had opened one of the sash windows in their bedroom at the top of the house and was leaning out. 'What are you doing?' he called down.

He looked crumpled, as if he'd been asleep. He was in his stripy pyjamas and his mop of greying, curly hair was sticking up round his head. She felt a rush of love.

'I'm coming!' she whispered.

She opened the heavy wooden front door, flung her briefcase down, raced up two flights of stairs and threw herself, panting, into his arms. He staggered slightly before righting himself.

'What is it, darling?' he asked, stroking her dark hair. 'What's the matter?'

His pyjama top smelled warm and comforting, of fabric conditioner – and Tom.

'It's nothing,' she sobbed, 'I've had a horrible day at work. I'm so glad to see you.'

He squeezed her to him. 'There must be something else,' he whispered. 'You're in such a state. Where did you go for dinner?'

'Nowhere special.' Her body was still shaking. 'Honestly, I've just had a terrible day, loads of hassle. I didn't want to go out this evening. I'm so tired. I just want you to cuddle me.'

'Of course I'll cuddle you,' he replied, helping her off with her coat and jacket.

She struggled out of her skirt and tights, pulled on the cream silk nightie under her pillow and checked that the alarm beside her bed was on. Force of habit.

She lay on her side facing the window and he put his arms around her. She pushed her bottom back into the curve of his body, clamping her arms over his so that he couldn't take them away.

'You silly girl,' he said, kissing the back of her neck. 'It's not like you to get so het up about work. Maybe you need a holiday.'

'Yes,' she whispered. 'Maybe. Hold me, Tom. Don't let me go.'

He kissed her again. She could feel his warm breath on her skin.

'You silly goose,' he replied. 'I don't know what's come over you. You're my wife and there's nothing that could ever separate us. We're together for ever, you and me. You know that.'

Chapter Thirty

❧

Nic was relieved when she was able to pull off the slip road on to the M4, heading towards Slough. She put her foot on the accelerator and signalled right into the middle lane, overtaking several cars in front. As the needle rose to 80 m.p.h. she felt her spirits lift slightly. She opened the window just a fraction and the cold wind whistled around her, making her blond bob blow about.

It was 9 a.m. on Friday morning and the roads were pleasantly clear. She turned on the radio. 'Do They Know It's Christmas?' blared out. She turned it off again quickly: 12 December already and she hadn't bought a single present, not even for Dominic.

The dull, throbbing headache that she woke up with most mornings had dispersed after several painkillers, but they couldn't obliterate the anxiety that gnawed away at her insides. She felt panicky all the time. It helped to be on the road, though, getting away from the house, leaving the empty bottles and the scene of her crime behind.

She felt for the mints on the passenger seat, eased one out of the tube and popped it in her mouth. That'd help mask the smell of alcohol on her breath. She must have drunk a heck of a lot last night because she couldn't remember much about it, not after she'd got Dominic off to bed.

She vaguely recalled Alan coming home and sticking his head round the door to say hello while she was watching TV. He must have spent the rest of the evening in his study because she didn't think she'd seen him again.

She also recollected squeezing the dregs out of that box of wine that had been left over from the party a few weeks before. She could picture herself on the sofa, her head thrown back, ripping the cardboard off to reveal the plastic bag inside and sucking at the nozzle to drain the very last drops. It had seemed funny at the time.

Well, it didn't seem funny now.

She had no idea when she'd gone to bed, just that she'd woken up in all her clothes – apart from her pants and jeans which were on the floor in an untidy mess beside her. Dominic was shaking her awake. Alan was nowhere to been seen; he must have left for work already. Thank God.

She shivered, remembering the shock of her discovery: 'Wake up, Mummy, we'll be late,' Dominic was saying. She'd moved her legs slightly and realised that she was lying in wet sheets, that it was damp all around her. At first she didn't understand; she must have spilled her glass of water. Or had Dizzy somehow jumped up without her noticing and made a mess? That seemed highly unlikely.

Nic had sniffed the duvet when Dominic turned away. She'd closed her eyes and waited as the truth rolled over her: she'd peed in the bed.

She checked the driving mirror and swallowed. This wasn't right. This was seriously wrong. She was in trouble. The road ahead started blurring up. She sniffed. She mustn't cry now; it was dangerous. She'd have an accident.

She'd managed to get up, strip the bed, shove everything in the washing machine and even pull the mattress off the base. She'd made a half-hearted attempt to wash the mattress with a flannel, but she knew it wouldn't work. She'd just have to leave it to dry. She was disgusting.

She'd had a shower and pulled on clean clothes: her See by Chloé blouse and her favourite black trousers. Downstairs, she'd tidied up the kitchen while Dominic was having breakfast, then she'd rushed him off to school before hitting the motorway.

She glanced to her left and checked that her notebook was on the seat with the mints. Good. She must focus on the *Mums* magazine interview, then she'd think about what she was going to do about the other thing. There were people out there who could help. Organisations. She'd heard of them. But then everyone would discover. Evie, Becca, Dominic. Mummy.

No.

She spotted the turning for Slough West, signalled and swung sharply off the motorway. A car behind her hooted. 'Fuck off,' she said.

It was strange to see Christmas trees in people's front windows as she left the dual carriageway and drove along residential streets again. She couldn't imagine going out and buying a Christmas tree and decorating it. Alan would have to do it. Poor Dominic.

She realised that she had no idea where to go from here. She pulled into a lay-by and set the sat nav. 'Cross the bridge and turn right at the roundabout in fifty metres,' the voice said. Thank God for sat nav. She'd be hopelessly lost otherwise.

Nic was pleased when she entered the wide, tree-lined street leading to Cookham Village and spotted the Thames drifting lazily along on her right. Various small boats were moored along the bank and a few people were out with pushchairs and dogs. They were wearing jackets and trousers, mainly, not coats and scarves; the weather was mild for the time of year and Nic herself was quite comfortable in just her silk blouse, though she'd put her jacket on when she got out of the car.

She noticed how slowly people were walking, as if they were in no hurry. It felt almost like another country after the hustle and bustle of London. She could quite see why you would choose to live here. She spotted the converted chapel, now the Stanley Spencer Gallery, on her left and turned into the High Street as instructed, passing what looked like an ancient Tudor pub and a shop called the Old Apothecary. After leaving the High Street she continued on for a mile or two to the outskirts of the village until she was instructed to stop.

She was outside a pretty Victorian house with a small paved front garden. Luckily, she could park right opposite the front door. Nic pulled on the handbrake, turned off the ignition and checked her face in the mirror. Now that the car was no longer moving she realised how bad she felt – weak and slightly nauseous. There were beads of sweat on her forehead and upper lip.

She reached for her bag on the floor of the passenger seat and dabbed her face with a hankie. Then she combed the knots out of her hair and put on her Mac pinky-brown lipstick.

Teresa, the woman she was to interview for *Mums*, opened the door before Nic had time to ring the bell. Nic was relieved. She wasn't in the mood for a tricky interviewee and Teresa looked comfortingly unthreatening.

She was in her late twenties or early thirties, plumpish, with short, sensible brown hair and a friendly smile. She was wearing an oversized, slightly grubby beige V-neck sweater which looked as if it might belong to her husband, pale blue jeans and sheepskin slippers. She seemed to have a very large bust owing, no doubt, to the fact that she was breast-feeding. Well, this was a feature about home births and Teresa's baby was only five months old.

The women shook hands. 'Excuse my appearance,' Teresa said, eyeing up Nic's Whistles jacket and silk blouse. Nic made a mental note to dress down before she went on another *Mums* interview. She ought to have known better.

'Please,' Nic said. 'I know what it's like with a new baby. I spent most of the first year in my pyjamas because there didn't seem to be time to get dressed.'

She smiled. Teresa's gaze lingered on the turquoise train tracks. Nic was used to it by now. 'They look a bit silly, don't they?' she said. 'The braces, I mean. I feel like an overgrown schoolgirl.'

Teresa grinned back, reassured. 'I'm quite envious, actually. I always wanted braces but I didn't need them. You're right about never having time to get dressed properly. I spend ages getting Archie ready, then I end up throwing on the same things I've worn three days running.'

She took Nic's jacket and led her into her little square drawing room at the front of the house. Nic cast an eye around. Archie was lying on a play mat on the floor underneath an activity centre. Various colourful objects dangled down from the toy, which the baby was batting with his little fists, drumming his legs in the air at the same time.

'He'll stay there for hours.' Teresa smiled. 'He loves it. Coffee?'

Nic nodded. There was a strong smell of nappy and biscuits. Her stomach reeled.

'Can you keep an eye on him while I put the kettle on?' Teresa said, disappearing.

It was hard to find anywhere to sit because the floor, surfaces and every seat were covered in toys and other baby paraphernalia: blankets, toys, items of clothing. Nic picked a stuffed giraffe and an elephant off the armchair under the bay window, put them on the floor and sat down gratefully. The baby gurgled.

'Who's a gorgeous boy?' she said half-heartedly. She loved babies but today she couldn't move. She was too shaky and fragile. So she sat there, trying to bond from a distance, praying that he wouldn't start crying.

Teresa came back with two mugs of coffee. Nic took a sip and winced. She hated instant coffee. There was no table to put her mug on so she set it down carefully on the carpet at her feet and pulled a notebook from her handbag.

'Thanks very much for agreeing to the interview,' she started. 'You know I'm speaking to three women who've had very different experiences of home births? The title will be "Would You Have a Home Birth?" We want to put the pros and cons.'

Her voice sounded awfully shaky. She hoped Teresa wouldn't notice. Teresa didn't seem to. She nodded, clearing a space on the flowery sofa opposite Nic so that she could sit down. The room felt very close. There was no window open. Nic rolled up the sleeves of her blouse.

'A bit of background first,' she said. 'Can you tell me what you do, what your husband does, that sort of thing.'

Archie started whimpering. 'I expect he's hungry.' Teresa bent down to pick him up and latched him on to her breast, where he made happy slurping sounds.

Nic tried to use her shorthand to jot down Teresa's background details before moving on to her home birth story. For some reason she couldn't remember how to write a lot of the words, though, and had to use messy longhand instead.

The other two women she'd interviewed had had good experiences, so Teresa was to represent the opposite view.

'It's not a happy tale,' Teresa warned, before launching into her account.

'I woke up at about four fifteen in the morning thinking these contractions were pretty strong but they weren't difficult,' she explained. 'I dozed for a while then I realised that I wasn't getting that much dozing in between these squeezes so I looked at my watch and found they were every three minutes or so and lasting for about a minute.'

Nic was scribbling furiously but her hand wouldn't seem to go where she wanted.

'I got up to see if they'd go away when I had a wee, but they didn't. I tried to wake Dave – that's my husband – but he was in a very deep sleep and I didn't have the heart to dig him in the ribs just yet.'

Nic's eyelids felt uncomfortably heavy. She wished that she could close them for a moment.

'At about four forty-five I thought that, even though this wasn't hard to handle, I possibly should phone my independent midwife, Bronwen, just in case. I hoped she wouldn't try to keep me talking long enough to time a contraction. Midwives see whether you can talk through it, and they use that information to gauge how quickly they need to get to you.'

Nic sat forward in her chair to keep alert. She knew she should ask questions, get to the point, but Teresa was enjoying herself. It seemed rude to stop her.

'Well,' she continued, 'even though these contractions weren't that bad, I didn't fancy trying to talk while dealing with one. I was very relieved when Bronwen asked if I wanted her to come now. I said yes. I had another go at waking up Dave but he was basically talking in his sleep! "Get up!" "Why?" "Because we're going to have a baby." "Can't you wait till morning?" "No I bloody well can't."'

Teresa transferred Archie to her other breast but he wasn't interested. He'd dropped off and was snoring lightly. All right for some.

'I decided I needed music to give me something to focus on,' Teresa continued. 'I had some relaxing birth music tracks. They were very soothing.'

Teresa's voice was soft and crooning, almost like a lullaby.

'Bronwen arrived at five fifteen and I was starting to have to lean over and sway my hips a bit during contractions, but was fine in between. However, when she arrived the "in between" bit disappeared and I had about four, one after the other.'

Nic felt her head drop. It hurt her neck. She jerked up again immediately and she had to sit back in the armchair. Otherwise she might topple forward on to the floor.

'Bronwen checked the baby's heart and said it was fine,' Teresa continued, 'and checked the position and said the head was fully engaged. She asked me if I wanted to go in the birth pool now. Fortunately it was all set up. I had the large, oval pool I'd ordered from *Mums* and it had a heater and filter unit, so the water was all ready . . .'

Something was pushing Nic's shoulder. She snapped her eyes open. Teresa's face was very close to hers.

'Are you all right?' she was saying, shaking her. 'Is something wrong?'

Nic sat bolt upright and looked around her. She was dazed, disorientated, and her mouth felt dry. She noticed Archie asleep on the sofa. Christ. She must have been asleep too. She had no idea for how long.

'No, no, nothing's wrong,' she said, running a hand through her hair. 'I'm so sorry, I had a bit of a late night . . .' She winked, hoping to make light of it.

It was a bad move. Teresa's face hardened. 'I'm sorry if I was boring you . . .'

Nic stood up and pulled down her blouse, which had bunched up round her waist. 'You weren't boring me at all. It was most interesting. I . . . it was my son's birthday,' she lied. 'We had a bit of a party.'

Teresa took a step back. 'A party? On a Thursday night? That's a funny day to have a party.'

Nic tried to smile. 'You know what it's like, lots of the parents stayed on for a drink . . .'

Teresa shook her head. 'Look,' she said, 'Archie will be awake soon and I need to get his lunch ready. I think it would be best if you went.'

Nic put her hand out to touch Teresa's arm but she backed away. 'Couldn't we just finish the interview?'

Teresa stared at her. Her eyes were cold and judgemental. She was so different from the soft, friendly woman of before. Nic looked away quickly.

'I don't think you're in any fit state . . .' Teresa started to say.

Nic wrung her hands. 'Please?'

'I'd like you to go,' Teresa repeated.

Nic nodded. There was no point arguing. She went into the hall, picked up her jacket and walked past Teresa in silence. She could sense the younger woman's eyes boring into her back. She had a horrible feeling that she knew what Teresa was thinking: lush, drunkard, piss-head. Nic raised her chin, straightened up and marched, as steadily as she could, down the garden path.

She'd find another woman to interview, it would be all right. It was just a bore, that's all, that she'd had a wasted journey. But bloody hell, what if *Mums* found out? She was about to turn, run back up the path and plead with Teresa not to say anything. She was a decent woman, maybe she'd take pity on Nic. Maybe Nic could persuade her that this was a one-off. She swung round at the exact moment that the front door banged shut.

Nic flinched and took a step back. The door was dark blue, with six black, expressionless windowpanes and a thin, letterbox mouth. She staggered slightly, as if she'd been struck.

A nasty feeling crept over her that maybe she wasn't going to get away with it.

She'd really blown it this time.

Chapter Thirty-One

❧

The mobile rang as she turned the corner into her street. Nic pulled over and parked underneath a tree. She needed to know immediately and she'd rather check here than at home. There was no one about. That was lucky, anyway.

It was a voice message. She realised that her hands were trembling as she pressed the button. She recognised the voice immediately.

'Nic. Can you call as soon as you get this. It's Annabel.'

That was it. No: 'How's tricks?' or: 'Hi honey, I've got a juicy fat commission for you.' She sounded formal and professional. There was a job to be done. Nic pressed the hache key to return the call. She counted five rings. Her heart lifted. Maybe she'd gone for a late lunch.

'Annabel Hadfield speaking.'

Nic could feel the pulse in her temples throbbing. 'C'est moi,' she said, trying to sound cheerful.

'Nic.' There was no warmth or pleasure in Annabel's voice. 'What *on earth* happened?' She emphasised the 'on earth'. Nic felt as if her body were getting smaller. She was crumpling up in her seat; her shoulders were caving in on her.

She swallowed. 'I'm sorry,' she said. 'I wasn't feeling well. I should have rearranged the interview.'

'Nic,' Annabel persisted, 'she said you were pissed. She could smell it on your breath.'

Nic felt sick, but she could use her charm; she'd make a joke of it. It would be all right.

She cleared her throat. 'Well, I may have had a glass or two last night but—'

'She said you were trembling and sweaty. You "absolutely reeked". Her words not mine.'

Nic laughed. 'It wasn't that bad. I had a bit of a hangover—'

Annabel interrupted again. 'You fell asleep in a chair with your mouth wide open. In the middle of the interview. Teresa was very upset. She said at first she thought you were ill and she was going to ring her husband. She nearly called an ambulance.'

'That's a bit of an over-reaction,' Nic chipped in. 'I only nodded off for a minute.'

Annabel ignored her. 'Then she realised you were rat-arsed. She said you looked wild and confused. She was actually worried about her baby.'

Nic was shocked. 'I'd never—'

'I know.' Annabel sounded softer now, less angry. 'But that's not the point,' she went on. 'The point is she was frightened, in her own home, by one of our writers. How do you think that makes us look?'

Nic was silent. She didn't know what to say.

'I'm afraid I've had to tell Julie.' Julie was the editor.

Nic gasped. 'But—'

'I couldn't cover up for you, Nic. It'd be my job on the line if I did.'

'What did she say?' Nic didn't want to know but she couldn't not ask either.

'She went ballistic – not surprisingly.'

'I'm so sorry.' Nic was crying now. Wet, salty tears were running down her cheeks and dribbling into her mouth. She sniffed. 'You've been so good about giving me work.'

Annabel sighed. 'Teresa said she bought *Mums* every month. She certainly won't be buying us again. At least she's only one reader.' Annabel laughed humourlessly. 'But honestly, Nic, what were you thinking of?'

'I don't know, I was stupid. I thought I'd be all right.'

'Well, you thought wrong,' said Annabel. 'What the hell were you doing last night anyway?'

Nic rubbed her eyes with her sleeve. A man walked past the car and peered at her strangely. She looked away.

'We had a bit of a party at home.' She was hardly going to reveal the truth.

'Bloody hell, Nic,' Annabel said. 'You seriously overdid things this time. I can't give you any more work, you know that, don't you?'

'Yes.' Nic's voice sounded very small. She felt about five years old. 'Did Julie say that?'

'She didn't phrase it quite so politely.'

'Do you think I should write to her?'

'I don't think that's a good idea.'

'Oh.' Nic felt numb. She'd known Julie for years, almost as long as Annabel. Julie had given Nic the deputy features editor job at *My World*.

'It was terribly unprofessional of me,' she whispered.

'Nic?'

'Yes.'

'Do you want some free advice from a friend?'

'OK.' She didn't really want it.

'Get help now, get yourself sorted out. For your family's sake, for Dominic, as well as for you. It's the least he deserves.'

Nic's face and neck felt hot. She wanted to lash out and hit somebody, or curl up and cry. She wasn't sure which.

She straightened up in her seat. 'Honestly, I don't need help,' she said brightly. 'I just had a bit too much wine last night and I've got a bug as well, which added to the problem. You know how it is.'

There was silence on the other end.

'We should go for lunch sometime,' she went on. 'A non-alcoholic one.' She laughed. 'It'd be good to catch up.'

'Bye, Nic,' said Annabel.

It was still only 2.15 p.m. Dominic was having tea with a friend. It was hours before she had to collect him. She fetched her laptop from the bedroom, put it on the kitchen table, plugged it in and started to type. Her fingers flew across the keyboard.

Fuck, if she couldn't be a journalist any more she was going to be a famous author. There was still six months to go before manuscripts had to be finished for the competition. She had time on her hands. She could do it.

'Beattie hated being back in London,' she wrote. 'She hated the rain, the drab, grey pavements, the way nobody caught your eye, nobody smiled. She longed to be back in Niger, despite the dangers. She longed to be in the arms of Adamou.'

Nic rolled her shoulders and stretched, glancing through the floor-length windows at the neat, symmetrical garden. It was getting dark. She'd been typing for two hours virtually non-stop. She felt quite excited. She was well over halfway through now and she knew where she was going.

This is what she should be doing, not writing for bloody *Mums* magazine. Stuff them. She felt bad about Annabel, though. Annabel was her friend. Annabel implied that she had an alcohol problem.

Nic bit her lip. She couldn't quite believe that she'd got herself into this situation. She couldn't understand why she'd thought she was somehow different, that she wouldn't become addicted like other people. It was arrogant, apart from anything else. Stupid.

She realised that her tummy was rumbling. Not surprising. She hadn't eaten all day. She always felt better, more human, as the hours wore on and her appetite returned.

She rose, stuck two pieces of bread in the toaster and waited for them to pop up before spreading them with butter and marmalade. She took her plate over to the laptop and started typing again. She hardly tasted what she was eating, she was focusing too much on the screen.

She felt powerful, in control of her plot and characters, a master creator. She wouldn't have a drink till after she'd picked Dominic up. And she'd have only one glass, that was it. Stop at one.

The phone rang. Bugger. Should she leave it? She picked it up.

'Nic? It's Evie.'

Nic pushed her chair back. She could afford ten minutes on the phone with her friend. She'd count it as her break. She smiled. 'Hey, how are you?'

Evie talked a lot about Neil. 'He thinks he can just come here any time he wants,' she complained.

'Can't you tell him not to?' They'd had this conversation so often. Nic wished Evie would stop being a victim and stick up for herself more.

'It's difficult, with the kids. I mean, it's important that we stay friendly for their sakes.'

'You can still be friends without him dropping by every day and treating the house like his own,' Nic pointed out.

'I know.' Evie sounded crestfallen.

'What does he think of Steve?'

Evie paused. 'He doesn't know about him.'

'Why not?'

'I don't know, I suppose I'm a little afraid of his reaction.'

'That's ridiculous,' said Nic. 'It doesn't matter what he thinks. You can't let him control you.'

Evie sighed. 'It's stupid, isn't it? When we were married he always told me what to do. I guess it's hard to break the habits of a lifetime.'

'Doesn't he ever call before he comes?'

'Rarely,' Evie replied. 'It's so unsettling for the children. By the way,' she said, thinking of something else, 'have you heard from Becca recently?'

Nic pondered for a second. They hadn't spoken since the November creative writing group. That was unusual.

'Not for ages. You?'

'No,' said Evie. 'She's probably just really busy at work. We'll see her on the twenty-first anyway. Hopefully she'll make it.'

'The twenty-first?' Nic was puzzled. Her memory was so bad these days.

Evie sounded almost cross. 'You know, the Creative Writing Group Christmas party? At your house – in case you've forgotten.'

Nic groaned inwardly. The party was to be in lieu of a formal December meeting. She'd volunteered to host it. It had seemed like a good idea at the time but it was bound to be a drunken affair. She felt as if everything was conspiring against her, as if everyone was determined to make sure that she remained pissed.

'Oh yes,' she said half-heartedly. 'Of course.'

She hadn't told Alan yet, not that it mattered. He'd either be out or working upstairs.

A shadow crossed her mind. 'Can I ask you something?'

'Sure.'

'Did Neil ever look at magazines – porn I mean? Or does Steve?'

'Not to my knowledge.' Evie sounded surprised. 'Why?'

Nic felt suddenly brave. 'I think Alan does sometimes – I found some magazines in his study.'

Evie giggled. 'What, *Naughty Nurses* or *Asian Babes* or something? I'm sure a lot of men like that kind of thing. They must, or there wouldn't be so many on the shelves.'

'But do you think there's any harm in it?' Nic persisted.

'Not really. I mean it's all just fantasy, isn't it?'

'What if the girls look very young?'

Evie hesitated. The hair on Nic's arms prickled.

'Well, they all look young, don't they?' Evie said finally. 'I mean, men are terribly predictable. Given the choice, they'd always pick a young, nubile thing over an old bag like you or me. It's just the way they are, the way they're wired. I don't think there's anything to worry about.'

Nic swallowed. 'I guess not.'

Chapter Thirty-Two

❧

'God, Nic, you stink of booze.' Nic was taken aback. Dr Kelly looked really concerned.

Nic had booked an emergency appointment. She was lucky to get it, given that it was only three days before Christmas, and many people had stopped work.

She'd stood naked in front of her bedroom mirror this morning and stared. One breast looked larger than the other, unless she was imagining it. She'd flattened her hands and run the palms over both her breasts and up into the armpits, feeling for lumps. The tissue felt soft and smooth as usual. But then, when she stood back and looked again, the right was definitely larger than the left. There must be something wrong.

'Pop over to the bed and take your top and bra off,' Dr Kelly had said, drawing the sickly pink and green striped curtain around Nic to preserve her modesty. Which was rather un-necessary, Nic thought, given that they were the only people in the room.

Nic had perched awkwardly on the edge of the bed while Dr Kelly looked carefully at both breasts. The surgery was warm, but Nic felt goose-pimply and vulnerable.

Dr Kelly raised an eyebrow. 'You do realise that it's perfectly normal to have one breast slightly larger than the other?'

Nic nodded. She guessed it was. She felt foolish.

Dr Kelly had come up close to examine Nic more carefully. 'This might feel a bit chilly . . .' She'd taken a step back and gasped. Presumably the stink of stale alcohol was oozing from every one of Nic's pores.

It had been the St Barnabas's Creative Writing Group Christmas Party last night and they must have drunk at least a bottle of wine each. Nic had also downed a bottle on her own before they arrived. Well, she'd had to. The others couldn't keep pace and it would have been embarrassing to top her own glass up more than everyone else's. Far better to get tanked up in advance.

Alan had been in the office all day catching up on work, despite the fact that it was Sunday. He'd come home when the party was in full swing and headed upstairs quickly. Dominic more or less took himself off to bed. Pamela and the boring members of the group had left at ten-ish, but Nic, Evie, Russell, Jonathan and, surprisingly, Tristram, had continued carousing until the small hours.

Nic, who was still naked from the waist up, looked at Dr Kelly fearfully. She crossed her arms across her chest, but that felt silly, so she uncrossed them again. 'I had a party last night,' she explained.

'You must have had an awful lot to drink because you still smell of it. And you look terrible. Your breasts are fine,' Dr Kelly added abruptly, passing Nic her clothes. 'But what about *you*?'

Dr Kelly was staring at Nic's face now, as if finally decipher-ing a code that had been written there for years. Nic flinched under the spotlight.

'Actually, you know, I think I might be drinking a bit too much. I'm not too sure,' she stammered.

'How much?' Dr Kelly said sharply.

'A bottle or so of wine a night.' Nic closed her eyes, waiting for some stinging rebuke. But none came.

'That's not good,' Dr Kelly said matter-of-factly. 'You should have told me about this before. But there are people who can help, you know, there are organisations that specialise in this. Shall I give you the number?'

Dr Kelly walked over to her desk to look something up in a book. Nic fumbled with her bra and top before joining her. She hovered awkwardly while Dr Kelly wrote something on a slip of paper and handed it across. Nic glanced down nervously. On it was written the name Alcoholics Anonymous and a tele-phone number.

Nic swallowed, folded the piece of paper into several pieces

237

and shoved it in the back pocket of her jeans. She'd heard of AA, but she didn't associate it with people like her. But Dr Kelly was right, she did need help.

'Thanks,' she said, genuinely grateful. 'I'll call them.'

Dr Kelly sat behind her desk and glanced at her computer screen, presumably to check on her next patient.

'Yes,' she said, 'they're the experts. And if you want to talk to me again about this you can make a longer appointment.'

Dr Kelly was a very good GP, but she had ten more patients waiting outside and Nic's allotted time was up. Nic staggered out of the surgery feeling dazed. So Dr Kelly thought she was an alcoholic. That was that then. It must be true.

She was confused, though. It wasn't supposed to happen to women like her, with husbands and money and nice homes and two cars in the driveway. She felt for the piece of paper in her back pocket. It was reassuring to know that it was there. But she wouldn't ring today, not with Christmas just round the corner and more parties to go to. There was too much going on.

She opened the door of her car and climbed in. She loved Christmas parties. She loved the decorations, the dressing up, that warm glow of goodwill that seemed to envelop all but the most curmudgeonly, the racing from one event to another with no time to think in between.

She excelled herself at Christmas parties, she was the life and soul, louder, more outrageous, funnier than anyone else. Christmas parties were her stage, her opportunity to perform. No, she wouldn't do anything right now, just before Christmas. She'd wait till early January and act then. That was the sensible thing to do.

She and Alan had been invited to three parties the next day, starting with drinks at noon with the Smiths in Kensington. Nic knew they'd be smart occasions. She wore a stunning multicoloured silk Roberto Cavalli halter-neck top with a ruffle neckline, along with black satin skinny-legged Philosophy di Alberta Ferretti pants and Jimmy Choo sandals. None of your Gap sale rail today.

They raced from the Smiths to the Dwyers in Richmond, where they had more champagne. Nic found herself standing next to a relatively well-known actor. She asked lots of questions; she knew actors loved talking about themselves.

They got on so well that she felt able to ask if she could interview him for a women's magazine. She didn't know which one, but she was sure that she'd find someone who hadn't heard of the Teresa debacle and blacklisted her.

The actor rarely gave interviews but agreed because, he said, Nic would be doing it. Normally he hated journalists, but she was different. He was a bit leery, in fact. He kept telling her that he thought her turquoise braces were cute. But Nic was delighted with her coup. She could handle a bit of leching in exchange for a scoop.

She was on a real high when they left the party around 4 p.m. But Alan, who was at the wheel, was tight-lipped as they drove away.

'You're drunk again,' he accused. 'And you were flirting outrageously with that actor. It was embarrassing.'

'I'm not drunk,' she lied. 'Why didn't you come and join us?'

'I didn't want to break up your intimate little tête-à-tête.'

'It wasn't an intimate little tête-à-tête. Don't be ridiculous. I was trying to persuade him to give an interview, which he did by the way.'

'Well done.' Alan stared at the road ahead. 'Just make sure you're sober when you meet up or your article won't make sense and you'll get even fewer commissions.'

Nic, wounded, felt obliged to defend herself. 'How dare you criticise my work? I'm not getting commissions for the simple reason that advertising is down and magazines are having to write far more in-house.' She bit her lip, remembering Teresa. Thank God he'd never know about that.

'Well, I'll tell you now, I'm not coming to the Bergs later,' Alan said. 'I've had enough of going to parties with you. You shouldn't go either. You'll only get even more drunk.'

Nic felt tears welling in her eyes. She poked the corners with her forefinger. She wanted to tell him that she was going to go to AA in January, that she'd sort herself out then. But she didn't dare. They spent the rest of the journey in silence and as soon as they got home, Alan went straight upstairs.

'Cup of tea?' she called after him.

'No.' He slammed his study door.

Nic went to find Dominic. She'd asked her neighbour's au pair, Anna, to babysit and they were both in Dominic's bedroom, sitting on cushions on the floor listening to music. There were a couple of Coke cans lying around, empty packets of crisps and dirty clothes. The usual stuff.

'Hi,' she said, putting out a hand to steady herself on the chest of drawers. She beamed. She was the perfect mamma, home from a party to see her beautiful boy. Who was she kidding?

'Hi,' Dominic replied, without looking at her. She was annoyed that he didn't get up to give her a kiss.

'Turn the music down so I can talk to you,' she said.

'What?'

He didn't seem pleased to see her.

'Turn the music down!' she repeated.

Dominic fiddled with the volume on the CD player at the foot of his bed. Now at least she could hear herself think.

She glanced around the room. Anna, who was Polish, rose. 'You have had nice partee?'

Nic, still upset about Dominic, ignored her. 'I'd like you to tidy up your room now, Dominic, it's a mess.'

He picked up a plastic Lego Transformer model that was on the floor and started pulling at its head. 'Later.'

'No, now.' She glared at him. Where was her hug and kiss?

Anna, clearly uncomfortable, took a step towards the door. 'You need me for anythink else or I go now?'

Nic pulled back her shoulders and managed a thin smile. 'No thank you. I've left your money on the hall table. I'll be down in a minute.'

'Bye, Dominic.' Anna smiled as she left the room.

'Bye. Thank you.' Dominic smiled sweetly back.

Stung, Nic turned to him again. He'd now pulled the head off his Transformer and was yanking at an arm. He still wouldn't look at her. She picked up a pair of jeans that were lying beside his bed, folded them roughly and tried to shove them in a drawer. It wouldn't close, so she kicked it with her foot.

'Durr, they don't go in there,' Dominic said, finally looking up. 'They go in the one above.'

'Don't be rude,' Nic spat. 'Don't talk to me like that. You're a rude little boy.'

'"Don't talk to me like that",' he said imitating her voice. 'Are you drunk?'

'What?' She must have misheard.

'I know you've been drinking alcohol because you're all clumsy.'

She narrowed her eyes and snatched the Transformer from him. 'What did you just say?'

He stuck out his lower lip sulkily. 'Daddy says you're always clumsy when you're drunk.' He was still sitting on the floor. He drew his knees into his chest so that he was in a tight little ball.

'How dare you speak to me like that!'

Their eyes locked. Nic could see both fear and defiance in his gaze. The fear made her want to cry. The defiance infuriated her. She picked up a CD that was lying on his bed and threw it against the wall.

'You're grounded, young man,' she said, 'for a very long time.'

At last Dominic started to weep. He sat there, snivelling, like a beaten animal. She was shocked; no one was allowed to make her darling boy cry.

'I'm sorry, poppet,' she moaned.

She stepped unsteadily towards him, holding out her arms. She wanted to hug him, to make things all right again, to claim the kiss that she'd been after all along.

'Go away,' Dominic said in a muffled voice. He was so young still – only nine. But he seemed much more grown up sometimes. 'I hate you,' he went on, his face buried in his knees. 'I can't wait to grow up and leave this house and then I'll never have to see you again.'

Nic felt as if she'd been thumped in the stomach. She cried out and staggered towards the door. She could hardly see through the tears. She loved Dominic so much. She put her arm against the wall to stop herself falling.

'I was going to ask if you'd like to come to the Bergs party with me,' she whispered. 'I thought we could have a nice evening together, just the two of us . . .'

'I don't like the Bergs.'

'Well, you can bloody well go to bed then.'

It might only be 6 p.m. or thereabouts, but she wanted him to suffer.

'I will,' he said, climbing into bed in all his clothes and throwing the duvet over his head.

Nic stumbled downstairs. The au pair had taken her money from the hall table and left already. Nic poured herself a large glass of red wine in the kitchen and gulped it down. Sod the lot of them, she thought. This wasn't supposed to have happened. She couldn't stay here, with this atmosphere. And she did want to go to the Bergs. It would take her mind off things. She'd just have to go on her own.

She walked slowly upstairs again and flung off her clothes. The door to Alan's study was still closed. That was a relief, for once. She didn't want him to know what had happened with Dominic.

She pulled her black cocktail dress out of the cupboard. It was sleeveless chiffon, empire line, with a low cut, scooped neck and a velvet bow below the bust. She wore high gold sandals with it and lots of gold jewellery. Then she pulled up her blond hair – it was hardly long enough, but she managed to catch just enough to fasten it with a clip – and applied more make-up. She wouldn't bother to get rid of the old stuff. She wanted big, smoky eyes with masses of brown eye-shadow and black mascara.

She checked herself in the full-length mirror. Her skin was very pale and she had dark circles under her eyes but she looked interesting, a little bit heroin-chic. She blew herself a kiss. 'You're gorgeous, sweetie, no matter what anyone says.'

Her head felt muzzy but another glass of champagne would make it better. She grabbed her handbag and car keys, slammed the front door and tottered to Alan's Merc in her high heels.

She chose the Merc deliberately. It was the car Alan always took to work. Good. She hoped he'd be really upset.

She lowered herself into the driver's seat, turned the key in the ignition and revved up the engine. With luck, Alan would hear. Then she accelerated – fast – down the drive, kicking up the gravel as she went.

Chapter Thirty-Three

She turned the CD up loud and started singing to Oasis. 'Fuck you, Alan, I'll do what I fucking well like,' she belted over the music.

There was a fair amount of traffic on the road. She was in the wrong lane for the South Circular heading for Clapham but managed to weave across the road. Several cars honked at her. She'd have to concentrate. There would be dozens of police about so near to Christmas.

She slowed right down, gripping the steering wheel, and tried to focus on the road ahead but it was difficult to keep in a straight line. It was as if the car had a mind of its own and was determined to veer off to the left.

When she reached Clapham Common, where the party was, she sighed with relief. Nearly there. A small blue car started to overtake on the right. She checked her speed: she was doing 20 m.p.h. Safest that way. But he was obviously in a hurry. He seemed very close to her, only a few feet away. She could see the driver's short brown hair and the leather watchstrap on his wrist. He was going to hit her, surely?

She swerved hard to the left. She needed to get away from him. Far too hard. The steering wheel spun right round. She hadn't meant the movement to be so extreme. There was a tree, a big old London plane, right in front of her. She tried to brake but her foot missed the pedal.

There was a crash. She ricocheted forwards then back then forwards again. She was going to die. The airbag inflated, cushioning the impact. She could hear glass smashing and there was a sharp pain in her neck, then the car stopped moving. She sat there, shocked. Her right shoulder was throbbing. She wiggled her arms, her toes and legs. They seemed to move all right. She wasn't dead or paralysed.

She managed to shift a little to the left and clocked that the windscreen had shattered. It looked as if the bonnet had crumpled right up in front of her. She could see tree bark. A branch was poking through the passenger side. The car must be in a terrible mess.

'Alan will be furious,' she giggled. 'Poor old Alan and his fucking car.'

There were people around her. A man yanked her door open. 'Are you all right, love?'

She tried to take off her seatbelt but couldn't. She was all fingers and thumbs. The man moved round to the other side of the car, opened the passenger door and managed to unclick her. She tried to get out but couldn't; the airbag was blocking the way.

'I must hurry, I'm late for my party.'

The man took her arm and pulled her out. Her high heel caught the edge of the car and she fell on to the road. She thought she'd hurt herself, hurt her face, but she couldn't tell. There was no pain.

She heard the man speaking to some other people round about: 'She's drunk.'

'Look at the state of her.' It was a woman's voice this time. 'Fancy driving in that condition. She could have killed someone.'

The man helped her up off the floor and she stumbled to the edge of the pavement and sat down. She wiped her face with her hand. There was blood, quite a lot of it. The man passed her a hankie: 'Here. You've cut your face.'

She took it and said nothing.

For a moment she saw herself through everyone else's eyes. She was in the air, looking down on herself. She was expensively dressed, small, thin and elegant, probably in her forties. She was roaring drunk beside her posh, crushed car.

'She should know better,' another woman tutted.

'Shocking, isn't it,' came a different voice.

Nic didn't blame them. She would have said exactly the same.

Drunk drivers should be locked up for a long time. It was a wicked thing to do.

She could hear police sirens now. She gasped. She had to get away, run away from all these people. She tried to rise but couldn't. Her limbs were like jelly; they wouldn't do what she wanted.

Alan's face took shape in front of her, then Dominic's. He looked so sad and worried. He was crying: 'Mum!' She started to weep noiselessly.

'Come on, let's get you up,' someone said. She looked up and there were police officers standing over her. Two men and a woman. She glanced to her left and there seemed to be at least a couple more standing further off. She was surrounded. The woman and a man took her by the arms and helped her rise.

'Looks like you've got a few cuts and bruises,' the WPC said. She sounded kind. 'We'll get the paramedics to check you over.'

Nic could hear an ambulance now. Soon she was half walking, half being carried inside. She felt strange and disorientated. This seemed to be happening to someone else. A male paramedic with watery blue eyes was checking for broken bones, dabbing her face gently with cotton wool and strong-smelling antiseptic. 'We'll soon have you cleaned up.'

He helped her back outside and a policeman produced a breathalyser. Nic's stomach lurched. She took a step forward, wanting to bolt. She'd never make it. They'd catch her. Besides, her legs weren't strong enough and she thought she still had her high-heeled gold sandals on, though she couldn't be sure.

'We need you to blow into this – one, long, continuous breath,' the officer said.

Nic blew, meek as a child. She wasn't going anywhere. The light went straight from green to red. She had most definitely failed the test. She didn't care any more.

'We're going to take you to Walworth police station,' a WPC said firmly. 'I'd like you to get into the back of the car, behind the passenger seat. Can you manage that?'

'What about my car?' Nic's voice sounded very far away.

'Don't worry about that, we'll take care of it.'

Nic swallowed. She thought they'd put her in handcuffs. Isn't that what they normally did with criminals like her? She was relieved they didn't. Maybe they thought she was docile enough not to need them.

'How long will I be at the police station?' she asked, clambering in.

'As long as it takes to go through the procedures.'

'I'm so sorry.' She hung her head. 'I'm just so sorry.'

She was aware of passers-by watching as they drove off, judging her. This would be something to tell their friends and neighbours. She didn't feel drunk any more. The shock must have sobered her up. She was able to walk into the police station unaided.

'Do you understand why you're here – because you've had a positive breath test?' the duty sergeant asked.

'Yes.' She gave him her name and address.

They went through the legal procedures. She felt as though she were in a dream. A solicitor was present when she repeated the breath test. She was three times over the limit and they charged her with drink driving straightaway.

'Can I go home now?' she said, when they'd taken all the details.

'Not till the doctor's seen you and says you're fit to be released.'

Nic made no protest when they removed her watch and jewellery, her belt and hair tie, and led her to the cell. It was just as she'd imagined: cold, basic, too bright. But it was no more than she deserved.

'My husband and son,' she said, panicky. 'They'll be so worried. Will someone tell them where I am?'

'We'll give your husband a call,' the police officer said. 'With luck you'll be out by early morning.'

'Thank you,' she said, grateful for his gentle manner. She hated herself enough. She didn't need abuse.

She slept fitfully, aware that someone was checking up on her every fifteen minutes or so. Perhaps they thought she'd try to commit suicide. It wasn't a bad idea, actually. And all the time she was thinking: What on earth is Alan going to say? What will Dominic say? I am so ashamed.

* * *

Evie received the call around 10 p.m.

'Evie? It's Alan.'

'Hello,' she said, surprised. Alan never phoned her. 'Get off!' She and Steve were on the sitting-room sofa together. He was nibbling her earlobe.

'I beg your pardon?' Alan sounded anxious.

'I'm sorry.' Steve was tweaking her nipple now, deliberately trying to distract her. She managed to stifle a giggle.

'I just had a call from Walworth police station,' Alan went on. 'Nic's been in an accident.'

'Oh God.' Evie sat bolt upright, pushing Steve into the corner. 'Is she all right?'

'Just a few cuts and bruises by the sound of things,' Alan sighed. 'Evie, she was drunk. She crashed my car into a tree. It's a miracle she didn't kill anyone – or herself.'

Evie put her head in the hand that wasn't holding the phone and rubbed her eyes. 'I knew she'd been drinking a lot. I feel so bad . . .' Her voice trailed off.

'It's not your fault,' Alan interrupted. 'I've spoken to her about her drinking time and again but she wouldn't listen.'

Evie glared at Steve, who got the message and skulked out of the room. She couldn't have a proper conversation with him there.

'Where is she now?' She had so many questions.

'Locked up – can you believe it?' There was a note of disgust in Alan's voice. Evie cringed. For a second, she thought she knew how Nic must feel when she was drunk. She wasn't sure that Alan's judgemental attitude would do much to help.

'How long for?' Evie asked.

'Overnight, or until four or five a.m. They have to wait until she's sobered up enough to be examined by a doctor. Apparently she was way over the limit.'

'Where did it happen?'

'Clapham Common. She was on her way to a party. I should never have let her go. We'd had a row about her drinking and she stormed off. I'm afraid I didn't try to stop her. I, well, I'd just had enough I suppose.'

Evie swallowed. She couldn't imagine her friend in a police cell. Nic would feel so frightened – and alone.

'What'll happen to her after that?'

'She's been charged with drink driving and she'll have to go to court. They said they'd explain it all when I collect her. Apparently the car's a terrible mess.'

Evie grimaced. She couldn't care less about the stupid car. 'What can I do to help?' She'd never liked Alan much but she wanted to be there for Nic.

'Actually that's why I was calling.' Alan sounded relieved. 'Do you think you could come over and look after Dominic while I go to the police station? I'm sorry to ask, right before Christmas. I've tried everyone else I can think of but they're all busy . . .'

Evie thought for a second. 'Of course. I can ask Steve – he's, er, my boyfriend – to look after my kids. I'll be with you in about half an hour.'

'Thank you.' Alan sounded really grateful. 'I can give you the spare room. It's just that I need you to be here when Dominic wakes up.'

Evie felt dazed as she wandered into the kitchen to find Steve. He was sitting at the kitchen table, a bottle of red wine and an empty glass in front of him, listening to some sort of chat show on the radio. She noticed that he'd opened the expensive Châteauneuf-du-Pape that she'd been saving for a special occasion.

'What's up?' he said, filling his glass. 'Don't tell me, Nic's got pissed again? Well, that's a surprise. What a lush.'

Evie felt her face go hot. 'Don't talk about Nic like that,' she spluttered. 'She's got a problem. She needs help.'

'I bet that boring old accountant husband of hers is upset.' Steve sniggered. Evie hated that snigger. He took a large slurp of wine. 'It'll be in the local paper.' He rubbed his hands together and grinned. 'He won't like that.'

Chapter Thirty-Four

'What are you doing, Mummy?'

Becca looked up from her laptop and smiled. Alice was standing at the door in her blue and white checked pyjamas with the daisy on the pocket. Her fair curly hair, so often pulled back in bunches or a ponytail, was framing her face, which was still pink from the bath.

'I'm writing my book,' Becca said. 'Did Monica remember to wash your hair?'

Alice nodded. Monica, the au pair, had agreed to look after the children while Becca worked.

'Come here,' she said, patting her knees.

Alice ran over and climbed on her mother's lap.

'Shall I read you a little bit of the story?' Becca asked.

'No, I'll read to you,' Alice said firmly. She was only six but you could tell she was very bright. She was always asking questions.

Becca smiled. 'Go on then.'

Alice peered at the screen and began to read slowly. '"The children ran across the field following Scruffy . . ." Who's Scruffy, Mummy?'

'He's the dog,' Becca explained patiently.

'"It was getting dark,"' Alice went on. '"In the distance they could see Farmer Scrubs's barn. There was a light on. 'I think we should go back,' H . . . Hed . . ."'

'" Heidi",' Becca said.

'Heidi,' Alice repeated. '". . . Heidi said. 'Don't be silly,' Josh replied. 'We need to see what Farmer Scrubs is up to.'"'

Alice leaned back. 'What is he up to, Mummy? Is Farmer Scrubs a bad man?'

Becca laughed. 'You'll have to wait and read the story when

it's finished. Now go and help Daddy with the Christmas decorations. I'll be with you in five minutes.'

'OK.' Alice hopped off her mother's lap and ran out of the study. Becca could hear her bumping down the steps on her bottom – she always did that – and thundering into the first-floor drawing room below. She made a big noise for a little girl.

Becca turned back to the screen and frowned. Farmer Scrubs *was* a bad man. Becoming increasingly so, in fact. It worried her a little that the story was taking a rather more sinister turn than she'd intended. She mustn't make it too frightening. It was a children's book, after all.

She put her thumb in her mouth and started to nibble on her manicured nail but stopped herself. Her weekly mani-pedis cost a fortune. She pushed the thumb further into her mouth, feeling for the rounded corner of the nail with her tongue. Then, quickly and deliberately, she brought her canine down and bit the corner right off. The lump of nail felt huge in her mouth. She grimaced – the clear varnish tasted bitter – and spat the nail into her other hand.

She stared down at the savaged nail that only a moment ago had been so hard, smooth and perfect. She ran her forefinger over the jagged, uneven edge. It pierced the skin slightly, which she liked. One by one, she bit little chunks off the edges of all her fingernails, crunched them up and swallowed them. Once she'd started she couldn't stop; it was addictive. She always used to chew her fingernails – back then. She'd forgotten how satisfying it was.

Alice didn't bite her nails. She was a happy, secure child. She loved her family so much. Becca had suggested that they spend Christmas at the Normandy farmhouse; it would have been a relief to get away. But Alice had been adamant. 'I want to stay here with all my toys.'

'But you'll have new toys for Christmas,' Becca argued.

But Alice wouldn't listen to reason. She'd frowned and crossed her arms over her chest. 'I like it here,' she insisted. 'It's cosier.'

But for how long? Becca shivered. She'd had a text from Gary the day after they'd had dinner in the pub in Kew and they'd agreed to meet again on 8 January. At least she had a couple of weeks' grace. Since then she'd heard nothing; with luck he was busy with his family. But every time her phone rang or an email plopped into her inbox her heart started hammering. This was no way to live but she could see no way out either.

Strange that she'd found herself using every spare moment she'd had since that dinner to get on with her book. It was a welcome distraction, she supposed, and also at the back of her mind, perhaps, was the thought that before too long she might be needing another career. She mustn't think about that, though. It was easier just to plough on, get stuck into her plot, lose herself in her characters. Work, work. She was like a little donkey, always working.

Something made her get up and walk to the window overlooking the street. The black Venetian blinds were closed. She separated them just a little and peeked out.

It was a clear, cold night. There were quite a few streetlamps around the green and she could make out several people walking across the middle of the flat grass, on their way to the pub or theatre, perhaps. They were well wrapped up.

She glanced over to the right and noticed a huddle of what looked like youngsters crouching on the grass under the trees. They were wearing a uniform of baggy trousers and hoodies. A number of them were smoking. She could see the glowing ends of cigarettes bobbing around in the darkness.

You often saw groups of teenagers on Richmond Green. They were too young to go to the pub; Becca supposed the Green must be one of the few places where they could hang out, and they did so in all weathers. Mostly they were no trouble but occasionally they'd become rowdy, a scuffle would break out and the police would turn up to move them on. Becca felt quite sorry for them. There should be youth clubs and things for them to go to.

She looked directly below her, on to the pavement beneath the window. Something caught her eye just across the road: a movement. There was a large tree with a thick trunk and branches that reached way up. She didn't want to but she felt compelled to stay fixed on the tree, waiting to see what it was that had attracted her attention. A fox, perhaps?

At last a shape half emerged from behind the trunk. It was clearly a man, dressed in some sort of dark jacket – leather probably. The collar seemed to be turned up against the cold. Becca remained stock still, scarcely breathing. After a few moments the figure stepped fully out into the clearing in front of the house, between two trees. He seemed to stare at the house for a few moments before looking up at her top-floor window.

The lamplight was bright enough for her to make out certain features: the receding hair, the sideburns, that same black and red rucksack over his shoulder. She gasped. Her whole body was frozen, a block of ice.

Gary. What do you want of me?

She snapped the blinds shut and staggered back several paces into the middle of the room. So he knew where she lived. She wondered how long he'd been there. Maybe this wasn't the first time. Maybe he was going to knock. Then it would all be over.

'Mu-ummy! Hurry up!' It was James's voice.

Becca was propelled back into the four walls of her study. She walked over to the laptop, logged off and closed it. Her fingers were trembling. She scrunched her hands into a fist, feeling the sharp, savaged nails digging into her palms. That helped to steady her nerves. She wondered if anyone would notice her ruined manicure. She could always file the nails down later.

As if any of that mattered now.

In other circumstances the scene that greeted her in the drawing room would have made her glow with pleasure: a giant, dark-green Christmas tree – eight feet high at least – was in front of the bay window that was obscured by thick, floor-length, red and gold curtains. There was a large, crackling, log-effect gas fire that made the room feel snug and warm despite the high ceiling.

Tom was on his hands and knees, making the final adjustments to the stand that held the tree in place. Becca noticed that he was wearing his Ralph Lauren jeans and the dark-green cashmere sweater that she'd given him last Christmas. It was a good combination. On his feet were his tartan Black Watch slippers.

However, there was an expanse of white back and a hint of builder's cleavage owing, no doubt, to the fact that the jeans were rather tight and he had to wear them below his paunch. He'd put on a bit more weight recently. She felt a surge of love. She used to chide him about his weight, try to force him on diets, but now, she realised, his chubbiness was part and parcel of what she loved about him. He seemed to be puffing and grunting a lot, but in a good-natured sort of way.

The children were taking decorations out of the two big gold boxes that they lived in when they weren't being used and turning them over in their hands.

'This one's beautiful!' Alice said, holding up a see-through glass bauble that looked like an icicle.

'Here's the reindeer!' James cried, examining the wooden toy that Becca remembered buying at a market stall in Vienna some years before.

Tom – or Monica – had put the King's College Christmas carols CD on. 'Glory to the newborn king!' trilled an angelic-sounding boy. There was a smell of pine, as well as cinnamon and nutmeg from the winter displays that Becca had placed on each of the mahogany consoles. All in all, it was a scene of perfect family harmony.

Tom got up at last and grinned at Becca, flashing the dimples in both cheeks. His face was pink and glowing from the exertion. 'What do you think?' he said, standing back to admire his handiwork. 'Is it straight?'

She eyed the tree critically. 'I think it might need to go just a little further to the left.'

He crouched again, uncomplaining, beneath the prickly branches. 'Can you push it?' he asked, his voice sounding slightly strangled.

Becca obliged. The tree moved a fraction to the left.

'There,' Tom said, pushing himself up to standing again with his hands. 'Happy now?'

Becca nodded.

'A glass of champagne for the lady?' He was in a very jolly mood.

'Can we have hot chocolate?' Alice asked, jumping up and down on the spot.

Becca moved swiftly to grab the silver bauble from her hand. It was from an expensive Harrods set. 'Careful, or you'll drop it.' Why was she bothering?

'Champagne would be lovely,' she said, turning back to her husband and managing a smile. 'Let's make a start on the decorations, kids, while Daddy gets the drinks.'

Becca needed the little step ladder from the library next door to put the angel on the top of the tree. It had a porcelain head and arms with a sheer white over gold silk skirt trimmed with marabou feathers, feather wings and a gold halo. She'd bought that in Vienna, too.

She wondered every year whether it was rather tacky, but it fulfilled a need: as a child she'd looked longingly at the exquisite angels on other children's real trees. Dawn had had to make do with a small, artificial tree and a miserable, plastic fairy that Mam had bought from the local tat store.

Mam . . . Mum . . . She flinched. What would she be doing now? And Jude. So long buried. Just rotting bones. Gary, everything that was happening: it was retribution of course. How vain, how arrogant she'd been to imagine that she could walk away and start all over again.

She felt giddy and wobbled on the ladder.

'Steady on,' Tom said. 'Are you all right?'

His voice brought her back to the present. She clutched on to the side of the ladder and stabilised herself. The dizziness faded. 'I almost lost my balance,' she said. 'Silly me.'

When she'd finished and Tom had turned the lights on, Alice gasped: 'That's beautiful.' Her eyes were saucers.

Becca climbed down from the ladder and wheeled it back into the library. Then she stood beside Tom, one arm lightly round his waist, the other holding her champagne glass, staring. He gave her shoulder a squeeze.

'Are you sure we want that manky old Father Christmas decoration?' he asked, pointing to a moth-eaten-looking cardboard and fabric figure near the bottom of the tree.

'Yeah, it's rubbish,' James agreed. He moved to take it off.

'No,' Becca cried. She was surprised by the shrillness in her voice. James stopped in his tracks.

'You made it at nursery school, don't you remember?' she told him. 'I love it. And the clay star over there with glitter on that Alice made when she was three. They're so precious, they're part of our family history.'

James looked at his mother incredulously. 'Mum, they're just rubbish old—'

Tom's laugh curled around them like sweet-smelling cigar smoke. For a moment, Becca relaxed.

'Mother says the dodgy old decorations should stay, so stay they shall,' he pronounced. 'More champagne, darling?'

It was late by the time they got the children to sleep – nearly ten o'clock. Alice would be tired tomorrow but at least she could sleep in. Becca lay on the handmade, creamy wool and silk rug in front of the fire. She'd had a quick shower and changed into her white cotton flannel pull-ons, a soft grey long-sleeved, ribbed T-shirt and pink cashmere bedsocks.

She hadn't looked outside again. He'd knock if he wanted to. He'd do what he liked when he was ready. She was in his hands.

Tom, who was still wearing his jeans and jumper, came and lay on the carpet beside her. He propped himself up, like her, on his elbow. Their heads were just a few inches apart, but their bodies fanned out and away from each other. Some Mozart was playing quietly in the background.

He smiled. 'This is nice. Peace at last.' He put a hand over hers. 'Your hands are cold.'

She frowned.

'What's the matter?'

'Nothing.'

'No, go on. I can see something is.'

She sighed. 'Do you think we should have gone to Normandy for Christmas?' The words came out in a rush. His hand was still there, warming hers.

'Why? Do you?'

She shook her head. 'Not really. Well, I just wondered if it would have been a good idea to get right away.'

It was his turn to frown. 'Why didn't you say so if that's what you wanted?'

She took her hand away. She couldn't keep still. 'I don't know. Well, Alice was so adamant that she wanted to be here and you didn't seem bothered and it's quite a lot of work to organise.'

He sat up and scratched his head. 'It's not that I wasn't bothered, Becks. It's just that you didn't mention it so I thought you'd decided you'd rather be here, too. I wish you'd make up your mind.'

She glanced up at his face. He looked almost hurt. She was sorry. She didn't want to spoil the moment. It was lovely to have him here, all to herself, without the telly on and with no newspapers to distract him either. She should savour it.

She sat up, too, and shuffled over to his side, her legs crossed, resting her head on his shoulder.

'I'm sorry,' she said. 'I didn't mean to sound dissatisfied. I'm happy we're spending Christmas in London. I've just had such a lot on at work recently, I think I'm worn out. I can't think straight.'

Tom put his arm around her waist and stroked her side. The cotton T-shirt she was wearing felt soft and soothing against her skin. His hand moved up under her armpit to the area where her bra would normally be. He seemed to be searching for the strap.

Finding none, she felt his body tense a little in recognition. His fingers snaked around under her armpit to her breast which was indeed naked under the T-shirt. The rest of his body was still but his breath became heavier. He found the nipple and began twisting it tentatively between his fingers.

Becca's head was still on his shoulder, one hand on his knee, the other on her own in front of her. She allowed his hand to roam for a moment, enjoying his enjoyment, feeling his body heat up like a radiator.

At last he turned and looked into her eyes. His own were so full of passion and longing that she wanted to cry.

She hated herself for having pick-picked at their relationship like a child with a scab. For having spent years examining his faults like a forensic scientist, turning them over and over,

257

exploring them from every possible angle, without ever stopping to think about all the things that were wonderful about him.

Maybe she'd stopped herself from loving him fully because, after all, love was another emotion and she'd learned to keep these under control. And now here she was about to lose him.

She knelt up, wrapped her hands around his dear, curly head and gently pulled his mouth on to hers. Their tongues performed a sort of dance, like a swans' courtship ritual, moving this way and that, in and out, in perfect synchrony.

She broke off suddenly: 'Monica,' she said, glancing towards the open door.

He got up swiftly and closed the door, turning off the table lamp on his way back so that the room was illuminated solely by the fire and the Christmas-tree lights. She raised her arms above her head while he removed her top. Then he took off his own, but she made him wait for her to unbuckle his belt and pull off his jeans.

She kissed the very tip of his penis and took him in her mouth, taking pleasure in his sighs of bliss.

'I love you, Becks,' he whispered.

She stopped what she was doing for a moment. When was the last time she'd said it?

'I love you so much, too.'

Chapter Thirty-Five

⁂

Nic looked terrible when she came through the door with Alan. Her face was ghostly white, her clothes twisted and crumpled, her shoulders bent, and there was dried blood on her lips, perhaps where the braces had rubbed. But Evie thought she noticed something else, too, something that she hadn't seen before: a strange calm.

She hugged Nic. 'Thank God you're OK.'

Nic's arms hung limply at her side. 'Thank you.'

She took a step back, her blond head bowed. She couldn't bear to catch Evie's eye. 'And thank you for looking after Dominic.' She glanced behind Evie, searching for him. 'Where is he?'

'Still asleep,' Evie replied. 'I haven't heard a peep from him.' It wasn't so surprising. It was still only 8 a.m.

Nic nodded. 'That's good. Thank goodness.'

'He'll find out,' Alan said sharply. 'You won't be able to hide it from him.'

Evie winced.

'I know,' Nic said wearily. 'I'd like to tell him in my own time, that's all.'

They sat, the three of them, sipping tea by the Christmas tree in the warm television room downstairs, the room where Evie and Steve had sat on the night of that famous party. There was a strong smell of pine coming from the tree, which was rather sparse. And there were too many red and gold decorations at the top and not enough at the bottom. She remembered Nic saying that she'd left it all to Alan. Clearly he didn't have Nic's artistic touch.

Brightly coloured Christmas cards were arranged higgledy-piggledy on every available surface. They knew lots of people.

259

Alan got up to make a phone call about the car – which had been towed to a nearby garage – leaving the two women alone.

'Evie?' said Nic, taking a deep breath. She was still in her party clothes from the night before, with a grey cardigan round her shoulders which Alan must have brought with him to the police station. She had no make-up on now, though, just a bit of smudged mascara round her eyes. She was hunched over and her thin little legs in opaque black tights were crossed. She looked fragile and old.

'Yes?' Evie said. She wondered what was coming.

'I've got a major drink problem,' Nic said quietly. She was twisting her wedding ring round and round on her skinny third finger. Evie noticed that her knuckles were red and bumpy and seemed too large for her hands. 'Will you stay with me while I call Alcoholics Anonymous?'

Nic looked straight at Evie. There was an honesty in her face that Evie didn't recognise. No more pretence. 'Of course I will. Thank God. I've been so worried about you,' she cried, giving Nic another hug. This time Nic hugged her back.

She wanted to make the call from her bedroom with the door shut, so there was no chance that Dominic would overhear. The two women sat on her bed with the antique French headboard. Evie admired the striking paisley wallpaper on the wall. The room felt so cool, elegant and ordered, she reflected, totally at odds with everything that was going on in Nic's chaotic life.

Nic talked and cried and talked a little more, while Evie flicked quietly through some glossy magazines on the bedside table. When Nic finally put down the receiver, she told Evie that someone was going to come round that very day, in a couple of hours. Even though it was Christmas Eve.

'Please will you stay with me? I'm sorry to ask you but I'm scared.'

Evie hesitated. She wasn't sure that she could leave Freya and Michael with Steve any longer. She didn't know what Steve's plans were. In fact, she realised that she had no idea what he intended to do for the rest of today or tomorrow, Christmas Day. She'd tried to pin him down but he'd been non-committal.

She rang the house phone on her mobile. They'd probably still be asleep, all three of them, but it wouldn't harm to wake them. Freya answered after what seemed like an eternity.

'Mum?' she sounded surprised. 'Where are you?'

Evie explained the situation swiftly. 'Can I talk to Steve?' she asked.

Freya yawned. 'He's not here. He left last night. He said something had cropped up.'

Evie started. The children were alone? Why hadn't he rung? She didn't mind Freya babysitting but she'd never, ever leave her and Michael on their own overnight. Her heart began beating faster. She thought rapidly. Her instinct was to go home straight-away but she was torn. Nic needed her, too.

'Darling, can you stay with Michael for just a little longer? I'm sorry but Nic would like me to be here.'

'No problem.'

'Are you sure you're all right?'

'Stop fussing. We're fine. Michael's still asleep.'

Evie swallowed. 'You won't let him go out anywhere?'

'Where would he go? Don't be silly, Mum.'

'There are a couple of pizzas in the freezer. You can have them for lunch.'

Freya yawned again. 'OK.'

Evie felt her shoulders relax. 'I'll be home as soon as I can. We'll go to Christingle this evening and have Christmas Eve supper together.'

She'd speak to Steve later, give him an earful. What the hell was he playing at?

'Not Christingle,' Freya groaned.

They went every year. Evie knew that the children were too old really, the service was aimed at small children, but it was one tradition that she couldn't bear to give up. They'd just have to swallow their irritation and go to Christingle for her sake.

Nic's doorbell rang around 1 p.m. Evie got up from the sofa in the television room to shake hands with a smartly dressed woman, who introduced herself as Celia.

Nic poured out her story while Evie listened, shocked to hear

261

that things were far worse than she'd ever imagined. Nic kept nothing back. Celia, well spoken, professional, explained how she, too, was an alcoholic who'd managed to keep off booze for three years. But she still took it one day at a time.

'Alcoholism is like a lift,' she said. 'You keep on going down and down, but you can get off at any level if you decide that's what you want. Or you can just stay on that lift until you hit rock bottom and literally lose everything: your home, husband, children. You can end up in the gutter. I've met plenty of people who have.'

Nic wept into a tissue. 'I so want to get better. Please help me.'

Evie left around three. She couldn't wait to get home. She was exhausted, but optimistic, too. Maybe this was Nic's wake-up call. Maybe this would set her on the road to recovery.

Neil's Alfa Romeo was parked outside. Evie swallowed. This was the last thing that she needed. She wanted to see the children, to hold them in her arms and make sure that they were all right.

She was also desperate to phone Steve and find out what he was playing at. It's true that he knew Freya often looked after Michael. It wasn't as if either of them were babies. But he shouldn't have left without telling her. He'd have to have a bloody good explanation.

She breathed in and out deeply. Calm, she told herself. Keep calm. Neil won't stay long. He'll be wanting to get back to his beloved, pregnant Helen. Once he'd gone, Evie could start thinking properly about Christmas.

Michael met her in the hall. Evie tried not to look at the crack on the wall which ran from ceiling to floor. It still upset her, every time she saw it. He was in socks and pyjamas still. His hair was uncombed and there were brown stains around his mouth. Breakfast Coco Pops? He looked small and slightly neglected. It tore at her heart.

She held out her arms and he walked into them. He was nine now; he had to pretend he didn't like cuddles.

'Where've you been, Mum?' he said sulkily. 'You've been ages.'

'I'm sorry, darling.' She wrapped her arms around him and squeezed tight. 'I wanted to leave earlier but Nic asked me to stay. She's not well. I had to help.'

'It's Christmas Eve,' Michael said, still resentful. 'It's supposed to be family time.'

Evie felt guilty enough already. She didn't need telling off. 'I know, and we're going to have a lovely Christmas from now on, I promise.' She kissed the top of his head and then pulled back, remembering. 'Where's Daddy?'

'Watching TV, I think.' Michael nodded towards the closed sitting-room door.

Evie's stomach clenched. Typical that Neil should be watching TV instead of spending time with the children that he professed to care so much about. She pushed the door open and strode in. He was sitting there, his feet on the coffee table in front, a pile of newspapers by his side. He looked as if he owned the place.

'Why is Michael still in his pyjamas?' she demanded. She couldn't help herself.

Neil looked up, a nonchalant expression on his face. 'Oh, so you've decided to show up, have you?' He picked up the remote and turned the volume down slightly, but not so much that he couldn't still hear the programme. 'That's good of you. I was shocked when Michael said you'd left them on their own all night. You shouldn't do that.'

He didn't look shocked, he looked rather pleased that he'd found her out. Evie could feel the blood pulsing in her temples. She wanted to hit him.

'It's a good job I came by,' he went on, turning back to the TV screen. 'Michael seemed to have no idea when you were coming home. I suppose you've been spending time with your new friend.'

He wrinkled his nose when he said 'new friend'. He could've been talking about something on the bottom of his shoe. The injustice of it hit her like a sledgehammer.

'What?' she blurted. 'So it's OK for you to shack up with some trollop but I can't have a boyfriend, is that right?'

She was aware of Michael hovering behind her. She ought

263

to stop but she couldn't. 'Don't you dare come in here telling me what to do with my children,' she went on. The words came at him like red-hot iron filings. 'You're lucky I let you see them at all after what you've done. You mean, lying, filthy little creep.'

Michael let out a sob. Horrified by her own outburst, Evie swung round to apologise, to comfort him, but he'd already dashed from the room.

Neil rose and snapped off the TV. 'You shouldn't speak like that in front of the children,' he said calmly. His sanctimony was sickening. 'Another time you want to spend the night with a man the children can stay with me and Helen.'

Evie thought she might spontaneously combust. She was a bull in a ring, surrounded by stupid, prancing matadors. 'I did not spend the night with some man,' she bellowed. 'Nic was in a car crash. She needed my help.'

Neil looked surprised. That was gratifying.

'And don't you dare imply that I'm sleeping around,' Evie roared. 'My boyfriend – though it's none of your business – is called Steve and I love him very much. In fact I think we'll probably get married.'

Neil was poker-faced but his eyes gave him away: he was stunned, no doubt about it. Evie realised even as she uttered the word 'love' that it was a lie. She wasn't sure that she loved Steve after all. Nor was she convinced that she was going to marry him, despite Zelda's predictions. But her words had hit home. She'd more than rattled Neil's cage: she'd sent the bastard flying.

He cleared his throat. 'Well,' he said, pretending to take it all in his stride. 'I didn't realise things were so serious. Congratulations. I'll need to meet Sam, er Steve, of course, before he has contact with the children. That is' – he looked at her beadily – 'if he hasn't already.'

Evie waited for a second, relishing her moment of power. 'I don't recall your discussing it with me before you introduced Freya and Michael to Helen.' She was quite calm herself now. 'And yes,' she went on, 'Steve has met them and I'm glad to say they like him very much.'

Neil's eyes narrowed. His face had turned an odd, puttyish

colour. 'Yes, well, I'd like to meet him all the same,' he said abruptly. 'I must go now. I'll say goodbye to the children.'

Evie stepped back to allow him to pass. He stopped at the door and turned around. 'Will Simon, er, Steve, be spending tomorrow with you?' He sounded young suddenly, faltering. 'Because I'd like to pop round at some point to give the children their presents?'

'It would be more convenient if you came on Boxing Day,' Evie replied. 'Around eleven a.m. would suit us.'

She could have punched the air when he left. She would have played this card so much sooner if she'd known the effect it would have. Neil was jealous, no doubt about it. He looked positively crestfallen. What's more, seeing him standing there, all winded and pathetic, she realised that she didn't fancy him any more. Not in the way that she once had, anyway. Not in that painful, all-consuming way that meant she couldn't think of anything else, couldn't focus on anyone else. This was progress indeed.

Now to sort out Steve.

Chapter Thirty-Six

'He does love you, you know, he's just got a lot on his mind.' Zelda paused. She was obviously having another drag on her cigarette.

'Yes, well, I've got a lot on mine too,' Evie replied, 'but I'd never have done what he did. The way he left without telling me was unforgivable – and now the fact that I can't even get hold of him . . .'

She was sitting on the edge of her bed watching the rain lashing past her window, bouncing off the grey pavements. Some Christmas morning. Some Christmas Day. She'd sneaked off to talk to Zelda after giving the children their traditional Christmas brunch of smoked salmon and scrambled eggs.

'You must be patient,' came Zelda's husky tones, 'it'll all become clear.'

Evie knotted one leg around the other. She was distracted for a moment by the pregnant young woman's gold wedding dress on the tailor's dummy in the corner of her room. She half closed her eyes, tipped her head on one side. It needed another row of crystals around the neckline. She'd had to buy more fabric and do a total redesign; they'd opted for a flattering empire line that would hide the bump. They'd need to wait until much nearer the time for the final fitting, though. Who knew how large the bump and the bust would grow?

'You still there?' Zelda asked.

Evie snapped out of her daydream. 'I've left countless messages,' she said, 'I don't know where he can be. And he hasn't even called to wish me Happy Christmas.'

She reached for a tissue from the box beside her bed and blew her nose. 'Are you absolutely sure he's The One?'

'Look, love, I can only tell you what I bin told.' Zelda sounded slightly scratchy. Evie had asked the same question so many times. 'But if you really want to find out more, to dig deeper, I'd advise regression.'

'What's that?' Evie was intrigued.

'It's very popular,' Zelda went on. 'A lot of my clients like it. I'm fully qualified, of course.'

'But what does it involve?' Evie had no idea.

'It's like therapy,' Zelda explained. 'Using hypnotism, you go back in time to a past life. You can find out how your past lives have influenced your relationships and make sure you don't make the same mistakes again, see.'

Evie shivered. 'It sounds scary.' There might be things in her past that she'd really rather not know about. She was fascinated too, though.

'It's not cheap,' Zelda said. 'It'll cost you seventy-five pounds.'

Evie sucked in her cheeks.

'It's up to you, darlin' . . .'

She knew she was going to do it.

'You'll have to book an appointment. It'll have to wait till the New Year.'

'The New Year?' That sounded such a long way away. 'But what am I going to do *now* – about Steve I mean?'

'Go and play with them kiddies of yours,' Zelda said firmly. 'That Steve'll turn up eventually with his explanation. Men always do.'

Evie put the phone down. The call hadn't exactly been satisfactory. She spent a fortune on Zelda but she really didn't feel that she'd had her full attention today – and now she was contemplating forking out seventy-five more pounds on this regression thing. Maybe Zelda was busy with Christmas arrangements, but Evie somehow doubted it. Zelda hardly ever talked about her own private life, but Evie had gleaned enough to know that she lived alone, had probably never been married and almost certainly had no children.

She could smell the turkey cooking downstairs. She thought Freya was in her room and Michael was probably watching TV. He'd be glued for hours if she let him. She bit her lip. She almost wished that she hadn't put Neil off. Last Christmas – their first apart – he'd been with them practically all day, probably because he felt so guilty. He cooked the meal and she nearly convinced herself that they were back to normal, that his leaving had all been a nightmare. She even remembered feeling happy, off and on.

Now she faced the prospect of spending the entire day alone with the children. They'd already opened their presents and there were hours stretching ahead that she'd somehow have to try to fill with Christmas spirit. She loved their company, that wasn't a problem. But it was hard having to do everything herself.

She tried Steve's number one more time. 'The mobile phone you are calling is switched off. Please try again later.'

Bastard. Tears sprang in her eyes. She threw the phone on the bed and stalked from the room. He was so cruel. She couldn't imagine an explanation in the world that would satisfy her.

She opened the sitting-room door. Michael was absorbed in some cartoon or other. She must think of him and Freya now, not herself.

'Hello, darling,' she said brightly, putting on her best happy mummy smile. 'I thought we'd have the turkey around five, OK?'

He grunted without looking up.

'Would you like to go for a walk?'

He ignored her. She repeated herself.

'In the rain?' he said at last, glancing over to the window. It was still bucketing down.

'We could put on cagoules and wellies. It's fun walking in the rain if you're well wrapped up.'

'Mu-um.' He gave her a look as if to say d'you think I'm three? before turning back to the TV.

The phone rang. She rushed to answer it in the kitchen. She was panting slightly as she picked the handset up.

'Eve, is that you?'

Her heart sank. It was her mother. She supposed she did have to speak to her mother on Christmas morning.

'How are you?' Evie tried to sound cheerful. 'And Dad? Are you having a nice day?'

'Not really,' her mother replied.

Evie sat down at the kitchen table. This was going to be a long one, she could just tell. 'Why's that?' she asked, not wanting to know.

'Your father's insisted on opening the shop so I'm all on my own.'

'Opening the shop?' Evie cried, 'but why, for Heaven's sake? Who on earth wants to buy furniture on Christmas Day?'

'I know,' said her mother gloomily, 'but you know what he's like. He says there might be people from other religions out and about – Buddhists for example. Or what's that religion that Madonna likes? Kabbalah, that's it. There might be some Kabbalah types.'

Evie laughed; she couldn't help herself. 'How many Kabbalah followers does he think will be wandering around Ottery St Mary on Christmas Day looking for furniture?'

'Well, you know he doesn't really like Christmas anyway,' her mother sighed. 'He'd rather be in the shop reading his book than stuck at home with me.'

Evie swallowed. She felt guilty. She could have taken the children to Devon, especially in view of the fact that they weren't now seeing Neil – and she wasn't seeing Steve. But the thought of being cooped up with her parents for several days was too much to bear. They'd spend most of the time criticising Neil – and her indirectly for having chosen him – and telling her how she should be managing her affairs.

'And you should get yourself a proper job,' her father would no doubt say. 'Your mother and I could help you find a decent franchise somewhere. Or you could join our business. This airy-fairy wedding-dress lark is all very well but it doesn't pay, never will.'

She was never, ever going to join their business. Not even if she were destitute. She'd rather slit her wrists. No, it was just as well that she'd refused their invitation for Christmas on the grounds that the children needed to see their dad. She was better off here. At least then she could wallow in her misery without her parents breathing down her neck saying, 'I told you so.'

* * *

wot u doing today beautiful?

Freya glowed with pleasure. *nothing much*, she wrote. *my mum's cooking. she's in a funny mood. i think she's upset about her boyfriend or sumthing.*

Freya's hair was annoying her. She scraped it up on the top of her head and fastened it with a scrunchie. That felt better.

why?

dunno. maybe cos he's not coming for christmas.

do u like him?

Freya got up, opened one of her curtains just a chink and peeped out. It was tipping down with rain outside. She closed it quickly. The room was almost pitch black, save for the muffled light coming from the little bedside lamp behind her which she'd covered with one of her black T-shirts.

hes a creep, she typed.

why?

She didn't want to think about him. Al was asking too many questions.

wot u doing anyway? she wrote. *where's your daughter?*

with her mum, Al typed back. *wish i was with u.*

Freya's insides ached. If only things were different. If only she'd picked a normal boy her own age.

mum and dad had a big row yesterday, she said. *I'm not seeing dad today.*

do u mind?

She thought for a moment. No, she didn't mind, she was relieved not to have to see the horrible girlfriend. She pictured Dad's smiling face. He was crouching down. She was a little girl running, running across the grass into his wide-open arms. He scooped her up and swung her round in a big circle. She swooped and swirled; she was a bird, flying in the sky.

She looked at the screen again. *a bit,* she typed.

wish i could c u. i miss u, he said.

well u can't. ur a middle aged man. its not right.

She regretted her words immediately. For an agonising few minutes she thought that he wasn't going to respond. At last he did.

love isn't always predictable Freya, he typed. *sometimes 2 people fall in love and to the outside world it seems completely wrong. only those 2 people know the truth.*

She scratched her head and shifted slightly in her chair. *yeah, i spose so.*

anyway, he said, *u r so grown up for your age. u don't seem like a child, u r so mature. if things were different id luv to take u away 4 a romantic weekend.*

A romantic weekend? Her tummy tingled. *where would u take me?*

maybe paris? he asked. *u ever been?*

Her heart started to gallop. She could see the Eiffel Tower, the shops and pavement cafés.

never, she replied. *ive always wanted 2 go.* She frowned. *but mum would never let me.*

she needn't know.

A thought crossed her mind. She waited, fingers crossed, willing him to read her. She was much too shy to suggest it herself.

At last his reply came back. She grinned, hugging her arms around her.

we could go to Disneyland 2 – if u like?

Evie was surprised to hear a knock at the front door. Neil? Her heart skipped. She checked herself and frowned. She'd specifically told him not to come today. This was very bad of him.

She opened the door. Bill was standing there in the porch clutching a brown paper bag. He was wearing his ancient-looking Barbour, but his head was uncovered and his face and silver-grey hair were sodden.

'Merry Christmas!' He smiled. 'I've brought you some potatoes from the allotment.' He thrust the paper bag into Evie's arms. 'They're Desiree, straight from the ground. They keep best there. They're resistant to pests, unlike other varieties.'

'Oh.' Evie was nonplussed. 'I was expecting . . .'

'I'll be off,' he said quickly. 'I only wanted to wish you a Happy Christmas and give you these. I've got masses, I can't eat them all and it seems a shame for them to go to waste. They're very good.' He started to go.

'Wait!' she cried. 'Come and have a drink. I mean, if you've time?'

'No thanks, I don't want to disturb—' He peered behind her, as if looking for someone.

'You're not disturbing anything,' she interrupted. 'It's just me and the children. Please, we'd love you to come and share some Christmas cheer with us. We need it, I tell you.'

'But I thought . . .'

Evie shook her head. 'I asked Neil not to visit today but when you knocked I thought he'd probably turned up anyway. You know what he's like.'

Bill frowned. 'He should respect your wishes. It's not on.'

She laughed. 'Respect my wishes? That would be a first.'

Bill hesitated. 'What about . . . ?'

Evie knew what he was thinking. 'Steve? Oh, let's not talk about him. He's in my bad books.' She peeped into the brown bag. There were five or six creamy brown potatoes in there, still with clumps of soil on them. 'They smell lovely,' she said, 'all earthy. We'll have them with our turkey.'

Bill rubbed his hands together. 'Turkey, eh? I'm having goose this year.' The corner of his mouth twitched slightly.

Evie cocked her head on one side. 'Any of the family with you?'

He shook his head. 'They did ask me to go and stay but to be honest, it's not good timing. Henry's in the middle of building work and the house is chaos and Robert's wife is eight months pregnant. She doesn't want her father-in-law around now. I remember how Jan felt when she was at that stage of pregnancy. She just wanted to be able to get on with turning out the cupboards and cleaning the inside of the washing machine.'

Evie laughed. 'I don't remember cleaning the inside of the washing machine when I was pregnant. But I did buy dozens of baby blankets and spend a lot of time rearranging them. Neil thought I was mad.'

'There you are,' Bill said, grinning, 'it's that nesting thing that women do. I'd hate to get in the way of a woman and her nesting.' He stamped his wellie-clad feet on the floor to keep warm. 'No,' he said, agreeing with himself, 'I'm in the best place, with my goose and my books. I'm rereading Trollope's *He Knew He Was Right*. Have you read it?'

She shook her head.

'Excellent stuff,' he said brightly. 'I'd forgotten how good he is on women and the inner conflicts caused by their position in Victorian society.'

'Bill!'

Evie swung round.

Freya was on the bottom stair. She beamed. 'Happy Christmas!'

Evie was startled. Freya rarely smiled, let alone at adults. Bill was blessed indeed. 'I was trying to persuade him to come in for a drink,' she explained.

'Please do,' Freya said. 'We need some company, don't we, Mum?'

Bill hesitated. 'Well, if you're sure? Just for half an hour . . .'

Evie grabbed his arm and pulled him inside. 'That's settled then,' she said happily. 'I've got homemade mince pies and a lovely bottle of mulled wine from M and S. You can try a little, Freya, it's delicious.'

They sat, the three of them, round the kitchen table, breathing in the roasting turkey smells and sipping mulled wine. Soon they were joined by Michael, clutching his Cluedo board. His eyes brightened when he saw Bill.

'Can we all play?' he said.

Evie glanced at Freya, expecting an immediate 'no'. She never played board games these days.

'Only if Bill does,' Freya said. 'He'll stop us arguing. We'll have to be polite if he's here. And only if I can be Miss Scarlet.'

Evie was flabbergasted. She looked at Bill. 'I like a good game of Cluedo,' he said, rubbing his thighs. 'But be warned – I get very competitive.'

Evie giggled. 'Well, so do I. In fact I always win, don't I, kids?'

Michael plonked himself down next to Freya. 'Rubbish,' he said. 'You're always so desperate to win you don't check all your clues, then when you turn the cards over you've got it wrong and ruined the game.'

273

Bill snorted. 'Does she really do that? Shocking.'

Evie felt herself blush. 'It only happened once,' she insisted. 'Well, maybe twice . . .'

Bill took another sip of wine, draining his glass. 'OK,' he said, leaning forward, 'I can see I'm going to have to have my wits about me if I'm going to thrash Evie. I'll be Reverend Green. I've always rather fancied myself as a country vicar.' He looked at her. 'Are you sure we've got time to play? I mean, I don't know when you're planning to eat?'

Evie put a hand on his. 'The turkey's going to be hours yet. Honestly. It's lovely to have you here.'

Michael stood up. 'I'll be Colonel Mustard,' he shouted.

Freya raised her eyebrows. 'Honestly, he always gets over-excited like this when he plays Cluedo.'

Michael glared at his sister.

'I refuse to be boring old Mrs White stuck in the kitchen,' Evie said firmly. 'I'll be Mrs Peacock. Now, who's going to go first?'

Bill wiped his mouth on his napkin, put it on the table and leaned back in his chair. 'Delicious,' he sighed, patting his stomach. 'The best Christmas pud I've had in years.'

It hadn't taken much to persuade him to stay for dinner. Evie couldn't bear the thought of him all alone on Christmas Day with only his books for company. But she wasn't just being charitable. It was much more fun having him there anyway. His green paper hat was perched at a jaunty angle on the top of his head and he had bits of silver streamer from Freya's party popper round his neck.

'I'm stuffed,' Michael announced, burping.

'Don't do that,' Evie scolded. 'It's rude. Anyone for dates or chocolate brazils?'

Bill, Michael and Freya groaned.

Michael found a spooky film for them to watch on TV called *The Orphanage*. Evie turned up the heating a little and drew the curtains. It was still drizzling outside: cold and black and miserable. She realised that she hadn't been out all day but she hadn't missed it; to her surprise, they'd had what she could only describe as a pretty perfect Christmas, despite Neil's absence. In fact she couldn't remember a Christmas when there'd been so much laughter.

'Sit down, Bill, please,' she said, motioning to the sofa, from where you had the best view of the TV screen.

'No, no.' He pointed to the rather battered green Lloyd Loom chair in the corner of the room, 'I'll sit there. It's perfect.'

Freya, who'd already nabbed the prime spot on the sofa, got up. 'No, you take the sofa,' she insisted, 'I prefer that chair.' She plonked herself down on the Lloyd Loom.

Her tone of voice was so commanding that Bill didn't argue. Evie was surprised at her daughter's good manners; she didn't know what had come over her. But she decided not to say anything.

She sat down between Bill and Michael. It was a bit of a squash, but it didn't seem to matter. She slipped off her shoes and wiggled her toes. Michael brought his bare feet up on the sofa and put one on her lap. 'Aren't your feet cold?' she tutted, putting her hand over his toes to warm them. 'Where are your slippers?'

He reached up and managed to click the standard lamp off, so that the room was in darkness. Evie shivered. She loved a good ghost story, but she was glad that she wasn't alone; she'd have been a nervous wreck. She furtively slid her tortoiseshell glasses out of her pocket and put them on.

The story was about a woman who bought her beloved child-hood home, a creepy old derelict mansion, with dreams of restoring and reopening it as a home for disabled children. But she became worried when her small son began playing with an invisible friend. Their games become increasingly disturbing, and then the boy vanished.

There was a crash of music. A door slammed, trapping the woman inside. Evie screamed. She leaped off the sofa.

'It's only a film,' Michael said, pulling his foot away in disgust.

Bill reached out and put his arm lightly round her shoulder. 'You can hang on to me if it gets too much,' he said, his eyes fixed on the screen. 'I'm pretty scared myself.'

'Thanks,' she whispered back, allowing his arm to remain

there. It was slightly embarrassing, but she liked it all the same. She hoped that he wouldn't think she'd misinterpret his gesture; she knew he was just being nice.

A window shattered. She squealed again and edged closer to him. There was just the faintest whiff of wood smoke on his woolly jumper – they'd probably had a bonfire at the allotment. Freya looked at her mother. She must have spotted that Bill had his arm round her but she didn't seem fazed.

'This is the scariest film I've ever seen,' she said, pulling her feet up on the chair and resting her chin on her knees.

'Come over here, will you, Freya?' Michael begged. He was petrified, too, but wouldn't say so. Freya rose quickly and sat down on the floor at her brother's feet.

'Pooh, your feet smell,' she said, leaning back against the sofa.

'Shut up,' he hissed. 'D'you think the mother's going to get killed?'

The phone rang. 'I'll leave it,' Evie said. It stopped ringing then started again. 'Blast. Who on earth can that be?'

Reluctantly she started to rise. Bill moved his arm away. 'I'll only be a second.' She pulled the door to behind her so as not to disturb the others. She felt cold without the warmth of Bill's body next to hers. The harsh, overhead light in the hall made her squint. She padded down the hall in her stockinged feet and reached the phone just as it stopped ringing. Typical. She dialled 1471 and her heart stopped. It was Steve.

She thought for a second. She could leave it. Wait for him to call again tomorrow, or never. She punched his number in.

'Hi, babe,' he said, cool as anything.

'Where the hell have you been?'

'Sorry, there was a problem with Jacob,' he said. 'His mum needed me to babysit.' He didn't sound at all sorry.

'I needed you to babysit,' she said. 'You left my kids on their own all night without even telling me.'

'I thought they were old enough.'

Evie thought her head might explode. 'Michael's only nine, Steve,' she hissed, 'something might have happened!'

'Look,' he replied, 'we can't discuss this on the phone. I'll come round and we can sort it out.'

'No, you won't come round,' she began to say, but he'd already hung up.

Bill came down the hall towards her. He looked concerned. 'Everything all right?'

She sniffed and wiped a tear away with her sleeve. 'Not really. It's just, you know, this man I've been seeing.' She felt embarrassed; she couldn't look Bill in the eye. 'It's a bit complicated,' she went on. 'He let me down badly and now he says he's coming round to sort things out but I don't want him to.'

Bill looked at her steadily. 'You can always say no, Evie.'

'I guess it would be good to say goodbye properly, to draw a line under the whole thing,' she replied quickly.

Bill glanced at his watch and frowned. 'I'll be off.' He hesitated. He looked as if he wanted to say something.

'What is it?' she demanded.

'There's something I've been meaning to ask you for a while. It's been on my mind but I didn't want to say it in front of the children. Have you got a moment before I go?'

She was surprised. 'Of course.'

'Can we go somewhere private?'

She had no idea what this was about but she led him into the kitchen and closed the door behind them. 'Sit down?'

'No,' he said, 'it'll only take a second.' He scratched his head. 'I hope you don't think I'm interfering. You'll probably think it's none of my business, but I wondered . . . is Freya all right? She's been fine today but it occurred to me that she seems troubled a lot of the time, more than the usual teenage angst, you know? She doesn't look all that well either.'

Evie swallowed. She wasn't expecting this. 'You know she's very upset about Neil and the baby . . .'

He nodded. 'Do you think it would help if she talked to someone? A counsellor, I mean? There's probably someone attached to the school who could help.'

Evie crossed her arms in front of her chest. 'I don't think she'd take kindly to the suggestion. She'd be appalled.'

Bill shifted slightly on his feet. 'I've come across quite a lot of young people in my time, as you can imagine, and I've always tried to point my students in the direction of a counsellor if they're having problems . . .'

Evie looked at her feet. 'I appreciate your concern,' she said, pursing her lips, 'but I don't think she's having problems. And she knows she can always talk to me if she needs to.'

Bill nodded. 'You know best, of course.'

He headed back down the hall and started to put his Barbour on.

'Why don't you stay and watch the end of the film?' she asked. She didn't really mean it. You could have too much of Bill.

He shook his head. 'Thanks for a lovely day. And say goodbye to the children for me, will you? I don't want to disturb them.'

Chapter Thirty-Seven

Carol left her bike at Richmond Station and walked down the two flights of steps to the platform. She held tightly on to the rail as she did so; she didn't want to stumble. She had her bag on one arm and a copy of the *Daily Mirror* under the other. She was rather looking forward to the journey. She didn't usually take the tube.

Luckily she wouldn't have to change. It was straight through on the District Line to Bow Road, then she'd walk to Griselda's place using her battered old *A–Z* for directions. It was years since she'd been there, so many years that she couldn't remember the last time. When she stepped out of the station everything felt alien: the buildings were completely different; even the people looked – and sounded – different. It could have been a foreign country. She couldn't imagine why Griselda had chosen to move so far away.

She decided to cut through Victoria Park to get to her sister's house. It was a crisp, bright December day between Christmas and New Year, the kind of day that Carol loved. There weren't many folk about. They should be taking the children for rides on their new bikes or kicking footballs about, she thought glumly. Probably stuck indoors in crowded shopping centres, every one of them, shopping being the new national pastime.

She skirted the lake feeling guilty that she hadn't any bread for the ducks and swans. She didn't feel sorry for the Canada geese though, horrible things. They were so pushy. She was in no rush, it was still only 10.30 a.m.

It took her half an hour to get to Griselda's and when she arrived, she stopped on the pavement outside and stared. The house was in a real state: the door and windows were all peeling and there were weeds growing through the black railings.

A big green wheelie bin in the front garden was overflowing with rubbish. She took a deep breath and knocked, hoping the inside wouldn't be as bad. But she reeled when Griselda opened the door into her little flat; the stink of tobacco smoke and old food was overpowering.

Carol looked around. There was a brimming ashtray on the dark wooden side table next to Griselda's tatty old armchair, which she'd pulled up in front of the electric fire. Carol nearly trod in a bowl containing the remains of what looked like tomato soup. There were blobs of greeny-blue mould on top. It must have been there for days.

The curtains were torn and sections had come away from the pelmet. There should have been a lovely view of Victoria Park, but the window was so grimy that you could hardly see out. Carol covered her face with her hands. This was her little sister's room she was standing in.

'Oh, Griselda,' she gasped. 'I had no idea. Why didn't you tell me?'

Griselda frowned. 'Dunno what you're talkin' about,' she said, shuffling over to the sink in the corner of the room and filling the kettle. 'Why have you come anyway?'

'To wish you Happy Christmas, of course.' Carol pulled herself together, fished in her bag and produced a shiny gold parcel with a card stuck on the top.

'Here,' she said. 'Your present.'

Griselda's eyes widened. She always did love a present. 'Can I open it now?'

Carol nodded.

Griselda tore at the parcel and a woolly red scarf and pair of matching gloves fell out. She picked them up, put them on and did a little waltz round the room. 'How do I look?'

'Lovely,' Carol laughed. 'You always suited red.'

Griselda stopped twirling and stared at her sister. 'No I didn't,' she said, taking the scarf and gloves off and putting them carefully on the windowsill. 'You were the one they said suited red, don't you remember? Mother said you looked really nice in that red cape when you were young. She said I could never wear red because of me skin tone.'

Carol looked puzzled. 'But that was so long ago. And skin tone changes. Anyway, I think you look really nice in them and they'll be so warm.'

Griselda didn't seem to hear. 'You always looked nice in everythin',' she went on. She seemed to be staring at a particular spot on the wall behind Carol. 'You were tall and blonde and pretty and you weren't shy, like me. All the boys were after you.'

'Yes, well, didn't do me much good, did it?' Carol said quickly. She looked around for somewhere to sit. There appeared to be only one chair.

Griselda snapped out of her daydream. 'Take that one,' she said, reading her sister's mind. 'I'll get another chair from the bedroom.'

She had a thick white parting but the rest of her hair was very black. Carol was reminded of the badger who sometimes put in an appearance in her garden. She felt the need to check the seat before settling down. She wasn't the world's tidiest person herself, but she didn't want to sit on an old sandwich or something. There was a hole in the chair and the springs didn't look up to much, but otherwise it was safe.

'Cuppa?' Griselda said, coming back with a little upright chair for herself from the bedroom.

'That'd be nice.' Carol hoped the mugs weren't too dirty.

Griselda made two cups of tea and passed one to her sister. 'So,' she said, giving Carol a funny look. 'What are you really here for? You're not foolin' me about Christmas. You never bin here at Christmas before. What's up?'

'You've never *been* here,' Carol corrected. She took a sip of tea. 'But you're right,' she sighed. 'There is another reason why I came. I wanted to talk to you about Evie. To ask your advice, really.'

Griselda stared. 'Ask my advice? Why?'

Carol sipped her tea cautiously. It tasted perfectly normal. 'Because you're my sister,' she said. 'And I thought, well, I thought you might be able to tell me something, to get some information from . . .' she paused, fiddling with the gold cross around her neck, '. . . the spirits.'

281

Griselda tipped back her head and roared with laughter, revealing several black holes where teeth had once been. 'The spirits, she says? I can't believe me ears. Never thought I'd see the day. You've never held no truck with spirits, always told me to shut up about 'em. My! You've changed your tune.'

Carol set her cup down on the little table to her left and cleared her throat. 'Yes, well, you know I don't like all that spiritualism business normally but' – she leaned forward to be closer to Griselda – 'but I'm worried about Evie – and Freya. I just thought you might be able to give me a little reassurance, that's all.'

Griselda's eyes narrowed. 'What are you so worried about anyway?'

Carol shuffled in her seat and looked at her hands. 'There's this man I don't like.'

Griselda took a sip of tea. She made a slurping sound. Carol winced. 'So?' Griselda said. 'She's a grown woman. You can't tell her who she should be courtin'.'

Carol felt her face go hot. She glared at her sister. 'I can't tell her anything, remember?'

Griselda grunted. 'I s'pose not.'

'Anyway, it's not just him,' Carol went on. 'There's also Freya. She doesn't seem right. She's not happy. She seems a bit, well, furtive. I see her most days at the bus stop, you see, and she's changed. My instincts tell me something's wrong but I can't probe. It's awful being so powerless.' Carol felt tears pricking in her eyes. 'I just hoped you might be able to shed some light on things.'

'Don't cry.' Griselda leaned forward and patted her sister's knee clumsily. 'Here,' she said, rising slowly. She had to lean heavily on the back of the chair for support. Her breathing was so bad. 'I'll fetch you a tissue.'

Carol blew her nose. 'So you will?'

Griselda drew the curtains. 'It's easier in the dark,' she explained. 'You just sit tight while I see who's around.'

She sat opposite Carol again and closed her eyes, breathing in and out deeply.

'Now,' she said, 'I just need a minute to connect. Ah yes, I can see you're worried, really worried. Poor you. You've got yourself in such a state. But there's no need, no need at all.'

Carol swallowed. She was tempted to say a quick Lord's Prayer, but she resisted. This sort of thing made her terribly nervous. Suddenly Griselda opened her eyes and looked Carol straight in the eye, making her flinch.

'Now you listen to me,' she said. 'You mustn't interfere. Evie's young man is going to make her very happy.'

Carol's shoulders relaxed. 'Are you sure? But he seems so, well, unreliable.'

'And Freya's just being a typical teenager,' Griselda went on. 'There's no need to fret. She's growing up nicely. She's hunky dory. Tip top.'

Carol clapped her hands, she couldn't help herself. 'What a relief! I'm so glad I came. I knew it was a good idea.'

Griselda reached across Carol and took the packet of cigarettes from the side table next to her. She lit a fag and peered into the distance, narrowing her eyes. 'Yeah, well,' she said, inhaling deeply, 'they're tellin' me clear as day. Couldn't be clearer. That girl's not in no trouble at all.'

Carol felt much happier on the tube going home. She knew it was irrational; she didn't really believe in Griselda's spirits any more than she believed in Father Christmas. Griselda was like a child. The spirits were her invisible friends that she'd never grown out of.

There again, just occasionally Carol would remember something Griselda had said in the past that would make her sit up straight, something that had come true. That's why, even though she was so sceptical, she still felt absurdly relieved if Griselda insisted that things would be all right. She certainly felt reassured now.

She pictured Griselda's dirty little room. It was sad to think of her living like that. But at least she seemed to be eating . . . well, if not properly, enough. And she seemed OK in herself. Barmy as ever, of course, but safe and reasonably healthy, despite her chest.

The train stopped at Stepney Green. Several people got on, including a young woman with a pushchair. The baby, a girl, stared at Carol and rattled a toy in her hand. She couldn't be more than a year old. Griselda had told Carol that she was pregnant long before she knew the truth herself. Now that *was* weird. Carol was furious at the time. She said Griselda was disgusting, a horrible little girl for saying such a dreadful thing.

'Well, I know what you've been doing,' Griselda had whispered. She didn't have her cockney accent back then. She had a nice voice, quite a sweet voice, but at that moment she sounded nasty and sneaky.

Carol shivered. It was a mean thing that she'd done, of course. Derek was Griselda's boyfriend. Well, sort of. But they were only young. Griselda was only, what, thirteen then to his seventeen or eighteen? You could hardly call it a serious relationship.

The train whooshed into the tunnel and rattled on for several minutes before stopping again at Whitechapel. A chap waiting on the platform reminded Carol a little of Derek. He was smallish and slight, neatly dressed, nothing to write home about. Derek had a squint. You were never quite sure if he was looking at you or not. She'd only gone with him because she was tipsy. She'd never have done it otherwise. She'd met him in the park on her way back from school. Griselda had got another detention and had to stay behind.

Derek was with a group of mates, talking and laughing. He'd broken off from the group and come over to say hello. Carol had her uniform on, her satchel over her shoulder. He said he had the day off from the garage where he worked and offered her a sip of his cider. She didn't normally drink alcohol, she didn't like the taste, but she didn't want to look stupid in front of his mates so she said yes.

She sat beside him on the grass and took off her satchel. It was a warm summer's day. She said she mustn't be long or Mother would be in a bate. He shifted his body very close to hers and they talked about Griselda. He said she was 'away with the fairies'. She remembered that phrase; she'd never heard it before. He said he was going to chuck her. Carol tried to defend her, but in the end she had to agree that her sister *was* peculiar. 'What do you think's the matter with her?' she asked. His mates got up and left.

She told him about their parents, how she felt she had to protect Griselda because she made them so angry. Derek seemed very kind and sympathetic. He held her hand and said she had beautiful long fingers. Then he'd kissed her on the lips. She'd never had a proper kiss before, though lots of her friends had. Derek smelled of cider and tobacco. His lips felt nice. He seemed very experienced.

The doors closed and the train started up again. The young man must have gone in another carriage because Carol couldn't see him anywhere. She stared at the poster in front and tried to focus: 'if u cn rd this u cld bcm a sctry and gt a gd jb.' It didn't work. Her mind slid back to the subject that she most wanted to forget. She could still picture Griselda's tear-stained face, her wild hair. She'd called Carol all the names under the sun and said she'd never speak to her again. Carol felt herself wince. But it had only lasted a few days. Griselda got over it.

When they found out that Carol really was pregnant and Mum and Dad hit the roof, it was Griselda who comforted her. And when she gave birth and they took the baby away, Griselda was the one who climbed into bed with her and held her all through the night while her body shook with sobs. Griselda's nightie was soaked through.

Carol sighed. It was unlucky that she'd got pregnant after that one time. So many regrets. But you couldn't live on regrets now, could you? Besides, if she hadn't bumped into Derek that afternoon there'd be no Evie, and Evie was her everything, her reason for living.

It's a good job Griselda was the forgiving type, that's all. Because it wasn't nice of her to steal her own sister's boyfriend, no matter how weedy he was. Well, it was all water under the bridge now.

Carol left the train and walked slowly back up the two flights of steps at Richmond Station and out into the fresh air. It was only 3.30 p.m. but it was getting dark already. The air was really cold now that the sun had gone in. She was pleased to see that her bike was still chained to the railings where she'd left it. She trudged over to unlock it. She was tired now, ready to put her feet up. And she missed Victoria and Albert. It was rare for her to be away from them for so long.

She'd padlocked her helmet to the bike. She unlocked it, put it on her head and clicked the fastening under her chin. Then she wheeled her bike on to the main road. With luck there'd be something worth watching on the television tonight, like a nature programme. She liked those. Otherwise she'd listen to something on the wireless and do a bit more writing. She licked her lips, which were dry and cracked.

She looked over her shoulder and pushed herself off from the pavement. The cold wind bit at her cheeks. She couldn't wait to be back in the warm. She must try to stop worrying about Evie and Freya now and stop interfering. There was no need.

All in all it had been a most satisfactory day.

Chapter Thirty-Eight

✥

'"A door slammed and Marcellus strode in. Cornelia caught his gaze; his eyes were ice-cold. Her stomach lurched. It was several weeks since she had seen him. He'd been away all this time in the country. She'd forgotten how tall and broad he was. He must be the same height almost exactly as Spiculus—"'

'But I thought Spiculus was the hero and Marcellus was the villain!' Pamela interrupted.

Evie took a deep breath and tried to smile. Her cheeks felt tight and inflexible. 'That's right.'

'Well, you can't have your hero being the same height as your villain,' Pamela went on. 'Spunkulus, or whatever his name is, has to be much taller and more handsome. It's traditional.'

'Rubbish!' Nic said. 'I know plenty of men who are short and very attractive. It's a myth that women are only attracted to very tall men.'

'She's not saying that her hero is short,' said Jonathan, the one who was writing about the sexual adventures of a young man in Spain and Italy. He was sitting right at the back of the class and had to shout. 'She's saying that he and the villain are both equally tall.'

Evie closed her eyes and braced herself. She'd had a productive couple of weeks on her historical romance and she was pleased with how it was going. Since the fallout with Steve at Christmas, they'd been seeing less of each other and although she hadn't actually broken things off, she'd been playing it deliberately cool.

He'd been ringing her every day, desperate to come round, but she'd insisted that she needed to get on with her writing. Really she just wanted to punish him, to make him realise that

287

what he'd done was completely out of order. But while she'd been tapping away at the keyboard, an odd thing had happened: she'd found herself going off Spiculus. It was as if the book was writing itself.

She'd decided that Spiculus was boring. He was very sexy, but that was all there was to him. Unless he was fighting in the Coliseum – or shagging Cornelia, which he was very good at – he was vacuous and, frankly, full of crap. A bit like Steve, really. Steve was a great lover, no doubt about it, but he didn't seem to be a particularly successful journalist. He had an awful lot of time on his hands. Evie couldn't help wondering how he managed to make ends meet.

Meanwhile, she'd found herself becoming increasingly interested in a character called Gracchus. He was a wise older man, a friend of Cornelia's father, who had become a bit of a confidant. She found herself pouring her heart out to him and he was a really good listener. Plus, he made her laugh.

Evie could almost imagine Cornelia falling in love with him instead, but she banished the thought. Cornelia had known Gracchus for years, he was almost like a father figure. She mustn't let the plot run away with itself.

The argument about men's heights seemed to have ground to a halt. 'Shall I go on?' she asked wearily.

Tristram nodded. 'Just to the end of the page please, then we're going to talk about choosing the perfect word.'

Pamela put her hand up.

'Yes, Pamela?' Tristram said wearily.

'I've just finished writing a passage which, though I say so myself, is rather good on the descriptive front,' she said, patting her stiff grey hair. 'Perhaps you might like to hear it before we begin our discussion.'

Evie was relieved to take her place between Becca and Nic again. She smiled at Nic, who winked in return. She was so brave, Evie thought. She hadn't really expected Nic to make it to the January meeting at all.

She'd been to court just a few days after the New Year and received an eighteen-month driving ban and a five-hundred-pound fine, because it was a first offence. She'd told Evie that she'd apologised unreservedly to the magistrates, who'd warned that the local newspaper were attending.

There was, indeed, a story in the *Richmond and Twickenham Times*. The headline – 'Wealthy Accountant's Wife on Drink-Drive Charge' – had brought tears to Evie's eyes, so she dreaded to think what it must have done to Nic. But Nic said later that she'd gone so low already it wasn't as big a blow as she might have expected. She felt desperately sorry for Dominic and Alan, though. What a lousy Christmas present. She said she didn't know how she could ever make it up to them.

Nic had told Evie over coffee one morning that the pair of them had been wary and mistrustful when she explained that she'd found out she had an illness, alcoholism, and was determined to get better. But for the first time in years she was waking up in the morning feeling happy – well, almost happy – after another booze-free twenty-four hours. She told Evie that she was going to succeed in kicking the habit for their sakes. And so far she was managing, though it was still very early days.

No one in the creative writing group had mentioned the article when Nic arrived, but there had been a few funny looks. Evie knew Nic had noticed them.

Pamela finished reading her passage and sat down. She exuded pleasure in her own brilliance. It was a piece about a man having an argument with his wife.

'Well, I thought it was verbose,' Carol said when Pamela had finished. 'Far too many adjectives and adverbs.' She and Pamela were no longer even pretending to get along; it was all-out war.

'What do you mean?' Pamela snapped.

'For example,' Carol went on, 'you said something like "'What do you mean by that?' he said belligerently." I think "belligerently" is "Show Don't Tell".'

'No it's not.' Pamela replied. 'It's a perfect word to use in the circumstances. "Belligerent" sounds cross and grumpy. It's very descriptive.' She turned around and gave Carol, sitting just behind Evie, a withering look.

Tristram cleared his throat. 'Actually,' he said, 'this is a very good example of what I'm going to talk about. Can anyone think of a way of rewriting that line that would *convey* the belligerence whilst letting the character and action speak for themselves?'

There was silence. Evie fidgeted in her chair. She hated moments like this, when they were asked to correct someone else's writing. Not that Pamela had a problem with it, so long as it wasn't *her* writing they were trashing.

At last Russell raised a hand. Evie was rather relieved that the goatee had gone. 'It's taken me a few moments to think about it,' he said, 'but I think I've got there. I've written something down. How's this?'

He cleared his throat and read from a notepad: '"What the bloody hell do you mean by that?' He took a step forward, his hands coiled into fists."'

Tristram beamed. 'Excellent, excellent,' he said. 'This is just what I mean. Let your characters' actions and words speak for themselves. They don't need you, the author, to interpret their feelings to the reader; they're more than capable of getting ideas across on their own.'

Pamela stood up. Her body was shaking. Even from behind you could tell that she was incandescent with rage.

'I don't agree at all,' she boomed. 'I'd never use disgusting swear words to convey an emotion. It's lazy and unforgivable.'

Tristram fiddled with the gold chain around his neck on which his glasses were dangling. 'No one's suggesting that you have to use swear words, Pamela,' he sighed. 'That was just an example of what you might do to convey your meaning. Similarly, we should all try to avoid using the word for an emotion to get across how our characters are feeling. So, for instance, instead of saying, "He was elated", find a way to show this to your readers through dialogue, actions and physical sensations. Can anyone think of a few ways to convey elation?'

When the meeting was over, Evie, Nic and Becca picked up their bags and left the hall in a hurry.

'Quick,' whispered Evie, 'we have to get away from Pamela or she'll collar us and start slagging off Carol. Then Carol will wade in and there'll be an almighty row. I couldn't stand it.'

She took them each by the arm and whisked them into a side street out of sight. She was surprised to discover that Russell had scarpered even more swiftly and was unlocking his bike just a few yards up the road.

'So what juicy stories have you got this month?' Evie called when she was certain that no one was following them.

Russell raised his dark eyebrows heavenward. 'You're such gossips,' he said. 'I really can't reveal any more confidential information.'

The three women waited. Russell pulled his collar up and looked left and right. 'But there was a woman who came in for a routine check-up,' he said, *sotto voce*. 'She had genital warts the size of miniature cauliflowers.' He paused, looking at each of the women in turn. The air hung heavily between them. 'And she had no idea!' he added with a flourish.

Evie put her hands over her mouth. 'The size of miniature cauliflowers?' she gasped. 'She must have known. Surely? It's not possible.'

Russell shook his head. 'Nope, gospel truth. When I asked, as delicately as I could of course, if she was aware of her problem she looked appalled. She couldn't have looked down there for a very long time.'

'But her boyfriend – partner?' Nic squealed. He must have . . . ?'

Russell put his helmet on. 'Thought it was quite normal. Probably has cauliflowers himself. They weren't particularly . . . well, you know. Put it this way, the lights were on but there was no one at home.'

The women stood quite still while they digested the information.

'Well,' Russell said at last, swinging a leg over the crossbar, 'must be off. Good luck with the writing and see you next month!' He vanished round the corner.

Evie turned to her friends and shook her head. 'I can't believe you could have something like that and not *know*,' she muttered. 'I just can't believe it.'

She glanced at Becca, who was looking up and down the alleyway as if searching for someone or something.

'Becks?' Evie said, 'it's all right, the others'll have gone by now. We're on our own. Anyone for a drink – a soft drink?' she added quickly. 'Do you realise it's five years since we went on the writing course? We should celebrate.'

Nic looked surprised. She was wearing a red wollen coat with a big fur collar that emphasised her daintiness. She had some amazing clothes. 'God yes, I suppose it is,' she said. 'It was around the end of January, wasn't it? I remember glancing around the room during that first session and realising that you two were the only sane ones there.'

Becca looked down at the two smaller women. 'Do you remember that mad man – Peter or David or something – who was writing the book about a teenage girl?'

Evie snorted. 'Yes, and it was supposed to be set in the modern day and he made her say things like: "Golly gosh, Pater, my stockings have laddered."'

Nic giggled. 'He was single and clearly didn't have a clue how kids talk. Why on earth was he writing about a teenage girl in the first place, for heaven's sake?'

'And what about that bonkers woman writing an incomprehensible book about her childhood in Turkmenistan?' Becca grinned. 'And horrible fat Louise who dumped us via email a few weeks later because she obviously decided we weren't intellectual enough.'

Evie felt laughter gurgling in her throat. 'The cheek of it! Who did she think she was? George Eliot or something?'

'George Eliot and Marilyn Monroe rolled into one.' Nic grinned, showing off her braces. 'Do you remember the bustier at dinner?'

Evie shuddered. 'Ooh yes, the bustier,' she whispered.

Becca pulled up the collar on her dark grey coat. 'I can't come for a drink tonight,' she said suddenly. 'I must get home. I'm off to Nashville first thing tomorrow. Sorry.'

Evie frowned. 'This isn't like you, Mrs Intrepid "I've travelled the world ten times over and jet lag is for wimps."'

Becca started walking back towards the main road. 'Yes, well, I don't feel very intrepid.' You could see the breath coming out of her mouth, it was so cold. 'All I want to do right now is get home, lock all the doors and windows, close the curtains and pull the duvet over my head.'

'Are you all right?' Evie asked, puzzled.

'Of course I am,' Becca replied.

Becca left Nic and Evie at the street corner. They were heading in the opposite direction, Evie towards the bus stop and Nic to the train station.

Becca found herself looking this way and that, right and left. Several times she glanced over her shoulder. She'd seriously considered getting a taxi but that would have been foolish; it was only a seven- or eight-minute walk.

Her high heels clacked along the pavement. She wished they wouldn't make so much noise, drawing attention to her. She dug her hands in her pockets and tried to focus on her breathing. This was ridiculous; she was turning into a nervous wreck.

It wasn't surprising. She tried to imagine Evie's and Nic's faces if they found out. They'd hate her, hate what she'd done and hate the mountain of lies. There was no way that Becca could explain or make it right; there'd be no forgiveness.

She tried to imagine Alice and James. The shock on their little faces. How could they possibly understand? Tom and Alice and James, a solid little unit, and her, the broken satellite, spinning ever further away until it was out of sight. She felt a cry bubble in her throat, threatening to burst out. She dug her bitten nails in the palms of her hands and the pain forced it down.

She rounded the corner at King Street and made her way towards the Green. In one way this was worse, because she'd left the main road and there were no other people about. But she felt her spirits lift slightly when she spotted the comforting, dark-blue iron railings ahead: her terrace of houses. She was nearly home. She quickened her pace. She was almost running.

'What's the hurry?'

Becca jumped so high and so fast that her hair, her skin and the flesh beneath seemed to detach from her bones. Only her teeth were left clinging to her jaw, jangling in her mouth. The eyes in their sockets had come loose, too.

She spun around. Gary was standing right behind her. Where had he come from? 'What are you doing?' she hissed. 'Why are you following me?'

Gary moved towards her, his arms open. Instinctively she hopped back several paces. He frowned. 'I need to see you,' he said. 'You cancelled the eighth. It's been too long.'

It was true that she'd managed to get out of the eighth. She'd pleaded work. He'd seemed to accept it. She hadn't mentioned seeing him through the study window on Christmas Eve.

'I said I'd call when I get back from the States,' she whispered. 'You mustn't come here. It's too dangerous. Tom and—'

'I'm in love with you, Dawn,' Gary interrupted. She flinched. He put his hands in his trouser pockets. He was standing very upright, his feet planted firmly on the ground. 'Don't you see? I've always loved you, ever since primary school. I don't care about Tom or Michelle. I only care about us.'

He stepped forward and put his arms around her. This time she didn't resist. She pressed her face against his black leather jacket and sobbed. Her whole body felt weak and powerless; she was made of wet clay. She needed him to support her or she'd dribble on to the floor.

'What do you expect me to do?' she said. 'What do you want?' She pulled her face away from him but his arms were still wrapped tightly round her. 'Are you going to blackmail me?'

It was his turn now to step back. He pushed her off. 'How could you think that?' His voice was raised. His eyes were black and fiery.

Becca folded her arms across her body. She was shrinking, occupying an increasingly small space. She might disappear altogether down a crack in the pavement.

'You could make a fortune,' she went on. She closed her eyes and clenched her fists, waiting for his tirade.

There was a pause. When he finally spoke his voice was surprisingly calm. 'I'm not interested in blackmailing you, Dawn,' he said. 'I don't want your money. How could you think that?'

'What *do* you want then? I don't understand.'

'I want you.'

She shuddered. She wondered how she could ever have found him handsome. He was mad. She must have been mad. 'But we hardly know each other.' She stared into his eyes, pleading with him.

His eyes were blank and unresponsive. 'We've been through this,' he sighed. 'I've told you I know all I need to.'

'I can't leave Tom,' she wailed. 'The children. Is that what you want me to do?'

He stepped forward, right into her body space. He was so close that she could feel his breath on her face and smell his warm, musky odour.

'Of course you can't leave now,' he said. She felt her body, her legs and shoulders, relax slightly. 'You mustn't upset the children,' he whispered. One arm was round her shoulders now, the other round her waist. She stayed stock-still, rooted to the spot. He brought his hands up and took her face in them. 'I just want to see more of you, then I'll be happy. Then we can keep your secret to ourselves.'

She felt as if she were someone else: an actor in a tableau; a marionette jerking to its master's command. His lips pressed against hers. She opened her mouth slightly and allowed his tongue to roam around. There was so much saliva; she'd never known so much saliva. She felt as if she were drowning in a pool of blood and saliva and tears.

Is this how Jude felt when she was on the point of dying?

I can't do this, her body was screaming. I've got to do something.

Her hands reached out and around her, scrabbling in the thin air, searching for something, an object, a memory. It was all coming back; her past present and future converging.

'Ye little cow, it's no more than ye deserve,' Jude spat back.

Chapter Thirty-Nine

'Have you been under a sunbed recently?'

Evie was on the floor on her hands and knees, pinning the hem of the bride-to-be's dress. She'd dropped Michael at school an hour before and had the rest of the day to herself.

The woman was tall, blonde and slender – a delight to design for. She'd look good in a binbag. There was just one small problem. Evie had been thinking about how she was going to raise the subject since her client arrived. It was important to be tactful.

'No,' the woman said. 'Why do you ask?'

Evie glanced up. She was a most peculiar, orangey colour. 'I just thought you looked very, erm, tanned,' she said.

'It's funny,' the woman replied. 'A few other people have said that. And look at the palms of my hands.'

She held them out so that Evie could see. They were an even darker orange than the rest of her body. Evie cleared her throat. This wasn't an isolated case – she'd seen it once before.

'Have you, um, been eating lots of carrots?' she said as nonchalantly as possible, continuing to pin the hem.

'Yes,' the woman cried. 'I'm on the carrot diet. I've lost five pounds already. Only another two to go.'

'Ah,' said Evie. 'That accounts for it. It happened to another lady that I made a dress for. Your body can only store so much vitamin A over a short time so it's showing up as an orange tint on your skin. It won't do you any harm but maybe you should try a different diet. Switch to sweetcorn or something.' She laughed.

'God, I will,' said the woman. 'I don't want to look like a satsuma on my Big Day.'

As soon as the woman left, Evie went into the kitchen, closed

296

the door behind her and put the kettle on. She fetched the small cafetière from the cupboard, put two heaped spoonfuls of fresh coffee in and filled it up with hot water. Then she warmed a third of a mug of milk in the microwave, mixed the coffee in it and sat down at the kitchen table.

The phone was waiting there expectantly. Her stomach fluttered. She blew on the coffee and took a sip before tapping in Zelda's number.

'Hello, Evie,' Zelda said huskily. 'I was expectin' you.'

Evie had been looking forward to being regressed. She'd booked the session several weeks ago, just after Christmas, and was intrigued by the idea of going back in time to a past life. She was nervous too, though. She didn't really know what to expect.

'How are you today?' Zelda asked.

Evie hardly heard the question. She felt goose pimples running up and down her arms. 'I must admit I'm a bit anxious. Are you sure this is a good idea?'

Zelda sniffed. 'I wouldn't recommend it if I didn't think you'd benefit, darlin', but it's up to you, of course. You're the customer.'

'I do want it,' Evie insisted. 'I'm just a bit jumpy, that's all.'

'You've got nothin' to worry about,' Zelda went on. 'It'll help with yer confidence, see? I'll connect you with people you've spent lifetimes with before and you'll be able to recognise who they are today. It's all about understandin' how yer past is still influencin' yer present, see? Then you can create yer future as you want it to be.' Zelda made a puffing sound on her cigarette. 'Are you ready?'

'Er, I think so.'

'Trust me, sweet'art. I'll put it on yer usual card, shall I?'

Evie swallowed. Seventy-five pounds was an awful lot of money, but if it really was as helpful as Zelda promised . . . She took another swig of coffee, rested her elbows on the table, clamped the receiver to her ear and closed her eyes.

'Now I want you to concentrate really hard,' Zelda said quietly. 'Clear your mind. Be aware of only yer face, yer forehead, yer eyelids. They feel heavy, really heavy. Yer shoulders and neck are heavy, and so are yer hands and arms.'

Evie felt her forehead and eyelids drooping. The kitchen was warm and Zelda's voice was velvety and soporific. The only noises she could hear were a slight whirring from the fridge and some builders working in one of the back gardens a few houses down. They had a radio on, but the music sounded faraway and indistinct.

'Now I want you to imagine you're in a tunnel,' Zelda went on. 'You're walkin' along the tunnel and it's all dark and silent. At the very end you can see a tiny pinprick of light. You want to get to that light.'

Evie could picture the tunnel quite clearly. She could feel its soft, earthy sides. She wasn't afraid, she was intrigued. She wanted to get to the end.

'You're walkin' along and the light is gettin' nearer,' Zelda went on. 'You really want to reach that light. I'm going to count backwards from twenty and when I get to nought, you're going to step right out into that light and tell me what you see.'

Evie's pace quickened. She was desperate to find out what was at the end of the tunnel. She was only vaguely aware of Zelda's voice, murmuring something. She tried to listen. 'Twenty, nineteen, eighteen, seventeen . . .'

She heard 'nought', summoned all her energy and leaped out into the white light. Except that when she got there it wasn't light at all, it was dark and oppressive.

'What can you see?' Zelda said. 'Tell me what's in front of you.'

Evie peered into the gloom. 'I can see a woman,' she said.

'What sort of woman?'

Evie screwed up her eyes. 'It's a young woman with a pale face and dark hair tied back in a sort of bun. She's wearing old-fashioned clothes: a long, shabby dress and an apron. I think it's me.'

'Yes,' said Zelda. 'Good. Where are you and what are you doin'?'

Evie scanned the room, a cold, dingy place with damp-looking walls. There was a dirty mattress on the floor and a couple of blankets, but nothing more.

'I'm in someone's house,' she said. 'My house.' She shivered.

'There are small children around me, my children, pulling on my skirt. And – oh! There's a baby crying in the corner. He looks so cold and hungry. The children are frightened. They need me.'

'How do you feel?' Zelda asked.

'I want to pick them up and cuddle them but I'm not looking at them,' Evie explained. 'I'm looking at myself in the mirror. It's an old, cracked mirror on the wall. I'm putting dark make-up round my eyes, rouge on my cheeks and I have bright red lips. I'm crying, too, but I don't want the children to see.'

'Why are you cryin'?' Zelda sounded concerned, soothing.

'I'm not sure,' said Evie. She felt uneasy. She wanted to get out of the strange room and back to her warm kitchen, to the present, but she couldn't.

'Why are you upset?' Zelda pressed. 'What's happenin' to you?'

Evie swallowed. She could see the pale reflection and the incongruous make-up. The staring eyes of her hungry children.

'I'm going out to try to get some money as a prostitute,' she said suddenly. 'I don't want to but it's the only way. The children are starving . . .' Evie felt a knot in her stomach. Her heart was thumping. 'I know it's dangerous. I don't want to leave them . . .'

'Where's yer husband?' Zelda said gently. 'Why isn't he lookin' after you?'

Evie paused for a moment, searched her mind. 'He's not here. I think he's dead. No, he's left us. He's gone off with another woman.' She clenched the phone in her fist.

'Has he now? That's interestin',' she heard Zelda say. 'Now why has he done that, do you think?'

'I don't know,' Evie moaned. Her chest was tight. It was a horrible, familiar feeling. 'I have no idea.'

'I wonder if you haven't bin lookin' after him properly, usin' yer womanly wiles to keep him happy?' said Zelda.

Evie's heart fluttered. 'No, no,' she said, 'it's not that. He's a womaniser, another woman caught his eye. I was busy with the children . . .'

Zelda's voice cut through the air. 'I can hear your anger.

299

Don't be angry, Evie, this is all part of the therapy. Just listen to me, darlin', don't try to oppose me.'

Evie felt her shoulders relax slightly. Zelda was right, this wasn't for real, she was supposed to be learning from it. It was therapy.

'Now,' Zelda went on, gently, 'I can see already that there's a pattern here. The husband from your past and Neil. You can't hang on to your men, can you? That's what the past is tellin' us. We need to find out what you're doin' wrong, then you can put it right, see?'

'But it's not my fault,' Evie cried.

'Oh, but I think it is,' Zelda whispered. 'You see, I think you have to change your ways, not be so selfish. Tell him how wonderful he is. Stroke him. Love him with all your heart . . .'

'But I did love him with all my heart,' Evie sobbed, 'I adored him.'

'Well, you didn't show it, did you?' said Zelda. 'You was obviously doin' somethin' wrong, otherwise he'd still be with you now. You must of drove him away.'

Evie tried to open her eyes but they were too heavy. 'I want to stop now,' she said desperately.

'You can't, you need to finish the treatment,' Zelda replied. 'Please . . .'

'Be calm,' Zelda went on. 'You're doin' very well, this is very revealin'. One of the best regressions I've done. Now I want you to imagine that you're back in the tunnel. But this time you're going to move forward from where you're at, ten, twenty, thirty years in time.'

Evie felt herself crawling through the tunnel now. It seemed much narrower and very claustrophobic. She couldn't stand up. She was desperate to reach the light again. She was wriggling along on her elbows and knees.

'Now,' said Zelda suddenly. 'You're outside again. What do you see?'

Evie blinked and looked around. At least she wasn't back in that dingy room. 'I'm in a street,' she said. 'There are lots of people and horses and carts going by. It's raining.'

'What sort of people?'

'Poor people,' she said. 'They look tired and dirty. Some of them have bare feet. I'm in a street near where I live, I know it. The houses are very close together. Everything is shabby and old.'

'What else can you see?' Zelda persisted.

'I must leave now,' Evie said. 'I don't like it here. I don't feel safe.'

'Just a few more minutes,' Zelda soothed. 'You must find out how it ends.'

'But I don't want to. I'm scared.'

'Look around you,' Zelda commanded. Evie didn't like her tone of voice. She sounded so cold. But she had to do as she was told. Zelda was in control.

'Can you see yourself?' Zelda persisted. 'What are you doin'?'

Evie glanced left and right, up and down. Her eyes fell on a pile of what looked like clothes lying in a messy heap in the gutter. The pile moved. She screamed. 'I don't like it, I want to go.'

'What can you see?' Zelda hissed. 'What are you lookin' at?'

Evie let out a cry. 'It's me. I'm lying on the ground. Everyone's walking past. I – I think I'm dying. I'm on my own. No one cares . . .'

A high-pitched squeak, like a car braking suddenly, followed by a series of bangs, sliced through her subconscious.

'Evie? What the hell . . . ?'

She opened her eyes and turned around. It took a moment or two for her to focus. Bill appeared to be trying to climb through her sash window. He was half in, half out, banging on the pane. He was struggling to push the bottom bit up high enough to accommodate himself. It always was a tricky window to open. The lock had broken years ago.

'Evie?' She was aware of Zelda's voice on the other end of the line, but she was too confused to answer. She sat, mesmerised, while Bill gave one final shove and tumbled on to the kitchen floor virtually at her feet.

'Evie?' he said, getting up quickly and brushing himself down. 'I was in the garden. I heard you scream. I thought something had happened. Are you all right?'

She put the phone on the table. 'Yes, yes,' she said, rubbing her eyes. 'I was doing regression therapy. I got a bit upset. I could see myself lying half dead in the gutter.' She realised that must sound ridiculous. She attempted a laugh.

'Regression therapy?' Bill's face had gone red. He snatched the phone from the table and put it to his mouth. 'What a load of bollocks,' he shouted. 'What kind of crackpot are you?'

Evie was shocked. She'd never seen Bill so angry before. In fact she didn't think she'd seen him properly angry at all.

'There's no need to talk like that,' she said, grabbing the phone back. 'Zelda's my friend, she's an expert in her field.'

'Your *friend*?' he protested. 'Funny sort of friend who terrifies the living daylights out of you.' He relaxed a little. 'What's this regression therapy supposed to do, anyway?'

Evie put her hand up. 'One moment. Zelda?' She listened for a second or two, but the line had gone dead. Not surprising. Zelda wouldn't want to hang around eavesdropping on an argument.

Disappointment washed over her. She'd never get to know, now, what it all meant. If she was regressed again, it might be to a completely different life with a whole new set of characters. Yet she felt she'd been close to understanding something really important.

She felt hot, despite the fact that the window was wide open. 'You shouldn't have barged in like that, Bill,' she said. 'I'd been hypnotised. You interrupted the treatment. It could have been dangerous.'

'Treatment?' Bill glared at her. 'It's absolute cobblers, all this psychic stuff, surely you know that?'

She stared at her feet. She felt as if she were a schoolgirl, being ticked off by the teacher.

'I'm sorry.' His voice was softer now. 'But you had me worried. I honestly thought you were being attacked.'

She shook her head.

'I just don't think this sort of thing is good for you, or for anyone,' he went on. 'Especially not when you've been through a bad—'

Evie pulled her hand away. 'Oh, I see. So you think I'm too

weak and fragile to cope with it, do you? Look, I appreciate your concern, but I'm not some stupid, impressionable little girl tampering with things she doesn't understand. I've been talking to Zelda for months. I know she's good, she's given me some fantastic advice. And if she helps me, what's the problem?'

Bill looked at her intensely with his pale-blue eyes, forcing her to return his gaze. 'I don't think you're a silly little girl. Quite the opposite,' he said quietly. 'I think you're a beautiful, intelligent, fully grown woman.'

She felt herself blush and dropped her gaze.

'But even clever, fully grown women make mistakes, and I'm absolutely sure that you're making a mistake with this Zelda woman. She sounds like really bad news.'

Evie remembered what Zelda had told her about the tall, handsome stranger. It must be true; she had to believe it. And all the money she'd spent, surely that hadn't gone to waste?

'You're entitled to your opinion,' she huffed. 'And I'm entitled to mine. Thank you for checking I was all right. Now, if you don't mind I've got work to do. I've a wedding dress to finish.'

Bill sighed. He glanced at the window. 'I'll use the door this time if you don't mind. Would you like me to repair the lock before I go?'

Evie hesitated. It would be nice to get it fixed. It always worried her slightly that it didn't lock properly. She peeked at him. His mouth turned down slightly at the corners, which made him look disapproving. He could be so bloody superior sometimes.

She straightened her shoulders and stuck her chin out. 'No thank you,' she said. 'I'll do it myself.'

'As you wish,' he replied.

Chapter Forty

Luckily the suitcases were in the spare-room cupboard at the top of the house, so she wouldn't disturb anyone. It was past midnight and even Tom would be fast asleep. She'd had several days to think. In fact she'd thought of little else. She could still taste Gary's saliva in her mouth.

She closed her eyes. It mustn't happen again. The consequences were too terrifying to contemplate. She remembered her fingers, scrabbling around in the air, searching for something. She felt sick. She had to get as far away as possible.

Becca tiptoed past her own and the children's bedrooms and Monica's room on the half-landing above. When she reached the top, she pulled a small black leather holdall off the highest shelf of the cupboard – she wouldn't need much – and carried it into the study. She opened the middle drawer of her filing cabinet and found her passport right at the front. Then she sneaked downstairs to the utility room.

The light was terribly bright, it hurt her eyes, but there was a comforting smell of washing powder and fabric conditioner and the washing machine was humming quietly. Monica must have put a load in before she went to bed.

It felt so ordinary and normal. Life going on as it always had.

It felt like the day that Jude died.

Becca's chest was heavy, as if there were a lead weight in there instead of flesh and blood. Concentrate, she told herself. Focus on the task in hand. She was relieved to see a pair of her jeans and a couple of sweatshirts in a pile on the tumble-dryer waiting to be ironed, as well as some clean knickers and a few pairs of Tom's socks. They'd do. Her toothbrush and face cream and so on were in the en-suite bathroom, beside where Tom was sleeping, so she'd have to buy new when she got there. She laughed softly to herself. She couldn't quite believe that she was thinking about face cream. Force of habit.

She switched off the light and slunk into the kitchen, where she found an A4 notepad and pen beside the phone.

'Darling Tom,' she wrote. Tears pricked in her eyes and dribbled down her cheeks. She wiped them with her sleeve. This was no good. She needed to be strong, in control. She continued writing:

> I've done something bad, which you and the children will find hard, if not impossible, to understand. I've gone away for a while. I think it's better if I'm on my own.
>
> I love you and the children so much. Please look after them for me. Tell them Mummy isn't well, tell them whatever seems best. But make sure they know that I'll always love them, they're the most beautiful, precious children in the world and I'm so proud of them.

Her eyes were so full of tears that she could hardly read the words on the page, but there was no time to lose. She resumed writing:

> Tell them always to work hard and do their best. And please say that what I did was a terrible mistake. I regretted it the moment it happened. I'll never, ever forgive myself.
>
> Tom, you've been a wonderful husband. I'm sorry that I've been grumpy sometimes and haven't always appreciated you or told you how much I love you. You're a very special man.
>
> Goodbye, darling.
> Becca xxx

There was a noise upstairs. It sounded like a door creaking. Becca froze. This mustn't happen. She waited for a moment or two but the house fell silent again. She found an envelope in one of the drawers, folded her note, put it inside and sealed the envelope. Then she wrote 'TOM' in capital letters on the front and placed it by the kettle.

Luckily she always left the house before the others were up anyway, so Monica would give the kids breakfast and take them to school as usual. School. She tried to imagine the scene. Them going off, all clean and shiny and full, scuffling in the hall for their bags, happy that it was Friday and the weekend tomorrow. Monica urging them to hurry. Then Tom discovering the note.

Maybe he'd wake early and find it before – and keep them home. She bit her lip. Please let them be protected for as long as possible, cocooned in their snug little world.

She sneaked into the hall, shoved a pair of trainers in her bag and pulled her black North Face anorak out of the coat cupboard. She was still in her work clothes but it didn't matter, she'd change later.

She paused for a moment in front of the hall mirror. Her face looked so strange and pale, almost ghostly in the half-light. Most of her make-up had worn off and there were dark smudges under her eyes. She licked her finger and rubbed the smudges off as well as she could; she didn't want to draw attention to herself.

There was one of Alice's red scrunchies on the radiator cover. Some of her long, fair hairs were stuck to it. Becca's chest tightened. She stared at herself again. Her own, dyed, nearly black hair looked so fake to her now, fake and ugly and obvious. She was a joke, a woman in a grotesque party mask. She couldn't understand how she'd got away with it.

She picked the scrunchie up and pulled her hair back into a tight ponytail. Then she put on the anorak, picked up the holdall and her handbag and stepped out into the night. Her warm breath was making curly patterns in front of her. She glanced quickly left and right, half expecting Gary to jump out from behind a tree. He must have gone now, surely? But she couldn't be sure.

The coast seemed clear. Her black Mercedes was just a few yards up the road. She walked quietly for a few steps until she was almost there, then she ran to the door and bundled in.

She locked the doors and checked her watch: 1.15 a.m. At this time of night, with no traffic, she'd be in Folkestone in about an hour and a half. There was only a limited service on the Shuttle at the moment but they still ran every ninety minutes. God willing, she'd make Calais before sunrise.

She remembered something and rootled in her bag for her BlackBerry. She must be quick. She unclicked her seatbelt, opened the door a little, leaned as far out as she could and threw it underneath the back wheel of the car.

She pictured Gary's face, crushed into a frown, punching in her number over and over again, his brain going into overdrive as he tried to figure out what was happening. He'd never guess, never believe that she'd give it all up, that she'd really do it. Ha! That gave her some satisfaction.

She put her foot on the pedal and reversed out of the parking slot. The BlackBerry made a delicious crackling sound as she drove over it – and away.

Nic's eyelids snapped open. It took her a moment or two to work out where she was. She listened for Alan's breathing, reached out under the duvet and felt across the bed but there was just a cold space where he should have been.

She sat up. The door was half open. The landing light was off but there was a yellow glow coming from underneath his study door opposite. She glanced at the electric clock beside her. It was 1.30 a.m. She groaned. What the hell was he doing?

She got up to pee, but decided instead to go and see him, to try to coax him to bed. It wasn't good for him to work so late. It wasn't normal. She remembered the magazines and shook her head, hoping to disperse the images. She was wide awake now; it'd probably take her hours to drop off.

She reached for her dressing gown, padded across the landing and poked her head round his study door but he wasn't there. His laptop was open, though, illuminated and making that gentle whooshing sound that signalled it was in use.

There was a clatter downstairs: the sound of cutlery on plates. Maybe he was making himself a snack; he hadn't wanted much supper. She thought about going down to join him, she'd quite like a cup of tea, but then her eye was drawn to an orange light that flashed up on the bottom right hand side of the screen: it looked like a message.

She moved closer to take a look, she couldn't help herself. There was a name – *Freya*.

Evie's daughter's name. Coincidence. She double-clicked on the message so that she could read it. *Freya says: r u bak yet? u r taking ages!*

There was a silhouette in the top-right-hand corner of the message: a featureless head and shoulders. Nic hesitated, her ears pricked. There was another clatter from downstairs. She shouldn't. She must. She leaned over the machine and began to type: *hi*

She paused. Nothing happened. She pressed enter; she wasn't totally useless.

Freya says: at last! wot did u eat? Nic jumped. No wonder it was called instant messaging. She'd heard of it, of course. It was mostly for teenagers. Dominic was too young.

She swallowed. Her fingers moved across the keyboard as if of their own will.

beans on toast, Nic said. It was all she could think of. *yum.*

nice, Freya replied. *am gonna go to bed soon, really tired.*

me too, said Nic. *you had school today?* She flinched, she didn't want to know the answer.

course. why u ask stupid question?

Nic tried to sound nonchalant. *yeah. when's your GCSEs?* She squeezed her face into a grimace. It was such a crass enquiry, so obvious.

IN THREE YEARS, YOU KNOW THAT CRETIN. IM YEAR 8!!!!

Nic felt wobbly, unstable. But she'd got her answer. This girl must be twelve or thirteen – just like Evie's Freya. Coincidences did happen.

She listened again. It had gone quiet downstairs. Alan might be eating. She didn't have much time.

She was poised to type again but *Freya* interrupted: *can't wait 2 c u.*

Nic's heart was hammering so loud now that she feared someone would hear. She tried to swallow but her mouth was completely dry. All the saliva had gone. She tapped: *me 2.*

don't care if u r old and bald, Freya continued. *luv u so much.*

So she knew about Alan, knew he was a man, anyway, not a boy. Did she know that he was her husband, the husband of Evie's friend, though? Nic breathed in and out. Her legs felt weak but it was important to hold herself together. This girl could be in real danger.

go on then – tell me where we're meeting? just testing! she wrote. She was amazed that she had the guts.

st pancras station by the bronze statue of the lovers. 11.30 a.m sat. see?!

Saturday? The day after tomorrow. Nic's palms felt sweaty. Alan had told her that he was going to Brussels overnight on business. There was a clamp around her skull; someone was screwing it tighter and tighter.

She could hear Alan moving downstairs. He'd be up any minute. She thought fast. This was the most important thing that she'd ever done in her life. A shadow passed through her mind. She just needed to be sure.

what about your mum, can't remember her name? she typed.

durr. evie freestone. she doesn't know anything.

Nic stared at the screen. It was a joke, some horrible, sick movie. Whatever happened, she must stop him going back to the computer or he'd twig.

go 2 bed now, luv u, see u sat, she managed to type. She was on overdrive now, functioning only with the help of some extra-high gear that she didn't know she had.

c u sat XOX.

Nic left the laptop as it was and crawled on her hands and knees out of the study to her bedroom door. Then she stood up, folded her arms and leaned against the door frame. Her whole body was shaking. She must control it; he mustn't notice. She needed to draw on every ounce of strength she possessed.

Alan appeared at the top of the stairs. 'What are you doing?' He looked startled.

She'd acted at school; she could do it. She rubbed her eyes and yawned. 'I can't sleep.'

He frowned. He was annoyed. Of course he was. She hovered a couple of inches behind him, peering round his shoulder while he went into the study. She wound her arms round his waist.

She was a temptress. 'Come to bed,' she wheedled. She could sense irritation oozing from his every pore, but she clung on tight. 'I'm lonely,' she whined, 'I need a cuddle.'

He tried to shake her off but she held fast.

He was lingering over his laptop. There was hardly any space between him and the machine but she slipped between them. Then, before he could stop her, she reached up and planted a kiss on his mouth.

'What are you . . . ?'

'Come to bed, gorgeous,' she murmured, a sexy, minxy smile playing on her lips. She wanted to punch him, slap him, grab him by the balls and squeeze. But her feelings were secondary. She knew what she had to do.

'I'm coming,' he muttered.

She waited right by him, her hands on her hips, watching closely while he shut down his laptop, closed the cover, wound up the cord and put it away in its special bag. As soon as she was sure he was asleep, she crept down to the kitchen and closed the door softly behind her. Then she sat, quite still, staring into the blackness.

She'd never felt so alone in her life.

Chapter Forty-One

'You look lovely!'

Evie smiled at Freya as she came into the kitchen. She was wearing her usual tight black jeans and white T-shirt under a black V-neck pullover. Her favourite black leather belt with silver studs was slung round her hips. But something about her was different. Her hair?

She'd clearly washed and coloured it this morning. It was a dark plum colour and all sleek and shiny, tied back in a French ponytail with wisps falling round her face. She had black eyeliner on, but no other make-up, and her eyes were sparkly pools of blue light. She was also smiling. She looked very pretty and young.

'What are you up to today?' Evie asked, turning the page of her newspaper and taking a bite of toast. She adored Saturday mornings. She'd just dropped Michael at football training; she had a couple of hours all to herself.

'Going to Camden Market.' Freya walked over to the fridge and took out a carton of orange juice.

'Who with?' Evie glanced at the headline: 'We Didn't Expect to be Dealing with Stroppy Teenagers Again'. It was a piece about two grandparents who were raising their teenage grandchildren after their daughter was murdered. She started to read: 'Daisy loves hanging out with her friends, loud music, going to gigs . . .' Sounded familiar.

'Lucy,' Freya said.

'That's nice.'

Evie read on: 'Hazel and Reg like gardening, watching television . . .' Typical pensioners, then.

'I'm staying at her house tonight.'

Evie looked up. Freya was sipping orange juice from the carton.

'Don't do that.'

'It's finished.' Freya threw the carton in the bin.

'Put it in the recycling outside.'

Freya ignored her.

'Be careful,' Evie went on, looking back at the newspaper. 'There'll be lots of pickpockets about on a Saturday.'

'I know.'

'What time will you be home tomorrow?'

Freya wandered over to the cupboard, took out a packet of muesli and started pouring some in a bowl. 'Late afternoon,' she replied. 'Lucy's mum's invited me for Sunday lunch.'

Evie opened her mouth to speak.

'Don't worry,' Freya interjected. 'I did all my homework last night.'

Well, that was a relief.

Freya got some milk from the fridge and began eating her cereal standing up. Evie looked at the photo accompanying the article. The grandparents had white hair, specs, brave smiles. They looked slightly bemused, as if this were happening to someone else; she felt sorry for them, sorry for them all. It must be such a difficult situation.

'Well done – about the homework,' she said, taking another bite of toast. It had gone cold. 'I hope you have a lovely time.'

Freya put her bowl in the sink.

'The dishwasher,' said Evie, pointing a finger in the vague direction. She was still only on paragraph three. There were so many interruptions.

Freya came over and kissed her mother on the cheek. 'Thanks,' she said. 'You have a nice weekend too.'

She went into the hall. Evie could hear her putting on her coat. She felt empty suddenly; she wished she'd paid more attention. Now she wouldn't see Freya again till tomorrow.

'You haven't done your teeth!' she called.

There was a pause. The door slammed.

Freya had gone.

Evie folded the newspaper and got up to put her plate and mug in the dishwasher. The clock on the oven door said 10 a.m.

There was another hour to go before she had to collect Michael. Bliss.

The phone rang.

'Nic? How are you?' Evie was just in the mood for a good old chat with Nic now that she'd finished the article.

Her knees started to give way. She slumped on to the kitchen chair. She couldn't understand what Nic was saying. 'Alan, paedophile, Freya, St Pancras, eleven thirty, police . . .'

'What are you talking about?' Evie shouted.

'I'm so sorry . . . so sorry . . . the statue of the lovers . . . I knew he liked young girls . . .'

'I don't understand.'

'I went to the police station this morning . . . They're on their way to you now . . . Need you to go with them to identify her . . .'

Evie dropped the phone, grabbed her handbag from the hallway and ran.

Carol jumped when she heard the commotion and turned around, narrowing her eyes. She ought to visit the optician; she needed new glasses. She was always squinting. She could see clearly enough who this was, though: Evie. She was on the other side of the street, running like a crazed thing towards the main road. She had no coat on and her fair hair was flying behind her. She'd left her front door wide open. Whatever could have happened?

Carol stopped stroking the neighbour's black cat and got up. Her knees creaked. She'd been squatting there for some time, half facing the house, her beanie pulled down over her eyes, hoping to catch a glimpse of the family.

It was spitting with rain. Good job she was wearing her waterproofs. But Evie would get so wet. Carol left her bike where it was against a fence and crossed the road to Evie's side. She looked around, uncertain what to do. Evie was often late. Even as a child she left things till the last minute. It was one of her less appealing characteristics. But Carol had never seen her in quite such a panic as this before.

She opened the gate and walked up Evie's front path. She saw someone leave their house a few doors down and head off in the opposite direction, but other than that the street was quiet.

She'd close the front door; she couldn't leave it open, someone might steal something. If Evie had no keys, well, so be it. Carol knew Michael had football this morning, but Freya might be in. Failing that, it was always possible that a neighbour had a key and if not, Evie would just have to wait till Freya got home. She'd rather that, Carol was sure, than have the house burgled.

Carol put her hand through the brass letterbox and started to pull. Something stopped her. There were frogs hopping in her tummy. She opened the door an inch or two again and peered in. She could see all the way down Evie's hallway to the kitchen at the back! She'd love to know what Evie's kitchen was like.

She hadn't seen the hallway properly before either, just glimpses of it from outside. It was nice and wide, with a lovely high ceiling, but the wooden floor was a bit shabby. There was a pair of dirty white shoes at the foot of the stairs where someone had obviously kicked them off before going up. They were trainers, child-sized. Michael's, no doubt. Tch. He should know better.

On the left-hand wall by the mirror there was a thin crack, running almost from ceiling to floor, which someone had tried to paper over. Carol swallowed. Poor Evie. She couldn't afford for anyone to sort it out properly. The whole place could do with a lick of paint, actually. Carol clenched her fists. It was outrageous, Neil leaving Evie so short of cash. He had a good job, he ought to pay for someone to spruce it up for her.

The kitchen units seemed to be made of some sort of dark wood. Carol could just make out the corner of what looked like a stainless-steel fridge, too. She checked left and right again and put a foot over the threshold. If anyone asked, she'd say she was Evie's friend from the writing group. She was just making sure everything was all right.

It was possible that Freya was in. Well, Carol would use the same excuse. Freya! Imagine having a proper conversation with her, instead of the usual few words snatched at the bus stop. Carol's head swam.

She stepped right inside and closed the door quietly behind her. Then she padded down the hallway to the kitchen. The house had its own, special smell – of toast, Carol thought, and, well, of the three of them. It was a lovely, warm smell. Carol felt a lump in her throat.

She stood in the kitchen and looked around. It was bigger than she'd imagined and not as messy. Evie wasn't so dis-organised, then. There was a newspaper neatly folded on the kitchen table and a plum-coloured cardigan hanging on the back of one of the chairs. Evie's. Carol had seen her wearing it at the writing group. She picked it up, she couldn't help it; she held it to her cheek and then sniffed. It smelled of Evie – that particular scent she always wore. Carol didn't know the name.

She was tempted to have a peek upstairs but it would be too risky, less easy to explain. The house was silent. It felt empty, but she couldn't be sure. Freya was probably out but there again, she might just be asleep; teenagers were notorious for sleeping in.

She checked the sink: a few dirty dishes and cups. Her eye was caught by a pile of papers beside the phone. It was on the L-shaped worktop that jutted out into the room. There was a bowl of fruit there, too. Some mangy-looking brown bananas. Evie should make banana cake with them. Carol could show her how. As if.

She glanced at the paper on the top of the pile. It said 'Honeymount Primary School'. Something from Michael's school. Beside it was a diary, open at the correct page: 24 January. Evie had scribbled a few things down. Carol recognised the handwriting; it was large and a bit messy. Arty would be a kinder description.

'Football', it said, and just below: 'Call Zelda to rebook regres-sion therapy.'

Carol froze. Zelda? She must have made a mistake. She read the note again. It definitely said Zelda. Must be another one. But how many Zeldas were there? It wasn't exactly a common name. Her stomach clunked. Zelda had once spoken of regression therapy; she'd said it was quite popular. Carol had probably sneered, as usual. She couldn't remember.

She started to flick back, page by page, through the diary. It was mostly full of one-line notes: 'Dominic to tea'; 'Freya parents' evening'; 'call Nic'. She stopped at Tuesday 20 January, four days before. There it was again, in capital letters: 'ZELDA. 11.30 a.m. Regression Therapy'.

She didn't understand, it made no sense. They both knew a Zelda, a Zelda who regressed people – or claimed she could. It was such a coincidence. Too much of a coincidence.

A shadow passed through Carol's mind. Zelda was a dark one, always had been, always would be. Carol would ring her the moment she got home and clear the matter up. There was sure to be an innocent explanation. She didn't like the idea of Evie doing this regression business, though. It could mess with your brain.

She flicked back to the correct page in Evie's diary and left the house quickly, looking right and left again as she walked down the path. She was disappointed about Freya but it was for the best, really. She might have been frightened, finding her in the house, and it was easier not to have to come up with excuses.

The bike was exactly where she'd left it against the fence. Carol climbed on. Whatever Zelda was up to, one thing was certain: she'd have Evie's best interests at heart – and Carol's, of course. She might even be able to shed some light on Evie's sudden departure and put Carol's mind at rest. Zelda might be peculiar but she was a good old stick really. She didn't have a bad bone in her body.

Carol pedalled as fast as she could down the street and back up Richmond Road towards home. Several police cars roared by in the opposite direction, their sirens wailing. She stopped for a moment and watched them turn into Evie's street. She frowned.

She jumped back on her bike, her head down, and resumed pedalling at full speed. She'd wanted to pick up some coley for the cats in the market but she could do it another time. She needed to speak to Zelda immediately, to find out what was going on.

*   *   *

Evie rocked backwards and forwards on the overground train willing it to go faster, to respond to her motion. All she could see was the face of her daughter, her beautiful Freya. Oh God, let her be all right. Please let her be all right. I'll never let her out of my sight again.

She couldn't believe that people were so slow. They ambled on and off carrying their stupid shopping bags, stupid smiles on their faces. She wanted to scream: 'Don't you realise what's happening?' But she wouldn't do that. They might call the police. Then she'd never get there.

The police. It'd be all right. They'd arrive on time. Nic said they were ready, waiting. Shit, was this really happening? Maybe it was all a nightmare.

She texted Bill. She could rely on him. *Please collect Michael from football. I'll explain later.*

What if Alan had tricked them and met Freya somewhere else, got on a different train? Alan. It was so hard to believe. Maybe Nic had gone mad. But she wouldn't lie about something like this. Evie let out a howl. Several people stared. She put her hands over her mouth to stop the noise and slumped over, her head almost on her knees.

'Are you all right?' The woman sitting next to her touched her arm. Evie shook her head, shook the woman off.

They should have arrested him straightaway, the moment Nic told them. They were using Freya. Evie didn't care if they needed the evidence, so long as her baby was safe.

She had to change at Waterloo and find the tube. She was tearing through the tunnels, shoving people aside and hurtling past. She didn't care what they said, they were just streaks of colour, blurred impediments. At last, St Pancras. The doors opened and she spilled out on to the platform, looking this way and that. Why weren't the signs clearer?

'Careful!' She'd stepped on a man's foot. No time to apologise. She was running, running up the escalator. She didn't need to stop for breath. She was power-charged. Some people moved aside to let her pass. Good job or they'd get hurt.

She reached the main concourse and paused for a second to search for the statue. Where was it, where was Freya? Her heart was thumping so hard that she thought it might split. Not till she had Freya safely in her arms . . .

She saw Nic first, hovering in front of a shop window. She made a wild gesture with her arms but Evie looked away. She didn't care about Nic, only Freya. Beyond Evie was the giant bronze statue, two lovers clasping each other, their foreheads touching in a tender embrace.

She cried out: 'Oh!'

Chapter Forty-Two

❧❧❧

'Zelda speakin'.'

Carol cleared her throat: 'It's me.' She realised that her stomach was fluttering. How silly she was being. This was her sister, for goodness' sake! She carried the phone over to the kitchen table and plonked herself down. The plastic cord just about stretched if you untwisted a few coils and yanked.

'Why are you ringin'?' Zelda demanded.

Carol was affronted. 'You could at least try to sound pleased.' But she was being deflected. She must get to the heart of the matter. 'I was over at Evie's,' she began.

'What do you mean?' Zelda could be so sharp.

'I'm about to explain,' Carol said, as patiently as she could, 'if you'll only wait.' She tried again. 'I happened to be outside Evie's house when I saw her rushing out without a coat on.'

'So what?' Zelda said. 'Not everyone wears coats these days. The weather's much milder than it used to be. You've said so yourself a hundred times.'

Carol gritted her teeth. Zelda could be most trying.

'I know,' Carol went on, 'but she did seem to be in a terrible flap. And she left the door wide open.'

'Really?' Now Zelda was interested.

Albert was coiling round Carol's ankles, purring. She reached down to give him a stroke. 'I was worried,' she said, 'so I decided to pop inside and check that everything was all right.'

Zelda cackled. 'You mean you went inside to have a good butcher's, you nosy cow?'

Carol straightened her shoulders. 'I was not being nosy. I was concerned.'

Zelda made a huffing sound, which Carol ignored. She

tickled Albert under the chin. 'There didn't seem to be anyone around so I went into the kitchen.'

'I hope you didn't open any cupboards.'

Carol frowned. 'No, I didn't open any cupboards, but I did notice something in Evie's diary by the phone.'

Was there a slight intake of breath at the other end?

'There was a note which said "Call Zelda to rebook regression therapy". What's this all about, Griselda? I think you owe me an explanation.'

Albert jumped on to Carol's lap. She pushed him off.

At last Zelda broke the silence. 'Evie *has* been phonin' me for advice,' she said slowly. She seemed to be considering her words very carefully. 'And I did regress her the other day. She found it very useful.'

Carol chewed on her lip. It was taking a moment or two to digest the information. 'But how on earth did she get your number?' Suddenly, there were so many questions that she didn't know which to ask first.

'I don't know. I thought maybe you'd given it to her.'

Carol pulled a face. She could normally tell when Zelda was lying. 'Don't be silly. I'd never do that. It'd be too dangerous. And besides, you know I don't like spiritualism.'

'Well, I haven't a clue,' Zelda went on. She sounded annoyed. 'She must've picked my card up somewhere – or maybe someone recommended me. I'm quite popular, you know. I must say I was surprised when I put two and two together and twigged who it was.'

Carol felt uncomfortable. Her chest was tight; she didn't know why. She shuffled in her seat. She was struggling to understand.

'But why didn't you tell me?' she asked. 'This is my daughter we're talking about, remember. I've tried to be tolerant about your funny ways and what you get up to in your own home is your affair. But Evie's a different matter. You should have told me the moment you realised who it was.'

There was a noise on the other end of the line, like a snort. Was Zelda laughing? Surely not. That'd be totally inappropriate. 'Look,' Zelda said, 'I've bin helpin' this daughter of yours with a few problems. I've bin doing her a favour, if only you knew.'

'What problems?' Carol started winding the telephone cord round and round her forefinger. 'Is there something you haven't told me? Why was she in such a state?'

'Stop fussin' will you?' Zelda replied. 'Everything's fine. Sometimes I think you smother that precious daughter of yours. She's a grown woman now.'

Carol stopped twisting the cord. 'Don't be ridiculous. How can I possibly smother her when she doesn't even know who I am? And she may be a grown woman but she's very vulnerable at the moment. You must stop talking to her. Promise me you'll do as I ask?'

There was a pause, the sound of a match being lit.

'Zelda?' said Carol. She pictured Zelda's lower lip; she'd bet it was sticking out. Zelda always stuck it out when she sulked.

'I promise,' Zelda said.

'At least that's sorted.' Carol sighed. 'But you've given me a terrible shock. You might have ruined everything.'

Zelda was silent.

'And you should stop smoking,' Carol chided. 'I've told you time and again it's bad for your health.'

'Two-faced bitch.'

Carol froze. She must have misheard. 'I beg your pardon?' The air between them stilled, every particle on hold.

'I have to go now,' Zelda muttered finally, making the atoms shake again in an agitated mass. 'I've got more important things to do than sit here all day gabbin' with you.'

Zelda put the phone down and rubbed her hands together. She got so cold, just sitting still like that. She glanced out of the window. It was raining now, too. Dull old day. She frowned. Not so dull, actually. She'd had a feeling when she woke up that something was going to happen. She'd better dig around a bit, find out what was up.

She rose slowly and moved over to the window to draw the curtains. They preferred it when it was dark, the spirits, like the inside of her brain; they could slip in and out without any trouble. They liked that.

She took the crocheted shawl from the back of the chair and

wrapped it round her shoulders. She fiddled with the coloured tassels round the edge, twisting them between forefinger and thumb. She wasn't looking forward to this, but curiosity always got the better of her. She was a nosy old cow. Just like Carol snooping round that kitchen.

She shuffled into her bedroom and took a book from the little shelf on the left-hand wall. She found the photo under the front cover and looked at it; it was the black-and-white, passport-sized one that Carol had given her all them years ago. It was a sweet-looking baby, she had to admit, wrapped in a blanket. Almost bald, with just a few bits of fair hair on the top of its head. She stroked its face for a moment. Its tiny hands were curled up in front in tight little fists and its eyes were only half open.

She swallowed. 'Derek's baby.' She took the photo with her back into the living room and plonked down in the chair, resting it on her lap. She stared down at the picture for a few moments before closing her eyes, her hands folded in front of her, and started rocking backwards and forwards rhythmically.

Something cold brushed against her cheek and the hair on the back of her neck prickled. A whisper of warm wind rustled against her ear.

She started to moan. 'Course I should of told her,' she muttered. 'But what she done to me wasn't nice either.' Her head rolled from side to side and her tongue sagged in her mouth. Her upper body felt rigid, like hardboard. 'You're not allowed to give 'em the really bad news,' she was saying, 'it's against the rules.'

They were pushing down on her chest, compressing her lungs. Where was her inhaler?

'Serves Carol right. Teach her a lesson. I know it's not Evie's fault but . . .' Her legs started shaking, flopping and jerking like a pair of fish on the end of a line. 'She probably couldn't of stopped it, even if I'd told her, told 'em both.'

She was twitching that much, she needed to lie down flat. But they wouldn't let her. They wanted their bit of fun. 'I'm sorry,' she gasped. 'I know I'm bad, I know I done wrong.'

They were pulling on her limbs, stretching the muscles until she thought they'd snap. 'I did tell Evie to be careful,' she cried. 'I did sort of warn her.'

They wouldn't listen, they weren't impressed.

'But it should have been my baby,' she cried. 'She had no right to take my baby, my fella.'

They didn't understand, they had no mercy.

She tried to stand but her arms and hands were trembling too much to push her up. She gave one final, violent shudder before slumping back in her chair and falling into a deep, dreamless sleep.

There were so many people, coming in and out of glass-fronted shops, checking watches, sipping coffees, wasting precious time. Every second contained so many milliseconds, each one loaded with significance, each one crucial.

Evie elbowed her way through the crowds towards the base of the statue. She could see clear space around it, a void waiting to be filled. She saw a man leave the crowd and walk into the space. He seemed to occupy the entire blankness. He stopped and looked around. He was waiting for someone. He was short, slight, wearing a dark raincoat, carrying two bags: a black computer case and a brown leather holdall. Evie blinked. It took a moment to register; he looked completely different somehow, a stranger, but it was definitely him: Alan.

She made to plunge towards him. She was going to rip him to pieces.

'Stop!'

She couldn't move; arms were restraining her. She struggled, kicked and squirmed but the arms held tight. She was a chained animal, a mad creature. 'Let me go! My daughter . . .'

She ceased struggling. She could only stare, mesmerised. Freya had appeared in the space; she looked tiny. Alan, though, seemed to be getting bigger, growing before Evie's eyes. There was a clamp around Evie's chest, squeezing her heart, crushing it beneath her ribs. It was like watching a film. She was powerless to change the sequence of events.

Freya had a rucksack on her back. Her overnight bag. She took several faltering steps towards Alan, who held out his arms.

'Get off!' Evie's scream bounced off the ceiling and ricocheted round the walls. She was spitting now, writhing. People were staring but she took no notice.

'It's all right, Mrs Freestone,' a voice was saying. 'We're here. Police. It's under control.'

She glanced to her right. One of the men restraining her was speaking to her but he was staring straight ahead, totally focused on what was unfolding before them.

There was a shout. Three men and a woman – all plain-clothed, in jackets and trousers – had appeared from nowhere, swarming towards the statue. The crowd seemed to have frozen; no one spoke. Evie tried to spot Freya but she couldn't see anything now; there were too many people, too many obstructions.

'My daughter! What's happening?' She was blind with terror.

'Keep calm,' her captor said. 'They've got—'

'This is a customer alert.' It was a man's voice on the tannoy. 'A suspect package has been located in the vicinity of St Pancras Station. The station is being temporarily closed while investigations are carried out . . .'

'Shit.' The police officer on Evie's left loosened his grip slightly.

'Passengers are requested to remain calm,' the announcement continued, 'and leave the station via the nearest exit. There is no need to panic; I repeat, no need to panic. All arrivals and departures are cancelled until further notice . . .'

The crowds started to move, slowly at first then faster. People were grumbling, pushing towards the exits. There was a shout: 'Bomb . . . hurry . . .' The pace quickened; the tension was palpable.

Evie swung around. The police officer on her left was speaking into his radio. Then he was shouting over her head to the officer on her right. 'He's made a run for it . . . He's got the girl . . .'

Evie's world was spinning, her legs were buckling beneath her. The police officer was talking into the radio again but she couldn't hear what he was saying, just fragments of words with splintered meanings.

A voice cut through the fractured sounds. She strained to understand. 'We've lost them – they could be anywhere . . .'

She could scarcely breathe. She needed air. She wanted to throw up. She wanted Freya.

'My baby!' she cried, before everything went black.

Chapter Forty-Three

Becca's fingers were so cold that she could scarcely get the match out of the box and grip tightly enough to light it. It took several attempts and when at last she succeeded, she held the flame to the piece of newspaper and watched it burn for a moment before putting it in the stone fireplace.

Luckily the wood was completely dry and caught straight-away. It had been sitting there in the basket for Christ knew how long. It must be months since they'd last visited the house. She was always too busy to enjoy it, really. The whole place felt dirty and unloved, despite the fact that Mme Mercier was paid to come once a week to clean.

Well, it was obvious that she wasn't doing that. Normally, of course, Becca telephoned several days before to warn of their arrival. There'd be milk, orange juice, chicken and croissants waiting for them, along with fresh flowers in every vase. The beds would be newly made and smelling of fabric conditioner, the shutters would be flung open and Mme Mercier would have turned the heating on well in advance to warm the place up. She'd get a shock when she realised that she'd been caught out. Served her right.

Becca sat back on her haunches and warmed her hands in front of the flames. She had no idea what time it was – it didn't really matter. She was glad that she'd decided not to have a landline installed. She was completely uncontactable, possibly for the first time in her working life. It felt good to be alone, just her and her thoughts.

A grey mouse with a very long tail scuttled in front of her and scarpered down a tiny hole in the skirting board. Well, just her and her thoughts and the mice. She didn't mind mice, actually. There'd been an infestation on the estate all those years ago.

Everyone made a huge fuss, including Mam. There was even a petition to the Council. There was a family of them nesting somewhere in Becca's room.

Jude screamed whenever she saw one. The memory made Becca smile. She'd pretended to be frightened, too, but secretly she had names for them: Fluffy, Henrietta – she'd read that name somewhere in a book. It sounded mouselike to her, sort of scratchy. She'd tried to encourage them to appear on Jude's side of the room by scattering crumbs of bread and putting tiny morsels of cheese in the corners. Jude never did find out.

Her stomach made a noise; she realised that she was hungry. She'd stopped in a village on the way from Calais to buy a few things: baguette, milk, a bit of ham. Not *her* village: she didn't want anyone to see her. She'd deliberately parked the car at the back of the house, behind the trees. But word travelled fast round here, you couldn't keep anything secret for long.

She bit the corner of her thumbnail; there wasn't much left to chew on. She'd been here a whole day and night now. The solitude had felt quite dreamy, muffled; it was almost like being underwater. She was grateful that she'd been allowed that space, but she was quite surprised that they hadn't tracked her down. She'd have to make up her mind quickly about what to do.

The fire crackled. The last time they'd had one here the children had toasted marshmallows that they'd brought from London. She imagined that she could see Alice and James's faces in the flames. Poor them. Poor Tom, too. Her heart hurt. Maybe it didn't have to be like this? Maybe there was some other way?

She remembered Gary's tongue, slithering eel-like into her mouth, and his impassive, staring eyes when she'd pleaded with him. She wished that she'd never got into the grammar school, never played hockey. She wished Jude had gone to her friend's that day instead of coming home. She wished Jude hadn't hummed so loudly and annoyingly in their bedroom, distracting her from her essay, that Mam had finished work earlier, that Mam hadn't drunk so much, been around more to talk about things.

Excuses, excuses. Becca had brought this on herself; she was a wicked person. Her time had come. The children and Tom were better off without her.

She got up slowly and crossed the stone floor to the kitchen. There was still half a baguette in the bread bin beside the kettle where she'd left it; she tore a chunk off, dropping crumbs over the floor, and ate mechanically. It was hard and stale but she didn't care. She needed to quieten her stomach. It was just fuel.

She wiped her mouth with her hand and walked slowly up the curved wooden staircase to the bedroom at the back of the house. The shutters were still closed. She ought to keep them like that but it was oppressive, so she opened them and stared out.

There was nothing ahead but flat fields, trees and the odd barn dotted across the landscape; there weren't even any cows. There was no hint of sunshine and everything looked grey, even the grass. She used to love that view but now she wondered why on earth they hadn't bought a house in Provence, or Tuscany. Tom would have preferred it but she'd argued that Normandy was easier to get to with the children.

Tom had wanted a ski chalet somewhere in the Alps as well; it would be a good investment, he'd said, and the kids would love it. But something in her had baulked at the idea. She'd pretended it was just the money but the real reason was that Tom was a good skier, he'd been often as a child. And the children were coming along nicely. She, on the other hand, was hopeless. It scared the living daylights out of her; she'd never master it. She didn't want to be the odd one out. She'd had enough of that.

The odd one out. It never really left you. Perhaps Tom would buy that ski chalet now.

She moved away from the window quickly and started packing the few things that she'd got out back in her bag. Her work clothes, she decided, she'd leave behind. She wouldn't be needing them now.

She picked up the black wool Vivienne Westwood jacket that she'd left on the chair and laid it carefully on the end of the bed. Then she did the same with the pencil skirt and her black tights. Her black, high-heeled, patent-leather court shoes she put on the floor, facing outwards. She stood back for a moment and admired them all. She loved the jacket in particular; she never could quite believe that it belonged to her. The clothes were remarkably uncrumpled; they seemed to be waiting for someone else to step into them.

Next, she took off her Cartier watch and her diamond stud earrings and put them on the bedside table. She'd feel silly and overdressed in them now. Girls from Benwell, Newcastle, didn't wear things like that. She straightened the rug and took one last look around. It was a lovely room, with low oak beams and thick uneven walls. The bed was antique, Louis XV-style French, with a softly curved headboard and footboard. Funnily enough, they'd bought it in London and she'd had it uphol-stered in a shocking pink silky material. She and Tom had enjoyed that bed.

She shook herself. It was definitely time to go. She picked up her bag and stepped out on to the landing. The children's bedroom doors were closed and the air was dusty and silent. She realised that she felt like an intruder in her own home. Perhaps she'd always felt like an intruder here. Well, the house would soon be left in peace.

She descended a few steps and stopped. Her ears pricked. There was the distinctive sound of wheels on gravel. Fuck. Someone was coming up the drive.

Her heart started hammering. If only she'd left sooner; she was a fool. She thought quickly. She had the car keys in her bag. Whoever it was would surely ring the bell first and wait for a few moments, buying her some precious time. If she was speedy enough she could dart out of the back door and escape via the side entrance to the house. She'd be away down the road before they'd realised what had happened.

The fire was still burning downstairs. She'd been silly to light it. She'd have to leave it now. For all she knew, Tom had called the police. The whole story might be out. She wasn't going to be there when her face was splashed across the newspapers, when the whole world knew what she'd done. She wouldn't give Gary the satisfaction.

She had no idea where she was going. Tuscany, now there

was an idea. She could drive down to Nice and flit across the border and after Tuscany – who knew? She thought she could hear scrunching – footsteps approaching the front door. She paused and listened. It sounded like just one set of footsteps. Tom hadn't set the entire local constabulary on her, then. But she couldn't be sure.

A thought crossed her mind: Gary didn't know about the house. At least, she didn't think so. And even if she'd mentioned it, there was no way that he'd know where it was, the exact location. He could never find her, it was far too remote.

He'd managed to get hold of her mobile number, though, and her Richmond address. She shuddered. She felt as if the massive stone walls of the house were closing in on her, the roof collapsing, threatening to crush her. She had to escape into the fresh air.

She slipped into the kitchen and reached for the back-door key on the shelf by the cookery books. It made a grating noise as she turned it, which made her wince. There was a loud knock. Her hand was wet and slippery as she tried to twist the brass knob. She dried her hand with the sleeve of her sweatshirt and tried again. This time, the knob slid round and she opened the door a little.

She glanced down just before squeezing through. There, in the corner, was the old axe that Tom used to chop wood. She bent down and reached for the end. It felt cool and hard in the palm of her left hand. She picked it up.

Luckily the path leading to the car was concrete rather than gravel. She tiptoed for a few yards then sprinted towards the black Mercedes parked beneath the trees. The axe felt heavy. She gripped tightly so that it wouldn't fall.

There was a shout: 'Stop!' She fumbled for the key in her bag with her right hand; why hadn't she got it out before? Her fingers settled on the round metal key ring and she pulled, zapping the button as soon as it was pointing in the right direction. The locks clunked open.

She threw her bag on the passenger seat. She could hear the blood whooshing in her ears and her temples were pounding. She wasn't even blinking, she was so focused. She transferred the axe to her right hand and started to lift her left foot into the car. She gasped. Fingers were already seizing her shoulders, grasping, restraining her. She struggled to shake them off but she couldn't.

She screamed: 'No!' Birds fluttered out of the trees and flapped wildly above her.

She paused a second. The axe hung limply. She opened her fingers. She could feel it sliding from her grasp. It was only a couple of feet from the ground but it seemed to take for ever. Finally, it hit the concrete with a thud.

It was done.

She looked up and her eyes met another pair of eyes; they were big and dark, framed by thick, close-knit brows. The man was panting hard and she could feel his hot breath on her face.

She lost her footing and plunged towards him, knocking him off balance. He staggered back a few steps but quickly rallied. Before she had time to react, his arms were round her, circling her completely, gripping so tightly that they hurt.

She closed her eyes. She was finished. She had no strength left. Her head was squashed against the man's chest. She could feel his heart heaving, could hear the booming and swishing of blood coursing through vein and ventricle. Their two hearts were pumping in unison, in perfect, mocking synchronicity.

She parted her lips: 'Tom!'

It was scarcely audible; she was choked with tears.

'I didn't do it,' she moaned. 'I dropped it this time. It's on the floor. I didn't do it.'

Chapter Forty-Four

Carol stared out of the kitchen window. She was deeply troubled about her phone call with Zelda. It seemed highly unlikely that Evie had just happened on Zelda's number and Zelda had offered no other explanation. More importantly, she hadn't explained why she'd failed to tell Carol about the conversations they'd been having. It was all most disturbing.

Zelda had said Evie was all right, but she sounded weird, as if she were concealing something. Of course, the likelihood was that she had no idea what was going on or why Evie was in such a rush. But then there were those occasions when Zelda had claimed the spirits had revealed something to her and she'd actually been right. Coincidence, probably, but it made Carol very nervous all the same.

She didn't like it at all. Her stomach was in knots.

She paced around the room a few times. She found she couldn't stay still for long. It was still raining outside but anything would be better than just hanging around like this, worrying. Victoria and Albert were sensibly curled up on the plastic kitchen chairs. It was always warm in here, especially when the heating was on.

Albert looked up at Carol for a moment and miaowed. 'You stay there,' she commanded. 'I won't be long.'

She hurried into the hall and started putting on her waterproofs, which were still slightly damp from earlier on. Then she opened the door and wheeled her bike down the garden path.

She was surprised when she arrived, panting, outside Evie's house to see a light on in the front room. Was she home now? Carol hesitated for a moment before leaning her bike against Evie's wall and padlocking it. She had a perfectly legitimate reason for calling: she'd happened to be passing and noticed that Evie's door was wide open and no one was there. She was just popping by to check everything was all right.

Her hands were trembling slightly as she rang the bell. It would be the first time that she'd admitted knowing where Evie lived. But they were friends, from the writing group. They lived near each other and Carol's story was perfectly plausible. There was no reason why things couldn't return to how they were, once she'd put her mind at rest and established that the family were safe.

There was the sound of heavy footsteps coming down the hall. Carol was surprised. Evie had a lighter tread. The door opened and a tall, handsome, middle-aged man with a weathered face and silver hair was standing in the entrance. Carol recognised him as Evie's next-door neighbour, who was often fixing things in his garden.

'Oh,' she said, trying to peer round his shoulder, 'where's Evie?'

He frowned. 'She's not here.'

There was something in his voice that made Carol even more anxious.

'I'm sorry,' she said, straightening up, 'I must sound terribly rude. I'm an old friend of Evie's – from her writing group. I happened to be passing earlier on and noticed that she'd left the door open. I wanted to check that everything was in order, that nothing had been stolen.'

The man's face softened. 'I see,' he said. 'An old friend.' He was still standing in the doorway, blocking the entrance.

Michael appeared from the right, which Carol thought was the sitting room, and stood beside the man, who put an arm around him. Carol was taken aback – she hadn't realised they knew each other so well – but Michael seemed relaxed. He sort of sank comfortably into the older man's side. His face looked pinched, though, not like his usual self at all.

She thought rapidly. 'Michael!' she beamed. 'I've heard so much about you. I was worried about your mother.'

She dropped her bag on the step and several items spilled out: her keys, a pen, a packet of tissues. She stooped down to pick them up. 'How careless! I'm such a butterfingers today. May I come in for a moment while I sort myself out?'

Michael raised his eyebrows but the man moved aside and Carol scurried in before he could change his mind. She pretended to rearrange her bag.

'I must admit,' she said, now that she was safely inside, 'that there are a few things about Evie that have given me cause for concern recently. I was hoping that you might be able to shed some light on matters.' She looked the man in the eye. He had a lean, intelligent face, she thought; sensitive and kind.

He sighed, turning from her to close the door. 'I'm afraid your instincts are correct.' He started to guide Carol and Michael towards the kitchen at the back of the house. 'I'm Bill, Evie's neighbour,' he explained. 'Something terrible has happened. You'd better take your coat off and I'll put you in the picture.'

Al's hand was clamped around her right arm, squeezing tight. 'This way.' He was pushing through the crowds, bumping into people. 'Hurry.'

'Where are we going?'

'Don't talk, I'll tell you later.'

Freya's heart was thumping so loudly that she could hear it. She didn't understand. He was Nic's husband. Why hadn't he told her? She didn't know what it meant or what to think. She'd seen two or three men and a woman approaching; she'd heard them say, 'Police.' Then the announcement, everybody starting to shove. She was afraid that she was going to fall over and they'd trample on her.

'I'm scared . . .'

'It'll be all right.'

'Where are we going?'

They were out in the open now, half walking, half running along the main road through a sea of people. 'Oi, be careful . . . stop pushing . . .' Al took no notice. His grip on Freya's arm was so tight that she couldn't get away if she wanted to.

'I want to go home . . .' She had a lump in her throat. He didn't hear, or if he did, he took no notice.

Someone trod on her foot. It hurt. She started to cry. She wanted Mum. People were talking about a bomb. That was why they were running away from the station. Maybe they were all going to get killed.

Everyone was hurrying, jostling her. Police cars with wailing sirens were trying to get past. Cars and buses were moving aside. She was tired. They seemed to have walked miles. There was a railway sign ahead saying Euston Station. He pulled her up the grey, concrete steps to the main entrance.

'Where are we going?' she repeated. They stopped in front of a ticket machine.

'Birmingham.'

'But I thought . . .'

He was fumbling in his coat pocket for something. His wallet? 'Wait while I get the tickets.'

'I thought we were going to Paris.'

'The train's been cancelled. You'll like Birmingham . . .' He shoved his credit card in the slot. 'We can go to Paris later. You've got your passport?' He sounded sharp.

'Yes.'

She noticed his hands. They had blue, sticky-up veins on the back. His neck, poking out of the top of his collar, was thin and slightly wrinkly. She'd known he was old; she shouldn't be shocked. She'd probably fancy him once they got to know each other properly.

'I love you,' she whispered tentatively. It sounded odd, as if someone else was speaking. But it was true, wasn't it – that she loved him? She'd written it often enough. Maybe if she kept saying it then she'd forget that he was forty-eight and skinny. She looked over her shoulder. The woman standing behind was giving her a funny look.

'Quick,' he said, glancing up at the departures board. 'We have to buy some things.'

He pulled her into Accessorize and grabbed a pink woolly cap and scarf. 'Keep the change,' he told the shop girl. He turned to Freya.

She started to protest: 'But I don't like—'

'Put these on.'

She did as she was told, pulling the cap down over her ears and wrapping the scarf around her neck, right up to her nose.

In another shop he grabbed a brown jacket for himself and a plum-coloured jumper. They were pretty gross. He kept tapping his hand on the counter while he waited for the credit card to go through. 'We'll miss our train . . .'

She watched while he emptied the pockets of his navy-blue raincoat and put the jumper and jacket on. Then he rolled up the mac and shoved it in the brown holdall. He looked at her properly for the first time since they'd met in front of the statue. 'The police are after us. We mustn't let them find us. If they do we'll never see each other again . . .'

'Oh.' Freya was shivering. She was in big trouble. Mum would be mad at her. She thought of Gemma and Chantelle. If they found out she'd gone off with someone's dad . . . the thought made her want to throw up.

'We'll talk on the train,' he said. He sounded nicer now, kinder. He squeezed her hand: 'You're beautiful.' Her cheeks glowed. Maybe it was going to be OK.

He pulled her down the platform and on to the train. 'In here.' She kept her eyes fixed on the ground. She was clinging on to his hand, which felt sweaty and strange. She hoped that he wouldn't try to kiss her. She didn't think that she'd like him to kiss her. Maybe there'd be a funfair in Birmingham. They could go shopping and stay in a posh hotel. Gemma and Chantelle would be dead jealous if she told them that. At least that was one good thing, anyway.

Evie looked up. There were strange faces around her, people in green and yellow uniforms. There was something over her nose and mouth, a mask. She wanted to rip it off but her arms wouldn't move. She started to struggle.

One of the people in uniform, a middle-aged man with grey hair and a moustache, smiled. 'You'll be all right, love. You had a bit of a funny turn. We're just going to check you out . . .'

She tried to speak but couldn't. Her whole body was tense. She needed to get up, to find Freya.

'Don't worry, they'll bring your daughter back,' the man said.

A woman paramedic on the other side of the stretcher stroked Evie's hair off her forehead. She flinched. It was a strangely intimate gesture. 'They've alerted all the airports, railway stations, ferries. It's on the radio and TV. There's no chance he'll get away . . .'

Evie felt her shoulders relax a little but her mind was soon racing ahead. Airports . . . railway stations. They might slip through the net. They could go anywhere, change names, their appearance. She might never see Freya again. She heard a moaning sound and realised that it was coming from her. He might have pills, or a knife. He might kill her, kill them both.

She was inside the ambulance now. It was dark and claustrophobic. She wanted to scream. They were putting something on her arm and her chest.

'We're going to take your blood pressure,' the man said. 'Looks like you've had a bit of a bump on the head . . .'

She registered for the first time that her head was throbbing. She thought it hurt somewhere at the back but she didn't care. She tried to pull free, to get up, kick her legs, thrash out. The man put a restraining arm across her middle. It felt heavy.

'What's your name?' the woman asked. She had a low, sympathetic voice and a slight Northern accent. She lifted the oxygen mask up for a moment.

'Evie.'

'Listen, Evie,' the woman went on, replacing the mask, 'I know you must be really frightened but try to keep calm. Struggling won't help.' She took Evie's hand and patted it.

Evie wriggled but the man's arm was weighing her down. She didn't want to listen to the woman, she just wanted to break free.

'The police are doing all they can to find your daughter,' the woman continued, still holding her hand. 'There's a national alert. He won't get away. I reckon you'll have her back in your arms by tonight.'

In her arms. It was what she wanted more than anything. Evie started to cry. The hot tears pricked her cheeks, making her face itch.

'We just need to check you're all right, then we'll take you back to the police and they can explain exactly what they're doing, OK?'

Back to the police, that would be something. It made sense. Evie nodded and stopped struggling.

'That's better,' the woman said, adjusting what felt like a sticky pad on her chest. The man took his arm away. Evie took a deep breath.

'There've been several sightings of them heading towards Euston Station.' It was a new voice, a man's – official-sounding. Evie couldn't see him, he was behind her at the back of the ambulance. There were sounds of a radio chattering. Sirens. Evie's stomach fluttered and turned over. She tried to get up.

'Wait a minute, love.' The male paramedic looked over his shoulder to speak to the man behind. 'She seems OK. We need to clean the wound on the back of her head. I don't think she'll need an X-ray.'

'What's up at St Pancras?' the woman paramedic asked. 'Do they know yet? Was it a bomb?'

'False alarm. Some mug left a bag in the women's toilet.'

The woman clucked. 'What a prat.' She squeezed Evie's hand. 'Be brave,' she said. 'The police are doing all they can.'

Freya was sitting by the window watching the scenery hurtling past. It was spitting with rain and everything was dull and grey. She pulled the pink scarf up over her nose. She hated pink normally, never wore it, but she liked feeling her warm, moist breath inside the wool.

Al was beside her. His left leg was touching her right one and their knees were rubbing. It made her feel slightly sick. He was pretending to be relaxed but she could tell that he was nervous really. He kept looking round and his small hands, clasped together on the table in front of them, were trembling.

He searched for her hand on her lap under the table and squeezed it, leaning over to whisper in her ear: 'It's going to be OK, gorgeous.'

He'd called her 'gorgeous' and 'beautiful' hundreds of times in emails, but it was weird hearing him actually *say* it. She realised that she hadn't thought about his voice. She'd tried to picture his face as it really might be often enough, but in her head he spoke like one of the boys at school. But his real voice was well posh. Like a headteacher's or something. She didn't squeeze his hand back. She'd be too embarrassed. Her face felt hot; it was probably red. She hoped he wouldn't see, he'd think she was well babyish.

'What are we going to do when we get there?' she asked, lowering her scarf and turning to him. She spoke very quietly so that no one would hear. The seats opposite were empty but the rest of the carriage was fairly full.

'We'll find a hotel,' he replied. 'Or we might catch a flight somewhere.'

She was surprised. 'Where? Paris?'

He licked his lips and smiled. 'We'll see.' She noticed that his teeth were small and slightly pointy and he had a little cut on his chin – from shaving, she supposed. Dad used to do that sometimes, cut himself.

'I have to be back soon,' she said quickly. 'My parents will miss me.'

'Sure.' He put his hand on her knee now and squeezed that. She wiggled a bit and he took it away.

She pictured Mum and Dad. They'd be so worried. But Dad had the new baby to think of. He didn't really care about her. Maybe Mum would have a new baby, too, with her boyfriend. She wasn't too old, probably. Yuck. Freya pulled her feet up on to the seat, wrapped her arms around her knees and rested her chin on them, curling herself into a little ball.

Steve would have to come and live with them if Mum had a baby. Freya didn't like him. He was creepy. He just pretended to be nice to her and Michael. He'd prefer it if they were out of the way. Well, he'd got his wish now. Maybe Michael would run off too, then he'd be *really* happy.

Michael. She'd miss him – and he'd be well sad without her. She wanted to cry. She tried to swallow back the tears, wiped her eyes with her sleeve. 'Am I going to school on Monday?'

Al put an arm round her shoulder and touched her hair with his lips. It made her scalp prickle. 'You don't have to go ever again if you don't want. I'll look after you.'

Never go back to that stinking hole or see Gemma, Abigail

and Chantelle? She straightened her legs out, uncurled. 'But I will see my mum again, won't I?'

'Of course – if you want to.'

Maybe Mum wouldn't want to see *her* now, she'd be too furious. Freya felt tired. Her eyes were so heavy. She wanted to go to sleep. She wished that she was at home, under her purple duvet, that none of this had ever happened. Too late now.

'Are you hungry?'

Freya shook her head. Her mouth felt dry. There was no saliva in it. 'I'm thirsty, though.'

'I'll get you a drink from the buffet.'

It was only next door. Freya could see there was a queue.

'What would you like?'

She thought for a moment. 'Coke. And maybe a Twix or something, please.'

She watched his back as he started to walk down the carriage. He'd taken his jacket off and was just wearing the plum jumper. She could see that his legs were quite skinny in his dark trousers, much skinnier than Dad's. His shoulders sloped and there was a little bald patch on the back of his head. He turned and mouthed: 'Stay there.'

There was an announcement: 'This train will shortly be arriving at Watford Junction. Please have your luggage ready and make sure that you take all your bags with you before leaving the carriage.'

Quite a lot of people stood up and started taking things down from the shelves above. Her heart pitter-pattered. She felt under the table for her backpack, she didn't know why, and pulled it on to her lap, clutching it to her chest.

'The train is now arriving at Watford Junction. This station is Watford Junction. Next stop . . .'

She arose, putting her hand on the back of the seat to steady herself. The train pulled slowly to a halt and she could hear carriage doors opening. There was a swishing sound in her ears, the blood pulsing through her brain. She turned towards the exit. Lots of people were in the aisle, blocking the way.

Her mind emptied. There was no time to think. She had no

idea where she'd go. She just knew she had to get out. 'Excuse me, please . . .'

A woman in front of her turned around. 'You'll have to wait your turn . . .'

They didn't understand, she must leave.

'Please, I have to . . .' She tried to elbow her way past, but the woman was having none of it. 'There's a queue – in case you haven't noticed.'

'Wait!' It was Al's voice, Al's heavy hand on her shoulder. Her stomach flopped this way and that. 'Sit down.'

He sounded angry. She felt tiny, three years old. She shrank back into the seat. 'I need the toilet.'

She glanced up and saw him smile at the woman in the queue. She didn't like the way his lips pulled back, revealing his pointy teeth. 'I'm sorry, my daughter should have waited.'

She bit her lip, trying to stop her eyes welling up. But this was Al, her Al, whom she was supposed to adore. It had all gone wrong, everything was wrong. Nothing in her life ever went right.

'I'm not your daughter . . .' she muttered under her breath. She was hugging her backpack. It smelled of her room, of Mum.

He sat down beside her, put his hand on her knee and brushed his lips against her cheek. They felt dry and cracked. 'My beautiful girl,' he murmured. His hand was a dead weight, pushing her down.

She clenched her fists, realising that she was shaking.

'You're my beautiful girl. My Freya. We're going to have such fun together, you and me. Just you wait and see.'

Chapter Forty-Five

❦

Tom walked slowly back to their farmhouse and Becca followed. She noticed the ivy growing all around the back door and windows. Had there always been that much? The whole place was covered in it. It must have been there years, possibly hundreds of years. It would be a big job to pull it all down.

Her body was shuddering but she'd stopped crying. He sat down on the dark-red sofa in front of the fire and she took her place beside him.

'I thought you might have done something stupid,' he was muttering. 'I was so worried. The children were frantic.'

She stared straight ahead at the fire, which was beginning to die because no one was tending it.

'You don't know what I've done,' Becca whispered. 'You won't want me when you know what I've done.'

Tom put a hand in his trouser pocket, pulled something out and held it in front of her. It was a rather crumpled, passport-sized photo of two young girls. They looked about ten or eleven. They were smiling into the camera, their heads touching. Both had shoulder-length, straight, light hair. You couldn't tell the exact colour because the photo was black and white. One of the girls appeared older than the other, though there wasn't much between them. She had a more knowing expression. The other girl had a longer, thinner face and a sweet, slightly upturned nose.

Becca gasped. 'Where did you get that?'

'I found it on the floor of your study,' Tom replied.

Becca swallowed. It must have fallen out of the filing cabinet when she got her passport. She never used to be so careless.

'I knew it was you as soon as I saw it,' Tom went on. 'The hair's different, of course, but your face hasn't changed much. Not to me, anyway.'

Becca shuffled away from him into a corner of the sofa. She didn't want to touch him, to feel his sense of contamination, revulsion.

Tom didn't seem to notice that she'd moved. 'It was Patrick who told me,' he continued, still staring at the photo as if trying to unravel a code. Patrick was Tom's best friend, a journalist also. 'I rang as soon as I found your note. I didn't know what to do. He came immediately.

'I'd left the photo on the kitchen table. He recognised these two little girls from old newspaper articles.' Tom turned to his wife. A look of infinite sadness washed over his face. 'He told me who they were, Becca, told me the whole story. He didn't realise that one of them was you.'

Becca sat completely motionless, her hands in her lap. 'So why are you here?' she whispered. 'I don't understand. Why didn't you let me go?'

Tom ran his hands through his curly, greying hair. 'I think you're the one who owes *me* the explanation.'

Becca jumped up. She couldn't stay still any longer. 'Why do you think?' she cried. 'Because you'd hate me, of course.' She clenched her fists. It was so cruel, making her spell it out.

'Sit down,' he said quietly. 'I can't talk to you when you're standing up.'

She did as she was told. She was gazing at a point on the wall beside the fireplace, staring but not seeing.

'Whatever you've done,' he said fiercely, 'whatever you've concealed from me all these years, you're still my wife.'

She turned and looked into his dark-brown eyes. She felt as if he were delving into her mind and seeking out her very soul.

'I killed her,' she said, her own eyes filling with tears. 'My own sister. I got a stick and beat her around the head and body until she was dead.' So there it was, the truth at last. 'I'm not who you think I am,' she went on. 'I'm not the woman you thought you married. I'm Dawn from Newcastle, Dawn the murderer.' She covered her face with her hands. 'I'm sorry.'

'It was a long time ago,' Tom said fiercely, 'a lifetime. You were a child. You've created two beautiful children, a home, a family. We can move on from this.'

She shook her head. 'I can never get away from it. I thought I could, but I can't.'

He opened his mouth to speak but she ignored him.

'At first, when I was locked away, I wanted to die like Jude. I thought that was the only fair thing to do, the only way to make amends. Then, as the years went by, I began to think that maybe my life wasn't over and I could start again in some way. I couldn't erase what I'd done but I could sort of parcel it up and pack it away. It was a part of my life that had been and gone and there was nothing I could do to change what happened. But I did feel that I'd changed as a person, that I wasn't the same schoolgirl who'd had so much anger in her. I decided rather than throw my life away, I might as well try to make something of what was left.

'I worked so hard,' she said, 'I worked and worked. I wanted to prove that I wasn't just Dawn the murderer, that there was some good in me, something worthwhile. I almost made myself believe it. Then I met you and we had the children and, well . . .' She lowered her eyes. 'I suppose I always felt at the back of my mind that it was too good to be true, that it wouldn't last. Then when Gary got in touch—'

'Gary?'

Becca realised with a jolt that of course Tom knew nothing about him. Well, there was no point hiding it now. Everything else had come out. She told him about the emails, their first meeting in the pub, the fact that she was strongly attracted to him – Tom flinched at that, but he didn't interrupt.

She explained how he'd somehow got hold of her mobile number and started calling.

'Did you leave your bag at any point?' Tom asked.

She racked her brains. She remembered going to the loo and asking him to look after her bag. She felt such a fool.

She described the evening in Kew when he'd called her 'Dawn' for the first time and she'd started to feel so afraid.

Tom shook his head. 'If only you'd told me then.'

Finally, she told him about the way that Gary had followed her back from the pub after the last writing group and how, when he'd kissed her, she'd felt as if she were being raped.

343

'I was terrified that I'd try to kill him, Tom,' she said. She realised that her teeth were chattering. 'I thought it would happen all over again. That I'd lose control, lash out, just as I did with Jude.'

Tom frowned. 'You were only a girl. There were reasons . . .'

'And now he'll ring the papers,' she went on. 'It'll be a huge story. Everyone will know. There'll be reporters camped outside our house, I'll lose my job, it'll be terrible for the kids and for you. It would be much better if I just disappeared. At least then you can say you knew nothing. You'll be spared at least some of the shame.'

Tom was resting his head in his hands, his elbows on his knees. He looked deep in thought. Suddenly he leaped up and punched the palm of his hand with his fist.

'I don't believe he's interested in money,' he said. 'From what you tell me about him – his charity job, his manner, his clothes, everything – I don't think it's money that motivates him at all. I think what he wants is power over you. He's got some sort of sick crush on you. It's an obsession. If we tell him that I know everything and that you're giving up your job and we're going to walk off with the children into the sunset, he won't have any power over you any more. I think he'll just evaporate.'

Becca looked doubtful. 'Won't he tell the papers anyway, just to get revenge?'

'I don't think so,' Tom said. He stroked his chin. There was quite a lot of stubble. 'But what do we care,' he went on, 'so long as we've got each other and the children? Sod the papers. We know the truth – it doesn't matter what anyone else thinks.'

Becca's body felt light suddenly. It was as if the weight of the world were being lifted from her shoulders. She thought that if she stood up she might float away.

'We could buy a bar in Spain or something,' Tom said. He seemed to be speaking as much to himself as to her. 'Or a small hotel in Greece or Italy.'

Becca wrung her hands. It sounded too good to be true. 'But what about your job?'

Tom shook his head. 'I'm bored with it. Have been for ages.

If we get a hotel, I could run it while you write your kids' book or whatever it is you're doing.'

So he did know about the writing, then. He had been paying attention.

'A series of children's stories eventually, I hope,' she said.

She was high on drugs, suspended in a pink bubble, surrounded by ridiculously happy, technicolor thoughts. The bubble burst. 'But can you really forgive me?' she asked. She thought she might wake up at any moment.

'Grab your bag and let's go to Calais,' he replied. 'We need to get home as quickly as possible and sort that bastard out. We'll leave the Mercedes and take my car. We can pick it up later. We can do this on our own. We'll talk about our plans during the drive.'

'Becca! Where are you?'

Gary sounded gobsmacked. This made Becca glow with pleasure; up to now, she'd been the one on her back foot, constantly dumbfounded by the things he did and said. She almost wanted to laugh – if only he knew! – but she knew she mustn't. She needed to appear desperate.

They'd just got off the shuttle near Folkestone and Tom had parked the car and was hovering while she ran to the call-box. It was after nine now and dark outside, but there was plenty of light in the waiting area.

'I'm in Kent,' she stammered. 'I've been driving around for the past couple of days thinking about what to do about Tom, the kids – you know. I think I've made up my mind. I really need to see you, Gary.'

'Of course,' said Gary. He sounded worried. Becca thought she could hear a woman's voice in the background. His wife? 'It's work,' he muttered. 'I'll take it in the other room.'

She could hear his breathing as he walked. It made her shudder.

'I'm running out of money,' she hissed. She needed him to hurry. She wanted to get this over and done with.

'Right, I can talk now,' he replied at last. 'I couldn't speak in front of Michelle.'

345

'Can you meet me in front of the National Gallery in, say, two hours?' Becca blurted. She thought she could hear his brain whirring. He wouldn't like the suspense, the not knowing. Ha!

'Yes,' he said, 'but tell me what—?'

'I can't say any more now. I have to go. See you there at eleven p.m.'

Chapter Forty-Six

❧❧❧

The coffee tasted vile – watery and bitter. Evie wished that she could spit it out, but the family liaison officer had scarcely left her side since they'd arrived at the police station. Evie had taken painkillers so that her head was no longer throbbing. She needed to think clearly. Every scrap of information was important as it might provide a vital clue as to where Alan and Freya had gone.

'Tell me about your family: siblings, grandparents. Is there any way Freya might try to contact any of them?'

The family liaison officer was sitting beside her on an easy chair next to a low coffee table. She had a pleasant face, shoulder-length blond hair and black, rectangular glasses. She was probably in her mid-thirties. She was wearing plain clothes – black trousers and a cream blouse – and had taken her jacket off and hung it on the back of the seat. Every now and again she jotted something down in a notebook.

Evie put her plastic cup on the table and shook her head. 'I'm an only child,' she said. The inside of her mouth felt gluey and clogged. Her tongue was sticking to her cheeks. 'Adopted. I've never got on particularly well with my parents and Freya hasn't seen them for months. They live in Devon. It's highly unlikely she'd ring them.'

'What about friends?' the woman said. 'Does she have a best mate?'

'Lucy,' Evie replied wearily. 'They were at primary school together and now they're in the same class at the comprehensive.' She thought for a moment. 'Lucy hasn't been to our house for a while.' She started to fiddle with the silver chain around her neck. It had a heart on it; Neil had given it to her years ago.

The policewoman crossed one leg over the other. 'Had they fallen out, the two girls?'

Evie rubbed her eyes. 'I don't think so . . . I don't know.' She thought again how little she really knew about what was going on in Freya's life and cursed herself for not asking more questions. She put her head in her hands. 'I feel so bad. I should have protected her . . .'

The police officer touched her knee. 'Try to keep calm. You need to hold it together for Freya's sake. We need a number for Lucy, and can you tell me about her other friends? Who did she hang out with, other than Lucy? Was she having any problems at school?'

In another room at a separate police station, Nic was talking to a different police officer, also a woman. 'Were there any other indications that he liked young girls, before you discovered the magazines?'

Nic's hands were trembling. A slideshow was playing over and over in her mind: she saw Evie's face screwed up in anguish – she couldn't begin to imagine how she must be feeling; Freya's bony little shoulders and peaky chin; Alan's brown eyes, preying on her. Where were they? What were they doing? They must be found. She'd kill herself if they didn't catch Alan, if he did anything to harm Freya.

Nic wanted a drink so badly. She'd cut off her right arm for a glass of wine, the whole bottle. 'Please may I have some water?' she asked.

The woman police officer walked over to the water dispenser in the corner of the room and poured her a cup. It made a loud gurgling noise. Nic shivered. She handed Nic the cup and checked her watch. 'You must be hungry. Would you like something to eat?'

Nic started. It seemed extraordinary even to think about food. 'What time is it?' She had no idea.

'Two fifteen. I can ask them to bring some sandwiches?'

Nic couldn't remember when she last ate. Last night? That seemed like aeons ago. She shook her head. 'I'm not hungry.'

The police officer sat down again on the other side of the table and scratched her head. She was an attractive woman with a narrow face and short, slightly spiky brown hair. She might be quite a laugh when she was off duty. 'I know what you mean,' she said.

Freya, scrunched in a little ball in the corner by the window, registered that the train was slowing down. Another station? There's no way that he'd let her out of his sight this time. She pulled the brim of the pink cap lower over her eyes, squeezed her legs tighter into her chest and peeped at the young man now sitting opposite them.

He was wearing a black bomber jacket, had a diamond stud in his ear and was reading *Nuts*. He was quite fit. He noticed that she was looking at him and smiled. She scowled.

'Fuck,' Al whispered. He started jiggling his skinny leg up and down.

A man in another seat groaned loudly. 'Not bloody signal failure again. Or leaves on the frigging line.'

'There's always some excuse.' It was a shrill, woman's voice. 'I'm sick to death of it.'

'Ladies and gentlemen,' came the announcement. The carriage fell silent. 'I apologise for the delay. There's been a bit of a hold-up but the train in front will shortly be leaving Coventry Station. Please remain seated; we should be moving soon.'

'Thank God for that,' said the woman who'd spoken a moment earlier. 'For a minute I thought they were going to make us all get off and walk.'

Al's leg stopped jiggling. Freya heard him take a deep breath. She shifted slightly in her seat. Her bum was stiff from being scrooched in the same position for so long. A carriage door behind them slammed. There was the sound of a radio crackling. Freya's ears pricked. Someone right behind them barked: 'Alan Quinton?'

It all happened so quickly. Freya spun round to see Al half up out of his seat, his hands on the armrests on either side. His knuckles were white. The next thing she knew, he was holding his arms out in front of him and someone was putting handcuffs on.

Her eyes swivelled left and right frantically. There were several police officers, two men and a woman, but she could see others coming up the carriage from the opposite direction. Loads of them. 'Please remain in your seats,' a woman in uniform was saying to the other passengers. 'This won't take long.'

She saw the back of Al's thin neck, poking out of his shirt collar underneath the plum jumper. He turned and caught her eye. She thought she'd never forget that look, not as long as she lived. His eyes were dark brown, smooth as glass, unreadable. What was he trying to say? She could see her own face reflected in his lenses.

'We're arresting you on suspicion of child abduction,' a male officer said. 'You do not have to say anything but it may harm your defence if you do not now mention something which you later rely on in court.'

'No!' Freya shouted.

Al shook his head.

Tears were pouring down Freya's cheeks. She'd wanted to escape; now she was terrified of losing him. She lurched forward and wrapped her arms around his waist, clasped her hands together, tried to pull, to prise him away. It was her dream that they were tearing to pieces; she mustn't let go of the dream. What would be left, then?

'Freya?' a woman police officer said. Her voice was kind. 'We need to take him to the police station. You're safe now.' She put a hand on Freya's arm.

'Get off!' Freya screamed. 'You don't understand. He's my boyfriend. We love each other.'

'You're confused,' the woman went on in her crooning voice. 'It's understandable. Your mum's been so worried. She's going to be so relieved to hear you're OK.'

Freya felt frantic, caged. She wanted to lash out. 'I hate Mum,' she yelled. Her grip loosened and Al stumbled forward. She spat at the woman police officer, but the spit didn't get anywhere near. 'I hate you.' She backed up to the window behind, leaned her shoulders against the glass and clenched her fists. If she'd had a rock she'd have smashed the window and run.

The woman came towards her and tried to put her arm around her shoulders. Freya was crying so much that she couldn't make out her features, just her bulky, blue form.

'Get off!' she hissed. She was beating her arms against the woman's chest, trying to shove her off.

'It's all right,' the woman said. She was big, much stronger than Freya. Her voice was low and soothing. 'Everything's going to be OK.'

Freya glimpsed one of the police officers talking into his radio. 'We've got him. The girl's fine.' He had a big, fat grin on his face.

She blinked the tears away and gave the policewoman one last kick. 'I'm not fucking fine,' she howled. 'Why do you have to ruin everything?' Her shoulders slumped. She allowed the policewoman to take her by the hand and lead her out of the carriage, back into the real world. 'I hate all of you, you're all losers. You don't understand. He's all I've got. I love him. We love each other. Just let me go.'

'Thank God you're safe.' Evie flung both arms around her daughter. She was kissing her head, her hair, making it wet. She couldn't let go. 'I've been so worried about you.'

Freya's body was rigid and unyielding. Evie had been warned that she was angry and bewildered, but the blast of cold air still came as a shock.

'I love him,' Freya said defiantly, 'and he loves me. We're soulmates. You've got no idea . . .' She tried to shake her mother off but Evie held on tight.

'We'll talk about this later,' she said. 'He'd been grooming you. That's what they do. He wanted to hurt you—'

'No!' Freya cried, struggling. 'He wanted to help me. He was my friend.' She started to weep uncontrollably.

The police liaison officer passed Freya a wodge of paper hankies, which she blew into. 'Your mum's right, I'm afraid,' she said gently. 'He's a bad man, Freya. The main thing is that you're safe now.'

'He was helping me,' Freya sobbed. 'He stopped the bullying at school, he got Gemma and Chantelle off my back. I could talk to him. I didn't know he was Nic's husband, he didn't tell me.' Her shoulders sagged. 'I've got no one now.'

Evie groaned and shook her head. 'I didn't realise . . .'

Freya had stopped struggling and her body slumped, exhausted. She rested her head against her mother's breast. Evie was careful not to move, so that it could stay there. They were quiet for a moment, just standing in the middle of the special interview room where Evie had spent so many hours. She felt as if she'd been there, hanging on, all her life.

She'd still been talking to the police liaison officer when they got the news: some woman had noticed Freya and Alan on the train. Then, when the woman got off at Watford, she'd heard a news flash on her car radio about a missing girl and an older man. She'd called the police immediately and given a detailed description. They'd swung into action and organised for the train driver to stop the train on a pretext.

It took a moment or two for the information to sink in, then Evie had broken down. While she was waiting for them to bring Freya back from Coventry she kept imagining that the car would smash. Now at last, with Freya in her arms, she could finally believe that the nightmare was over.

She heard a car honking its horn outside. How strange, she thought, that people were going about their normal, everyday lives while her whole world had turned upside down.

'I'm sorry, Mum,' Freya said in a small voice, her head still resting on the same spot, her body limp.

'No,' said Evie, more fiercely than she'd intended. She lowered her voice. 'I'm the one who has to say sorry. I should have looked after you, been there for you. You're my precious daughter. You've no idea how precious you are. I've been so wrapped up in my own stupid, selfish problems that I didn't see what was under my nose. I didn't realise how much you needed me.'

Freya made a choking sound. 'I know it's been so hard for you with Dad leaving.'

'No,' Evie repeated. 'Lots of people's marriages break up. I'm not the only woman in the world whose husband's left. I've been wallowing in self-pity and I wasn't there for you. I've totally failed.'

'Don't . . .' Freya was still trying to protect her mum, Evie knew that. She'd allowed it to happen for far too long.

'Yes,' Evie said firmly. 'But things are going to change now, I promise. Whatever your problems are, we'll sort them out, one by one.' She took Freya's peaky little chin in her hand and pulled it gently up, forcing her to look her mother in the eye. 'We're going to tackle this together, OK?'

Freya nodded, sniffing. She didn't appear convinced. 'What about school?' she asked tentatively.

'Bugger school,' Evie snorted. 'You can leave; we'll find somewhere else. Whatever it takes to make you happy. I tell you, there's nothing we can't resolve.'

Freya looked brighter, but then frowned. 'What about Al?' she asked. 'What will happen to him?'

'I hope he'll go to prison for a long time,' Evie hissed.

She realised immediately that she'd said the wrong thing. She cursed herself for her insensitivity.

Freya started crying again and buried her head in her mother's chest. 'Will I ever see him again?'

'Oh, my poor baby,' Evie said, 'you'll get over him, truly you will.'

They sat down on one of the easy chairs, Freya on her mother's lap like a little girl. She was scrunching the paper hankies into a ball, picking at them with her fingers.

'I really love him,' she whispered. There was a pause. 'And I'm sure he loves me. He told me loads of times.'

'I know, darling,' Evie replied. She thought she could feel her daughter's heart hurting. Her own was aching in sympathy.

'He was going to take me to Euro Disney except the train was cancelled,' Freya said.

Evie flinched. She felt a pounding in her temples, but she managed to keep her voice soft and gentle: 'Because he knew that was somewhere you'd like to visit. It was a way of luring you from home.'

Freya thought for a moment. 'Will you tell Dad?'

'I had to, sweetie. He needed to know.'

'Is he mad at me?'

Evie kissed her daughter's wet cheek. 'No, darling,' she said.

'He was sick with worry. No one's mad at you. Not one little bit.'

'What about the police?'

'You're not in any trouble, I promise. Everyone's just so relieved you're OK.'

Freya was shivering. Evie grabbed her black duffel coat from the back of the chair and wrapped it round her daughter.

'Nic must hate me,' Freya said suddenly.

Evie hadn't given Nic a thought, not since she'd rung that morning with news of the assignation. God, was it only this morning? She wondered, for a second, how Nic must be feeling. And poor Dominic. He didn't deserve this.

'Of course she doesn't hate you,' Evie said. In truth, though, she had no idea what Nic's views were. In fact she didn't feel that she knew Nic any more at all. What had she said on the phone this morning? Something like: 'I knew he liked young girls . . .' What did that mean? That she might have known that he was a paedophile and done nothing about it seemed incredible. Grotesque. Evie couldn't believe it. It was too much. She couldn't make any sense of it. Right now she must put Nic to the back of her mind. Freya was her only concern.

'It's not your fault, none of this is,' Evie whispered. 'You're only a child. You've been in a bad way, a dark place for a long time. I realise that now. I've neglected you and let you down big time. But we'll talk everything through and get as much help as we need. Things are going to get better.'

They sat in silence for a few moments. It was dark outside and Evie thought that she could see Alan's face reflected in the windows. She closed her eyes, but his image slowly transformed in her mind into obscene pictures of what he might have done to Freya.

She squeezed her daughter again, breathing in her familiar smell of soap and, she thought, the fresh, slightly lemony scent that she often wore. It helped Evie to block out the pictures – but she knew that they'd return to haunt her in her dreams.

Chapter Forty-Seven

Nic stepped out of the police car and blinked. She'd been warned that there were reporters outside her house but she hadn't expected this many. The cameras were flashing almost continuously, blinding her. She covered her face with her hands and stayed close by the police officers flanking her.

'Have you spoken to your husband?' someone shouted. 'Did you know about his email relationship with Freya?'

'What does it feel like to be married to a paedophile?' a woman cried.

She hurried up the front drive and into the house, slammed the door shut and turned and collapsed back against it. She couldn't cry. She felt drained. She'd leaked emotion all day; now there was none left.

She let go of her handbag and slid on to her bottom on the floor. She didn't know if she had the energy to move; she thought she might stay there all night. She had no idea how long she sat there. After a while she became aware that Dizzy the dog was scratching at the kitchen door, yelping. She must be hungry, poor thing; Nic supposed she should eat something, too, but didn't think she could. She'd had a few bites of a ham sandwich and a cup of tea some time after she'd heard the news that they'd got Alan and that Freya was safe. She could still taste the butter in her mouth. Her stomach keeled.

She leaned over on to her hands and knees and pushed herself up. Best get to the bathroom; she thought she might be sick. Once upright, though, she felt less nauseous. Still in her coat and boots, she staggered down the hall.

The house felt cold and empty. She wished Dominic were there; she desperately needed a hug. But it was just as well that he was staying at a friend's. She was in no fit state to explain things to him now.

Quite what she was going to say to him she had no idea. No one could prepare you for something like that. Dominic was still so innocent; he might have been warned about 'bad men' but he certainly didn't know what they really did. She wished that she could protect him from the full horror but she knew that would be impossible. It would be in all the papers and on all the TV channels tomorrow. His cosy little world was about to be shattered.

The knotty lump that had been in her throat on and off all day reappeared. She thought it would probably never go away.

Dizzy was howling; she sounded desperate. She'd been on her own all day. Nic opened the kitchen door and reached up to put a hand over her nose and mouth. The room stank. It was only to be expected.

'Good girl,' she said, half-heartedly patting the dog who was barking and running around her in circles.

She turned on the light, walked slowly over to the glass doors at the far end of the kitchen and pulled them open. The cold air whooshed in, diluting the stench. Dizzy raced outside, yapping, before bowling back in and jumping up at her ankles. Nic staggered. She had to steady herself on the wall. 'I'll clean up the mess then I'll feed you,' she said. Her whole body felt leaden; she could hardly muster the energy.

Afterwards she went into the sitting room. The cleaner had been yesterday and everything was immaculate: pale cream walls, polished wood floor, cushions neatly lined up on the olive-green sofa, flowers on the console against the far wall.

Something made her walk over to the console and pick up a photo in a silver frame beside the vase. She peered at it, as if trying to decipher something.

The photo was of her and Alan on holiday in Greece before they married. They were sitting on a wall with the azure-blue sea behind them, grinning into the camera. It was clearly windy because her blond bobbed hair was flying about.

They were in casual holiday clothes: she was wearing sandals and a pale-pink sundress with spaghetti straps, he was in a beige polo shirt and white chinos, one leg casually crossed over another. He had his arm around her. Their faces were young, much younger – hers was certainly rounder – and very tanned.

She touched his eyes, his nose, the small, smiling mouth. Were they happy? She frowned. She couldn't remember. They certainly looked happy in the photo, but even then she'd been drinking too much, trying to drown her sorrows. It hadn't worked, of course. Colm, her first husband, the handsome Irish reporter who'd dumped her, had never been far from her thoughts.

Ironic that she'd run from one cheating bastard straight into the arms of a paedophile. She considered the word, turning it over in her mind. It was cold and hard, like a medical term, a description of some disease, perhaps. Funny that the root of the word was the same as that of paediatrician, given that one made children better while the other defiled them.

She flipped the photo over, took it out of its frame and ripped it to shreds.

'Animal,' she said, scattering the pieces on the floor. 'Disgusting, filthy, perverted animal. I hope they make you suffer in prison. I hope they tear you to pieces.'

She staggered from the sitting room back into the kitchen. Dizzy was still finishing her food, pushing the ceramic dish around the floor to lick up the last scraps. Nic opened the cupboard to the right of the sink, took down several clean glasses and pulled out a bottle of red wine which was tucked away behind them. She'd considered throwing out all the wine when she gave up drinking but had decided against it; after the accident she'd felt so determined: no temptation, she'd thought, would be too great. Well, that was a joke.

She unscrewed the cap, filled one of the glasses to the brim and took a gulp. It was so good, she'd forgotten how much she loved the taste. She drained the glass, refilled it and then carried the glass in one hand, the bottle in the other, up to the bedroom, taking big slugs as she went.

The room was just as she'd left it this morning: spotless. She remembered how she'd opened the curtains, folded her white nightdress, put it under the pillow and smoothed the green bedspread. Afterwards she'd had a shower and dressed in her dark-brown corduroy skirt, brown tights and a black polo neck. Then she'd put on her make-up, tidied her dressing table and gone downstairs to kiss Alan goodbye.

'See you tomorrow,' he'd said, brushing his dry lips against hers.

'Have a good time,' she'd called after him as he crunched down the driveway. As soon as he was out of sight she'd turned, her heart hammering, hurried into the kitchen and phoned the police.

Nic realised that she was still wearing her winter coat and boots but she didn't have time to take them off now. She grabbed the duvet and started pulling off the white cotton cover, which she threw on to the green carpet followed by the pillowcases. She topped up her glass and swallowed some more wine. She eyed the bottle; there was plenty more in the cupboard.

She glanced at the built-in wardrobe, to the right of the bed. It was white, the same as the walls. Alan had one half and she, the other. She flung open the doors on his side and looked in. The hanging section was full of suits and shoes, and to the left were shelves stacked with neatly folded shirts and jumpers, pants and socks. There were dozens of ties in different colours on a special tie rack on the inside of one of the doors.

She opened the big sash window overlooking the back garden, returned to the wardrobe, pulled out a bundle of shirts and flung them on to the grass below. She took another glug of wine, draining the glass, and tipped in the remains of the bottle.

She carried pile after pile of his clothes. He had more than she'd realised; odd, since he wasn't remotely interested in fashion. She laughed as she hurled them out into the night. Then she went into the bathroom and took his dressing gown from a hook on the back of the door, swept his aftershaves, shampoos, toothbrush off the shelves and chucked them out, too. Quite a few bottles fell on to the bathroom floor and smashed. She went back and picked the unbroken ones up. The bits of glass and spilled liquid, she left.

Next she emptied his bedside table. There wasn't much in

the one drawer: a comb, reading glasses, the book he picked up occasionally – a thriller. At last, when there were no traces of him left in the room, she leaned right out of the window and stared down at the heap of trousers, jackets, shirts, jumpers, bottles of this and that on the ground beneath.

'I hate you!' she screamed. Her voice sounded surprisingly loud and piercing in the darkness.

She started to run downstairs, slipped on one of the steps and crashed into the wall at the bottom, banging her head against the windowsill and hitting her shoulder. She winced, but the pain wasn't too bad. She managed to push herself up and staggered into the kitchen, where she grabbed more wine from the cupboard, unscrewed the lid and slurped straight from the bottle.

Matches. Where were the matches? She opened a drawer under the worktop and scrabbled around. She was sure she kept them there. She pulled the drawer out and tipped the contents on to the floor. There was a big box of household matches in amongst the sticky tape, string and glue. Bingo!

Dizzy was sniffing at the contents of the drawer. 'Come and watch!' Nic slurred. The little dog followed her into the garden. Nic was still in her coat and boots. She went round to the back of the house and tried to light a match. There was too much wind. 'Shit.' She lit another, and another. No luck.

She leaned over the pile of clothes and shoes, picked up a bottle of aftershave and opened it, splashing the contents over the heap of Alan's things. This time she opened her coat and lit the match inside. Gingerly she took the lighted match out and chucked it, still just burning, on the pile of clothes. Instinctively she jumped back. There was a gratifying boom as the pile caught light.

'Burn, burn!' she shouted as the flames leaped into the sky. A spark must have landed on Dizzy. She squealed and ran inside. Nic hardly noticed.

She stood, mesmerised, watching the fire spit and crackle. Every now and again there was a loud flash as more aftershave ignited. Nic picked up the bottle of wine at her feet and gulped. Her face was boiling hot but she didn't step back from the flames. She wanted to feel their intensity.

The phone started ringing but she ignored it. Black smoke caught the back of her throat and made her choke. Her eyes were watering so much that she could scarcely see. She poured wine down her gullet. It spilled over and trickled down her face. She wiped her mouth with the back of her arm.

She could hear shouts. People in the garden next door. 'What's going on?'

'I'm having a bonfire,' she screamed, without turning round. The fire was roaring so loudly that she wasn't sure if they'd hear.

'Call 999,' someone cried. 'It's out of control.'

Nic could see two fires now. The world was lurching from side to side. She could hardly stay upright. She left the blazing fire and staggered back inside, opened the front door wide so that the fire brigade could get in. She vaguely registered that there were no reporters; they'd be back soon. She groped her way into the TV room and plonked down on the sofa. Dizzy jumped on to her lap, whining, and pushed under her hands with her nose, wanting to be petted.

'Good girl,' said Nic, stroking mechanically. The little dog's body was trembling – or was it Nic's hands? She wasn't sure which.

'Good girl,' she said again, staring at the blank TV screen in front of her, half expecting the house to explode, scattering herself and its entire contents into the night sky.

Chapter Forty-Eight

It was after 10 p.m. when Evie and Freya finally arrived home. A police officer took them right to the front door and waited while Evie found her key. Bill hurried down the hall to greet them. His shirt was hanging out, he had Evie's blue and yellow checked apron on and was brandishing a wooden spoon. She might have laughed if she hadn't been so worn out and traumatised.

'Evie! Freya!' he called. 'You're back!' He glanced at the wooden spoon and lowered it. 'I, er, I was making scrambled eggs for Michael,' he explained.

Evie started to take off Freya's coat.

'You must be exhausted,' he went on. 'Cup of tea?'

Evie managed a smile. 'I can't think of anything I'd like more.'

She did a double take when she entered the kitchen with Freya following close behind. There was Carol from the writing group, of all people, sitting at the table beside Michael. They seemed to be playing some sort of board game. Michael got up and ran to his mother, who folded him in her arms. Then he gave Freya a hug.

'You all right?' he mumbled.

'Yes.'

There was an awkward silence.

'We're both absolutely knackered,' said Evie. 'But the main thing is that Freya's safe. It's too late to talk about anything now. We'll discuss it in the morning.'

She stood, sipping tea, while Bill finished the scrambled eggs and talked a little about his afternoon and evening with Michael. She was grateful; Bill knew that now wasn't the time for analysis. He was sensitive like that.

'He's very good at chess,' he said, ruffling Michael's hair and putting a plate of food in front of him. 'And I've discovered he's mad about *Star Wars*. He and Carol watched a film while I made the casserole.'

'You made a casserole?' Evie said. 'You're amazing.' She couldn't even be bothered to ask why Carol was there. It seemed quite in keeping, somehow, that there should be an unexpected person sitting round her table on an extraordinary day like today.

'I rather enjoyed it.' Carol grinned, showing off her stained teeth. 'Michael seemed to know everything that was going to happen. He warned me when there was going to be a scary bit so I could close my eyes.'

She gave Evie a lingering look that made her recoil. Carol clearly knew, then. Evie didn't know how she felt about that. She didn't think she'd want everyone to know. There was Freya to think of.

Freya was still hovering just a few inches from her mother. It seemed, after talking all day, that she'd finally realised that she'd been in real danger. Now she was afraid to leave Evie's orbit. That suited Evie just fine. She wasn't letting Freya out of her sight for a long time. She glanced at her daughter, who had big black circles under her eyes. They'd both been questioned extensively and there were a lot more questions to come. They'd need counselling, too, family and individual therapy, social services visits. The ramifications were huge. It was hard to imagine that their lives would ever be the same.

Evie hadn't seen Nic since St Pancras Station. The police had taken her with them, apparently, to identify Freya. Evie was supposed to do it, but she'd been too fast for them; they'd arrived at her house after she'd left.

'I must get Freya to bed,' Evie said. 'She can hardly stand up. Would you mind settling Michael down for me, Bill? You've been so kind already—'

'Of course,' he interrupted. 'Do you still like a bedtime story, Michael, or are you far too grown-up for that sort of thing?'

'I've got a *Star Wars* comic,' Michael said hopefully. Evie would never read him comics, she said they were boring.

'All right, we'll have that then,' said Bill, picking up Michael's plate and running it under the tap. 'Go and do your teeth and

I'll be with you in two ticks when I've finished stacking the dishwasher.'

Carol rose slowly, pushing herself up from the table with her hands. 'I'll be off then,' she said. 'Thanks for everything, Bill.' She spoke in an odd, loaded way. Evie didn't like it. Suddenly she wanted Carol out of the house this instant. What was she doing here anyway? Bill shouldn't have let her in.

'I'll see you to the door,' Bill said. They glanced at each other. Something passed between them that Evie didn't understand. There was a familiarity, a knowingness that made her cross and curious at the same time. She decided that she couldn't see the back of Carol soon enough.

'Come on, my love,' Evie said, taking Freya's hand, which felt small and frail. Guilt washed over her for the hundredth time that day. She'd failed Freya and failed as a mother. How could she not have spotted the danger signs? From now on, Freya came first – and Michael too, of course. The pair of them were her absolute priority.

Carol patted Evie on the shoulder in the hall as she and Freya started to go upstairs, but Evie ignored her.

'If there's anything I can do . . .' Carol said.

'No thank you,' Evie replied, without looking back, 'we just want to be alone.'

'You've been a saint,' Evie said when she finally came downstairs.

Bill was on the sitting-room sofa looking at the newspaper. He put it down the moment she spoke. 'Glad I could help.' He started to rise. 'Is Freya asleep?'

She nodded.

'I should think you're ready for bed now yourself,' he went on.

She rubbed her eyes. 'I am absolutely exhausted, but I'm not sure I'll be able to sleep.'

Bill frowned. 'Do you want to talk?'

She shook her head. 'You've done quite enough for me today. You must be exhausted, too. You go home. I might have a bath. That'll help me relax.'

He started to put on his coat, which was in the hall. His shirt was still hanging out and he tucked it in.

'Oh Bill,' she said, flinging her arms around him. 'You were so brilliant with Michael. He was happy as anything when I came in. You did a fantastic job of keeping the home fires burning.'

Bill gave her a squeeze.

'I've been a rubbish mother to Freya,' she went on. 'I've let her down hugely. I've been so wrapped up in my own problems that I couldn't see that she was crying out for help. Even you saw it, Bill.'

He was silent.

'I remember at Christmas when you said she seemed troubled and suggested she talk to a counsellor. If only I'd taken your advice . . .'

'The main thing is that she's all right,' he replied. 'You can get her all the help she needs now.'

For a moment they stood there, her cheek on his chest. It felt right somehow, as if this were her own, special place. He gave her another squeeze and pulled away.

'I'll be off,' he said, zipping up his Barbour. 'Busy day tomorrow.'

'What are you up to?' Evie crossed her arms and cocked her head on one side. She hadn't even thought about tomorrow; it had been hard enough getting through today. Tomorrow seemed like another planet.

'I'm doing a tutorial, nine till one,' Bill replied, putting his hands in his pockets. 'Then I plan to spend some time on the allotment, weather permitting. Fence is falling to pieces, needs repairing and creosoting.'

'English tutorial?' Evie asked. 'GCSE or A-level?'

'Neither.' Bill scratched his head. 'She's a mature student. Ukrainian. Doing an Open University degree. Working nights in a bar and studying during the day. She had a very disrupted schooling and she's trying to make up for lost time. Wish all my students were as diligent as her.'

'Oh,' said Evie. 'Is she clever?'

'Very bright, yes. Excellent English. Doing a dissertation on T. S. Eliot. I'm just giving her a few pointers, that's all. The OU's a bit impersonal. She seems to be blossoming, I'm glad to say.'

'How old is she?' Evie asked. It just popped out.

'Ooh, I don't know. Late twenties?'

'Married . . . children?'

Bill shrugged. 'No idea. We tend to stick to T. S. Eliot.'

'But you must know if she's married or not,' Evie persisted. 'Doesn't she wear a ring?'

Bill laughed. 'I'm not as nosy as you, Evie,' he said. 'I haven't noticed, but I'll make a point of looking tomorrow if you like.'

She felt herself redden. She hoped he wouldn't notice.

'Well, I'll be off,' he said, opening the door. 'I hope you get a decent night.'

He pecked her on both cheeks and started to walk down the path.

'You too,' Evie called after him. 'Thanks again for everything. And good luck with the tutorial tomorrow.'

Tom parked the car in St Martin's Street and they walked side by side towards Trafalgar Square. It was strange to see central London so deserted; Becca was used to going during the day when the place was humming.

Her heart was beating loudly. She was glad that she was wearing trainers: high heels would have heralded her approach and she didn't want that. Tom's soles were soft, too.

He stopped when they reached the corner. She gave him one last look: 'Don't leave me!' He gave her a thumbs up and she turned into the square on her own. If Gary saw them together he might bolt. They needed him to hear what they had to say first.

She glanced at Nelson's Column towering darkly above her; he seemed to be presiding over the whole square. He must have seen a thing or two in his time, she thought.

She started when she spotted Gary, already waiting, his back to the gallery. But it was a relief, really. It would have been agony to have to hang around; she might have lost her nerve. He was in the black leather jacket that he always wore, with the black and red rucksack over his shoulder. What did he keep in there? She didn't want to know.

He walked swiftly towards her. She noticed that he was frowning. 'Becca, what the hell are you playing at?' He put out his arms as if to grab her but she dodged away out of reach.

'Tom knows everything,' she said quickly. 'About my past, about you. It's over, Gary. You can't threaten me any more.'

Gary stopped in his tracks. He seemed to be processing the information. 'Dawn . . .' He looked over her shoulder and his mouth gaped. 'What the . . . ?'

Tom was beside Becca now. 'That's right, Gary,' he said coolly, 'I know all about Dawn. It doesn't make any difference. She's my wife.'

'The papers,' said Gary desperately. 'Everyone will know.'

Tom shook his head. 'We've had enough of our London life anyway. We'd always planned to live abroad. You can tell the papers what you want, we don't care.'

Gary's face clouded over. His shoulders drooped and he seemed to shrink before Becca's eyes. He looked small and gaunt in the lamplight. How could she have ever feared him?

'We should be going, Becca,' Tom said. 'It's late.'

He jabbed a finger at Gary, suddenly aggressive. 'And if we see you ever again, you little shit, we'll call the police, d'you understand? We'll tell them you've been stalking Becca. She's kept a diary, everything's there. Just get out of our lives and fuck off back down your stinking drainpipe.'

They spun around and headed back in the direction of the car. Becca felt about ten feet tall; she didn't look back once. It had all been so easy, so much easier than she'd imagined. She felt like singing; she felt like going up to complete strangers in the street and hugging them. Life was so beautiful.

Tom opened the car door for her.

'Thank you,' she said, turning to him. She opened her arms to embrace him but he was already moving round to the driver's side.

She clambered into the passenger seat and did up her seat-belt. She couldn't wipe the smile off her face.

'Let's get the hell out of here,' Tom said, lowering himself into his seat and starting up the engine. 'I want to go home.'

Chapter Forty-Nine

Evie arrived deliberately late for the March creative writing group. She slunk in and sat down right at the back of the church hall, nearest the door. Several people turned and looked at her impertinently, she thought. She shivered. She'd never get used to the stares from those who thought they knew so much about her from the press. She wanted to scream at them not to believe all they read, that much of what had been splurged across the papers was inaccurate. But she knew there was no point.

Since the nationwide alert, everybody seemed to think they were qualified to talk about the Freestones, including neighbours whom she'd never even spoken to. The quotes were so conflicting, it would have been almost funny if it wasn't so hurtful. Some people said what a 'nice, normal' family they were and what 'lovely, polite children'. Others, though, were damning.

Evie had been particularly stung by a stranger who, it turned out, lived at Number 22, who said she'd noticed that the children were often alone. Evie, said the woman, was frequently out with her 'long-haired boyfriend' and the father only visited rarely. Well, that was a lie. She made Freya and Michael sound like latchkey kids.

There again, Evie couldn't deny that she'd often left Freya to babysit, and when Nic had had the accident and Steve had buggered off without telling her, Freya and Michael had been alone all night. Had the neighbour's curtains been twitching? Maybe she deserved to be pilloried.

Evie had tried to stop Freya reading the papers, watching the TV news or listening to the radio but she'd picked things up all the same. She'd gnashed her teeth when she caught sight of Chantelle smirking in a TV report and claiming that they were 'best friends' at school. 'I knew she had a boyfriend, but she never let on how old he was.' When the reporter had asked Chantelle what kind of girl Freya was she'd said: 'Cool. Really popular.' Evie had had to stop Freya throwing her glass of orange juice at the screen.

Even some of the mums whose sons played football with Michael on a Saturday morning had put in their tuppence ha'penny. Michael, one of them said, was 'very outgoing'. She'd obviously never tried speaking to him, then.

It was Nic, though, Evie had to admit, who'd borne the worst of it. Many newspaper columnists – mostly women – had insisted that Nic must have known that Alan was a paedophile, grooming young girls on the net.

'Is this the most wicked mother in Britain?' screamed one headline, above a picture of Nic looking dazed outside her front door. The columnist argued that Nic was evil because she'd put her son at risk of being abused himself. She'd also called her a 'pathetic lush, who thought only of herself and where her next bottle of wine was coming from'.

Evie hadn't spoken to Nic, but she couldn't reconcile this portrait of depravity with the woman she knew and had spent so much time with. And whatever else she might have done, she'd never knowingly have put Dominic in danger. Evie knew that much.

Fortunately, since Freya had been found, the papers had largely respected Evie's request for privacy and hadn't camped outside her door, though they'd certainly doorstepped friends, neighbours and relatives. But Nic had had bricks thrown through her front window and 'paedophile' sprayed across the walls. She and Dominic had been forced to move to a safe house nearby while the furore died down. As far as Evie knew, Dominic was getting a taxi to and from school.

Evie was glad that it was Russell sitting next to her on her left. He squeezed her hand. 'Good to see you. You OK?' he whispered. She nodded, aware that her bottom lip was quivering.

It was at times like this, she reflected, that you really found out who your friends were. 'He's been droning on about bloody

Matron again,' Russell went on, nodding in Tristram's direction. 'You haven't missed a thing.'

Evie managed a half-smile.

'She made the most delicious cocoa,' she heard Tristram say. 'It was almost worth being ill because she'd bring you a mug of the sweetest nectar in bed . . .'

Evie glanced around now that all heads were turned back to the front. Carol was in the middle row, wearing her peculiar Afghan coat. And to her surprise, she spotted Becca's dark head near the front. She'd said she probably wouldn't make it tonight.

Evie felt hurt. Becca was one friend that she thought she really could rely on but she was acting most peculiarly. She'd phoned Evie a few times to check that she was OK but said she'd been through some sort of a crisis herself and couldn't visit. Evie struggled to understand; what sort of crisis could possibly be bigger than the one she herself was going through? She tried to remind herself, though, that Becca was normally Ms Cool and Unflappable. If she said that she'd had a crisis then it must be bad.

Evie realised that she was only mildly interested in knowing what the problem was, though; she felt that she couldn't take any more trauma now, she'd rather listen to small talk. Interestingly, her novel had turned out to be a refuge in the past few weeks. She'd found that burying herself in writing had helped to take her mind off things. That was one reason why she'd been determined to come to the writing group tonight. She'd missed last month's and she hoped, once she'd got over the embarrassment of seeing everyone again, that coming back would act as a bit of a spur.

'This month I thought we'd talk about characterisation,' Tristram said. 'Writers often fall into the trap of making their characters either black or white, but in real life most people have light and shade. Characters are far more interesting if they're a mixture of good and bad.'

Pamela, in the front row, harrumphed. 'Would you like to say something?' Tristram asked patiently.

'No thank you.' She shook her stiff helmet of grey hair.

Russell leaned over and whispered in Evie's ear again.

369

'She was thinking that she, unlike the rest of us, hasn't got any shade,' he sniggered, 'but she obviously thought better of saying so.'

Evie reflected on her main characters: Cornelia, Spiculus, Marcellus and, increasingly, Gracchus. She'd started out wanting Marcellus, Cornelia's husband, to be the baddie who was really a goodie, and Spiculus the lover to be the goodie who was really a baddie. Then, after Neil's baby news, she'd had to change that. But Tristram was right, in real life, most people had a bit of both in them: sunshine and shadows. Maybe she'd been too simplistic.

Thinking of baddies and goodies, she was surprised by how supportive Neil was being over Freya. There's no doubt that he'd been worried sick when she went missing and Evie knew that he, like her, had been through a lot of soul-searching since about how little he'd understood or really listened to his daughter.

If one good thing had come out of all this it was that he was now putting aside time to do things with Freya on her own, away from Evie or Helen. They'd been to the cinema twice and out for a long walk. So that Michael wouldn't feel sidelined, he'd taken him to football on Saturday morning, too. If Helen was fed up, she wasn't showing it. Or at least, Neil wasn't letting on.

He and Evie had managed to have a couple of constructive talks which hadn't descended into rows and recriminations. It seemed they'd both realised that they had to put their own feelings aside and work together for Freya's sake. It was weird, though, Evie thought, that the change hadn't made things worse for her; she didn't long to be back in his arms. She was just so glad that he was doing his best for his daughter. If only it hadn't taken a crisis for it to happen, for them both to see sense.

'What about physical description?' said Tristram. 'How much do you like?'

Pamela's hand shot up.

'Yes, Pamela?'

'A lot,' she said. 'When I'm reading I like to know exactly what each character looks like, the shape of their face, type of nose and so on. Otherwise if there are lots of characters you get confused.'

Tristram nodded. 'Good point,' he said, 'physical description helps to embed characters in the reader's mind.'

Pamela's back looked smug, Evie thought. She'd never realised backs could appear self-satisfied.

'What does everyone else think?' Tristram asked.

There was silence for a few moments and then Angela, the mousy one, raised her hand. Evie was surprised. Angela rarely spoke, unless it was to point out that none of them was going to win the national creative writing competition.

'I'm the opposite,' she said, pushing her large glasses up her nose.

'Can you speak up?' Tristram asked, cupping a hand round an ear.

Angela repeated herself, this time raising her voice. She looked most uncomfortable. Evie guessed that Angela rarely spoke above a whisper. She was a very timid creature.

'Interesting. Why's that now?' Tristram asked. 'Can you stand up, please, so that we can all hear.'

Angela looked around hoping, perhaps, that someone would come to her rescue. Evie smiled at her encouragingly but she was too far away to notice.

'I just think . . .' Angela stammered, 'I just think that I prefer to leave things to the reader's imagination. I like *some* pointers myself – for instance, is the character dark or fair, tall or short and so on – but I don't want to know everything.' She looked down. 'It's a personal thing, I suppose . . .'

'Very valid point,' Tristram said. 'How much should we leave to the reader's imagination? Very interesting.'

Evie thought that perhaps some of her physical descriptions were superfluous. She had mentioned Cornelia's 'almond-shaped eyes' rather a lot. Not to mention the dangling cherry-red lips that Pamela had so objected to all those months ago. Maybe she'd remove the references to Cornelia's 'pert breasts' as well. She'd never really been sure about them.

When the class was over Evie rose quickly, hoping that she could shoot out before anyone nabbed her.

'Fancy a drink?' Russell whispered.

She shook her head. 'I need to get back.' Neil was at home with Freya and Michael. He'd said he wasn't in a hurry, to take her time, but she didn't like to stay away from her children for too long these days.

'How's your daughter?' Russell asked, putting on his dark navy-blue donkey jacket.

'She's doing all right,' Evie replied. 'Thanks for asking.'

She started to do up the toggles on her duffel coat. There was a tap on her back. Damn, she hadn't been quick enough. She swung round.

'Can I have a word, dear?'

Bugger. It was Carol. Her face was inches from Evie's. She could see the pores on her nose and smell her musty Afghan coat.

'I'm in rather a hurry . . .' Evie mumbled.

'It won't take long.'

Russell thrust a piece of paper in Evie's hand as he rose to leave. 'My mobile. If you fancy a drink, or just a chat on the phone. I'm a good listener.'

Evie was surprised but touched. She didn't know him very well; he didn't need to do that. 'Thanks,' she said gratefully, stuffing the piece of paper in her coat pocket.

Before she knew it, Carol was clambering over the back of the chair next to hers and sitting down. 'It's a bit warm in this coat,' she puffed, smoothing her straggly grey hair off her red face. She didn't take the Afghan off, though.

Evie noticed that Becca was hovering on her own at the end of her row of chairs, a tall, thin, isolated figure with that pale face. Evie crossed her fingers, hoping that she'd come to her rescue but she made no move. What was she up to?

'I just need to know how you're doing, dear,' Carol said, patting Evie's arm.

Evie flinched. Carol was the last person she felt like talking to now. 'All right. As well as can be expected,' she replied sullenly. She was still standing, she wasn't going to sit down. It was one thing for Russell to offer his support, but she didn't want to be cross-examined by Carol. She noticed that Tristram was picking up his pile of papers from the table at the front. Good. He'd ask them to leave the hall soon so that he could turn out the lights and lock up.

'I hope your parents are being a help? Have they been up from Devon?' Carol persisted.

Evie felt hot suddenly and loosened the toggles on her coat. She swallowed. What the hell did Carol know about her parents anyway? And how did she know they lived in Devon? It was none of her business. 'I've asked them not to come,' she said. 'We need to be on our own at the moment.' She was aware that Carol was looking up at her closely but she refused to meet her eye.

'Of course,' Carol said. She shuffled slightly in her seat. 'I'm so glad you haven't sent Freya back to that dreadful school. She doesn't like it, you know. She's been very unhappy there.'

Evie's cheeks and neck burst into flame. She took a step back. 'Really, I don't need you telling me—'

Carol reached out and touched her arm again. 'Don't be angry, dear. I know you've been through so much. I only want to help.'

Evie relaxed slightly. Carol was shockingly nosy but she didn't mean any harm. She just said the first thing that came into her head. 'It's kind of you,' Evie said. 'I just can't talk about it at the moment.'

She picked up her bag and headed towards the door. She was aware that Carol and Becca were following. She felt like the bloody Pied Piper.

'Goodnight!' Tristram called. 'See you next month.'

It was spitting with rain outside. Evie pulled up her hood. Carol was right beside her.

'I'm glad Neil's there for you,' she said. Her straggly hair was sticking to her head and rain was trickling down her nose. 'But if he can't babysit, I can always look after Michael if you want to go out alone with Freya. You musn't leave her with that boyfriend of yours. She's not at all keen on him.'

Evie was gobsmacked. She couldn't even bring herself to reply.

'Evie . . . ?' She turned with relief to Becca, who'd opened a black umbrella.

'I'll be off,' Carol said.

The sooner the better, Evie thought.

'I'm sorry I've been such a rubbish friend,' Becca said, once Carol was out of hearing.

Evie looked at her. There was something different about her; she couldn't put her finger on it.

'It's been pretty difficult—' she started to say.

'Can we talk?' Becca interrupted.

'What, now? I have to get back.'

'I'll come with you. I can get a taxi home. Please?'

There was an urgency in her voice that Evie couldn't ignore. 'All right.'

She had no idea what this was about but her mind was racing; maybe Tom and Becca were splitting up, or she'd lost her job? It could be anything. Evie wasn't sure that she was the right shoulder to cry on; she'd got too many problems of her own. But she couldn't turn Becca away.

'The car's round the corner,' Evie said. 'Don't tell me anything now. Wait until we get home.'

It was half past ten by the time they walked through the door. Evie was grateful that Neil had got Michael to bed and he and Freya were in the sitting room watching repeats of *The Catherine Tate Show*.

Freya looked up and smiled when Evie poked her head round the door. 'How was your meeting?' she asked. She looked so small and young, sitting there in her yellow spotty dressing gown. She seemed to have regressed, Evie reflected. She was like a little girl again, timid and unsure of herself. Evie had taken to tucking her up in bed at night and leaving the landing light on.

Freya had been seeing a counsellor, sometimes alone, sometimes with Evie and Neil. They'd all been told to take things slowly. They'd agreed that Freya wouldn't go back to the same school and Evie and Neil had made a few enquiries about alternatives. But she wouldn't go anywhere until after Easter. She simply wasn't ready. Luckily she had Lucy; she'd called round a lot and they'd once gone swimming together but that was all. Mostly Freya seemed content to stay at home, at her mother's or father's side.

'Becca's here,' Evie told Neil. 'She wants to have a chat. Would you mind . . . ?'

He rose. 'C'mon, Freya. Time for bed.' She didn't even protest. He smiled at Evie. 'I'll let myself out.'

She and Becca went into the kitchen and closed the door. Evie fetched a bottle of white wine from the fridge. She had a feeling that they were going to need it. 'What's up?' she asked, filling two glasses.

Becca made a funny noise. Evie looked up and stared. She'd never seen her friend like this, ever. Her eyes were wide and wild; haunted.

'I've got something to tell you,' she said. 'It's going to change your opinion of me totally.'

Evie's legs felt weak. She didn't know if she could cope. She sat down shakily.

'I'm not who you think I am,' said Becca. She spoke slowly and deliberately, in that precise way that she had. 'My real name is Dawn Mackey. I had to change it because when I was twelve years old I killed my sister. I battered her to death with a hockey stick.'

Evie sat and listened, spellbound, as Becca – or Dawn – spilled her story. She started with her background, described the grim council estate in Newcastle where she'd grown up; her father, who'd abandoned them; her boozy mother who used to get beaten up by various boyfriends while Dawn and her sister, Jude, hid in the bedroom pretending not to hear. She described Jude, older than her by two years, with a different father and completely different in looks and character. She was always teasing Dawn about her 'posh friends' at the grammar school, picking on her, trying to get her into trouble.

'I desperately wanted to get out of the council estate, out of Newcastle,' Becca/Dawn explained. 'I was determined to make a better life for myself and I saw education as a means to that end. I worked like crazy at school.'

Then she came to the murder. Evie sat very still while Becca recounted that terrible afternoon in 1978 when she'd completely lost it. Time seemed to be suspended.

'I just saw red,' she whispered. 'I can't explain it. It was like a madness that came over me; I didn't know what I was doing. I just kept hitting and hitting.' She wiped her eye with the sleeve of her black cardigan. 'I didn't mean to kill her.' She looked at Evie pleadingly.

Evie stared back; she couldn't give Becca the comfort that she imagined she was craving.

'I thought she was going to kill me at first,' she went on. 'She was on top of me, bashing my head against the floor again and again. But then I found the hockey stick and pulled it out from under the bed. I hit her several times. It was self-defence, really. But then I carried on.' Becca hung her head. Her black hair fell in front of her face.

'I'll never really understand why I didn't stop. Psychologists told me I had this anger stemming from my background that had been burning away inside of me for years. It was like a ticking time bomb. But lots of people have difficult childhoods, and they don't all turn out to be murderers.'

Evie felt sweat trickling from her armpits. She wanted to squeeze Becca's hand, to reassure her that she understood and it was all right, but she couldn't. Her stomach was straining. 'So why are you telling me this?' she asked.

Becca explained about the trial; the verdict of manslaughter; the judge's summing up: he said that she was dangerous and should be watched very carefully.

Evie started when she heard that; the hairs on the backs of her arms stuck up. Dangerous? It didn't seem possible. She put her elbows on the table and rested her chin in her hands; she felt that she needed the support.

Becca came to the correctional institute and her new identity. She spoke very fast, scarcely stopping for breath until she got to the bit about Gary and her flight to Normandy. 'I thought Tom and the children would be better off without me,' she said.

Evie was finding it hard to process so much information. 'So you're telling me that Tom knew *nothing* about your past?'

Becca shook her head.

'How did you manage to keep up the lie for so long?'

Becca winced. 'Lie, yes,' she said. 'But I felt I had to, you see.'

Evie noticed for the first time that Becca's perfectly mani-cured nails were gone. They were bitten down to the quick. And the skin around them was red-raw. She started picking at a scab on the edge of her thumb. Evie had to look away.

'I'd been warned when I left prison that if anybody ever found out – anybody at all – my cover would be blown and it would be a massive story. There'd be people out to get me – lunatics. You know what they've been like with Nic.

'I'd have to move, change my name, my looks, start all over again. I suppose I got so used to being careful, to watching my back all the time, that it became second nature. Then, when I found Tom, I was convinced that if he knew what I'd done he'd dump me. There were so many times when I did want to tell him, it was such a massive burden, but I just couldn't.'

Evie took a slug of wine. 'But he knows now? How has he taken it?' She still couldn't believe what she was hearing.

Becca ran a finger round the rim of her glass. 'He's been amazing. He says we've got so much going for us and we'll get through this as a family.' She glanced at Evie. 'It seems almost too good to be true.'

Evie took a deep breath. 'He must love you an awful lot.'

Becca smiled. 'I feel incredibly lucky.'

'What's it like between you?' Evie wanted to know. 'I can't imagine. It must be like strangers getting to know each other for the first time.'

'We've talked a lot,' said Becca. 'He's being so strong.' She hesitated. 'There's just one thing . . .'

'What?'

'He's hardly touched me, not since I told him. He makes excuses, tries to avoid it.' She tucked her hair behind her ears. 'I guess it's not surprising really.'

'It'll come,' Evie replied. 'Give it time.' She topped up their glasses. 'Your story's safe with me.' She shivered, remembering the neighbour at Number 22 who'd been so eager to talk to reporters about her own family. 'I won't tell a soul.' She took another sip of wine and cleared her throat. 'But I still don't understand, you haven't explained. Why have you told *me*?'

Becca looked at her hands. Those pale hands with long,

slender fingers that had grabbed a stick and beaten someone to death. 'Because you're my friend.'

There was a pause. Evie wasn't sure who owned the silence: her or Becca. For a second she found herself imagining what Becca must have looked like with fair hair. How she must have appeared when she was clubbing her sister again and again until she stopped breathing, until there was blood everywhere. Was her face contorted with rage – or pleasure? Did she enjoy it?

Evie felt sick with revulsion. Even in their angriest moments, during one of their fiercest rows, Freya and Michael would never, ever do that to each other. They wouldn't be capable of it. But Becca grew up surrounded by hardship and violence, there were extenuating circumstances. She'd changed now, she was lovely and clever and funny and kind. Becca and Dawn were two different people.

Could a person really change as completely as that?

'Thank you for sharing this with me,' Evie whispered. 'It must have been really hard.' It was all that she could manage right now.

'Thank you for listening,' Becca replied.

Chapter Fifty

Evie dropped the letter in the letterbox. With luck, the advertisement would arrive in time to appear in next month's issue of *Brides-to-Be* magazine. It had cost rather a lot but she was determined to get her business back together and start earning proper money. It was time to stop whingeing and get off her backside.

Back home she made herself a cup of tea before going into the sitting room to resume sewing. She'd moved her tailor's dummy from her bedroom a few days ago so that she could admire the spring flowers in the front garden while she worked.

Something made her ears prick up. She peered out of the bay window and squinted, wishing that she had her glasses to hand. Normally she loved feasting her eyes on the miniature daffodils and tulips that she'd planted a few years before, and the purple hyacinths in her window boxes were at their very best.

But today she hardly noticed them; she was too busy trying to get a better look at the young woman walking up Bill's front path clutching a folder and a notebook in one arm, and carrying an orange plastic shopping bag in the other hand. The woman, who appeared to be in her mid to late twenties, was tall, slim and attractive, with long, silky brown hair. She was wearing brown boots, a rather jaunty pink and brown flowered skirt and a pale blue denim jacket.

Evie guessed that she was Bill's mature Ukrainian student. She'd seen her coming and going quite a lot recently, and she often stayed longer than three hours. Evie wondered what was in the orange plastic bag. Lunch for them both?

'Hi, babe!'

She spun around. Steve was standing in the doorway with

just a pair of Neil's old stripy pyjama bottoms on. He must have found them in the cupboard. He had a serious case of bed-head, and his chest and feet were bare. He'd clearly just woken.

Evie glanced at the clock: ten forty-five. All right for some on a weekday morning. She'd already taken Michael to school, got back, booked a doctor's appointment for Freya, cleaned away the breakfast dishes, tidied the kitchen, hoovered the hall, started pinning the hem of the wedding dress. And she'd got another client coming round this afternoon for a fitting. It was all go.

Steve's chest looked rather white and puny, Evie thought, and his arms were very long. He reminded her of a spider. Amazing how he'd wheedled his way back into her life. How had that happened? She hadn't even noticed, and here he was right at home again.

'I fancy poached eggs,' he said, running his hand through his long, sticking-up hair.

'Do you?' Evie replied. 'You know where the fridge is.'

She resumed her position at the window. The woman had disappeared into Bill's house now. Evie sighed, plumped up the cushions on the sofa and turned back to her tailor's dummy in the corner of the bay. She could hear Steve rattling plates and cutlery in the kitchen. 'Where's the butter?' he called.

'By the bread I expect,' she shouted back. He was hopeless at finding things.

She pricked her finger on a pin. 'Ow.' It was no use, she wasn't in the mood just now. She'd make a mistake. She got up off her knees and caught sight of Freya's black sweatshirt on the Lloyd Loom chair. She picked it up, started to fold it, sniffed. It smelled of Freya and that fresh, lemony scent she wore. Evie hugged the sweatshirt to her, thinking how different things could have turned out.

It was three months since that dreadful day in January and, thank God, things were slowly improving. Freya had swapped schools after Easter and seemed to have enjoyed her first week. She was going to have to re-do a year because she'd missed so much, but she said that she didn't mind. She'd admitted that she hadn't been working properly for months and needed to go through the syllabus again. She seemed to be enjoying her subjects more this time around, though it was still early days, and the therapy sessions were certainly helping.

She and Evie had been in the shopping centre one Saturday afternoon when they'd spotted Gemma and Chantelle. Freya had stopped dead in her tracks. Evie could sense her fear. They'd scurried into Claire's Accessories but the girls had followed them in.

'Hi, Freya, how are you?' Gemma had smiled. 'Do you want to come round my house and listen to some music?'

Freya had mumbled something about being busy. After the girls left, Evie whispered: 'They want to be your friend now.'

'Because they think I'm famous,' Freya replied through gritted teeth. 'No chance. I'll never forget what they did to me.' But she'd seemed, at last, to accept that they were no longer a threat, that they couldn't hurt her any more.

Neil's baby was due any day and Evie did worry that it would set Freya back. On the other hand, father and daughter were getting on better and it might even give Freya something else to think about. Although Freya still professed to hate Helen, Evie did think that she could detect a slight softening.

Evie thought of Nic. They hadn't been in touch but Evie had seen Russell from the writing group a few times. He'd been talking to Nic too, and had passed on some of her news. Thank God Alan was where he should be: locked up. At first Evie had been so angry with Nic, so furious, that she couldn't see beyond that. How could she have ignored the signs and put Freya in such danger? But Russell had pointed out that it had taken a lot of courage for Nic to do what she did in the end and turn him in. She'd shown what she was really made of. And, of course, she'd lost so much in the process.

She and Alan were getting divorced and money was a major worry. She'd had to take Dominic out of his private school, where he was happy and secure, and she was going to need to sell the house.

As for Becca, well, Evie still found it hard to absorb. The fact that she'd led this secret life for all those years, concealed her past so brilliantly, was difficult to take on board. She'd found herself googling Becca – or Dawn – repeatedly, poring over the facts of the case and the newspaper stories written at the time and subsequently, trying to connect this disturbed girl from Newcastle with the Becca that she now knew, or had thought she knew.

Evie had tried to convince Becca that their friendship was unchanged but in truth, both recognised that it would and could never be the same. Becca said the whole story would probably come out some day, one way or another, but of one thing Evie was sure: she wasn't going to be the one to spill the beans.

Becca had resigned from her job and the Richmond house was on the market. She and Tom were looking for a suitable property in Spain which they could turn into a hotel. Evie would miss them but she could understand their logic. They'd certainly stay in touch; you couldn't share a secret like that and not remain inextricably bound.

She strolled into the kitchen. Steve was busy buttering some toast. She noticed that he had dirty fingernails.

'Much work today?' she asked. She didn't know why she bothered. She knew what the answer would be.

'Nah, there's not much about at the moment.' He licked his fingers. Evie shuddered. He did have some revolting personal habits. 'Thought I'd hang around here today, if that's all right with you, read the papers, watch a bit of TV.'

Evie's face felt hot. 'No it's not all right with me,' she said. '*I* have work to do. I've got a wedding dress to finish.' He shot her a hurt expression. She softened. 'I'm sorry,' she went on, 'but it's distracting trying to work when you're around. I can't concentrate properly. I make loads of mistakes.'

He shrugged. 'OK then, I'll be off – soon as I've finished this.' He plopped two poached eggs from the pan on to some toast and plonked his plate on the table.

He looked cold, sitting there without a shirt on. His shoulders were very thin. Evie felt guilty suddenly.

'I'll see you early next week, shall I?' she asked. 'Once I've made some progress with the dress.'

'I'll be back before then,' he replied, taking a mouthful of food. 'I'm meeting a mate over this way tomorrow night, it'd be easier for me to stay here.'

Evie swallowed. 'Ah,' she said. 'I see. OK, tomorrow night then.'

She tramped slowly upstairs and flopped on to her bed. She couldn't understand these negative feelings that she was having about Steve. Not when Zelda was so insistent that he was The One. It simply didn't make sense.

Zelda had gone a bit funny recently. She kept insisting that Evie shouldn't tell anyone – not a soul – that they were having these conversations. But who was Evie likely to tell anyway? Certainly not Bill. He'd say loftily that it was all a load of rubbish and she was wasting her money. He could be so arrogant and dismissive.

Evie grimaced. Zelda seemed to be taking an age to answer the phone. That was annoying, too. Where was she? It wasn't as if she had anything much else to do. She wasn't much cop at her job, either. She'd totally cocked up as far as Freya was concerned. Hadn't seen it coming at all. What use was a medium if she couldn't even see seismic events like that around the corner?

Evie checked herself. She was expecting too much of Zelda, who never claimed that she could see everything. She, Evie, really was in a miserable mood today. She'd better snap out of it or no one would want to talk to her.

'Zelda speakin'.' She sounded slightly out of breath. 'Oh,' she puffed, 'I've just got in from me walk. I wasn't expectin' you till tonight.'

Evie sat back on the bed, propping up the pillows behind her. 'I need to talk to you about Steve.'

'What about him?'

'I've gone off him.'

'Gone off?'

'Yes.' Did she have to spell it out? 'I mean, I don't fancy him any more.'

There was a pause while Zelda lit a fag. 'So, what's that got to do with it?' she said at last.

383

Evie was exasperated. 'It means I can't bear the sight of him any more. I think he's a lazy, sponging, unattractive creep.'

Zelda took a drag of her cigarette. Evie imagined that she could smell the smoke wafting out of the receiver. 'That's a bit strong, darlin'.'

'Well, I can't hide my feelings any longer,' Evie huffed. 'I'm going to have to say something. He can't be The One you told me about. Anyway, didn't you say his name began with a T, a P or a W? You must have made a mistake.'

Zelda tut-tutted. 'Oh no, darlin',' she said, 'there's no mistake. You're just going through a bad patch, that's all. You should have a weekend away together without the kiddies. That'll put the romance back.'

'But I don't want to go away for a weekend with him,' Evie cried. 'In fact I can't think of anything worse.'

She put her hand over her mouth. She couldn't believe she'd just said it. What on earth was she thinking of?

'Look, darlin',' Zelda hissed. The tone in her voice startled Evie. She sounded quite angry. 'I'm tellin' you straight. This Steve o' yours is the one for you and no mistake. It's Steve you're gonna marry.'

Evie gasped. 'What if I don't want to marry him?' she said. 'What if I've changed my mind?'

'You can't change what's written,' Zelda replied. 'No one can do that. So you'd best just buckle down and get used to the idea.'

It wasn't easy to follow someone on a bike. Carol didn't think it was quite her thing. It would be difficult enough on foot but with a bike it was even harder. She tried to go as slowly as possible, so as not to overtake him, but that made her wobble precariously. Then she had to stop and walk for a bit, doing her best not to bump into pedestrians and thus draw attention to herself.

Steve was on the same side of the road heading towards the town centre. Carol guessed that he was going to the station but she couldn't be sure. He stopped once at a shop to buy a newspaper, calling goodbye as he left. She hated the way he was so familiar with the place and the people. He'd spent the last few months insinuating himself back into Evie's life and it looked as if he were now in danger of becoming a permanent fixture. Carol shivered. Not if she could help it.

He walked with a stoop – he didn't have a nice, flat back like Evie. And his long, straight hair, flecked with grey, was hanging down around his face in greasy strings. It needed a good wash. What a nasty, unsavoury-looking character, Carol thought. She couldn't imagine what on earth Evie saw in him.

She crossed the road quickly as they neared the train station and left her bike against the fence. There was no time to lock it. She'd just have to keep her fingers crossed that it wouldn't get nicked. Good job it was one of those old, sit-up-and-beg varieties with a big, wicker basket on the front. Not exactly trendy.

She trailed behind him into the ticket hall and watched while he paid for his ticket; she had a pass. Then she kept close while he went through the barrier and up the ramp on to platform three. He stood and studied a train map on the wall while she sat down on a bench and sighed with relief. Maybe this was going to be easier than she'd feared. Most of the time while he was walking he'd had his head down, staring at his feet. Luckily he was the unobservant sort.

She sat several rows back on the train; there weren't many people about so it wasn't difficult to keep an eye on him. Meanwhile, he stared out of the window; hadn't he got a job to go to? Carol was contemptuous. He'd be a hopeless provider, not what Evie needed at all.

The train stopped at Clapham Junction and Steve got out, followed by Carol, and headed up Lavender Hill. Fortunately his pace was pretty slow. Not in any hurry, she thought disapprovingly. Not like *proper* men with important business to attend to.

Halfway up Lavender Hill he crossed the road and turned right. Carol was relieved; he must be near his destination now. There were fewer people off the main road and she feared that at any moment he might turn round and spot her. But he carried on until he reached a dingy-looking Victorian semi with a 'To Let' sign outside, where he stopped.

Carol hung back and peered at him round the corner of a privet hedge. She was surprised to see a youngish woman with a small boy on her hip, marching out of the house and down the path towards him. She'd left the front door wide open.

'Where the fuck have you been?' the woman shouted.

Charming. Carol didn't have to strain at all. The man mumbled something which Carol couldn't hear.

'Fine example you're setting your son,' the woman went on. 'Disappearing for nights on end. And how am I supposed to find somewhere else for us to live if you never give us any money? We can't live on thin air, you know.'

Steve put his arm on her shoulder. He seemed to be hoping to hustle her inside, but she wasn't having any of it.

'Take your hands off me,' she screeched, shaking him away. 'I'm sick with worry. We're being kicked out of our home and do you care? No you don't. All you can do is fuck around with whoever it is you're fucking when you're not with me.'

Carol winced. She wasn't used to language like this. It really was most disagreeable. Steve put his hands in his pockets. His shoulders were drooping even more than usual and his chin was practically scraping the floor. Carol couldn't hear what he said next, but she guessed it was some sort of apology.

'I don't care what you say,' the woman screeched, 'you're not coming in here, no way. I've had enough of you and your empty promises. You can fuck off. I never want to see you again.'

She turned on her heels and marched back towards the house, with Steve in hot pursuit. But before he could get his foot in the door, she'd slammed it in his face.

Carol wanted to cheer, but she managed to contain herself. He rang the bell a few times and she was willing the woman not to answer. She didn't. Then he went to the front window and started banging on that, and throwing pebbles up to the window above. At last, when he got no joy, he went to the side gate, climbed on to the next-door neighbour's wall and tried to jump over, but it was too high. Carol was immensely relieved.

Money or no money, that poor woman would be better off without him.

When he'd finally given up, Carol watched Steve sloping off down the road in the other direction, his mobile clamped to his ear. A nasty thought crossed her mind: he was probably ringing Evie to fix up his bed for tonight. She checked in either direction that no one was coming and stepped out from behind the privet hedge. She'd have to act fast.

She took a deep breath, straightened her shoulders and hurried back down the hill towards the station. She didn't know if she could do it; she thought she'd never been so nervous in her life. But she was sick of watching from the wings, of knowing full well what was best and not being allowed to say it. She'd done it for too long; she owed it now to Evie to act.

Her underarms and the palms of her hands were sweaty and her heart was racing. She was frightened but excited too. After all, she'd been dreaming of this moment for the past forty-two years.

The time had almost come to step out of the shadows.

Chapter Fifty-One

'What's the matter?'

The young woman had obviously been crying. Her eyes were red and she was clutching a paper hankie. Evie ushered her into the sitting room, picking up a plate from the floor that she'd used for her lunchtime sandwich and putting it on the Lloyd Loom chair. 'Sit down, please.'

The woman plonked herself on the sofa and blew into a hankie. Her Big Day was in a month's time. Pre-wedding jitters, Evie supposed. It wasn't unusual.

'I've finished the lace now,' she said kindly. 'The dress looks beautiful. Would you like to see it?'

'No!' The woman started sobbing. Evie sat down beside her and put an arm around her shoulders.

'What is it?' she said. 'What's happened?'

'He's called it off,' the woman wailed. 'He says he's changed his mind, he doesn't know if he loves me any more. But' – Evie got up and passed her a box of tissues that were on the windowsill – 'we've been planning this for a whole year. I don't understand why he didn't tell me before!'

'I'm so sorry,' Evie said. 'Do you think he means it or is it just pre-wedding nerves?'

'He means it,' the woman said. Her body was trembling. Evie instinctively reached up and stroked her thick auburn hair. 'He's cancelled the church and the reception and said he's going to ring round this morning to tell everyone.'

'My God,' Evie said. 'You must be devastated. Was there any indication at all that this was coming?'

It was 2.30 p.m. before the woman left. Evie had tried her best to be helpful, to offer sound advice, and she felt wrung out. The poor woman was in pieces. Evie wondered what on earth to do about the dress. The fabric had cost a lot and she'd spent hours making it, but she didn't know if she'd have the heart to charge for it. She badly needed the money, though. She'd think about it later.

She was annoyed when the doorbell rang. She didn't want to talk to anyone.

'May I come in, dear?'

Evie had great difficulty concealing her irritation. This was all she needed: first a distraught, jilted bride and now Carol on her doorstep. It really was the last straw.

'I can't be long,' she said, checking her watch in a very obvious way. 'I have some work to finish before I pick up Michael.' She raised her eyebrows. 'The school day's so short. I'm sorry I haven't time to make coffee.'

Carol stepped over the threshold. 'That's all right, dear,' she said, 'I don't want any coffee but I do have something to tell you.' She glanced around, clearly expecting to be invited to sit down.

'In here,' Evie sighed, leading Carol into the sitting room. What on earth did the woman want?

Sunlight was streaming through the window and you could almost smell the hyacinths in the window box. Carol settled down on the sofa while Evie chose the Lloyd Loom.

Carol cleared her throat. 'There's something you need to know about that man you're seeing: Steve.' She rubbed her hands on her legs as if to warm them, though it wasn't cold.

Evie's stomach flip-flopped.

'I saw him with his wife – or girlfriend or whoever she is – and their baby.'

Well, so what? Evie knew about his ex and their little boy.

'They're still living together, or they were up until this morning when she kicked him out for – excuse my language . . .' Carol lowered her eyes, '. . . "fucking around" and not paying the rent.'

Evie stared at Carol's lips. They were opening and closing but the sound seemed to be coming from somewhere else. 'You must have made a mistake . . .'

'No, dear, no mistake,' Carol said. 'I saw him outside his

house in Clapham. They were having an argument. She was using terrible language. He's definitely been living there up till now.'

Evie sat quite still for a moment, digesting the information. In a way this didn't surprise her. He'd always said that he didn't want her coming to his place because it was too small and poky. But she supposed she'd had her doubts, though she'd chosen to ignore them. Funny that she'd had that conversation with Zelda about him earlier. She wondered what Zelda would say about this. She frowned. She couldn't expect Evie to marry him now.

Marry. How foolish she was. She was never going to get married again. She wasn't the sort of woman you wanted to marry – that's why Neil had left her, that's why Helen was about to have his baby.

Carol's voice shattered the silence, making her jump. 'I'm sorry to give you such a shock.'

Evie came back to the present. Who was this ugly woman with long grey hair? She shouldn't be here, she was intruding.

'What business is it of yours what Steve does and who I go out with?' Evie said quietly. She started picking at a loose thread on the sleeve of her jumper. 'I don't know how you know him but it's got nothing to do with you. You shouldn't poke your nose in where it's not wanted.'

'Oh, but it is my business.'

Evie looked up. She didn't like the tone of Carol's voice. She wasn't an amusing eccentric, she was creepy. 'What do you mean?' The hairs on Evie's arms prickled.

'I mean,' said Carol, 'that I'm your mother.'

Evie froze. 'That's a wicked thing to say . . .' She wanted to get up but she couldn't. Something was binding her to the chair.

'It's true, Evie,' Carol went on. 'I was just sixteen when I had you. My parents – they weren't very nice people – wouldn't let me keep you so you had to be adopted.'

Evie stared at Carol. She wasn't joking. She was leaning forwards eagerly, almost excitedly, in her chair, her fingers working away like a tricoteuse.

'It was the saddest day of my life when they took you,'

Carol continued, 'but I've kept an eye on you all these years.' Her face broke into a smile. 'I was there on your first day at school, when you started Brownies, when you got married and had the children. You didn't know it but I was always there, making sure you were all right.'

The cord binding Evie to the chair snapped and she jumped up. 'What are you saying? That you've been stalking me since I was a child?' She laughed. 'I don't believe you. Is this some sort of joke?'

Carol fumbled in her bag and took out what looked like a small, pink notebook with a plastic cover. She opened it and out fell a pile of photographs.

'Here,' she said, fumbling with the pictures, trying to sort them into a pile. Evie didn't want to look but she couldn't help it. Her eyes were drawn to them like magnets. She gasped. There was a fuzzy picture of a little girl in uniform coming out of school – her; another of a bride and groom standing on the church steps – her and Neil.

She snatched one of the photos that had fallen on to Carol's lap. 'That's Freya!' she cried. 'How dare you take pictures of my daughter. That's illegal. I could have you locked up.' There was another one underneath of Michael aged about two. Evie seized that, too, and held it to her chest.

Carol gazed at her sadly. Evie looked into the older woman's eyes for the first time, properly absorbing them. A spark of recognition shot through her that made her shudder.

'I thought you might be like this,' Carol said, shaking her head. 'I know it's a lot to take in. I just want you to know that I've loved you always and I still love you. I've only ever wanted what's best for you.'

Evie saw flashes of red and orange in the corners of her vision. 'What's best for me?' she shouted. 'Where have I heard that before? My parents were always telling me what was best for me only they didn't have a clue. They just wanted me to be something I wasn't.

'I had a horrible childhood,' she went on, 'and now you're stirring things up and claiming you're my mother and trying to tell me what to do about Steve. Well, I don't want another mother. One's more than enough for me. And I certainly don't want advice about Steve.'

Carol wiped a tear away with her hand. 'I've only ever wanted to hold you in my arms and tell you I love you.'

'You should have thought about that before you gave me away,' Evie shrieked. 'It's too late now. Much too late.' She tried to pull Carol off the sofa but she was too heavy.

'Zelda never told me about this,' Evie ranted. She was almost talking to herself. 'Zelda said Steve was The One, too. I hate you, I hate everyone.'

Carol stared at her. 'Zelda? When did she say that? You shouldn't listen to her—'

'I've told you, stop telling me what to do,' Evie raged. 'Get up.'

Carol managed to stagger to her feet and Evie half pushed, half pulled her to the door.

'Get out of my house right now,' she yelled.

Carol was cringing like a cornered animal. She stumbled off the step and nearly fell. Evie stood with her hands on her hips while she tottered down the path. She was a pathetic sight but Evie didn't care. This was all too much.

'Push off,' she roared at the top of her voice, 'and don't ever come back.'

Carol glanced back, an injured look on her face.

'I never want to see you again.'

Bill heard the commotion and came running out of his house. 'What on earth . . . ?'

He saw Carol trying to unpadlock her bike and then start to cross to the other side of the street, but before he could say anything she'd pedalled off.

Evie heard her call something to him over her shoulder. She watched Carol's not insubstantial form getting smaller and smaller. She was wobbling rather a lot. Upset. Evie felt a twinge of guilt but Carol had given her such a shock. Evie couldn't believe it was true. There again, there was something frighteningly plausible about her story.

She flicked back through various scenes in her mind,

remembering the way Carol had made a point, after one of the writing groups, of asking Nic and Becca to look after her. Evie had just heard that Helen was pregnant and must have been looking strained, but it had seemed odd at the time, over-friendly; Carol had also made that peculiar to-do in the pub before Christmas when Evie had told everyone about her feelings for Steve. They'd all agreed that Carol was way out of order.

Now Evie thought about it, Carol had always sat close to her in meetings, too, and asked so many questions about her and her family, and she always seemed to know little details about Evie's life that she didn't remember telling her, such as where her parents lived and which school she went to. Occasionally it would bring Evie up short, then she'd reason that she must have mentioned it to Carol at some stage and forgotten.

The truth was, Carol had always seemed unusually interested in and concerned about her but Evie had put it down to kindly eccentricity. And she couldn't deny that she had felt this strange affinity towards her. She couldn't quite put her finger on it but there was something about her that had seemed, well, familiar somehow. It was very strange.

She walked towards Bill, hugging her arms around her. She was shivering despite the mild weather. She must look a fright, she thought, all staring eyes and wild expression.

'Are you all right?' he asked, giving her one of his intense looks.

Evie shook her head. 'She just told me she's my birth mother,' she said, nodding in Carol's direction. She laughed. 'Fancy coming round here and saying that. It's too much on top of everything else. I can't handle it.'

She started to cry. Bill put his arm round her and gave her a hug.

There was a pause.

'It's true, Evie,' he said gently. 'She told me on the day that Freya went missing.'

Evie gasped. 'What?'

'She came to your house – remember? – ostensibly to check you were all right because you'd left the door open. I told her about Freya and she was terribly upset. Then while Michael was upstairs in his room for a while, it all came out. Her facts were correct: your birth date, the names of your adoptive parents, where you lived as a child, everything.'

Evie broke away. She was shocked. 'But why didn't you tell me? How could you keep it from me?'

Bill looked serious. 'She asked me not to. She made me promise.'

Evie shook her head.

'Also, I didn't think you were in any fit state to take on board something as big as this. You'd got enough to think about with Freya. You needed to be focusing on her. I thought it was best if Carol told you in her own time, as and when she felt the moment was right.'

Evie's face crumpled. 'So she decided that the right moment was just after she'd told me that Steve was still living with what I supposed to be his ex-wife. And now you tell me that you knew all along and you were hiding it from me?'

Bill was about to say something when they were disturbed by a noise next door.

'Bill? There you are! I didn't know where you had gone.'

Evie's heart sank. A tall young woman with long brown hair was advancing towards them. It was the Ukrainian student.

'I'm sorry,' she said in a strong accent. She looked oddly at Evie. 'Have I disturbed something?'

'Not at all,' Evie said. She turned to Bill. 'You'd better get back to your tutorial.'

He frowned. 'Could you give us a moment, Galina?'

'Of course.' The young woman pointed to his house. 'Shall I put the kettle on?'

'Good idea.'

'I have brought cakes. We can have tea and cakes.' She smiled at Evie. 'Would you care for a cake? They are chocolate eclairs. I had never tasted one until I came to England.'

'I'm on a diet,' Evie snapped.

'Oh.' The young woman's eyes widened.

'That would be nice,' Bill said. 'I'll just be a moment.'

Evie gritted her teeth, waiting for the Ukrainian to leave.

'You were rather sharp,' said Bill, once Galina was out of earshot.

Evie felt uncomfortably hot.

'Look, it's a bit difficult now but I'll come round later,' Bill said. 'When I've finished teaching. We can talk things through then.'

'Don't bother,' Evie said, deadpan.

'It'll be all right,' Bill persisted.

Evie stared at him. His blue eyes were trying to convey something but her insides felt hollow.

'I have to go now,' he went on. 'It's not fair on—'

'Just go then,' Evie snapped. 'I've had it up to here.' She did an invisible sign on her forehead with her hand.

'Evie?'

She turned on her heel and marched back into the house. She was aware that Bill was standing, watching her, right up until the moment that she slammed the front door.

Chapter Fifty-Two

Zelda was sitting on a wooden bench by the big round pond in Victoria Park, staring at the ducks and geese. She didn't look up when Carol approached. 'I thought you'd come today,' she said, her eyes fixed straight ahead.

Carol lowered herself down beside her sister. 'Why did you do it?' she asked simply.

Zelda shrugged. 'I don't know what you mean.'

Carol clenched her fists. She wanted to lash out. It took a moment or two to compose herself. 'How did Evie get your number?'

'Easy. I put a card through her door. She rang the next day.'

'Did you know about Freya? Could you tell what was going to happen?' Carol was fiddling with the tassels on her brown woollen poncho. It was helping her to keep calm. She needed to know this. It was really important.

Zelda laughed. 'I can't believe I'm hearin' this. You who always said you didn't hold no truck with the spirit world. P'raps you shouldn't have written me off like that.'

'But did you?' Carol stared at her sister, willing her to meet her gaze. She might know more if she could look into her sister's eyes.

At last Zelda turned. 'I can't see everythin',' she answered, her face very still. Her pupils were round, black and unfathomable. 'I might be good at what I do but I'm no miracle-worker. If the spirits don't feel like tellin' you somethin', they won't.'

Carol swallowed. Zelda was still holding her gaze. Carol didn't know if she believed her sister or not. She felt so confused. She couldn't tell what Zelda's eyes were saying.

'But what about Steve?' Carol said at last, breaking the spell. 'You made Evie carry on with him even though you must have known he was bad news. She told me you'd said he was "The One". Why did you do that?'

Zelda snorted. 'Look, I couldn't force her to go with anyone. She's got a mind of her own, that girl. Besides, I thought he was good for her. She was lonely; she needed a new man to help her get over that two-timin' husband of hers.'

'You continued talking to her, advising her after I'd specifically asked you not to.'

'Yeah, well, she kept callin' me. She was desperate. What was I to do? Dump her? I couldn't do that, it wouldn't have been nice.'

'I don't believe you,' Carol said. 'I don't believe you had her best interests at heart.'

Zelda shuffled in her seat. 'You can believe what you like,' she said, 'it's the truth.'

'I feel betrayed,' said Carol. 'I can't believe my own sister would go behind my back like that.'

Zelda crossed her arms. Carol noticed that she was wearing her royal-blue fluffy slippers: the ones she'd given her for her birthday.

'That's a laugh comin' from you!' Zelda retorted. 'Some sister you were, stealin' my man and next thing I know you're havin' his bloody baby!'

Carol widened her eyes. 'But that was so long ago!'

'Not to me it isn't,' Zelda replied. 'Seems like yesterday to me.'

Carol stared at the pond. Some mallard ducks were lazily dipping their heads in and out of the water, their tales waggling, looking for food. The drakes had emerald-green feathers; it was the mating season.

'You know Evie's the most important thing to me in the whole world,' she said quietly. 'You know how much I love her. It was wrong to go meddling in her life like that. She got far too involved with this man – she took her eye off the ball and neglected Freya. She could have been raped, or worse, murdered.' Carol shook her head. 'That was bad of you, Zelda—'

'Bad? Just listen to you!' Zelda interrupted. 'And I suppose it's not bad to steal yer own sister's man – the only man I ever loved? What do you call that, then?'

Carol stopped fiddling with her poncho and sat quite still, her hands in her lap. 'He was going to leave you anyway.'

Zelda jumped up. She was surprisingly quick on her pins. 'Leave me? Don't give me that,' she laughed. 'He comes to me house most nights, talks to me on the end of me bed. He loved me, you fool. He says you were just a playthin', you satisfied an urge, that's all. He needed it and you gave it to 'im.'

Carol flinched.

'He never had no feelin's for you,' Zelda continued. 'If you hadn't of gone and got yourself pregnant—'

'Sit down,' Carol commanded, pulling on Zelda's sleeve. She did as she was told. 'I didn't get pregnant deliberately, don't you understand? It was a mistake, I was young, he seduced me.'

Zelda grimaced. 'Here we go, Miss Goody Two-Shoes.' There was a nasty tone in her voice. 'You knew perfectly well what you was doin'. Don't give me that "I was an innocent little girl" bollocks. You wanted to get pregnant so you could get married and get out of that shithole of a house we was livin' in. Start a new life. Only it didn't work, did it?' She laughed. 'They wouldn't let you keep the baby. You hadn't bargained on that, had you? Thought they'd be delighted to get shot of you. You weren't so clever after all!'

Carol was weeping now, she couldn't help herself. She wiped the tears away with her sleeve. 'I suppose I did think, well, maybe Derek and I would marry . . .'

'See?' Zelda said triumphantly. 'I knew it! I knew what was going on in that sneaky little mind of yours.'

Carol swallowed. 'But I was so young,' she pleaded, 'I didn't see things clearly. I just thought: He's older, he's got a job. Maybe he can get us out of here. I'd have taken you with us, Griselda, that was my plan.'

Zelda growled. 'You must be flippin' bonkers if you think I'd of gone to live with you and Derek and yer precious baby. Besides, like I said, it was me he wanted really. You was just a distraction.'

Carol shuffled in her seat. 'Be that as it may,' she said, 'I still can't believe that you'd deliberately put the happiness of another person at risk and maybe the safety of a child, too, just to get some sort of . . .' She paused. '. . . some sort of sick revenge.'

Zelda turned and grinned. Her mouth was a black, gaping hole interspersed with a few crooked teeth. 'Well, you know what they say,' she said. 'Revenge is sweet. I was pleased you was worried about Evie. I wanted you to sweat a bit. Shame she ain't going to marry that no-good man of hers but you can't have everythin'.'

Carol felt light-headed suddenly. The world started to spin. She closed her eyes and after a moment or two, the dizziness passed. 'All these years,' she said, 'that I've cared for you. Thought about you. Wanted the best for you. It was me, remember, who stood up for you against Mother and Father when we were children. I may not have believed all that psychic stuff but I never judged you. I was your only friend.

'And now I find you've been trying your best to hurt me and my family. I don't understand how you could do it. Doesn't the fact that we're sisters, that we have the same blood, count for anything?'

Zelda wrapped her blue shawl more tightly around her. 'When you stole Derek,' she said, 'that was it, as far as I was concerned. You wasn't me sister no more.'

Carol put her hands over her face and hung her head. 'I had no idea,' she said, 'absolutely no idea.'

Zelda rustled in a plastic bag on the bench beside her, fished out a bit of bread and threw it at the pond. It didn't quite reach. Several Canada geese heaved themselves out of the water and waddled towards it, squawking loudly.

'I don't know why you're cryin',' she mumbled. 'Everythin's all right now, ain't it? Evie's not goin' to marry that man you dislike; Freya's safe. It's all hunky dory. You can just toddle off back to that precious family of yours. You won't get no more hassle from me. I've settled a score, I'm happy enough. I ain't bothered with you.'

Carol took her hands away from her face. 'It's not that simple,' she replied. 'I've told Evie I'm her mother and she doesn't want to know.' She reached in her back pocket for a hankie to blow her nose on but there wasn't one.

'You follow her around all them years and then she don't want to know you?' Zelda cackled. 'Priceless! That's kids for you.'

Carol started to cry again. 'I don't know what to do.'

Zelda rose. 'Nothin' you can do,' she said, matter-of factly. 'If a kid don't want to know you, that's that I should think. I don't blame her. I mean, at the end of the day you did give her away. You left her to her fate.'

Carol jumped up. 'That's so unfair,' she shouted. 'You know how upset I was. I'd have done anything to keep her.'

Zelda tut-tutted. 'Yeah, well. It ain't no good tellin' her that is it? Far as she can see, you turned your back on her and that's that.' She picked up the white plastic bag and tipped the rest of the bread beside the water's edge. 'I must be goin'.'

Carol's stomach lurched. Her chest felt hollow. 'Will I see you again?' Her voice was very small.

Zelda turned to look at her sister. Her eyes were cold and hard. Carol flinched. 'I doubt it,' she said. 'I don't think there's anythin' more to say, do you?'

'Can't we forgive each other? Call it quits?' Carol was desperate. 'We are sisters, after all. We're all we've got.'

Zelda laughed. 'You should of thought of that before you did what you did. Too late now, darlin'.' She scrunched the plastic bag up into a ball and put it in her cardigan pocket before turning and walking slowly away.

Carol sat and watched until her sister had disappeared from view. She didn't look back once. A mother and toddler in a bright-red cardigan stopped and watched the geese eating their bread. One of them waddled towards the small child, who started crying.

'Shoo,' the mother said, pushing the goose away with her foot. She picked the small child up. 'It's all right,' she soothed. 'Mummy won't let that naughty goose hurt you.'

Carol couldn't see any more. Her eyes were blurred with tears. She got up, adjusted her poncho and set off slowly in the opposite direction from her sister towards the tube.

* * *

'"Your parents are coming to collect you this weekend," Heidi's mum, Stella, said to Josh and Katie. Scruffy barked.'

Becca paused for a moment and glanced out of the window before continuing to type.

He started jumping up and down, yapping madly.

'Stop it Scruffy, I can't think what's got into you,' Stella said crossly. 'You're putting dirty paw marks on my nice clean apron.'

'Look, he doesn't want you to go,' Heidi cried. 'He's asking if you can stay for another week.' It certainly seemed to be the case. He had a beseeching look in his eyes.

'Woof?' he said, his head on one side. 'Woof?' Everyone laughed.

'Come here, Scruff,' Josh said, giving the dog a tickle under the chin. 'Don't you worry, we'll be back next summer – if we may?' Josh looked at Stella, who beamed.

'Most certainly,' she said. 'Summers at Breamwater just wouldn't be the same without you, would they?'

The children shook their heads.

'How's it going?'

Becca started, her train of thought broken. She spun round on the chair and smiled at Tom, who was wearing jeans and his old navy-blue jumper with the hole in the sleeve. She rolled her shoulders. She must have been hunched over the laptop in her study for several hours.

'Well,' she replied. 'I've got the wind in my sails at last. I'm romping towards the finish.'

'Great!' he said, peering over her shoulder.

Their arms brushed momentarily and he took a step back. She pretended that she hadn't noticed. It was Saturday afternoon. He'd been making flapjacks with the children downstairs, giving Becca time to crack on with her children's story. She was on the penultimate chapter; she was wrapping everything up. It was the final week in April so she'd have a month or so to reread the manuscript and polish it to a shine before the 1 June competition deadline. She'd never thought she'd make it; she'd amazed herself.

She had no idea if it was winning material, but she was pleased with the way the storyline had turned out; for a while her thoughts had been so black that she wasn't sure if she could bring the plot to the happy conclusion that she'd planned so many months before. Events seemed to have veered off in a most unpleasant direction.

But in the past four weeks or so she'd rewritten the blackest bits, toned them down, and she felt that all the different threads had come together nicely. It was exciting.

'Sorry to disturb you,' Tom said. 'Shall I bring you up a cup of tea?'

Becca shook her head. 'I think I've done enough for today. I'll come down now. Those flapjacks smell delicious.' She paused and looked at her husband seriously. 'By the way, I've found a couple of possible places to stay.'

He rested against the edge of the desk and crossed his arms. 'Really?'

She nodded. 'There's the Marriott, which has an indoor swimming pool. It's not far from Newcastle city centre and there's lots of parkland round about. I think the children would love it; I want them to have a nice time and get a good impression of the place.'

Tom cocked his head on one side. 'Are you sure this is a good idea?'

She sighed. 'I have to do it, Tom. I'd prefer to go with you and the kids, but if you'd rather stay . . .'

He put up his hand. 'No,' he said, 'you're right. This is something we should do together, as a family. We can talk about what we say to the kids later. You go ahead and book. I'll support you in every way I can.'

Chapter Fifty-Three

❧

'Evie suggested the café in the corner of the market place. Eleven o'clock.'

'Oh,' said Nic.

'All right with you?' Russell asked.

'I guess so.'

'Don't forget it's the April creative writing group tonight,' he went on. 'Would you like a lift? I can easily swing by. Seven thirty, say?'

'Thank you.'

'You haven't had a drink?' He sounded concerned.

'No.'

Although Russell was a stalwart of the creative writing group, Nic had only really got to know him well in the past couple of months. He'd been kind enough to ring when he'd heard the news about Alan and read some of the lurid headlines about her. 'If I can be of any help . . .' he'd said. 'I'm a good listener.'

Well, she'd needed to talk all right and a doctor had seemed as good a person to confide in as any, even if Russell did have rather a peculiar specialism. In fact he was just about the only person she felt that she could open her heart to.

Evie, obviously, wasn't speaking to her and Becca, well . . . Becca had called round one evening about two weeks ago to drop her bombshell, but unfortunately Nic had already consumed the best part of her second bottle of wine.

She'd been drinking practically every night since the bonfire. She'd managed to restrain herself when Dominic was there, but as soon as he'd gone to bed she'd cracked open the wine. Sometimes she'd been able to stick to just one or two glasses, but often she'd drunk herself into a near-stupor. She hated herself for it, but she didn't seem to have the will to stop. She'd been in no fit state to listen to Becca's confession. Nic was ashamed of it now, but she'd actually laughed.

'It's true, Nic.' Becca's eyes were pleading.

Nic felt sweaty. Trapped. 'I can't talk about it,' she'd said, swatting an imaginary fly. She wasn't so drunk that she didn't register the look of hurt on Becca's face.

'Please . . . ?'

'I'll call you,' Nic had replied, using the arm of the sofa to push herself up. 'I need to go to bed.'

Since then she'd gone ten full days without booze, not even a glass with her nighttime sleeping pill to knock her out. It was Russell who'd finally brought her up short. She owed him big-time.

'You'll lose Dominic if you carry on like this,' he'd said a couple of days after Becca's visit. 'Is that what you want?'

'No.'

'He's already lost his father. He needs you, Nic.'

Later, Marie, her oldest friend, had dropped by unexpect-edly. The one she'd talked to in Paris that time, who'd convinced her that she wasn't an alcoholic. Marie was a big drinker; her father had died of it.

'I've quit, Nic,' Marie had said. So she'd had a problem, too. She'd made out that she was fine but she hadn't been telling the truth. 'I was worried that I was going to end up like Dad.'

Well, the penny had dropped. If Marie had packed it in then she could too. Nic had had her bender. It was time to get sober – for Dominic's sake. She'd started going to AA meetings again. She'd go every night if she needed to. No more excuses. She needed to sort this out once and for all; it was imperative.

She knew that Russell had been in touch with Evie after last month's creative writing group, the March one. Nic had thought about sending flowers, or presents for Freya, maybe. Her fingers had been poised so many times on the keyboard to look up suitable gifts on the internet. But it might seem to them so pathetically inadequate, an insult even. She didn't want to upset either of them more.

'Go and see her,' Russell had urged. 'Talk to her. You're friends, you need each other.' He'd had to act as intermediary,

404

though, to set up the rendezvous. Nic was too scared to pick up the phone herself. She took a sip of tea from the mug beside the phone. It had gone cold.

'Why are you doing this?' she asked.

'Dunno really.' Russell laughed. 'Must be mad. I guess I just like you both.'

She put down the phone, walked upstairs slowly and changed out of her jeans into a light-blue denim shirt dress, tied with a belt at the waist, and her flat brown suede boots; it wasn't quite warm enough for sandals. Then she sat at her dressing table and put on some make-up.

She wasn't looking too bad, she thought, pushing her blond hair off her forehead so that she could apply some light foundation. Not considering what she'd been through. Her face was a little gaunt, her cheeks rather hollow, but she seemed to have lost that ghastly, yellowish tinge. Even just ten days without alcohol must have done her some good.

She went back downstairs and checked her watch: 10.05 a.m. She'd better go. She didn't know how often the trains ran to Kingston. Everything took so much longer without a car. She checked through the window; it was drizzling. She put on her beige trenchcoat, a brown canvas hat with a little brim which, she hoped, would act as some sort of disguise, and grabbed her handbag. She had butterflies in her stomach. She felt as if she were about to sit a crucial exam, or attend a job interview. Or both.

Evie was already there, sitting facing the door at a table by the window overlooking the busy market square. She had a cup of coffee in front of her. She looked small and forlorn, Nic thought. Her fair hair was tied back in a ponytail and she was wearing little or no make-up.

'I hope you haven't been waiting . . . ?'

'No,' Evie said without smiling. 'I was early.'

Nic went up to the counter and ordered a cappuccino. Most of the tables were full. She pretended not to notice when the woman making her coffee nudged the waitress next to her in the ribs and whispered something. She was getting used to being recognised. She just hoped they wouldn't cause a scene.

When she returned to the table, Evie was staring into space.

'How's Freya?' Nic asked, sitting down with her back to the middle of the room, taking off her hat and running her fingers through her hair.

Evie started. She'd been miles away. 'Not too bad,' she said, looking at her nails. 'She's changed schools and she's finding the therapy helpful, I think. We all are.'

Nic nodded. 'I wish I could turn the clock back . . .'

Evie shook her head. 'Don't. It won't do any good.' She glanced at Nic for the first time, who noticed that there were tears in her eyes. 'When I was waiting there in that police station for news,' Evie said, 'I honestly thought I might never see her again. All I wanted was to have her back, hold her in my arms again. I realised that since Neil left I'd thought of no one but myself, really. I failed her big time.'

Nic's eyes pricked, too. 'You're being very hard on yourself. You should blame me, not yourself.'

Evie's eyes narrowed. 'I do.'

Nic stirred the froth in her coffee but didn't take a sip. 'Can I tell you something?' she said at last.

Evie nodded.

'I don't know how to say this. I don't want to cause you any more pain.'

Evie grimaced. 'I'm getting used to it.'

Nic took a deep breath. 'I'm not trying to justify what I did.'

'Good.' Evie sounded hard.

'I just want to say . . .' Nic told Evie about the magazines and how shocked she'd been. 'Alan and I never had a great sex life but I had no idea he was interested in children – until then. And even then I thought it was just fantasy. I didn't imagine he'd act on it.'

She talked about her drinking and how frightened she'd been of losing Alan, that she feared without him she'd sink. 'I know I was wrong to turn a blind eye. It's something I'll have to live with for the rest of my life.'

She recounted how she'd crept into his study and seen Freya's messages on his laptop. How at that point, she came to her senses and knew what she had to do. 'If he'd done anything to Freya, hurt her, I honestly think I'd have killed myself.'

Evie was silent. They both were after that.

'I went through hell,' Evie said finally. 'Who knows what he might have done to Freya when he'd finished with her?'

'Sorry's such an inadequate word,' Nic whispered. 'But for what it's worth, I really am.'

The women stared at each other for a moment. Nic wished that she could open up her soul, spread it out in front of Evie for her to examine, turn over, pull apart. She could do anything to it, so long as she believed that Nic's remorse was genuine.

At last Evie took a deep breath. 'How's Dominic?' she said quietly.

Nic was grateful. 'He misses Alan terribly and he's also furious with him.'

'How much does he understand?' Evie wanted to know.

Nic shrugged. 'He's nine. You can't pull the wool over his eyes; he understands pretty much everything.'

Evie winced. 'God, it must be terrible for him. Have you taken him to see Alan?'

Nic shook her head. 'I won't – and anyway Dom doesn't want to see him. To be honest, he's in turmoil.'

Evie picked at a piece of thread on the cuff of her faded grey sweatshirt. 'I'm sorry he's having to change school on top of everything else.'

'It's so hard for him.'

Next, Evie told Nic about Carol's revelation.

Nic swallowed. 'I'm really sorry.'

Evie waved a hand dismissively. 'It's minor in comparison with this, with what we've both been through.'

'But it must have been a terrible shock.'

Evie sighed. 'I could have done without it,' she agreed. 'I can't get my head round it, the fact that she's been following me all these years, spying on me.' She hesitated. There were so many issues swimming round her head, jostling with each other for space, such a lot to think about. 'Becca's told you?'

Nic nodded. 'It's hard to take in, isn't it? She must have been through hell all these years, hiding a secret like that. It sounds as if Tom is being amazing.'

'Incredible,' Evie agreed. 'I'm not sure if I could be so forgiving, if Neil had kept something like that from me. She looked straight at Nic. There were deep creases running from Nic's nose to the corners of her mouth. 'You were very brave, to do what you did, to call the police. Thank you.'

Nic cleared her throat. It meant a lot, that.

There was another pause. Nic wondered whether to say it or not. She straightened her shoulders. 'One good piece of news: I'm off the booze again. I'll never go back. That part of my life is over.'

Evie touched her arm and gave the flicker of a gap-toothed smile. 'Well, thank God for that.'

Evie was pleasantly surprised as she kissed Nic lightly goodbye and stepped out of the café into the market place. The rain had disappeared and the sun had come out. There were quite a few people wandering around without coats. She took off her own dark-brown corduroy jacket and pushed up the sleeves of her grey sweatshirt.

She stopped at a market stall to buy some black grapes for Freya and Michael. Then she popped into a chemist's to buy hair conditioner for herself. All the while she found herself repeating the conversation with Nic in her mind, picking it apart, delving into her subconscious and marvelling at the green shoots of forgiveness that she discovered there.

It was only a fifteen-minute walk to her house and as she strolled up her street she spotted a tall man with silver-grey hair coming out of his house carrying a pile of things which he put in the boot of his car: Bill.

Her stomach lurched. She hung back for a moment waiting for him to finish. He went back into the house, only to come out a moment later with another pile of stuff. Damn. Since he'd dropped the bombshell that he knew about Carol somehow or other they'd managed to avoid speaking to each other. She'd seen him a few times and he'd looked as if he might have wanted to say something. But she'd scuttled off and he hadn't followed.

She imagined that he was too busy with his Ukrainian, who was still a frequent visitor, to bother about her. Evie missed him a lot – but it wasn't *her* job to grovel. As far as she was concerned he was the one who needed to say sorry but he was so arrogant, he probably never would.

She was wondering if she could time it so that he was going into the house again as she scurried into hers, when he turned and spotted her. She was only a few yards from him now. For a moment their eyes locked. She glanced down quickly and clocked that he was carrying a pile of books. He bent down and put them on the pavement in front of him.

When he got up she saw that his red and blue checked shirt was open. His chest had just a small amount of silver-grey hair on it. His khaki trousers, though belted, were falling off his hips and she couldn't help noticing that his stomach was lean and flat.

She looked up again quickly and swallowed. He wiped his sleeve across his forehead.

'It's hot,' she said unnecessarily.

'Yes,' he replied. 'I'm taking a load of stuff to the dump.' He nodded at the books on the pavement in front. 'Dunno why I've kept these old textbooks. They're out of date.'

'Oh,' she said.

'Doing a bit of a spring clean,' he went on. She glanced to her right, through his front door, and noticed that the hallway, once littered with books, was now clear. The wooden floor was a warm, honey colour and there was a little vase of bluebells from his garden on the oak table.

She often peeped out of the window at his back garden; it was a lovely, English cottage garden, full of rambling roses, foxgloves, lavender and hollyhocks at the right time of year. It was much loved but not over-tended, a little bit wild; a haven for birds and butterflies.

He must have followed her gaze. 'Would you like some?' he asked, meaning the bluebells. 'I've got masses in the back.'

'Thank you,' she replied.

He didn't move. She noticed that his Adam's apple was quite prominent. His chin was squareish and there were beads of sweat on his upper lip. He cleared his throat. 'I thought I'd have the place decorated,' he said.

'Good idea.'

There was an awkward silence.

'I might be getting a lodger.' He scratched his head. 'Just for a month or two.'

'Ah.' She was trying hard not to look again at his chest. Her eyes fell instead on the area just below his tummy button. There seemed to be a trail of light brown hair . . . She pulled herself together. She'd only half heard him. 'A lodger?'

'Yes,' he said. 'Galina needs somewhere to stay and it seems . . .'

Galina the Ukrainian? Evie snapped out of her daydream and pursed her lips. 'Sorry,' she said, 'I'm in a hurry. I need to . . .'

She side-stepped the pile of books and rootled in her jeans pocket for her keys.

'Evie?' he called but her back was already turned and she pretended not to hear.

Chapter Fifty-Four

❦

Nic stayed close to Russell as they walked through the heavy oak door of the church hall and took their places beside Becca and Evie in the back row. She was aware of an uncomfortable hush as people turned and looked at her for a moment or two longer than necessary, and then spun back to the front.

She caught Carol's eye and was surprised, in a way, to receive a sympathetic sort of smile. Nic hadn't known how Carol would react, given the extraordinary news that she was, in fact, Evie's mother and Freya's grandmother. Carol might have been angry with Nic, like Evie.

Nic was momentarily overcome by the feeling that she'd stepped out of a spaceship into an alien body; that she was entering a new and unknown landscape. She swayed slightly in her chair. Russell, on her right, must have sensed it; he turned and looked at her, raising his black eyebrows.

'You OK?'

She nodded. The soles of her feet were touching solid ground again.

'Good to see you *all* here,' Tristram said, puffing out his chest and smoothing down his red silk tie. He emphasised the 'all'. His words were weighty with meaning. Nic felt it; she knew that everyone in the room did, too.

'How are we doing with our manuscripts?' he asked. 'Not long till the deadline.' He peered over the top of his gold-rimmed glasses and grinned. 'Adding the finishing touches now, are we?'

There was a collective groan.

'Well, I've finished,' said a shrill voice at the front. It was Pamela of course.

There was another groan.

'"Art is never finished, only abandoned." Leonardo Da Vinci.'

411

Nic jumped. It was Russell, next to her. His voice was very loud. Lately, she'd found that she couldn't stand loud noises.

'Very good,' said Tristram. 'I think that's true, don't you? You could go on polishing and making changes for ever but there comes a point when you just think: enough. Imperfect as it is, it's time to lay it to rest.'

Pamela was silent. She wouldn't like that, Nic thought. She, no doubt, reckoned that her work *was* perfect.

'This evening I thought we'd talk about dialogue,' said Tristram. He picked up a book from the table in front of him and started leafing through. 'I have a book here about writing by the author Jane Wenham-Jones. She says: "The art of writing good dialogue lies in capturing the essence of what people say in real situations without necessarily including all the detail."'

He scanned down the page. 'She goes on:

Make sure your characters are not droning on about what they had for breakfast, to fill in the time before the next piece of action, but are actually telling us something we didn't previously know . . . Also, try to avoid long chunks of speech by the same person without some respite . . . I find it very helpful to not only hear my imaginary characters in my head when I'm writing dialogue, but to actually visualise them and see what they are doing. This also helps to prevent one from stating the obvious . . .

'Interesting,' Tristram went on. 'Now, I'd like a brave volunteer to read out a passage of their dialogue.'

There was a deathly silence.

'Come on,' said Tristram. 'Don't be shy.'

Jonathan, sitting two rows in front of Nic, raised his hand.

Nic perked up. Jonathan was the one who'd spent years abroad teaching English as a Foreign Language and was writing a novel about a young man's sexual adventures.

'Excellent,' said Tristram. 'Stand up please, so we can all hear.'

Jonathan rose to his feet, a wodge of papers in his hand,

412

swept his blond hair off his face and twiddled his moustache in that way that he had.

'Let me see,' he said, leafing through his papers. 'Ye-es. This'll do. A bit of background: Ralph, my main protagonist, is giving a lift to Pilar, the beautiful Spanish girl that he met in a bar. Here goes . . .'

Jonathan cleared his throat and started to read: '"Ralph looked around him. 'Oh bugger! The car has broken down and the next town is miles away.'

'"'Oh no. I can feel a panic attack coming on,' said Pilar. 'What are we going to do?'

'"'I can think of plenty of things,' Ralph said, winking . . .'"'

There was a noise at the front of the class. It was Pamela shuffling in her seat, her chair legs squeaking. She usually had an urgent call of nature when Jonathan started to read.

He looked up. 'Sorry,' he grinned. 'It gets a bit steamy in places.'

'In places?' Pamela snapped. 'It seems to me that it's pornography all the way through.'

Tristram glared at her over the top of his gold-rimmed glasses. 'Please,' he said. 'Let Jonathan finish.'

Jonathan looked down at the page again: '"'. . . like take off your bra for starters. You've got the most beautiful pair of breasts.'

'"'I don't think my mother would approve,' said Pilar. 'She's warned me about men like you. Well, go on then, kiss me, kiss me hard. Hurry before I change my mind.'"'

Russell nudged Nic in the ribs. She giggled, she couldn't help it. She put her hand over her mouth and stared hard at her feet.

'Have you finished?' Tristram asked politely.

Nic marvelled at his sangfroid. She glanced at Evie, sitting next to her on her left and she, too, appeared to be shaking with mirth.

'Thank you, Jonathan,' Tristram went on. 'Now, who'd like to comment?'

Carol raised her hand. 'I don't think someone would say: "I'm going to have a panic attack," I think they'd just have it,' she said, waving her arms around in an exaggerated fashion to demonstrate.

Several people tittered.

'Right,' said Tristram. 'Well spotted. She'd be more likely to clutch her throat or wave her arms around or something. Anything else?'

'Yes,' said Carol. 'In my experience men don't ask if they can take off your bra, they just get on with it.' She hooted with laughter.

'Honestly,' Pamela tutted. 'How vulgar—'

'No, I'm with Carol again,' Tristram interrupted. 'How else could Jonathan have done it?'

Russell stood up. 'How about this: "'I can think of plenty of things to do,' said Ralph, fumbling with the fastening of her bra, which pinged open with a gratifying pop."'

Nic snorted.

'What?' said Russell, looking down at her innocently.

'Bras don't pop open – at least mine don't.' Nic looked at Becca and Evie. 'Have you ever had a bra that pops open? Maybe you can get them with poppers but I've never seen them.'

Several members of the class turned to each other to discuss the matter. The volume in the hall rose.

'Ladies and gentlemen,' Tristram said loudly. 'We're not here to discuss the finer points of corsetry.' He paused. 'Though I'm sure the other gentlemen here will agree that it's a most entrancing subject. But no, we're here to talk about dialogue, remember? Now, does anyone else have anything to say about Jonathan's example?'

Nic was in an excellent mood by the end of the meeting; she hadn't laughed so much in months. She turned to Evie and Becca. 'Well, that was entertaining.'

Evie frowned and ran her hands through her shoulder-length fair hair, which looked as if it had just been washed and straightened. 'Why are you looking at me like that?' she asked.

Nic was startled. 'I wasn't. I mean, like what?' Was Evie trying to pick a fight?

Evie leaned forward. 'Does my hair look funny?' She seemed deadly serious.

'No.' Nic didn't know what she was talking about.

'It looks nice,' Becca chipped in. 'Have you done something to it?'

Various people had started to leave the hall. Russell, who was at the end of the row, got up. 'I need a word with Tristram. I'll just be a moment . . .'

'I washed it before I came out,' Evie explained. 'Only by mistake I used hair-removal cream instead of conditioner.'

'What?' Nic squeaked. She put her hands over her mouth. 'You didn't?'

Evie nodded. 'I was in a hurry and I reached for what I thought was this new conditioner I'd just bought, only it had the same coloured top as my Veet.'

'Ohmigod,' said Becca. She started rooting in Evie's hair like a monkey searching for nits. 'I can't see any bald patches. You might be all right.'

Evie sat quite still while Becca continued to burrow. 'Are you sure?'

'I think so,' Becca replied. 'I think you've got away with it.'

'Thank God,' Evie sighed. 'I rinsed it really carefully as soon as I realised. I probably had the longest shower I've ever had in my life. I was petrified I'd end up looking like a Mexican Hairless Dog.'

'A Mexican Hairless Dog? What's that?' said Nic, trying to keep a straight face.

'They're completely bald, with just a few tufts of hair sticking up on top like a coconut.'

'That's awful,' Nic replied. She was having difficulty controlling her mirth. 'How long was the Veet on for?'

Evie thought for a moment. 'Only a few minutes, I reckon. Two or three?' She nudged Nic in the ribs. 'Stop laughing at me. This is a serious matter. I don't want to go bald.'

'Certainly not,' Nic replied. 'But I've got some nice hats if you want to borrow one.'

Being at the back of the hall, Nic had hoped that she'd be able to sneak out quickly without speaking to any of the others. But as she rose to leave, she realised that Tristram was scooting towards her, calling her name.

She felt suddenly hot. She was glad that Becca and Evie were still with her. Tristram reached her side and leaned over.

'I just wanted to offer my condolences,' he said in a low voice, squeezing her arm. 'The press can be animals but well done for coming tonight. Keep your chin up.'

Nic was touched. A lump appeared in her throat. 'Thank you.'

Tristram stood up straight, rubbing his back as if it hurt, and pulled a face. 'How's the writing coming on?' His voice was louder now. 'I hope you're getting cracking. Not long to go.'

Nic grimaced. 'To be honest, I'm only about three-quarters of the way through. I'll never finish in time.'

'Nonsense,' Tristram replied. 'Knuckle down and you'll do it, even if you have to write two or three thousand words a day right up till the last moment. It'll be tough but you're quite capable of it. You know how much I admire your writing. You'll kick yourself if you let this opportunity go by.'

He was right, she thought. It would be a mistake to throw in the towel now that she'd got this far. Tristram moved away to talk to another class member.

'Drink anyone?' Russell asked. He was standing at the end of the row.

Nic, Evie and Becca all shook their heads.

'Evie, dear!'

Nic heard Evie groan. Carol was clambering over the chairs in front, swinging a basket full of things; clearly she couldn't be bothered to wait for the people at the ends of the rows to move. Her shoulder-length grey hair looked awfully straggly and she was huffing and puffing. She was still wearing her big Afghan coat even though it was April.

'Evie, can I have a word?'

There was no way Evie could avoid her. 'What is it?' she growled.

Nic winced.

Carol was in the row in front now; there was just a chair between them, acting as a sort of barrier. She put her basket on the seat and scrabbled for something. At last she pulled out a thin wad of papers, slightly curling at the edges. The top sheet had black smudges on it.

'My book,' she said, brandishing it in front of her. 'The first draft.' She focused at a point on the wall behind, uncharacteristically shy. 'I wondered if you'd read through it for me.'

Nic glanced at Evie, who was frowning. 'I don't know . . .'

'I'd be ever so grateful,' Carol persisted. 'I haven't shown it to anyone yet.'

Evie grabbed the pile of papers. She held them in one hand, slightly away from her body as if she were scared she might catch something.

'All right,' she said. 'But I don't know if I'll have any useful comments to make.'

'I don't expect a critique or anything like that,' Carol replied. 'I'd just like you to take a look, that's all. If you would.'

Chapter Fifty-Five

Nic reread the last few lines that she'd written:

> Beattie pointed the gun right between Adamou's eyes. 'One move and you're dead.'
> Adamou took a step forward. She hesitated for a second and pulled the trigger. She didn't have time to look. She thought she caught him out of the corner of her eye staggering like a drunken sailor and then, when she reached the door, she heard a thump.

Nic typed 'THE END' and reread it several times, savouring the feeling. After a moment or two she checked the word count: 124,400 words. She sighed, pressed 'save' and closed the document, then she moved the mouse until the arrow was on 'organise' and scrolled down.

She took a deep breath. 'It's got to be done.'

She clicked 'delete'. A message came up: 'Are you sure you want to move this file to the Recycle Bin?' She paused for a moment before hitting 'yes'. The file disappeared. Then she went to the Recycle Bin and emptied it.

That was that, then. All those months of work down the pan. She'd have nothing to enter for the competition. Her dreams of winning were at an end.

Her stomach tingled. She wanted to laugh. *This* dream was over, but she could start another book, something completely different. This time, she thought, her work would be gritty and real. She had such a lot to say. She'd leave it for a month or two, let the dust settle and then start afresh.

She got up slowly and rubbed her eyes. She'd been writing solidly more or less every day since last month's creative writing group when Tristram had urged her to finish. She'd been in danger of flagging again until Becca made more encouraging noises at the May meeting a week ago. Nic doubted she could do it, but there was still time to meet the 1 June deadline, Becca had insisted. She herself was right on target, as were most of the others.

Finishing, for Nic, had been slow and painful, like pulling teeth. But it was over now. She didn't have to put herself through it any more. *The Girl from Niger* had been doomed from the start. It was stupid, self-indulgent and had too many bad memories. It was definitely time to move on.

She thought of Evie, as she so often did, wondered how she was getting on with her writing. She hadn't made the May meeting. Not surprising, given the news. Neil's baby had arrived and Freya was finding it very difficult; having rediscovered the father that she felt she'd lost, he was now too busy to see much of her.

Nic had phoned Evie, trying to be supportive, but she knew that she wasn't the right person to talk to. In fact it was amazing that Evie was willing to talk to her at all.

That familiar wave of guilt rolled over Nic, knocking her sideways. She'd never forgive herself. Yet she must keep going, look forwards – for Dominic's sake. She was all he had. She wasn't sure that she'd ever let him see Alan again.

Alan. She shuddered. These days she tended to refer to him as A. She didn't want to think about him. Fortunately she didn't have to see him or to speak to him. Along with his clothes and other belongings, she'd destroyed every photograph of him that she could find.

He'd been sentenced at the crown court last week and given five years. They reckoned he'd serve three to three and a half. He'd pleaded guilty to attempting to meet a child after sexual grooming on the internet. They'd also found 269 indecent images on his laptop. His main interest, they said, was girls aged seven to eleven, but he liked young teenagers, too. He'd be on the sex-offenders register for life.

It was a relief to know that he'd been put away but she continued to question herself and there were plenty, she knew, who would always judge her and condemn her. She had to accept that. But she'd made an important decision after the verdict that had surprised even her: she'd agreed to give one interview to a Sunday newspaper.

Her main reason for coming forward wasn't to try to gain sympathy but to alert people to what 'just looking' can lead to. The terrible pictures found on A's laptop were of real children. That knowledge had shocked her to the core. It had made her fear and loathe secrecy in families, in relationships. She felt that she'd had enough secrets for one life.

If one person could learn from her tale and voice their fears rather than sweep them under the carpet, then speaking out and telling the world about her experience was worthwhile. And whilst she abhorred the increased exposure that had resulted from the article, there had been one welcome and quite unexpected outcome: she'd received a surprising number of letters of support, including one from Evie.

She went downstairs to the kitchen and put the kettle on. Dizzy, who was snoozing in her basket, looked up and thumped her tail.

'Good girl.' Nic smiled. 'Dominic will be home soon, then we'll go walkies!'

Dizzy got up and trotted over to her mistress, who bent down and gave her a stroke. 'We'll go to Richmond Park, shall we?' Nic was speaking half to the dog and half to herself. She glanced through the open glass door of the kitchen into the garden. The late sun was casting a rich, golden glow over walls, paving stones and flowers. 'It's a beautiful evening.'

It occurred to her that the azaleas would be blooming now in the Isabella Plantation within the park; May was the best time to go, though the woodland garden was beautiful all year round. Maybe they'd walk there.

She and Dominic had taken to having an evening stroll together now that the weather was so much better. For some reason he seemed to open up on their walks. He talked about his dad, about his new school and friends more than at other times. Maybe it was the fact that they walked side by side. Perhaps it seemed less scary and intense to him than if they were opposite each other at the supper table. Whatever the reason, Nic had tried to make the walks a regular evening activity. It was their quiet time together and they both seemed to value it.

The doorbell rang. Nic glanced at her watch: seven p.m. Her heart gave a skip. She realised that she hadn't even noticed when it turned six, the time when she'd been accustomed to having her first drink.

She missed alcohol, of course, but she didn't miss being enslaved, always looking for the next drink, waking up anxious, depressed, the black pit waiting to engulf her. Besides, she needed all her strength to cope with what lay ahead. She couldn't afford to fall apart again.

'Mum!' Dominic bundled her into the hallway followed by Toby, a friend from his new school, who started to take off his shoes.

'Come back, Toby!' his mother scolded. 'We can't stay now. We've got people coming for supper.'

Nic smiled, registering the surprise in the other mother's eyes; she must have forgotten about Nic's turquoise train tracks. 'They've obviously had a good time then?' Nic said.

'Great,' Toby's mother agreed. 'They built a den in the garden.'

Later, after their walk, Nic read Dominic a chapter of *Harry Potter*. He pretended that he was too old to be read to but he liked it really. When she'd finished the final paragraph he propped himself up on his elbows.

'You're all right, aren't you – without Daddy, I mean?' he asked anxiously.

She ruffled his hair. 'Yes, darling. I'm all right.'

'What if something happened to you, too. What if you got cancer or something. Who'd look after me then?'

She frowned. This again. 'Nothing's going to happen to me, Dom.'

'But what if it did?' he persisted.

She pulled the duvet back and climbed in beside him. 'Move over.'

'Tell me,' he said again. He wouldn't give up.

She put her arm around him. 'If something did happen to

me – and it won't – you'd live with Grandma, or Aunty Jacqueline. But I promise you I'm not going anywhere.'

He thought about this for a moment. 'If I went to live with Aunty Jacqueline would I have my own room?'

Nic smiled. 'She's got a big house so yes, I'm sure you would. And she'd take very great care of you. She loves you very much.'

He shivered. 'I don't want to live with anyone else.' He was starting to cry.

Nic sighed. It was so difficult to reassure him. She'd give anything to make him happy, secure again, but she didn't know how.

'Do you want to come in my bed?' she asked. She'd been hoping to watch a TV programme.

He nodded.

'Come on then.'

She undressed, switched on the radio, turned out the light and curled around him, her chin resting on the top of his head, her knees in the hollows of his. She held him tight until he drifted off to sleep, the sound of chatter drowning out his thoughts.

He cried out in his sleep a few times. His whole body was sweaty and trembling. She whispered in his ear: 'Mummy's here, Mummy's with you,' over and over again like a mantra until he seemed to believe her and was finally quiet.

Evie put her head in her hands and closed her eyes. She was in an awful muddle and she knew it. She was, she reckoned, nine-tenths of the way through her book and she still didn't know how it was going to end. She was sure that famous authors like Marian Keyes and Jodi Picoult always knew exactly how their novels would conclude before they'd written so much as a single word; she'd bet they did very detailed synopses.

The problem was that Spiculus, the gladiator-turned body-guard, had turned out to be a love-rat after all and Cornelia had rightly dropped him. Evie had thought that she could twist the plot around so that Marcellus, the neglectful husband, would prove to be a hero. But somehow Evie just couldn't bring herself to make Cornelia fall in love with him again. It wasn't how she wanted it to end.

One of the difficulties, she realised, was that she was relying far too much on her own feelings for Neil; she just couldn't help it. There again, perhaps it wasn't surprising, given that she'd modelled Marcellus and Spiculus on Neil right from the start, right down to their looks, mannerisms, even the way they peeled apples with a knife and cut them into little pieces before eating them. Whom had she been trying to kid?

She hadn't intended Marcellus to be Neil, it had just happened. And in view of the fact that it was less than a week now till the June deadline, she hadn't time to go back and make Marcellus completely different.

Then there was Gracchus, who had become Cornelia's confidant. He kept sort of forcing his way into the writing, even when Evie didn't mean it to happen. The original plan – such as it was – was that he'd be a subsidiary character, very much in the background. But somehow he'd become one of the main protagonists and Evie didn't know quite what to do with him, how to wrap it all up. She really should have done a proper synopsis right at the beginning, she thought. She'd know next time.

She closed the document and shut the lid of her laptop. She'd taken to working on the kitchen table recently rather than in the bedroom where she often did her sewing; she found it too distracting to be constantly reminded of the other work she ought to be doing.

She walked upstairs and heard giggling coming from Freya's room. She knocked on the door.

'Come in!'

Evie poked her head in. Freya was sitting on the bed, a magazine on her lap, her mobile clamped to her ear.

She held the cover up for Evie to see. '*Heat*,' she explained. 'I'm talking to Lucy.'

'Have you done your homework?'

'Don't nag,' said Freya. 'I'll do it later.'

Evie frowned. 'I'm not nagging . . .' But then she smiled. It was a relief to see Freya acting in a normal, feisty, teenagerish way. She'd been so withdrawn and docile lately.

'I have to leave in half an hour,' said Evie. 'Dad should be here soon. Are you sure you're all right with it?'

Freya nodded. 'No probs. I'll make him watch *Big Brother* with me.'

'Homework,' Evie reminded her.

Freya gave her one of her looks before resuming her chat.

Evie pulled the door to and walked up the next flight of stairs to her bedroom. She opened her wardrobe and peered in. What the hell was she going to wear? She wished, now, that she'd bought something new. There again, it might be too obvious. She didn't want Steve thinking that she was excited about seeing him or anything.

She pushed a few hangers aside, pulled out the French Connection top that she'd picked up in the sales last summer and examined it critically. It was made of a fine, cream-coloured cotton material with thin, barely visible silver stripes. It had a V-neck with a soft ruffle around the edge and no sleeves. She could wear it with her black, cashmere cardigan and jeans. Perfect. Pretty and fun, she decided, without being provocative.

She undressed quickly and turned the shower on next door. The warm water whooshed over her, making her skin tingle with pleasure. She lowered her head so that the jet hit her in just the spot where her neck ached. She could almost feel the muscles and ligaments starting to lengthen and relax. They were practically purring.

She washed herself carefully all over with the olive-oil shower cream that Freya had given her for her birthday, thinking all the while about Steve and what tonight would bring. He'd called her so many times since that Wednesday when Carol had dropped the bombshell – both about him and herself. At first Evie had refused even to speak to him; she was far too upset. Then, gradually, like a queen granting an audience, she'd allowed him two and, later, five minutes of her time.

In the end, she supposed, he'd simply beaten her into submission. She'd felt obliged to listen just to get shot of him, except that once she'd heard what he had to say, her mood had begun to soften somewhat.

It was the lies, she'd said, that were so unforgivable. 'But I felt I had to lie or you'd dump me.'

Why, she'd asked, was he still living with the girlfriend anyway if, as he'd claimed, it was all over? 'She's the mother of my child. I felt guilty. I felt I had to get them settled into somewhere new before I could make the final break.'

Were they still sleeping together? 'No.' She didn't believe him. 'Well, just once or twice,' he admitted. 'But it didn't mean anything. It was just to keep the peace, really.'

Were you, she wondered, ever going to bother to tell me that you and she were still living together when we met? 'Of course – eventually,' he replied. 'It's you I love, Evie. You're the woman for me.'

That was the bit that really got her. Love. She needed that. She felt so alone, now that Helen had had the baby. Neil hardly ever dropped by these days. He only came by arrangement, to see the children and babysit when Evie was going out. It's what she'd wanted – for him to leave her alone. But now that it had happened there was an empty space in her heart that she thought nothing could ever fill.

Carol was desperate to step in and plug the gap but Evie wasn't having any of it. Since Carol had broken the news, Evie had felt as if she were grieving – for the mother she never had and once thought she so desperately wanted. All these years, she realised, she'd had this picture in her mind of what her real mother would be like: warm and caring, beautiful, clever, fault-less.

Her adoptive parents had told her virtually nothing about her past. Whenever she asked, they'd look all hurt and say: 'Aren't we good enough?' So Evie had woven fantastic stories about her birth mother. Maybe she was a famous actress – or an Eastern European princess! And now Carol had come along and shattered the dream.

Mad Carol, who'd been following her around, taking photographs of her and the children. Evie still had her manuscript. She'd stuffed it under the bed; she couldn't face looking at it. In some ways Evie did feel sorry for her: what a wasted life, forever yearning for the one thing that she couldn't have. But the fact was that Carol had abandoned Evie, left her to her inadequate parents. And something else was troubling Evie, too: Carol's desperate need. Evie had this feeling that if she let Carol into her life, if she opened up her heart and home to her, Carol would slowly swallow her up. For self-preservation, for her own sanity, she felt that she must keep her birth mother at arms' length.

Evie finished getting dressed and sat down to put on her make-up. The top looked nice, she decided, examining herself in the mirror. It was slightly transparent, but with her white lacy bra underneath you couldn't see too much.

'Bye!' she called as she hurried past Freya's room. She was running late. 'Michael will be back from Isaac's at around eight p.m.'

She caught the bus a few stops up the road to the parade of shops. She'd decided to suggest somewhere close to home – Steve could do the travelling. She was ten minutes late but he hadn't arrived yet so she waited for him on a bench outside the Indian restaurant. She didn't want to sit inside on her own. It was a warm evening and she'd enjoy watching the world go by.

There was a fair amount of traffic on the road: people heading off for their Saturday night out, probably. She watched, with some interest, while a youth in a hoodie came out of the off-licence carrying a four-pack of cider.

'It's party time!' he shouted down his mobile and punched the air, only to be stopped by a pair of what turned out to be plain-clothed police officers. They asked his name and age and he admitted that he was only sixteen – too young to be buying alcohol. She could hear the conversation quite clearly. He also handed over a packet of cigarettes and some fake ID.

He had an intelligent face and didn't sound like a delinquent. But he'd been caught red-handed. The police officers put on purple gloves and frisked him. They tipped his cider down the drain, confiscated the cigarettes and fake ID and took down his name and address. 'We'll be writing to your parents,' they said sternly.

The youth looked stricken. Evie felt almost sorry for him but he had been silly, drawing attention to himself like that. He'd never do it again, that's for sure.

She checked the time on her mobile phone. Steve was half an hour late. She'd been so engrossed in the hoodie incident that she hadn't realised. A familiar sense of misery washed over her; surely he wouldn't stand her up again? She couldn't imagine what excuse he could possibly come up with this time.

She checked her text messages to make sure that she hadn't missed one from him. There was nothing. She was beginning to feel cold now. The sun had disappeared completely and her black cardigan was only thin. She wondered whether to go home; she'd give him ten more minutes. The train might have been delayed. Maybe there was signal failure or something. But he could have rung.

'Evie!' She swivelled round. A handsome, broad-shouldered, middle-aged man was walking towards her carrying a bottle of wine in each hand and one under his left arm. He had a crisp-looking, pale-pink shirt on which was rolled up to reveal strong forearms.

His silver hair was neatly cut around the ears and his tanned face suggested that he'd been abroad somewhere – or he spent a lot of time outside.

She was taken aback. 'Bill!' she said, standing up. 'What are you doing here?'

Bill raised a hand with one of the bottles in it. 'Going to a party,' he said. 'Might I ask the same of you?'

'I was waiting for someone,' she replied. She noticed that Bill's eyes were very blue. 'But he's late and I can't be bothered to wait any more.' She shrugged. 'I think I'll go home.'

Bill cleared his throat. 'Look, Evie, I'm sorry about Carol, the way you found out. It wasn't fair. I should have talked to you. I wanted to apologise but you were so angry, I couldn't get anywhere near you—'

She raised a hand. 'Please don't. I was upset, I overreacted. It wasn't your fault that she chose to blurt it out the way she did. Anyway' – she shifted on her feet – 'you were probably right. It would have been a mistake to tell me just after we'd found Freya. I wouldn't have been able to take it in. I'm sorry I was so cross,' she added.

He shook his head, looked at her quizzically. 'Have you spoken to Carol since?'

'I see her at the creative writing group.'

'How do you feel about her?'

Evie sighed. 'Angry, shocked, sad. All sorts of things, I guess. I expect we'll have some sort of relationship eventually but I'm not going to be pushed into anything. If she thinks there's going to be a happy-ever-after ending she's sorely mistaken.'

They started to walk towards home. 'Where's the party?' she asked, only half wanting to know. She suspected that the Ukrainian might figure somewhere in his plans. She was still a regular visitor to his house, though she didn't appear to have moved in yet.

'Allotment,' he replied. 'We tend to have one at this time of year – if the weather's good enough.' He nodded at the bottles of wine. 'Great three-for-one offer at that off-licence.'

'What have you got growing now – in your allotment?' she asked, mildly interested,

'Asparagus. Masses of it. I should get a good crop of peaches and greengages this year, too.' He scratched his chin. 'I need to plant out the French beans and train the runners and I haven't yet prepared the beds for the sweetcorn and tomatoes. I must get a move on.'

Evie giggled. 'Prepared the beds? It sounds like you're planning to tuck them in and read them a story.'

'You're not far off actually,' he replied. 'I don't know about a story but they do like being talked to.'

Evie raised her eyebrows. 'You talk to your tomatoes and sweetcorn?'

'Of course,' he said seriously. 'They thrive on it. By the way, how are the wedding dresses going?'

'Really well,' Evie said. 'I put an ad in *Brides-to-Be* magazine and got a very encouraging response. I'm farming them out to a machinist now. I haven't got time to sew them all myself. It's nice that the business is making some money at last. I should have got off my backside ages ago.'

She hadn't even noticed when they got to her garden gate that they'd walked all the way home.

'Here you are,' he said, hanging back.

Her mobile phone pinged. There was a text message, which she opened. It was from Steve. 'Running late – sorry. Call me.' She deleted it.

'What are you going to do now?' Bill asked. She didn't need to tell him who the message was from.

'Oh,' she shrugged, 'I'll miss him for a while but I'll get over it. I thought he was The One, you see.' She looked into Bill's blue eyes. 'But I was completely and utterly wrong.'

Bill smiled. 'We all get things wrong, Evie. We'd be inhuman if we didn't.'

'But I was a fool,' she said. 'I couldn't see what was in front of my nose.'

Bill put the bottles of wine on the pavement beside him. She wondered what he was going to do next. She wasn't sure if he made the first move or she did, but before she knew it they were in each other's arms, her lips pressed against his, his warm, sweet breath on her face. The neighbours might be watching but she didn't care. Let them gossip!

When at last she came up for air there were only two words on her lips: 'The Ukrainian.'

'Who? Galina?' he asked, surprised.

'I thought she was . . . you were . . .'

He laughed. 'She's a student, you silly thing. I told you. I felt sorry for her and I wanted to help. You didn't really imagine . . . ?'

Evie sighed and rested her cheek against the hollow of his breastbone, the special place that she liked so much – her special place.

She frowned. 'I don't know anything about T. S. Eliot. Isn't that what she's doing her thesis on?'

'I'll read you some of his poems if you like, tell you a bit about him.'

'I'd rather see your allotment first.'

A big grin broke over his handsome face. 'Really? We don't have to stay long.'

She nodded. 'Really.'

He picked up the wine, plonked a bottle in each of Evie's hands, took one himself and wrapped the other arm around her shoulders.

'To the allotment, madam,' he said, guiding her past his house and up the road.

She stopped suddenly. 'Oh!' she cried. The penny plopped into the well. 'Bill. William. Is your real name William?'

'William Edward,' he said proudly. 'But no one's ever called me that.'

'A P, a T or a W. Of course!' she squealed. 'It's Gracchus. Cornelia has to marry Gracchus!'

Bill stared at her. He must have thought she'd gone mad. 'I beg your pardon?'

Evie smiled at him. 'Nothing. Well, it is something actually. I've just thought of a brilliant ending for my book.'

'That's fabulous,' said Bill, giving her a squeeze. 'I'd love to read it sometime – if I may.'

'Definitely,' she replied, 'but right now I want to admire your runner beans and greengages.' She gasped. 'I hope that didn't sound . . .'

His blue eyes twinkled but he didn't reply.

'To the allotment,' she added quickly.

Chapter Fifty-Six

It was the weekend and Becca wandered around Newcastle city centre in a daze. So much had changed. She hardly recognised the old riverside, now connected to Gateshead quayside by the flashy Millennium Bridge. And she found it hard to take in all the smart new shops and wine bars.

As well as wonder, she felt a keen sense of loss. It didn't feel like *her* city, the one that she'd once known and loved. It's true that as a child she'd thought her shoe box on the council estate a dump; she couldn't wait to get out. But the city centre she'd always found beautiful and majestic, magical almost.

Now, however, it was an entirely different place, full of smart-looking cosmopolitan types in suits and shiny shoes bustling to and from their posh offices. The place didn't feel cold or bleak any more. She realised, with surprise, that she missed the *grimness*.

They climbed the steps of Castle Keep, built by Henry II, in the oldest, most historic part of the city and looked out over the River Tyne, the cathedral and Newcastle Central Station. They took the children to Blackfriars, the remains of a thirteenth-century priory, and wandered down the Bigg Market.

Becca was relieved that although the shops had changed, this street at least still felt the same. She half expected to see Jude walk by with a gang of raucous girls, wearing nothing but a tiny dress and high heels even in the depths of winter. Jude used to go there most Friday nights, but not Becca. She was too young. She wouldn't have got served.

When they reached Eldon Square, she realised that Alice was tugging on her sleeve: 'I'm hungry.'

Becca's skin pricked with irritation. Was that all Alice could think about: her stomach? She checked herself. Alice had no idea how important this trip was for her mother. Why would she? Becca and Tom had told both children very little.

'We'll have lunch soon,' she promised. 'What do you fancy eating?'

'Pizza!' Alice and James chorused.

'All right,' Becca said, 'why don't you look out for a Pizza Express? There's bound to be one here somewhere.'

After lunch, they headed back to the car park. Becca's heart had started to thump. Funnily enough she could remember the exact address of Gary's mother, June – she knew that she hadn't moved because Gary had told her. But Becca had no idea how to get there any more, so she'd bought a map.

She didn't know if Gary had mentioned to June that he'd seen her, but she had a feeling that he wouldn't have. Becca planned to make up a story about being the daughter of a friend of her mother's family and try to get her own mother's address that way.

There was every chance that June would work out who she was – and then, of course, there was the possibility that she might go to the press. But it was a risk that Becca was prepared to take. Her mother could be anywhere in the country; the quickest way of tracking her down was through June. She needed to find Mam and speak to her. She knew now that it was the only way she could ever find peace.

'I'd like to go to the cemetery first,' Becca said once they were in the car. She found West Road on the map.

'Ooh,' said Alice, 'will there be ghosts?'

Becca turned around and looked in the back. Alice's blond wavy hair was loose and her big blue eyes were very wide.

James made a scary face. 'Wooo, wooo!'

Alice started to cry.

'Stop it, James,' Becca scolded. She looked at Alice. 'No, darling, there won't be any ghosts, just gravestones. And you can put a little bunch of flowers there for my sister – your aunt.'

'How did she die again?' James asked.

Becca swallowed. 'I told you, it was a tragic accident. I'll explain more when you're older.'

She turned back to the front, relieved that he seemed to have accepted her explanation – for the time being at least. He was too young to hear the truth. They were right by the car-park exit now. Tom put the ticket in the slot and the metal barrier swung open.

'Left here,' she commanded. 'Then we need to go right at the roundabout. It shouldn't take long.'

There was plenty of parking space at the crematorium.

Tom looked at Becca carefully. 'Are you sure you want to do this?'

She nodded. She was quite surprised by how easily they found the gravestone. Alice and James thought that it was great fun to dodge among the little paths, looking for the name. 'What did you say she was called?' 'How do you spell it again?'

It was James who spotted it. 'Here it is!' he called delightedly. Becca felt her heart start to race. She ran to his side and read the name quickly: Judith Jane Mackey. It was her all right. She felt giddy, unstable, and widened her legs to steady herself.

Tom approached and gently pulled Alice and James back: 'Let Mummy look first.' He knew that Becca needed a few moments to herself.

She knelt down and examined the stone first, before the writing. The plaque was quite small and square, made of black granite, and looked surprisingly new. There was a built-in vase for flowers on the side but it was empty. Becca had a little bunch of red roses in her hand – they'd stopped at a florist on the way – but she wouldn't put them in just yet.

She read the inscription slowly, reverentially, silently mouthing the words:

Treasured Memories of Judith Jane Mackey.
Died 18th May 1978 aged 15 years.
For ever in our hearts.

At the bottom of the tablet was a short poem:

Memory is a golden chain
That binds us till we meet again.

Becca felt a painful tugging in her chest. Had Mam chosen the poem, corny as it was, out of hundreds of possible verses because it offered a crumb of hope? Or perhaps she was too shocked and grief-stricken to be able to think straight.

Maybe friends and neighbours had done it for her. She wasn't a religious woman, so it was surprising in a way that she'd wanted something that suggested an afterlife. There again, didn't most people turn to God – whether they believed in Him or not – in times of misery? Becca laid the flowers at her feet and put her hands over her eyes.

'Why is Mummy crying?' she heard Alice ask, but the words only half registered. Tom whispered something that she couldn't understand.

She squatted there for several minutes, listening to the silence, before opening her eyes.

'I'm sorry, Jude,' she murmured. 'Really I am. I wish I could turn back the clock. I wish I hadn't been so angry, so full of hate. I wish I was the one that died, not you. I hope you're at peace, now, wherever you are.'

A little gust of warm wind brushed against her face, like a sigh. She laid the back of her hand against her cheek. She kissed the roses and arranged them in the vase, which was half-filled with rainwater. Then she got up.

She turned and smiled. 'Your turn now, James and Alice. You can put your flowers in the vase with mine if you like.'

James stepped forward. 'I'd rather put them by the stone,' he said firmly. 'I think yours should be the only ones in the vase.'

'Me too,' Alice copied, coming out from behind her father's leg.

They laid their posies side by side on the grass in front of the plaque.

Becca turned to Tom. 'We can go now.'

'Are you sure?' He started: 'Look!'

At first she didn't know what he meant. He was pointing. She turned around and followed his finger with her eyes. When they fell on the place where he wanted her to look, she gasped: 'No!'

434

How had she missed it? There, right beside Jude's grave, on another stone in big bold letters was the truth:

Maureen Elizabeth Mackey
Born 4th February 1938
Died 11th April 1989
Rest in Peace

Becca stared. She couldn't take it in. Mam was dead. She'd been dead for twenty years.

All this time Becca had been wondering what she felt, whether to try to get in touch, fretting about what she'd say if she did. But it had been pointless, wasted emotion, because Mam had no feelings at all, she didn't care. She was just dust and ashes.

Becca thought back: she would have left university and started her first job when it happened. Why did no one tell her? Not the probation officers, not anyone? She wondered how Mam had died, whether she'd thought of Becca in her last moments. Had she cried out for her – or just for Jude? Becca felt a fool for never considering even for a second that she might be gone.

Grief washed over her, threatening to break her body into little pieces. She felt herself stagger; the world started to spin and the ground seemed to crumble beneath her.

'Becca!' Tom caught her as she fell. 'Sit down . . . put your head between your knees . . . you'll be all right.'

She heard his words but he seemed to be speaking another language. What did it all mean? He was forcing her head between her knees, pushing down firmly. She heard Alice crying.

'I'm OK,' Becca kept repeating, 'I'm OK.' But she didn't mean it. She'd never see Mam again, speak to her again. She'd never get the chance to prove to her that she was different now, that she'd changed, made something of herself. She'd never be able to make her proud.

She looked up. Alice was right beside her, a look of confusion on her face. 'What's the matter, Mummy?'

Becca tried to sit up. She felt peculiar and shaky but she must be strong – for Alice, for them all. 'I've just found out that my

435

mummy's dead,' she tried to explain. 'I didn't know. It's made me very sad.'

Alice plonked herself firmly on Becca's lap and put her arms around her neck. 'Don't worry,' she said. She sounded like a wise old woman, a hundred years old. 'You've got us – me and James and Daddy. We'll look after you.'

Becca hugged her daughter tight, burying her tear-stained face in Alice's baby-soft hair. 'I know, darling,' she said, 'I've got you and I'm so, so lucky.'

Tom and Becca held a child's hand each as they walked slowly back to the car park. The sky had clouded over and it was starting to feel chilly.

Tom stopped by the car and looked at Becca. 'You can't go on beating yourself up,' he said steadily. 'You've said you're sorry. There's nothing more you can do except live your life as well as you can. Raise your children to the best of your ability. Be kind.

'Your mother could have got in touch before she died but she didn't. That was her choice. It's between her and her maker now. I couldn't imagine either of us behaving like that with Alice or James, but I guess she came from a harder, less forgiving era.'

He was right. Becca could picture Mam now: her tough, care-worn expression; the deep lines carved into her face by years of boozing, chain-smoking, being slapped about by various boyfriends; the cheap clothes; the hands rough and calloused from being constantly in and out of water, cleaning other people's houses – rich women's houses.

She'd had no one to support her, no therapists to help her come to terms with what had happened, no decent education to broaden her mind, no Mr Carr to teach her the power of reasoning and to enable her to see things in the round.

Mam had viewed the world in black and white; there were no shades of grey. Becca's dad had walked out on them just after Becca was born, so he was bad; Becca had killed Jude, so Becca was wicked, never mind the circumstances, the excuses. She'd ruined Mam's life and that was that.

In truth, Mam had never had much time for Becca anyway;

she'd not had a lot of love to give. They'd all been surrounded by violence but the difference was, Becca had got out. Maybe Mam blamed her for the fact that her dad had walked. Jude's dad – who was a different man – had also scarpered, but maybe Mam preferred him, ergo she preferred Jude. Who knew, now, how her brain had worked?

'Let's go home now,' Tom said, 'to London.'

Becca was surprised. 'What, now? What about our bags? And it'll be so late by the time we arrive.'

'It doesn't matter,' Tom replied firmly. 'We'll grab our bags from the hotel, settle the bill and head off straightaway. We've seen all we need to.'

The children were virtually silent as they pounded along the motorway, heading south. Alice fell asleep for a couple of hours but James just sat there, listening to the radio and staring out of the window. Becca didn't think she'd ever known Tom drive so fast, but he was steady and focused. She wasn't afraid.

At last, when they were just outside London, James spoke. 'Mum? Do you miss your sister?'

'Yes.'

'Were you very sad when she died?'

'Yes.'

'Did you like her – when you were a little girl, I mean?'

Becca paused while she thought about this. 'I loved her,' she said at last, 'but I'm afraid that I didn't like her. We were very different.'

'You didn't like your own sister?' He'd never heard such a thing. He was astounded. Becca was glad.

'It happens sometimes,' she said quietly. 'But thank goodness you and Alice are good friends. I think that'll be my greatest achievement' – she said this more to herself than to him – 'if you and Alice grow up to be good friends.'

James pondered for a moment – Becca knew quite well what he was up to – but in the end he decided not to make a facetious remark.

'Will you go to her grave again?' he piped up.

'I think so,' said Becca. So many questions.

'Did it make you feel better – going, I mean?'

Becca wiped away a tear and blew her nose. She turned to look at James in the back. It was dark outside but she could still make out his familiar features.

She smiled. 'It's something I should have done a long time ago, darling,' she whispered. 'Of course I'm sad that she died. I always will be. But yes, in answer to your question, yes, I think I do feel better.'

'I've kept the photo,' Tom said. Becca was surprised. She didn't realise that he'd been listening.

'Which one?'

'The one of you and Jude in the photo booth.'

'Good.'

The car fell silent again.

Becca decided that she'd find a frame tomorrow. It would have to be a very small one. Then she'd put it on the mantel-piece, beside the other family photos, where it belonged.

Chapter Fifty-Seven

✦

'Quiet please, I have an important announcement to make.'
Tristram peered over his gold-rimmed spectacles at the seated
gathering.

It was the December meeting of the St Barnabas's Creative
Writing Group. Six months had passed since the 1 June competition deadline and Evie had virtually forgotten about it. So
much had happened since then.

She glanced around her. She had Nic and Becca on either
side, as usual. Russell and Jonathan were beside each other in
the front row, next to Pamela, in her usual spot bang in the
centre.

There was no mousy Angela tonight but Tim, the car enthu-
siast, was here. Evie had already had a chat with him about
how well his Toyota Yaris was running. She was pleased for
him, really she was, but she did wish that he wouldn't go
on so.

Her own Renault Espace had all but given up the ghost and
she found that she could hardly care less. She seemed only to
use it for shopping these days and, really, she could order that
online. Bill's influence seemed to have rubbed off and she was
turning surprisingly green. She tended to cycle or go by bus
now.

Several new people had joined the group, perhaps lured by
the prospect of future competitions. Tristram said that the one
they'd entered had been such a success, with a vast number of
entries of a very high standard, that the organisers were already
planning another.

Evie turned around quickly and caught sight of Carol right
at the back of the class keeping her distance. Good. She seemed
to have got the message about giving Evie plenty of space,

literally and metaphorically. These days, Carol wouldn't dare make interfering comments about any aspect of Evie's life.

Tristram cleared his throat. 'I have the results of the creative writing competition.'

An excited ripple ran around the room.

'And I'm delighted to say,' Tristram went on, 'that I have some rather good news.'

Evie's mind started to race. She didn't believe for a moment that she'd won anything. She'd finished *The Roman's Wife* with two days to spare and she was pleased, in the end, with what she'd achieved. But she knew in her heart that it wasn't prize-winning material and she doubted very much that she'd find an agent or a publisher. Never mind, it had been a challenge and she was glad that she'd done it. She'd achieved a lot and, in fact, she'd already started researching and writing a second historical romance: *The Viking's Honour*. She felt that, with the experience she'd gained, this one would be an altogether better, more professional product.

'Can you wait a moment, please?'

There was a rustle of annoyance. Pamela had stood up and was smoothing down her skirt.

Tristram took off his glasses. 'Really, this is a very in-convenient . . .'

'I need to powder my nose,' Pamela said, making for the door of the ladies' room at the side of the church hall.

Nic nudged Evie in the ribs. 'She thinks she's won. Silly old bat. There's no way.'

Becca was sitting very still, her hands in her lap. Evie admired her hair from the side. It was looking very shiny. She'd had a semi-permanent, dark blond tint put in while it grew back to its natural light-brown colour. Then, she said, she thought she might have subtle highlights to disguise the grey beginning to peep through.

The colour looked much better on her. Softer. Her eyebrows were no longer black, either. In fact her whole air had changed. She seemed less pent up, more relaxed in looks and manner. Evie shot her a reassuring smile. She knew that Becca was quietly hopeful about the competition. She seemed very pleased with what she'd written, though she hadn't allowed anyone else to read it.

She was leaving just after Christmas for a new life with Tom and the children in Spain. She'd handed in her notice at work and this was to be a fresh beginning. She and Tom were going to run a small hotel, but Evie realised that Becca must be thinking how wonderful it would be to have the boost of a win under her belt before they left – and an agent, to boot. That way she could begin to take herself seriously as an author and set aside some serious time for writing.

Nic, of course, had scrapped *The Girl from Niger* with nary a backward glance. She, like Evie, had begun something new. She'd still be intrigued, though, Evie thought, to find out who in the writing group, if anyone, had won something. It was all rather thrilling.

They chatted among themselves for a few minutes while they waited for Pamela to reappear. Every now and again Evie could hear Carol's voice rising above the hubbub. She caught the odd phrase: 'Who does she think she is?'; 'Selfish nincompoop'. She could imagine whom Carol was discussing. Evie sniggered inwardly. After going through a rather subdued period, Carol seemed to have regained some of her tell-it-as-it-is streak.

At last Pamela reappeared, with lots of lipstick on in a rather startling shade of baby pink. She'd clearly sprayed her stiff grey hair, too. The smell could knock you down at fifty paces. Evie reckoned she must be a fire hazard.

Pamela gave a prim little smile – but no apology for having kept everyone waiting – and sat down again.

'Now,' said Tristram irritably, 'let's have no more interruptions, please. I received a letter from the organisers this morning to say that . . .' He looked up from the sheet of paper he was holding in front of him and scanned the entire room, deliberately drawing out the suspense. '. . . to say that one of our members has WON THE COMPETITION!'

There was a sharp intake of breath.

Evie jumped up. She couldn't help it. 'Oh, but who, who? You've got to tell us!'

Pamela swung round and gave her an icy stare. 'He's coming to that,' she hissed.

Evie sat down again.

'Patience!' Tristram beamed. He was enjoying his moment of power. 'I'm coming to that. The winner,' he said, pulling back his shoulders and puffing out his paunch, 'is someone whose writing style has developed a great deal in the past year.

'The winner' – he looked up again and smiled: he wasn't going to give the sex away – 'has a mesmerising style full of fast turns, dynamic leaps and boundless humour. He or she has well and truly mastered the art of "Show Don't Tell". But most of all,' he went on, 'the judges praised this person's extraordinary imagination. They said he or she has written, I quote, "a highly inventive debut novel . . . a welcome new voice rising up amongst the great voices."'

Evie turned to Becca, who was twisting her wedding ring round and round her finger. Nerves. 'It's not me,' Becca whispered. 'My writing's good, I think, but I don't have an extraordinary imagination.'

Evie took a quick look at Pamela, who was sitting up, ramrod straight, quivering with anticipation. But did Pamela have it in her to write something 'highly inventive'? Evie seriously doubted it. Maybe it was Russell, clever old Russell. Though personally she'd always found his work rather obscure.

God, it couldn't be car-mad Tim, could it? Or Jonathan's account of a young man's sexual romp through Spain and Italy? Or maybe it was gloomy old Angela's tome about self-harming.

Tristram took a step forward, drew himself up to his full height and grinned. 'You've been very patient and now I'm going to tell you the name.'

Evie thought she might be sick.

He straightened his red silk tie at the neck, ran his hand down the length of it and over his ample tum. 'The winner of the national Creative Writing Competition, 2009 is . . . Carol Tyndall for *Miaow*, her fabulous novella about a houseful of talking and remarkably clever, philosophical cats!'

'NO!'

All eyes swivelled to the front row.

Pamela had stood up and was leaning right over, practically breathing in Tristram's face. He took a self-preserving step back.

'No,' she repeated, 'you've got it wrong.'

Tristram raised a hand. 'I can assure you . . .'

'You're not telling me that stupid old fool has won. It's a joke. The whole competition's a complete farce.'

'Really, Pamela,' Tristram stuttered, 'this isn't a very nice attitude. One should be noble in defeat.'

'Pah!'

Pamela turned round to the front, her face pinched with fury. Evie sensed everyone lean back slightly in their chair.

'I'm leaving,' she snorted, bending down to grab her handbag from underneath her chair, 'and if you've got any sense you will, too. There's an excellent creative writing group in Surbiton which they've been begging me to join for months but out of loyalty I've said no. But now that I can see how things are run here, how devious and corrupt it all is, I realise that my loyalty has been entirely misplaced.'

'Wait a minute,' Tristram said, grabbing Pamela's arm, 'that's not fair, I had nothing whatever to do with the—'

She tried to shake him off. 'Unhand me at once, sir, or I'll call the police!'

Tristram did as he was told. He looked as if he'd been scorched.

Pamela marched towards the exit, her chin in the air, turning one more time before she opened the door.

'And if that lunatic creature,' – she nodded in Carol's direction – 'imagines that she's written a good book she should go and see a doctor. It's a fix, the whole thing's a fix. Goodbye.'

'To Carol!' said Russell.

Everyone raised a glass. 'Carol!'

They all took a slurp of champagne.

'Well, I never imagined this.' Carol grinned, revealing her stained teeth. 'Not in a million years. I thought if anyone was going to win it would be Becca.'

They'd managed to squash around the long, dark wooden table next to the Christmas tree in the corner of the pub. The entire class had turned up, excluding Angela and Pamela, of course – about fifteen in all.

Becca shook her head. 'Nah,' she said. 'Your story's much more inventive. But the last time I spoke to you, back in, what, about March, you said you didn't think you'd finish in time and you were only really doing it for fun, anyway. What happened?'

Carol sipped her drink. 'I had a big spurt in April.' She glanced at Evie and quickly looked away. 'Honestly, I think I wrote most of it in a month. The words just flowed. But I'm truly staggered that I've won. I thought the judges would dismiss *Miaow* as too eccentric.'

Evie smiled. 'They clearly loved it. Well done,' she said, raising her glass again.

Carol looked grateful. 'Thank you – all. I'd like to buy another couple of bottles of champagne. Would someone mind going up and ordering for me?'

Russell rose.

'Here's my purse.' Carol delved into her bag, pulled out a battered-looking brown leather purse and thrust it into his hand. 'See if they have some nice nibbles, too,' she suggested. 'Or should I say canapés?' There should be enough cash in there. Can't think of a better way to spend it.' She winked. Everyone laughed.

Becca squealed. Evie spun round to look. Becca was pointing at Nic. 'You've had your braces off! I hadn't even noticed.'

Nic parted her lips to reveal a set of perfect, straight white teeth. 'Nice, eh?' she grinned. 'They came off on Tuesday.'

'Lovely,' Evie marvelled. 'You look like a Hollywood film star.'

'Gorgeous,' Becca agreed. 'Are you pleased?'

Nic nodded. 'It's been worth it. I wasn't sure at first because of the discomfort, but I always hated my snaggled tooth.'

Everyone was silent while they examined Nic's dental work.

'Well,' said Tim, who normally only talked about cars. 'They look jolly good to me – not that I know anything about that sort of thing.'

Nic smiled gratefully. 'Thanks,' she said. 'I feel like a new woman.'

'A new woman? Ah, that reminds me.' Russell had come back with a cooler containing a bottle of champagne. The other was still on the bar. 'I had an interesting patient this week,' he said, 'a very pleasant woman who, er, who used to be a man . . .'

Evie leaned forward. 'Tell us,' she pleaded.

Russell shook his head. 'I really can't, one must be discreet.'

'Oh, for goodness' sake!' Nic said crossly. 'We know about all your other patients. I don't see why this one should have special treatment.'

Russell took the bottle out of the cooler. 'May I do the honours?'

Carol nodded. 'Go on, please.'

He pointed the bottle away from the table and twisted the cork, which came off with a loud and satisfying pop. Tim had risen and was holding two empty glasses, which Russell quickly filled.

'Give me the others, quick,' he said. 'Oh all right, if you insist,' he continued, filling the other glasses which people were passing up the table. 'Well, this gentleman-turned-lady had a bit of an infection. She'd had the full op – you know – but the interesting thing was' – Russell looked up and twinkled – 'that the wife came into the examination room with him, er, her.'

'The wife?' Becca spluttered. 'You mean they're still married?'

Russell nodded.

'Very good relationship apparently. Several kids. She seemed most concerned about the infection – but not at all worried about where it had come from. Clearly they have an open relationship. They still share a bed, though.'

Carol tutted. 'It wasn't like this in my day. No one had ever heard of transvestites, transsexuals, whatever you call them.'

'Rubbish,' Jonathan chipped in. He'd clearly got over the fact that his book hadn't won the competition and had squished into his favourite place next to Nic. He was practically sitting on her lap. They looked very cosy. She was pretending not to notice. 'Think of Quentin Crisp – and the English journalist and travel writer Jan Morris in the 1960s. You must have heard of her?'

Carol harrumphed. 'Still, it wasn't common, though. These people seem to be two a penny nowadays.'

Evie laughed. 'Hardly. Anyway, I think it's nice that he, er, she and the wife are still good friends. Must have been difficult for the wife to come to terms with, though,' she added darkly.

Nic took a sip from her glass. She was on orange juice and lemonade. She seemed to be coping amazingly well without alcohol, Evie thought.

'What news of the baby?' Nic asked quietly. The others were still discussing Russell's transsexual.

'Mia? I caught a glimpse of her in the car the other day,' Evie whispered. 'She's very sweet. Helen and Neil were looking a bit rough, though.' She gave a naughty, gap-toothed grin. 'Evidently not getting much sleep.'

'Poor Neil, poor Helen.' Nic smirked. 'What's Neil like with Bill?'

'Chilly,' Evie replied. 'Bill's always charming, though.'

'I bet he is. And I bet Neil finds it infuriating.'

Evie laughed. 'I think he does. But you know what?' she said, tipping her head to one side. 'The lovely thing is that I really don't care what he thinks. So long as he turns up on time for the children and looks after them properly when they're with him, I'm happy. I wouldn't be in his shoes, though.' She shivered.

'Why not?'

'The children tell me Helen's awfully bossy. She makes him cook supper the minute he gets in from work. Says she can't look after the baby and make a meal at the same time. And they never go out in the evenings now because she doesn't trust anyone to babysit.'

'Ha, serves him right!'

It was midnight by the time they left the pub. Carol had clearly thoroughly enjoyed the evening and looked a little flushed from the champagne as well as her success.

'Congratulations, and be careful!' Evie called as Carol clambered on to her bike and wobbled off down the street.

She waved a hand without looking round. 'I will!'

Becca turned to Evie and Nic. 'Who'd have thought it?' she said. 'Carol winning the prize. She's done so well!'

'I know,' said Nic, 'and with a good agent now, she'll no doubt find a publisher soon. It's amazing.'

Evie nodded. 'How do you feel?' she asked Becca. 'Are you very disappointed? We all thought you were going to win.'

Becca smiled. 'You know what? I think there's something rather marvellous about the fact that the judges opted for a really unusual book instead of plumping for something more obvious, don't you?'

The other women nodded in agreement.

'I can't wait to read *Miaow* properly,' Becca went on. 'We've only heard short extracts up to now, haven't we?' She looked at Evie. 'Didn't Carol gave you a copy a while back? Did you read it?'

Evie shook her head. 'I couldn't bring myself to. It's still under my bed.'

Nic raised her eyebrows. 'Aren't you curious? I would be.'

'Kind of,' Evie said seriously. 'But I'm scared, too. I'm sure I will one day, when I'm feeling strong enough.'

'I can understand that,' Nic replied. She glanced down at Evie's feet and squeaked: 'What on earth are those?'

Evie was wearing her black duffel coat on top of a pretty, slightly hippyish brushed-cotton dress with an aubergine and brown pattern that Nic had admired earlier. However, on her feet were a pair of large muddy green wellies. Nic couldn't believe that she hadn't spotted them earlier.

Evie looked embarrassed. 'I was helping Bill at the allotment this afternoon,' she explained. 'I was in a rush to get out this evening and I couldn't find my shoes . . .'

'So you shoved those on?' Nic snorted. 'An interesting look. You could start a new trend – or not.'

Evie flashed another gap-toothed smile. 'I never imagined I'd get into this allotment lark but actually it's rather compulsive. You should come and visit us down there sometime. You might catch the bug.'

'I can't quite see that happening.' Becca grinned. 'Or at least, not that sort of bug. But I'll come and sample some of

447

your cabbage wine or whatever it is that you allotmenteers go in for.'

'Cabbage wine?' said Evie. 'I don't think so. But we're going to have a marvellous crop of—'

'Oh God, here she goes,' Nic said, raising her eyebrows, which was now possible as the Botox had long since worn off. 'Give her the merest hint of encouragement and she's off. She'll be going on about her bloody compost heap next.'

Evie clapped her hands. 'Compost heap? I nearly forgot to tell you, we're building a wormery! We've got four hundred worms arriving on Friday. Bill says worm wee is an excellent fertiliser.'

Nic shook her head. 'Mad. She's gone absolutely mad.'

'You can have some if you like,' Evie offered. 'We should have plenty.'

'Er, maybe not,' said Nic.

Chapter Fifty-Eight

It was cold and dark and Becca was grateful that the porch light was on when she got home. She had some difficulty squeezing past the cardboard boxes on either side of the hallway. She caught sight of the address scribbled on top of one of the crates as she passed – Goodall, Villa Dolores, Avenida de las Palomas, Málaga – and felt a familiar tingle of excitement. Not long now.

She took off her shoes, hung her coat on the bannisters and tiptoed upstairs. She was surprised to see the light on in the first-floor drawing room; she'd expected Tom either to be asleep or watching TV in bed. She'd tell him about Carol's win and Evie's wormery. It would make him laugh.

He had his back to her facing the bay window that over-looked the green. The curtains were drawn and his hands were clasped behind him. The room felt chilly; the heating must have gone off and the fireplace was cold. He was still in his suit trousers and a white shirt. His curly hair, surprisingly grey now, flicked up at the collar. A stranger would take him for a solid, respectable, middle-aged gentleman – until he turned and gave his cheeky, dimpled smile. He seemed to be deep in thought.

'Tom!' she said. 'What are you doing?'

He swivelled round and she could tell immediately that something was the matter. His eyes were dead and his mouth was turned down at the corners. His face, normally ruddy and animated, was a strange, pallid colour.

'What's wrong?' she cried, hurrying towards him, her arms outstretched. 'What's happened?'

His hands remained behind his back and his body was rigid. She stopped in her tracks and put her arms down.

'I'm sorry, Becca,' he said, shaking his head. 'I can't do it.'

Her heart started beating faster. 'Can't do what?'

'You and me. Spain. It's not going to work.'

She stared at him, uncomprehending. His dark-brown eyes were unreadable. Was he joking?

She laughed nervously. 'What do you mean?'

He closed his eyes. He wouldn't look at her. 'I thought we could get through it as a family, I thought I could move on. But I can't.'

She clutched her throat. 'I don't understand. Why have you suddenly changed your mind?'

He paused. 'It's not a sudden thing. I've been thinking about it for the past year.' His eyes were still closed.

She couldn't believe what she was hearing. 'Why didn't you say – before we made all these plans?'

He shrugged, opened his eyes and stared at the palms of his hands. 'I wanted to keep the family together. I wanted us to start a new life. I thought if I believed hard enough that I could forgive and forget then I really would. Mind over matter, I suppose.'

'But it didn't work?'

He hung his head. 'No.'

She stood, frozen to the spot. 'I thought it was too good to be true,' she said quietly.

He swallowed. 'It's the not knowing, too.' Still he wouldn't look at her. 'The constantly checking over your shoulder wondering if someone will find out who you are, waiting for that knock on the door . . .'

'Tom,' she said, 'I've lived with it for thirty years. It is possible.'

He didn't seem to hear. 'What if Gary decides to cough after all this time – or he has a row with his wife and she scurries off to the tabloids? I can't handle it, I can't live my life like that. Even if we were abroad I'd still be on edge the whole time. I'd go mad.'

She put her hands over her face. She felt so alone. 'I knew this would happen. It's why I lied to you. I knew it would destroy us. You shouldn't have come after me. You should have left me in Normandy. It would have been so much easier.'

He walked over to an armchair in the corner of the room

and sat down, his elbows on his knees, staring at his feet. Becca chose to remain standing.

'What'll you do?' he asked simply. 'The children . . . it's such a mess.' He wiped his forehead with his sleeve.

She thought rapidly. They were due to leave in two weeks' time. The house was sold, the new one bought, the children had places at a school in Málaga.

'Tom?' she pleaded, taking a step towards him.

He flinched and put his hands up like a barrier. 'Don't.'

She'd tried so hard to ignore the way that he avoided touching her, to convince herself that it would pass. It hurt so much. She should have listened to her instincts. 'I don't know. I suppose I'll go anyway.'

He shifted slightly in his chair.

'What about you?' she asked.

He looked up. His eyes and nose were red. 'Shift on the nationals, I guess.' He laughed grimly. 'They might even give me my old job back.' He hated that job, he'd been desperate to get away. 'I won't expect anything from you – financially, I mean.'

She took a deep breath; it seemed such an irrelevance, how they'd work out the money side of things. 'The children will be devastated,' she whispered.

He hugged his arms around his chest. 'I'll visit as often as I can. And once I get my own place—'

'Stop.' She couldn't bear to look that far ahead. Just getting through the next twenty-four hours was going to be hard enough. 'Think about it, Tom,' she pleaded. 'We've got two weeks. We can delay. You don't have to make a decision now. You might feel differently . . .'

He shook his head. 'I've made up my mind. I can't do it. We've reached the end of the line.'

A thought occurred to her. 'Is there someone else?'

'No.'

'But you were so kind,' she went on, 'after I told you. You've been so gentle, so understanding. Don't you love me any more?' She needed an answer. She had to be sure.

He unfolded his arms. It seemed an eternity before he replied. 'I love the woman I thought you were, the one I thought I

451

married. I can't love Dawn. I've tried so hard but I just can't. When I think about what she did . . . what you did . . .' He screwed his face up. He looked as if he were in pain.

She felt sick. 'What?' she commanded. She had to hear it. 'Finish what you were about to say.'

He stared at her for the first time, looking deeply into her eyes. His own eyes were sad but she couldn't reach out to him.

He spoke very quietly. 'I feel disgusted.' He looked away quickly, shaking his head. 'I'm sorry.'

Becca staggered slightly, as if she'd been struck, but she managed to steady herself. 'We're the same person, Tom,' she whispered urgently. 'Dawn and Becca, Becca and Dawn. And I wouldn't be the woman you fell in love with if I hadn't—'

'It doesn't matter,' he interrupted. 'I can't explain.'

She thought about how different her life had looked just ten minutes before when she was stumbling over the boxes in the hall. Spain, the sunshine, the four of them together, a whole new adventure. So it had all been an illusion.

Had she ever truly believed that she'd get away with it – that she and Tom could start again? Maybe, like him, she'd just *wanted* to believe it. Real life wasn't like that.

She thought about kind Mr Carr at the correctional institute who'd tried so hard to convince her that she could put the past behind her. She pictured Jude on the day she died, straddling Dawn, thumping up and down on her stomach as hard as she could, her long nails scraping down her cheek, making her eyes water.

She remembered Jude's words: 'I hate ye, I'll always hate ye. Ye think ye're so fuckin' clever but ye're not.'

'Please, Jude,' Becca muttered.

'What?' said Tom.

Becca shook her head, raised a hand to hush him. 'Please, Jude, can't we make up now?'

But there was no reply.

Jude had got her revenge after all.

Zelda lit another fag and inhaled deeply. It was well after midnight and she'd been on the phone all evening. She was

452

exhausted. It had been a bad night. She hadn't been able to find anyone, not even her usual suspects. Probably off somewhere having a knees-up, the buggers.

But she couldn't say that to her clients, now could she? The woman whose daughter had died in a car crash had been particularly wearing; she'd gone on and on, blubbing away, asking so many questions. It was tiring having to make it up. Still, she shouldn't complain. Business was booming. She'd picked up several new clients thanks to them leaflets she'd had printed.

She got up slowly and went to fill the kettle. A nice cup of tea, that'd be the ticket. She wouldn't go to bed just yet, not when her mind was still racing. She needed to unwind first, unclog her brains. She opened the tin of teabags and peered in. Nearly empty. Tch. She'd have to go to the shops tomorrow. She looked at the picture on the side of the gold tin. It was of a little girl in old-fashioned clothes, Victorian or something. She had curly hair and a big, red parcel in her arms. She was smiling.

Zelda frowned. Another of Carol's stupid Christmas presents. It had come full up with lots of fancy teabags with weird names. Well, Zelda had got rid of them quick and put normal ones in instead. What was Carol thinking of, giving her smelly tea like that? She should have known she wouldn't like it.

That funny, gnawing feeling in her belly again, like a rat nibbling away at her insides.

She filled her cup with boiling water, dunked the teabag a few times before chucking it in the sink. Then she sniffed the milk – force of habit – and added just a little, not too much, and two sugars.

It had been an effort to get on the tube and go all the way across London to deliver them leaflets, she thought, sitting back down. She didn't like the tube, the way people stared at her and made snide comments. But Carol would never find out what she was up to. At least now there were possibilities. You never knew who might bite. After all, it wasn't such a big place. Coincidences happened.

The phone rang. Blast. She could always leave it, but there again . . .

She picked up the receiver: 'Zelda speakin'.'

'I hope I'm not calling too late?' It was a woman's voice, anxious, quavery. She sounded posh, middle class, but there was a slight lilt in there too, a hint of something that Zelda couldn't quite place. She knitted her brows. She was good at accents. You could always hear them better on the phone. It wasn't Welsh, for sure. Or Scottish.

'No, darlin', I'm always up late,' she said. 'How can I help?'

'I got your leaflet through my letterbox.'

Zelda sat up. The woman lived in or around Richmond, then.

'I've never done this before,' she went on.

'That's all right.' Zelda put on her most reassuring voice. 'I won't bite.'

'There's someone – two people actually – that I really need to speak to,' the woman explained.

Zelda reached for her cigarettes and lit one. 'Yes, darlin'?'

'It's my mother, you see,' she said. 'And my sister. They're both dead.'

'I'm sorry, sweet'art,' said Zelda. 'You must miss them somethin' terrible.'

'I do,' the woman answered. It sounded as if she was blowing her nose. 'They died a long time ago.'

Zelda paused. The woman's voice had a very faint, sing-songy quality. Geordie? That was it. There was a hint of Geordie in there. She must have lived in London for years, though, or had elocution lessons or something.

'Can you find them for me?' the woman went on. 'It's really urgent.'

'I can't promise it but I'll try,' Zelda replied. 'What's your name, darlin'?'

'Becca. Becca Goodall.'

Zelda hesitated. That name rang a bell. Her mind started to race.

'Have you got kiddies, darlin'?' she asked. She was playing for time while she racked her brain.

'Yes, two. Ten and seven.'

'I thought so.'

Ten, the same age as that Michael, Evie's boy. She was sure she'd heard Carol mention some Becca woman in relation to Evie.

She'd always listened carefully to what Carol said about that girl of hers, stored it away for possible future use.

'And you're married, yes?' Zelda asked.

The woman hesitated. 'It's difficult . . .'

Marital problems, then.

'Best friend's name begins with an F – or an E,' Zelda went on. 'That's it, an E.'

The woman gasped. 'Evie? How did you know?'

Zelda chuckled. She was enjoying herself now. 'I know lots of things, darlin',' she said. 'You'd be surprised.'

She put out her fag and lit another immediately. Funny, she wasn't a bit tired any more.

'But can you really . . . talk to the dead? I never used to believe in that sort of thing—'

'But now you're willin' to give it a go?' Zelda interrupted. 'Don't worry darlin', I have a lot of clients like you. They start off all unbelievin', then when they see what I can do they change their minds. It's all right, I'm used to dealin' with unbelievers like you.'

The woman paused. 'So do you think you can really help? I wouldn't ask, only I'm desperate to get in touch.'

Zelda listened carefully. She was hiding something, for certain. Interesting.

'There's something I need to talk to them about,' Becca went on. 'It's really important. My husband says he's going to leave me . . .' There was a catch in her throat. 'I need their help to win him back. I know I can do it, if only they'll let me. I have to speak to them, to explain.'

Zelda inhaled and exhaled deeply. 'Trust me, darlin',' she said softly. 'You're in good hands. Now close your eyes, sit back and focus on your mum's face. That's right . . . good . . . I can feel somethin' comin' through . . . I'm seein' somethin' more clearly now. What's your mum's name?'

'Maureen,' Becca whispered.

'Good evening, Maureen,' Zelda said. 'I've got someone here who's bin wantin' to speak to you for a very long time.'

Acknowledgments

I drew on the knowledge and experiences of many truly remarkable people to write this novel. Thank you Clare Fawcett, Emma Lewis, Kate O'Connor, Julie Brack, Peter Cox, Sgt Ian Bishop, Fiona Putty and Paola Carr-Walker for their insights and advice.

Nor would it have been possible without the kindness and patience, not to mention the invaluable literary and technical expertise, of my wonderful editor, Rosie de Courcy. And a great big thank you to my fantastic agent, Heather Holden-Brown, for her wisdom, wit and friendship.

A big kiss goes to my children, Georgia, Harry and Freddie, for making themselves scarce when it really mattered, and to my husband, Kevin, for rising so graciously to the role of chief cook and bottle washer when circumstances demanded.

My dear father, Christopher Burstall, died just before *Never Close Your Eyes* was published. Sadly, he never got to read it, but his loving inspiration is present in every page.